Alexander Fullerton
Russian interpreter, sh
lisher. Through nearly all these periods he has also been a writer – he has lived solely on his writing since 1967 and now has several bestsellers among the thirty novels to his credit. *Bloody Sunset* draws its inspiration and its convincing background from the two most basic elements in his own knowledge and experience – the Royal Navy and Russia.

Also by Alexander Fullerton

SURFACE!
BURY THE PAST
OLD MOKE
NO MAN'S MISTRESS
A WREN CALLED SMITH
THE WHITE MEN SANG
THE YELLOW FORD
SOLDIER FROM THE SEA
THE WAITING GAME
THE THUNDER AND THE FLAME
LIONHEART
CHIEF EXECUTIVE
THE PUBLISHER
STORE
THE ESCAPISTS
OTHER MEN'S WIVES
PIPER'S LEAVE
REGENESIS
THE APHRODITE CARGO
JOHNSON'S BIRD
LOOK TO THE WOLVES

The Everard series of naval novels

THE BLOODING OF THE GUNS
SIXTY MINUTES FOR ST GEORGE
PATROL TO THE GOLDEN HORN
STORM FORCE TO NARVIK
LAST LIFT FROM CRETE
ALL THE DROWING SEAS
A SHARE OF HONOUR
THE TORCH BEARERS
THE GATECRASHERS

The SBS trilogy

SPECIAL DELIVERANCE
SPECIAL DYNAMIC
SPECIAL DECEPTION

ALEXANDER FULLERTON

BLOODY SUNSET

A *Warner* Book

First published in Great Britain in 1991
by Macdonald & Co (Publishers) Ltd
This edition published by Warner Books in 1992

All characters in this publication are fictitious and any resemblance to real persons, living or dead, is purely coincidental.

A CIP catalogue record for this book is available
from the British Library

ISBN 0 7088 5447 8

Printed and bound in Great Britain by
BPCC Hazells Ltd
Member of BPCC Ltd

Warner Books
A Division of
Little, Brown and Company (UK) Limited
165 Great Dover Street
London SE1 4YA

BLOODY SUNSET

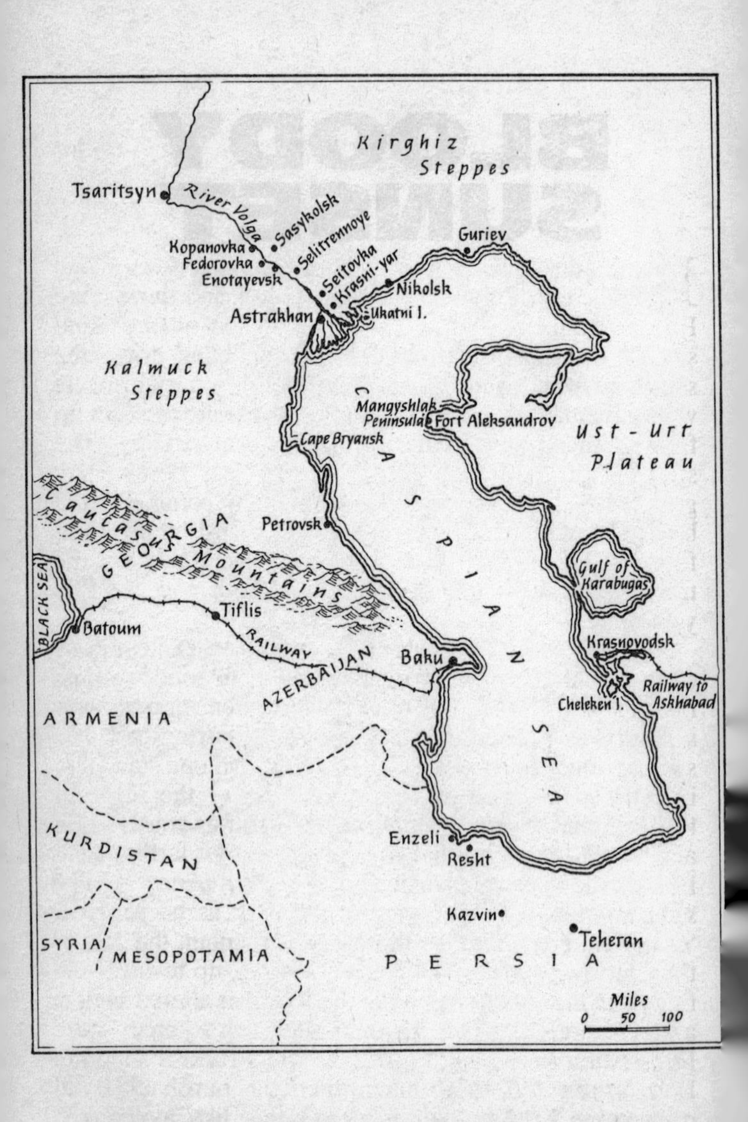

Kirghiz Steppes
Tsaritsyn
River Volga
Sasykolsk
Selitrennoye
Kopanovka
Fedorovka
Enotayevsk
Seitovka
Krasni-yar
Guriev
Nikolsk
Astrakhan
Ukatni I.
Kalmuck Steppes
Mangyshlak Peninsula
Fort Aleksandrov
Ust-Urt Plateau
Cape Bryansk
CASPIAN SEA
Caucasus Mountains
GEORGIA
Petrovsk
Gulf of Karabugas
BLACK SEA
Batoum
Tiflis
RAILWAY
AZERBAIJAN
Baku
Krasnovodsk
Railway to Askhabad
Cheleken I.
ARMENIA
KURDISTAN
Enzeli
Resht
Kazvin
Teheran
SYRIA
MESOPOTAMIA
PERSIA
Miles
0 50 100

1

Earth and stones erupted as shells plunged down along the crest of the rising ground ahead, and those were Russian gunners — their battery would be on the blind side of the ridge, Bob guessed — scrambling down the slope this way. 'Getting out from under' — a manoeuvre which seemed to be their almost invariable reaction to finding themselves under fire or direct attack. The sergeant of the North Staffs on the seat beside him gestured — helplessly, wordlessly, his only comment that brusque gesture and the expression of disgust on his blunt features. He shouted now with one hand ready on the truck's door — 'This'll do us, sir — thank you, near as you'll get, I—'

A shell's scrunching whistle ended in an explosion so close that the shower of debris came with solid, rattling impacts in the blast, the truck's windscreen miraculously surviving as Bob brought it to a sliding, jarring halt at a slant of about thirty degrees. The wheels on one side were in churned dirt and the others on rock — the sergeant being absolutely right, this was about as far as you'd get on any wheels, and in all the circumstances a lot farther than Bob should have chanced it. But — in for a penny ... The sergeant shouted back over his shoulder as he jumped, 'Come on, boys, *out*!' — then he was running, the rest of them following and spreading as they ran, up towards the ridge and the fall of shot while the Russians altered course away, diverging to their right, as unwilling to meet these Englishmen as they were to stand up to Turkish shellfire. Bob turning the truck meanwhile, the ramshackle old conveyance lurching this way and that like a drunken camel but still miraculously not bogging down — yet — and with the battle all astern now, he had in his mind's eye those poor bloody riflemen so ready to assume the role of gunners — if they got that far, lived that long — some of them, a lot wouldn't, you could bet — toiling into it up the ridge with their set, desperately youthful English faces ... The road wasn't far ahead now — thirty yards, with a bit of a bank to get over, a haze of other fighting over and around the oilrigs of Binagadi about two miles to the north and — here, closer, and as concerned his own fortunate self — the high ground, cliff-like escarpment, he'd be climbing it in a minute, touch wood — towering all along on his right, the south, that great bulwark protecting Baku town. Bulwark for the time being — until the Turks got up there ... Over the low bank: crashing over, listing wildly with a noise like jolting scrap iron, the old rattletrap lifting and crashing down again, one side and then the other; as he dragged the wheel over he saw three Russians in the road ahead, two of them with a wounded man dragging between them, swinging half-round to face him now as they heard the truck coming up behind them and obviously taking it for granted that he'd pick them up. But there was a first-aid station only a few hundred yards away — he'd noticed it on the way here, just minutes ago, and searching that way now he could see a tent's sloping roof, the scarlet cross. Then he was pounding past the three Russians — one head hanging, the other two open-mouthed, disbelieving ...

Poor beggars. But it was nothing new, that tactic of ducking smartly out of awkward corners. Just a few days ago General Dunsterville had personally witnessed a whole Russian battalion taking to its heels, and he'd written to the Baku authorities — the Central Caspian Dictatorship, they called themselves — stating bluntly that if local troops continued to run away whenever they were shot at, he — Dunsterville, head of the British military mission — wasn't going to continue wasting British lives, he'd evacuate Baku and let them take their chances.

Which would mean the Turks would walk in, virtually

unopposed. Apart from the handful of British troops here, the only fighting men worth a damn — apart from the Turks themselves, of course — were Colonel Bicherakov's Cossacks, but they were about 300 miles north-west, holding Petrovsk and its environs against the Bolsheviks in the north and west.

The blunt-nosed truck was grinding uphill now. Gradient steepening until the track had become a series of hairpin bends up the face of the escarpment, and Bob resolving not to breathe a word about this to anyone — since he'd had no business being here, no right even to have been behind the wheel of this antique vehicle in the first place. Not that he could very well have refused to stop and pick up those soldiers, after their sergeant had waved him down and begged a lift, their own lorry having given up the ghost. They'd been off duty — in some billet in the area of Cherniye Gorod, presumably — and there'd been a panic call for any available reinforcements to be rushed up to the Binagadi/Mud Volcano section of the thinly-held defences, and Bob Cowan, Lieutenant RNR, who'd been on an unauthorized visit to — well, to a young lady, in Cherniye Gorod, the oil town two miles east of Baku itself — had happened along, in the event seemed even to have made himself useful.

But in fact — he realized this now, with time to think about it — it was all of a piece, parts of one picture. His purpose in visiting Leonide had been to urge her to get out of Baku before the Turks fought their way in — with consequences that would be truly dreadful, indeed had been seen elsewhere in recent months. Turks, with Tartars at their heels, thirsty mainly for Armenian blood but not being all that particular, and anyway Leonide was half Armenian, through her mother. Dunsterville hadn't been issuing any idle threat in that letter to the local bigwigs, at this stage it did look like touch-and-go whether he'd hang on or pull out, and without the British stiffening — British taking the brunt of the fighting and casualties, in fact — these others wouldn't stem the tide for more than ten minutes. It was plain lunacy for her to stay and risk it, especially since she didn't even belong here. Her family home was on the other side of the Caspian, at Krasnovodsk; she was in Baku only to fix things up domestically for her recently widowed uncle, set him up with a good housekeeper, and so forth, then go back home. This uncle, George Muromsky, was a big noise in the oil business, while Leonide's father Sergei in Krasnovodsk also traded in oil but more importantly was a member of the Trans-Caspian government.

Which was how Bob had met her. In Krasnovodsk he'd been required to attend an official reception given by Colonel Peter Fleming, the British military commander in Krasnovodsk, and Sergei Muromsky had been the guest of honour, accompanied by his wife and daughter. Daughter Leonide Sergeyevna Muromskaya being petite, dark-haired, dark-eyed, vivacious and exceptionally pretty, as lively and talkative as Bob himself was taciturn — at any rate this was how others thought of him, he knew, although the truth as he saw it was simply that he didn't chatter much — and both she and her parents had been intrigued to meet this rather large young Englishman who when he did feel obliged to do more than smile, nod or grunt was able to do it in absolutely fluent Russian. While from his own point of view, she was a refuge and relief from the monastic and professional seclusion of naval life; and having the advantage of the language, being in fact half Russian himself — well, why not?

In the Baku dockyard he parked the truck where it had been earlier this morning, behind a go-down they'd taken over for Royal Navy stores, and shut its door quietly, intending to walk away and with luck have nobody even aware the truck had been made use of; but actually thinking more about the fighting he'd just come from, hoping to God the Turks would be repulsed again this time, and wondering how long it would take — if they weren't — to complete the evacuation: and from this back to a natural concern for Leonide. Not that she was in any way his responsibility; but neither she nor her uncle seemed to appreciate just how precarious the military situation had become, that they could *not* rely for ever on a mere handful of British troops holding off a whole Turkish army ... Deep in thought, he'd barely turned his back on the truck when a voice called jarringly from an open doorway, 'Took a little joyride, did we?'

The West Country tones of Mr Dewhurst, Gunner, were unmistakable. Bob paused, saw the tall, ginger-headed Warrant Officer as he emerged from the shed with a look of triumph on his pink, long-nosed face.

'Morning, Guns.'

'Any time you've a hankering for my department's transport—'

'You weren't here to ask. Bit early in the day for you, I dare say.' He saw the dig go home ... 'And I was in a rush.'

'You're in the rattle now, I reckon.'

'In the rattle' meant 'in trouble'. A man up on a disciplinary charge was 'in the rattle' ... Dewhurst elaborated, 'Been shoutin' for you all over. Past hour or more ... Well, I saw the truck was gone, and I drew me own conclusions, but—'

'You didn't let on. You're a pal, Dewsy. Who wants me and what for?'

'Better ask the Admiral. He's still on board, far as I know.'

On board HMS *Zoroaster*, this had to mean. And by 'the Admiral' the Gunner meant Commodore Norris, Senior Naval Officer Caspian. *Zoroaster* was one of eight merchant ships which the Royal Navy had commandeered and armed with four-inch and four-seven guns hauled overland on trucks and tractors and camels' backs from Basra on the Persian Gulf. A major undertaking and a hell of a journey, by river barges most of the two hundred miles from the head of the Gulf to Dizful, and from there another four hundred over deserts and mountains via Hamadan and Kazvin to Enzeli, transporting not only guns but the ammunition for them, as well as a mass of other naval stores and one forty-foot CMB — Coastal

Motorboat — plus depthcharges, searchlights, wireless-telegraphy equipment — all the gear they'd needed to transform eight old rustbuckets into warships — of a kind . . .

They were flying the White Ensign now, anyway. Their commanding officers were British, with an assortment of British and Russian officers and crews. The letters HMS still looked and sounded a bit odd when prefixed to such ships' names as *President Kruger, Emil Nobel, Allaverdi, Slava, Babiabut, Zoroaster* — this last-named and the *Kruger* being currently in Baku, the others either at Krasnovodsk or on patrol.

Four of the flotilla of eight were constantly at sea. The Bolsheviks held Astrakhan, at the top end of the Caspian and the mouth of the Volga, with a sizeable naval force, some of which had recently been transferred from the Baltic by way of that mighty Russian river; and since Comrade Trotsky had mentioned Baku as being high on his acquisition list, the maintenance of an efficient watch at sea was obviously essential.

Bob climbed the gangway to the deck of HMS *Zoroaster*, saluted the side and asked the quartermaster, 'Commodore on board?'

'Gone ashore, sir.' The leading seaman added, 'But he was wanting you, sir — *everyone's* been—'

'CO on board?'

'In his cabin, sir.'

To be wanted in a hurry wasn't all that unusual. Bob had been appointed to this circus for sea duties with interpreting as a sideline, but as things had turned out it was very much the other way round. There was a shortage of Russians who could manage a little pigeon-English, let alone British with even a smattering of Russian, whereas Bob had been born and raised in St Petersburg — known for the last four years, since the outbreak of war in 1914 in fact, as Petrograd — and he was probably the only man in Baku at this moment who was equally at home in either language.

He knocked on the cabin door, heard a gruff 'Come in',

and pushed the door open.

'Morning, sir.'

'Well ...' Lieutenant-Commander Eric Barker — RNR, his nautical background was Merchant Navy like Bob's — was a heavy-set, prematurely balding man in his middle thirties. Small blue eyes glittering in reflected sunshine as he glanced up from his desk ... 'Well, at last!'

'No idea — until a minute ago. I gather the Commodore—'

'He went up to the Europa half an hour ago, had to collect some Russian there. General Dunsterville wanted him and you—'

'Take the stores truck, may I?'

'If it's available — I suppose — and if —' He'd checked suddenly, and slapped his own forehead. 'Damn it. Clean forgot, you'd have gone without it. Here.'

Handing him a buff-coloured 'OHMS' envelope with *Lieut. Cowan RNR* scrawled on it in the blue indelible pencil invariably used by the Commodore's yeoman of signals. A signal therefore, or cable by landline — communications with the outside world still had to be routed via Basra — and very likely passed to him for translation into Russian, for the Commodore to pass on to someone or other ... Bob ripped it open: focused on its signalese address and opening words with a sense first of surprise, then shock, then — dismay.

He was sitting — not having been conscious of the act of doing so, only finding himself in the round-backed wooden armchair ...

'Bad news, Bob?'

He'd leant forward: shutting his eyes, crumpling the sheet of signal pad between clenched fists. Seeing in memory the final line of the last letter he'd had from his father, a letter written from a town called Vologda ten or eleven weeks ago: and he was *hearing* that line from the letter, in his father's low, rasping tone ... *That'll have to be it for a while, then, old lad. See you in Blighty before too long, God willing ...*

God had not been willing. The old man had been

taking passage from Archangel in the cruiser HMS *Splendid*, bound for Rosyth, and she'd been lost with all hands — either mined or torpedoed.

'Bob?'

He looked up, nodded to the man behind the desk. 'Sorry.' Pulling himself together: a process which included remembering where he was, and that he was required up-town, had been about to leave — and at that, in a hurry. He paused at the cabin door: 'I'll — take the stores truck. Thank you, sir.'

His father had been 'getting a bit of trouble from the old ticker' — so he'd written in the letter from Vologda. Nothing to worry about, he was good for a few years yet, but he was being sent home 'just to be on the safe side'. In any case there hadn't been much useful work for him of late, in the drastically changed circumstances since last year's revolution and the Bolshevik takeover that had followed it. In 1914 he'd been recruited by the Foreign Office and appended to the British Embassy staff with special responsibilities for war supplies and shipping: having been in trade in Russia for nearly fifty years he'd been worth his weight in gold. Then all the Allied embassies had moved to Vologda a few months ago, when Lenin had transferred the seat of government from Petrograd to Moscow: Vologda being on the railway and well placed geographically for a getaway either north to Archangel or east through Siberia, if evacuation of diplomatic staffs became desirable.

It wasn't 'the old ticker' that had finished him off, anyway. Either a mine or a torpedo, the Admiralty had said. It didn't seem to matter which — not all that much . . .

If it was true. Suppose he'd been late getting to Archangel, left in some other ship instead . . .

Out into sunshine like a furnace. Returning the QM's salute. Rattling down the brow to the jetty.

Accept it. The old man's dead. Drowned. Accept it, come to terms with it . . .

The truck was where he'd left it. Rumblings of gunfire

from the north like distant thunder. He wondered how those North Staffs boys were getting on, whether they'd managed to get the abandoned guns into action, and how many of them might by this time be dead or wounded. Shouting into Mr Dewhurst's doorway 'I'm taking your truck, Guns!' Then stooping, grasping the crank-handle: with that signal in his pocket, a physical reality, undeniable, unchangeable …

The engine fired, spluttered, roared unevenly. About the only thing there was no shortage of, here at Baku, was petrol. There were oceans of it. All the ships were oil-fired, too. The oil was of course the chief attraction of the place, to the Turks and their German allies. Well, to everyone … But the strategic situation wasn't just that simple. Oil was part of it, and the Central Powers would certainly have loved to get their hands on these gushing wells, but — looking further, across the Caspian and over the Ust-Urt Plateau and the Golden Road to Samarkand — apart from the oil, this was a vital way-station on the Turks' route eastward into Afghanistan and thence into British India via the North-West Frontier. The Bolsheviks had ratted on their allies, signed their own peace treaty with Germany at Brest-Litovsk — in March of this year, 1918, just a few months ago — which was why Britain had had to send in military missions to organize and support local military resistance, and a naval force to secure the Caspian.

The Caspian was the door eastward; it had to be kept shut and barred, policed by the Royal Navy. That was the object of the naval presence, the reasoning that had lain behind the decision to mount that extraordinarily ambitious overland trek — an experience which he, Cowan, had enormously enjoyed.

At the Europa he parked the truck, hurried into the hotel foyer, looked around and spotted the Armenian manager.

'Commodore Norris here?'

'Ah, Lieutenant Cowan! What a *pleasure*—'

'Is Commodore Norris in the hotel?'

'Ah, no, sir. But I believe he left a message ...'

The message was to the effect that from here he'd been going to the Dunsterforce HQ, and Lieutenant Cowan was to report there at his earliest convenience. The manager murmured at Bob's elbow, 'They are saying there is a battle in progress now. Does the lieutenant have any information as to—'

'No. None at all.'

He'd noticed a certain tension in the staff and in the polyglot crowd of customers milling around this foyer and in and out of the hotel. Heads had turned as he'd come thrusting in: they were all jumpy for news of the fighting — even for news of a British evacuation, if that was what it had to come to. In which event, as well as mass panic there'd no doubt be instant readjustments of allegiances and attitudes. This town had, after all, been Bolshevik-governed until only a few weeks ago when the Dictatorship had taken over and asked for British help. Dunsterville had been kicking his heels down in Persia then, but he'd immediately sent off a small advance party and then followed — by sea from Enzeli in the *President Kruger* — with the rest of his force.

That operation might be put into reverse at very short notice now, Bob guessed, as he gunned the truck's rattly old engine, pulling out around the hotel and setting course for the military headquarters, a big villa on the northern edge of town which had been placed at the general's disposal by its rich owner, one of the Dictatorship or one of their oil-rich supporters.

There were plenty of very well-heeled citizens in and around Baku. All of them with a lot to lose. And evacuation *could* be imminent ... Remembering his experiences in the earlier part of the morning, seeing again the taut anxiety in some of the faces in the Europa — and knowing how keenly tuned these people's ears and instincts so often were.

Not that there'd been a shred of anxiety in Leonide, earlier on. Recalling her surprised, almost indignant response to his own quiet pleading ... 'But — surely there can be no real danger — with your British army here to protect us? Your General Dunsterville surely wouldn't just walk away and leave us to the mercy of the Turks?'

She'd laughed at such a preposterous notion. He'd tried to explain: 'There are very few of our troops, you see. Really, just a handful — and the deuce of a lot of Turks. Odds of something like ten to one, or worse.'

'But we have Russian battalions as well, surely?'

He'd baulked at telling her that her own people were more of a liability than an asset. It would have taken a lot of explaining, however carefully one had been able to approach the subject and even if she'd have been prepared to listen — which he didn't for a moment think she would have been. What he'd have put to her — or tried to — was that nobody could accuse the individual Russian soldier of cowardice: Russians could, often *had*, fought like tigers when they were properly led. But they had no real leadership here, no discipline or sense of motivation, very little idea of what if anything they were fighting for — let alone might be fighting for tomorrow.

In fact his visit to her had been something of a fiasco. He'd gone without prior warning or invitation, and found that she already had a caller — an Armenian of about Bob's own age, well dressed, sure of himself, obviously not short of roubles. Name of — he stretched his memory — keeping his father's image out of it, or at least no more than shadowy in the background — and got it: Gavril. Surname elusive . . .

Then outside — Bob had said at once that he couldn't stay, had only been passing and looked in on the off-chance, and she'd come out with him to the curve of white steps that fronted this rather grand house — she'd asked him, 'Come this evening? Please do. My uncle would appreciate it very much, Robert Aleksand'ich, he truly would. Please?'

'I don't know. I mean — that I can get away. But listen . . .'

He'd told her what he'd come for — to persuade her to go back to Krasnovodsk before this place fell open to the

Turks — and so on, so forth; they'd had that brief and clearly non-productive conversation between the front steps and his truck.

Well — Mr Dewhurst's truck . . .

Dunsterforce HQ was in sight ahead now, set well back from the winding, uphill road amongst luxuriant gardens and with the Union Flag drooping from a slightly askew flagpole in front of the columned portico. He drove the truck into a space amongst other vehicles on what might until recently have been a croquet lawn, climbed out and headed for those front steps.

'Lieutenant Cowan, sir?'

A sergeant of the Royal Warwicks: he had one arm in a sling, doubtless the reason for his soft number here. And Bob's naval whites stood out like a sore thumb, of course, in the military environment. The sergeant told him, 'Been watching out for you, sir. I'll pass the word you're here. The Russian officer's just along here, sir — you're supposed to join him.'

'Very well. Thank you, Sergeant.'

'In here, sir.' He pushed a heavy door open, and stood aside. 'Captain — er — Sullivitsky, sir . . .'

Bob saw a slightly pained look on the face of the uniformed Russian who'd been semi-reclining on a plush-covered sofa in this small anteroom. He was pushing himself up now: by the look of him might well have been asleep. Tallish, slim, with thick brown hair which he was smoothing back with both hands now, and regular, handsome features. He said in Russian, 'I suppose you are Lieutenant Cowan. My name is Solovyev — not whatever that fool said. Captain Count Nikolai Petrovich Solovyev.'

They shook hands. Bob slow to speak: still preoccupied although he knew he had to clear his mind and concentrate on present business: whatever the hell it might turn out to be . . . 'I'm Bob Cowan. Robert Aleksandrovich Cowan, if you like.' He'd said it in full consciousness of its meaning: *Robert son of Alexander* . . . 'I've no idea what this is about.'

'I know you haven't. I'm expected to explain it to you,

so that then you can brief your naval commander and the General. I've already given him the bones of it, he knows why I'm here and — I *think* — what's at stake. But his knowledge of Russian is — er — limited, eh?'

'It is, rather.' Solovyev was sitting down again, and waving Bob to a nearby chair, as if he was the host here. Which perhaps he *was*, in one sense ... There was an attaché case on the table close to him, and a folded map on top of it. He was right about General Dunsterville anyway; the General was reputedly competent in the Russian language, but the competence didn't extend far beyond a formal, purely social usage.

Bob asked the Count, 'Do you speak any English?'

'Oh, my dear fellow — I can say *please*, and *thank you*, and *how are you today* ... May I ask how it is that you speak Russian as well as you do?'

'I was born and brought up in St Petersburg. My father settled there — from Scotland — when he was still a young man. And my mother was Russian.'

'Are they still—'

'No. No, they're not.' He dropped into the chair. 'Tell me what we're here for?'

'At least what *I* am here for ...'

Bob guessed, settling down to listen, that Solovyev was probably a few years older than him. Thirty or so. Same height, near enough, but slimmer. More — the word might be 'elegant'. It was not an adjective he'd ever have thought of in relation to himself, but it applied to this fellow, he thought. A twinge of frustration accompanied the notion that Leonide would undoubtedly find him attractive — with his brown wavy hair, regular features and that air of sophistication. And of course his rank — despite the fact that counts in Russia came at about a guinea a baker's dozen. But you could see, too, that he'd been through it, that he was a soldier, not a courtier — as he was confirming, at this moment: 'I've been with the Volunteer Army on the Don for the past seven or eight months. Notably in the fighting around Rostov — I'm glad to say we did rather well. But — if you'll forgive my coming straight to the point — here's what concerns us, at least what I hope and pray will concern your commanders here.'

He paused, looking hard at Bob — with anxiety in his greenish eyes, as if Bob could possibly have set his mind at rest, or influenced anything here in any way ... Frowning now: 'I should mention to start with that I came down from Petrovsk last night, in the gunboat *Ardaghan.* Before that, I had made my way overland to Petrovsk — yes, through that murderous rabble ...'

Through the Bolshevik army in that sector, was what he was saying. And from General Denikin's base in Don Cossack territory — probably all of five hundred miles, Bob guessed. Hearing him explain, 'I brought with me a request from Denikin to Bicherakov that he should send me on to you here as fast as possible. That's how I come to be talking to you, now.'

'Quite a journey you've made.'

'But listen, now. I received — nearly five weeks ago — a visitor. And my God, *his* journey ... At that time we were re-grouping for the assault on Ekaterinodar — which when I got to Petrovsk I was delighted to learn has now fallen to us ... But this visitor — messenger — when I'd last seen him was in Petrograd. He'd become a naval cadet just before the revolution: and my sister and this boy's sister are the closest of friends. Anyway, he was now about nineteen years old, and he'd come from my family's country house — what *was* our house might be nearer the truth — near Enotayevsk ... D'you know where that is?'

Bob shook his head. 'Not the foggiest.'

'I'll show you in a minute.' Glancing towards the map: then reaching to it, opening it out as he continued. 'He'd come from there, anyway, with a message to me from my mother — from my sister, in fact, it was my mother's message but she was ill, it was my sister who'd sent Boris ... My mother incidentally is the Countess Maria Ivanovna Solovyeva. I had heard nothing from her or of her since — well, a year, at least — but she and my sister must have found each other somehow. Oh, and this boy's sister was with them too — and also, most importantly of all—'

He'd checked. 'I must explain to you first that my mother was First Lady-in-Waiting to the Dowager Empress Maria Feodorovna.'

'The Tsar's mother . . .'

Solovyev nodded solemnly. 'Yes. And the message which this young man brought was to inform me that my mother and sister and Boris's own sister, *and the two children* — were in hiding in — well, in some part of our house, and at the time he set off with this message my mother was gravely ill. I don't know what kind of illness, only she couldn't move from there. But — well, reading between the lines of what Boris could tell me — he was not at all articulate, as in a minute I'll explain — they'd had a truly frightful journey down to Enotayevsk — by what route, with what privations, one can only guess but I suppose they had some reason to imagine they'd be safe there . . . You have a question?'

Bob nodded. 'You mentioned children. Relations, or—'

'*Good* question.' A nod . . . 'I asked Boris Nikolai'ich the same — *what* children? — but by this time he was — wandering, in his mind and speech. He'd arrived with a badly infected wound — you could smell the gangrene a mile away and he was just skin and bone, hardly a breath left in his body. It looked to me like a bayonet wound — here —' Solovyev touched his upper thigh, close to the groin — 'and the doctor agreed with me. But also that the boy was' — he hesitated — 'not long for this world. From what he'd told me when he first arrived I deduced that he'd been a very long time on his way — may have been a month, two months even — and I *believe* he said that he'd been forcibly enlisted at one stage in some Bolshevik unit. In which case he must have got away from them after he was wounded. He may have been left for dead — or as no further use to them — I wouldn't put *that* past them. He'd certainly had no medical attention — and either no food at all, or scraps . . . He had my sister's message off by heart, or so it seemed, the way he whispered it — two or three times, exactly the same — and nothing else ... And within two days he was dead. I was present, and the doctor was fighting to save his life or at least bring him back to consciousness — at my urging, I have to admit it was mostly in the hope he'd tell me something about these children. But—' the Count shook his head — 'no such luck. Luck enough to have got to me and delivered the message, I suppose. Then his strength gave out. It could have been only force of will that had kept him alive, I suppose the knowledge of the others relying on him for *their* lives.'

Solovyev had stopped again. Gazing across the room ... Then abruptly: 'I went to see General Denikin. You won't have got the point of this yet, but believe me, this was now a great deal more than just my personal concern for my mother and sister. I believed by that time, as I do now, that I have been entrusted with — well, in my own conviction, with the lives of two of their Imperial Majesties' daughters. In all probability the only two surviving members of the immediate family. Of course you will have heard the various rumours — that they've all been murdered, that they're prisoners, that they're living in disguise as peasants in this or that district ... Nobody knows, do they. But personally I wouldn't have bet on any of them being still alive — until this message. You see, here's the crux of it: my mother would never have named the children, *if* they are who I believe they must be. As I've told you, my mother was in close relationship with the mother of His Imperial Majesty — these girls' grandmother. What could be more likely than that in all the confusion and danger besetting them, if the family were having to split up, my mother would have been the person to whom they'd have entrusted them. D'you follow me? And besides, if 'the two children' were anyone else — young cousins, or children of friends, whoever — why would she *not* have named them? Huh? D'you take my point? I feel certain that this was her way of telling me — her *coded* message to me. Do you see it, as I'm trying to explain how *I* see it?'

He nodded. 'Except — correct me if I'm wrong — are any of those four Grand Duchesses exactly children, now?'

'In what would have been my mother's use of the word — yes. In fact the youngest, Anastasia, is now I suppose seventeen. The others nineteen, twenty-one — that's Tatiana — and then Olga about twenty-three. But in any case they are *Their Majesties'* children. Also it's not unlikely she was referring to the two youngest — the Grand Duchesses Anastasia and Maria.'

'All right. You'd know a lot better than I can, but — I agree, it holds water.'

'Of course it does. In fact it can't be interpreted any other way. This was also the view taken by General Denikin, I may tell you. We discussed it from all angles — and what might be done and how, and by whom ... But you see, to get there, to Enotayevsk — through not only the Bolshevik lines but through hundreds of miles of territory which at present they control — well, one man alone — even young Boris, just a boy, God rest his soul, and not particularly robust — but for an individual, or a team of fit men — fine, why not, with a bit of luck and nerve? But then — to come all the way out again — with women and children?'

Bob agreed. 'Impossible.'

'But now look here.' Solovyev leaned forward, shook the map open and spread it on the table. 'Here. Here now — Enotayevsk. Exactly — *here* ... The house is in fact a few versts to the south of it — about here. Right on the water's edge. Very beautiful surroundings, by the way.'

Bob focused on that area. Then checked against the distance scale. Getting an idea finally of what this was about, what was being proposed or was about to be proposed.

'Must be — what, a hundred miles up-river?'

'About that.'

Up the Volga. A hundred miles north of Astrakhan, the Bolsheviks' stronghold on the Caspian.

Commodore Norris glanced at the Count, then back at Bob. 'So what exactly is he asking us to do? Mount some sort of raid?'

'No, sir. I've explained — and he understands — that there's no question of being able to get up-river. What he's hoping is that we'd put him ashore — well, anywhere it can be managed, really, but obviously he'd prefer it to be somewhere inside the delta — and then to pick him up — with the ladies, touch wood — at some later date. Timing obviously subject to planning detail, and presumably a series of alternative dates, but — something of that sort.'

'Hmm.' Drumming his fingers on the map. 'Just him — one man alone ... Does he have a plan, any idea of how he'd get them out?'

Bob turned back to the Count, to put this question to him, but the General arrived at that moment: bursting in, slamming the door shut behind him: 'Well, Cowan? Got it all straight for us, have you?'

'Sir.' Bob had stiffened momentarily to attention; the others were on their feet as well, the Commodore asking 'How's the battle going, sir?'

'Battle's over.' A quick shake of the head, a scowl: 'At much too high a cost, but — well, main thing is we've sent 'em scurrying — with their tails between their legs. If Turks have tails. Wouldn't surprise me if they did.' He laughed, a bark of laughter that filled the room, had them all chuckling with him. Lionel Dunsterville, major-general, was a smallish man with a narrow, bony face and a configuration of prominent nose and deep-set eyes that gave him a distinctly hawkish look. His last command had been of the 1st Infantry Brigade, on the North-West Frontier; and as a former schoolfellow at Rugby of Mr Rudyard Kipling he'd been the original 'Stalky' of Mr Kipling's famous *Stalky and Co.* He told Bob, nodding towards the Count, 'Ask him whether he knows if Turks have tails or not ... No — on second thoughts, don't. Intriguing subject, but we haven't time for it. Give me the gist of what he wants of us — or of you, rather, it's a naval matter, isn't it?'

Bob went over it all again. It was evident from the General's quick and unsurprising acceptance of the story that he'd had a fair grasp of its basics before this, from his earlier talk with Solovyev. He'd be better at understanding Russian than at speaking it, no doubt. The part that did require careful explanation was the detail of the message where it mentioned children, the Count's reasons for believing that his mother had been telling him a lot more than anyone else could have guessed.

'His point being, sir, that his mother would hardly have sent a message to him that would have had no meaning for him. The reference to unnamed children had to mean *something* — and she'd know that he'd puzzle over it, and—'

'Yes. Got it.' The hawk's eyes blinked two or three times. 'And that's a tip to us on the importance of keeping the whole business very much under *our* hats. Eh? The Bolshies want the Tsar's family off the face of the earth — off Russian earth, anyway — so if they got as much as a sniff of this, Norris—'

'You're absolutely right, sir.'

'Second point — before I leave it with you — is we're talking about our own King's close relations. Sent a cruiser all the way to Archangel, didn't he, to pick up one of his aunts, or somesuch? Huh? Well, what I'm saying is if we do have it in our power to help this chap save their lives . . .'

Solovyev asked Bob, 'What is he saying?'

'Hang on. Tell you in a moment.'

' — if it looks to you like a practical proposition, we'd have no business *not* to have a shot at it. Eh, Norris?'

A nod. 'We'll have to look into ways and means, of course, there are some problems involved, but — yes, one way or another . . .'

Bob said quietly in Russian, 'We're going to try to help', and the Count's eyes gleamed. Then the lids covered them: he murmured, '*Slava Bogu . . .*'

'What was that?'

'He said "Glory be to God", sir.' The Count was on his

feet by this time, thanking the two senior officers profusely. Bob wondering, while he more or less automatically interpreted a phrase or two here and there, what it was about the Russian that he'd just discovered he didn't trust. Then it was gone: other thoughts were crowding up, and on top of everything else the Commodore was telling Dunsterville, 'I think I'll put Cowan in charge of this, sir – having the lingo he's the best man for it, to liaise with the Count here, work out some kind of scheme . . .'

2

Over breakfast next morning Johnny Pope, 23-year-old skipper of the flotilla's one and only CMB — coastal motorboat — asked Bob curiously, 'So what's behind this sudden interest?'

Interest in his CMB, he meant. Bob had asked him whether the boat was ready for sea, and when Pope had told him of course she was, he made damn sure she *always* was, he'd asked a few more questions — about her range and fuel consumption, for instance — and then mentioned that he'd very much like a trip to sea in her.

Mr Dewhurst, at the other end of the table, began to chuckle and shake his ginger head ... They were in the wardroom — formerly the saloon — of HMS *President Kruger.* The *Kruger* was being held in Baku now on Dunsterville's orders, on stand-by against the possible contingency of short-notice evacuation. She had room enough in her for the whole of Dunsterforce, and meanwhile she was available as a mess and accommodation for shore-based flotilla staff.

Pope asked Dewhurst, 'Something amusing you, Guns?'

'Definitely.' A jerk of the head, towards Bob. '*That* feller. Proper caution, he is. Ask him what he's *really* after, why don't you?'

'Well?'

Bob shrugged. 'God knows.'

'Certain party in Cherniye Gorod?' Dewhurst winked. 'Not of the male — er — gender, should I say?' He reached for the honey. 'Well — she gets rides in my departmental transport, so — stands to reason, don't it? —

next item on the programme's a jaunt on the ocean wave. Am I right, Bob?'

He stared at him for a long moment. Recalling some of his conversation with Leonide's uncle last evening, George Muromsky's attempt to question him on his career prospects and finances. It had occurred to him while he'd been parrying these questions that if he'd stated baldly, 'My father's dead and it leaves me fairly rich', the oil man would immediately have warmed to him as to a prospective member of the family ... He remembered the instant dislike he'd felt for him then. First because he'd have willingly given everything he had if it could have brought the old man back to life, and second because the questioning had been an irrelevance and quite unwarranted, since at no time had he had any such notions in his own mind, or said or done anything to suggest that he might have. In fact that clear indication of Muromsky-type priorities tended — perhaps unfairly — to make even Leonide rather less attractive.

Back to earth: or rather, to *Zoroaster*'s wardroom. Nodding to Mr Dewhurst ... 'Tell you the truth, Guns, nothing of the sort had crossed my mind. But it's not at all a bad idea.' He looked at Pope then: 'Re my *real* interest in your CMB, Johnny — spare me a few minutes after breakfast, would you?'

He'd glanced over his shoulder — letting Pope understand that the proximity and sharp ears of the Armenian steward was reason enough not to pursue the subject here. And having in mind the Commodore's strictures about secrecy: he'd told Bob to report directly to him, consulting any of the staff from whom he might need advice or information, in the course of putting an outline plan together, but to tell nobody any more about it than he had to. He'd told him this when they'd been leaving the headquarters villa, about to go their separate ways; then he'd stopped, glanced round to make sure they were alone ... 'Look here, Cowan. I saw the — the private communication you had this morning. As you must know, it's routine that I'm shown such messages. I want to tell you how *extremely* sorry I am. There's next to nothing one can say on these occasions that's of any real use or comfort — time's the only healer, isn't it — but — well, I do know — from my own experience, as it happens — what a *frightful* blow—'

'Yes, sir. Thank you. But — it's all right, I—'

'You're very much a key man in this flotilla, Cowan. Well, obviously, your particular talents are quite invaluable to me, but beyond that I'm more than satisfied with the way you've been carrying your several responsibilities. *More* than satisfied ... And this Solovyev business now — if you can make a success of it — strictly between you and me, Cowan — I'd eat my hat if some form of recognition were not forthcoming.'

The implication had been — presumably — promotion or a decoration. But whether the Commodore's motivation in telling him this had been an extension of that expression of sympathy — a kind-hearted attempt to cheer him up, in fact — or whether it might have derived from Dunsterville's assumption in regard to HM the King's interest in saving his young Russian cousins' lives — well, there might have been elements of both. While Bob, saluting as the Commodore — immaculate even if semi-strangled, in his high-necked No. 6 uniform jacket — strode away towards his Ford motorcar, was hearing his father's voice, the hoarse, gravelly tones that furnished most of the sound-effects to all his earliest recollections, the old man telling him — four years ago when he'd changed his Merchant Navy stripes to RNR ones — *If you're ever tempted to get up to any heroics, lad, make bloody certain someone sees you doing it!*

But for God's sake — all one was about to do was take a man in a boat and deposit him on a beach ...

Anyway — Operation Nightingale — Bob's label for it, the Russian word for nightingale being *Solovyei* — was scheduled to set out from Baku tomorrow evening, which of course put an unalterable limitation on the time available for planning and essential preparations. Even this wasn't soon enough for the Count. He'd been moved out of the Europa Hotel into the headquarters mess now, with the cover story that he'd come with despatches from Bicherakov and would be returning to Petrovsk as soon as telegraphic answers to questions raised by the Cossack leader had come back to Dunsterville from London. This justified his presence at headquarters and would explain his disappearance tomorrow; but meanwhile he was complaining bitterly at not being allowed to set out immediately. On the face of it, ridiculous — forty-eight hours, to set the whole thing up from scratch — but seeing it through his eyes the impatience was understandable. An hour's or a day's delay *could* make all the difference; and as he'd pointed out, it was something like three months now since his mother and sister had sent off their message. It might already be too late; even before that boy had staggered into the Volunteer Army's lines, the women might have been found and arrested.

In which case, they'd be dead. And knowing Bolshevik ways with aristocratic prisoners, it might be better for them if they were.

Last night in George Muromsky's house at Cherniye Gorod, Leonide had had a young cousin with her, a rather plain girl of about fifteen called Adriana. They'd sipped at glasses of tea, and Leonide had done nearly all the talking — telling him for instance how she'd always longed to visit England, and advancing a number of what he'd thought were rather inconsequential reasons why if things went badly here — which they wouldn't, of course, she was certain that in the long run everything was going to come out right — *if* the worst came to the worst, why England was the only other country to which she felt she could happily transplant herself. Adriana had agreed with everything her cousin had said, in giggly whispers and taking care never to let her eyes meet Bob's; and what with one thing and another, by the time the uncle joined them, bringing with him a decanter of a local firewater called *Kishmishkova* — it was a vodka made from raisins — he'd felt more than ready for it. Adriana had immediately retired — it was obvious she'd only been left there so that Bob and Leonide wouldn't be alone together — and

Leonide left the room with her, promising to be back shortly. Then, in the ensuing conversation — partly to change its direction, as Muromsky had been starting on his cross-examination about Bob's future plans, financial prospects and so forth — Bob had asked him whether he had any really authentic information concerning the fate of the Imperial family.

The older man had looked startled. 'Why do you ask me this question?'

Part of the reason of course must have been that he'd had Count Solovyev's story in the back of his mind. He'd answered vaguely — truthfully, as it happened — 'Oh, some of us were discussing it earlier on. Wondering which of the stories one might believe — if any.' He'd shrugged. 'They all seem to contradict each other, don't they?'

'Indeed. But it's not a subject I find pleasant to discuss, Lieutenant. If you don't mind . . .'

Leonide had returned in time to hear the last part of this. She'd murmured, setting down a tray of caviar and thin toast, 'Alapayevsk . . . What they say was done there seems to me — believable.'

She'd said it to her uncle, but she was offering the caviar to Bob now. Adding in a murmur, 'God rest their souls, poor darlings.'

The uncle asked her — challengingly — 'Where did *you* hear of it, may I enquire?'

'Oh.' She gestured — eastward, across the Caspian. 'At home everyone was whispering about it. I suppose because it sounds so real, so detailed, each of the poor creatures named so specifically.' She looked at Bob. 'Did you not hear it?'

'No. But I'd like to.' He added, 'That is, if you don't mind, sir.'

'Why should he mind?'

Muromsky told her heavily, 'Because it is not a fit subject for a young girl to speculate upon.'

'Oh, Uncle, *really* . . .' She'd moved impatiently. 'What we know, we *know.* We don't create evil by acknowledging its existence, nor do we eliminate it by pretending it's not there. So please, permit me . . . Bob, you *must* have heard the report that their Imperial Majesties together with their children and attendants had been murdered at Ekaterinburg — early in July?'

'But —' Bob had glanced at the uncle, then back at her — 'didn't the *Sovnarkom* issue a statement to the effect that only the Tsar had been shot?'

'What if they did? Would you believe a single word from *that* source?'

'I suppose not. But there were some other rumours too, weren't there. For instance, a rescue by — well, I forget . . . But the story I heard was that they weren't shot at all, that was just a red herring while in fact the Bolsheviks had agreed to hand them over to the Germans — in return for German support of the regime? And then —' he went on quickly, forestalling interruption — 'that the train carrying them was intercepted by this White Guard officer — whose name — is it Bulygin?'

'I have no idea.' Leonide seemed impatient. 'As you said, there are so many conflicting accounts. And — yes, for all we actually *know* they might all still be alive . . . Except that — well, this other report — rumour if you like — is that on the day after — at Alapayevsk, which in case you don't know is about a hundred miles to the north-east of Ekaterinburg — they'd imprisoned there the Grand Duchess Elizabeth, Grand Duke Sergei Mikhailovich —' she'd begun ticking them off name by name, on her fingers — 'oh, the three sons of Grand Duke Constantine — and one other . . .'

George Muromsky muttered as if unwillingly, 'Vladimir — Grand Duke Paul's son.'

'Yes. I knew it was six . . . Bob, they took them to this place outside the town where there's a disused mineshaft, and — threw them into it, one by one.'

'Except for Prince John.' Muromsky spoke in a low tone, without looking at either of them, gazing at his own clasped hands. 'Grand Duke Constantine's eldest son. He insisted on — as I heard it, anyway — throwing himself into the shaft — after encouraging the others, assuring them that they were going to a better life, to their Eternal Father.'

Uncle and niece had crossed themselves, and both were silent. Bob waited until Leonide stirred before he said quietly, 'It doesn't have to be true, Leonide.'

'No, but — listing them like that, name by name, makes it *seem* true. One can —' she paused — 'almost *see* it happening. Those poor, *poor* people . . .'

What Bob saw — recognizing it quite suddenly — was the tension and distress in her. It was in her voice first, then a barely discernible physical tremor that seemed to pass right through her like a spasm of pain or an electric shock. If he'd been alone with her he'd have gone to her and taken her in his arms, tried to comfort her; he *wanted* to, but Muromsky's eyes were on him and he could only sit there — stifled, useless — and Leonide was hurrying from the room, one hand pressing a tiny handkerchief to her eyes while Muromsky — burly, pudding-faced — growled, 'There — you see . . .'

It was all suppressed, he'd realized — *contained*, inside them. The Imperial family's fate was only one piece of it, a talking point because the Romanovs were who they were — the figureheads, potential rallying point, which of course was why the Bolsheviks needed to eliminate them. But murder, torture, every disgusting form of brutality and licence had been commonplace and widespread — still was, and they were all too starkly aware of it, but — he was looking at Muromsky but in his visual memory seeing again Leonide's involuntary reflex, that momentarily visible symptom of the terror she was so desperate to keep hidden — they *all* were, all clinging frantically to the pretence of normality.

She'd assured him — again — that she was in no danger here. George Muromsky had said the same, emphatically. He'd told Bob that if the situation deteriorated he'd take her to Krasnovodsk himself: he'd have adequate warning time — he wasn't totally out of touch with what was happening in his own town, for heaven's sake — and there was always plenty of room in the steamers on that regular ferry route. And so on, so forth ... And — Bob thought — perhaps for Muromsky, with the authority he carried in this community, warning would be given and berths *would* be found. But there'd be panic, too — Muromsky probably lacked the imagination to foresee this — thousands of them in a blind rush to force their way into anything that floated.

He arrived at the CMB berth in an inner basin of the Baku dockyard at exactly 2 pm; he'd arranged this with Johnny Pope after breakfast. Since then Pope had been sent for by the Commodore, who'd told him that he and his CMB were to be employed on a special operation, details of which would be confided to him in due course by Lieutenant Cowan, with whom he was meanwhile to co-operate. Norris had also stressed the need for very strict security.

Pope — tall, slim, fair-haired, known to some as 'DD', standing for 'Debs' Delight' — strolled towards him. 'So you're our big white chief now, Bob!'

'I've got a lot of donkey-work to do, that's all. And it's all pretty vague so far, I haven't cleared any of it yet with the Commodore ... But—' he'd stopped, looking downward and along the side of the jetty to a stern-on view of the forty-foot CMB. Cigar-shaped, and with the tail-end of her single torpedo protruding above the low, fantail-shaped stern. 'You won't be needing that torpedo, anyway. Better land it, Johnny, after this outing. You'll be carrying some extra weight — and what's more—'

'Passengers, would the extra weight be?'

'Yes. Well — later on, second trip — in a week's time, could be ten days or a fortnight — but for the first one anyway I think we might load you with a skiff — on that torpedo stowage?'

'Skiff, eh.' Pope raised his eyebrows. '*Very* cloak and dagger. But — why not. As long as it's well lashed down and chocked. We crash around quite a bit, you know — well, you'll see for yourself, in a minute. If there's the least bit of a chop, any high-speed stuff—'

'We shouldn't need your full forty knots. But let's pray for a flat calm anyway . . . All I'm asking for now, incidentally, is to be shown how everything works and how to handle her — because at a later stage I want to take Chris Henderson's place. Oh, and look — your spare CMB officer — Willoughby—'

'He's currently a watchkeeper in *Zoroaster*.'

'We'll be taking him along. And there's another Motor Mechanic, whose name I regret to say I don't—'

'Name's Keane. Working in the dockyard, supervising a bunch of hamfisted locals.'

'We'll want him too.' They were strolling up the jetty, towards the patiently waiting Sub-Lieutenant Henderson. Bob stopped, looking down at the CMB again. 'I'd better sketch it out for you, Johnny. Otherwise you won't know what's wanted, and we might miss out on something. After all, you're the expert.'

'Kind of you to say so.'

'It's called giving the devil his due . . . But — in a nutshell, there's a man to be put ashore up in Bolshy territory, and then — touch wood — picked up again a week or two later, by which time he should have some other people with him. The exact point of landing and pick-up hasn't been settled yet, but it'll be up at the top end, wouldn't be practical therefore to shoot you off from here — impossible, in fact, especially the pick-up later — so the answer is for your boat to be taken up north in tow.'

'In tow of what?'

'*Soroaster*. She's due to sail about 6 pm tomorrow, to relieve *Allaverdi* on patrol. So if you push off at about seven — an economical speed being twenty knots, you said — you could rendezvous with her off the end of the peninsula — well, off Zhiloy island — say, 9 pm. Allowing her fifteen knots, that is. Better than sailing from here in company — broad daylight and the locals' eyes on you — especially if some Bolshevik agent knew a certain passenger had embarked. It's no secret *Zoroaster*'ll be heading north, it's a routine change-over; a clever spy might put two and two together.'

'Do the Bolshies *have* clever spies?'

'The Germans do. Plenty of their agents about. The Dictatorship may think they've locked 'em all up, but ...' He shrugged. 'And they're hand-in-glove with the Bolsheviks, aren't they? Anyway, our mystery man will be on board, and so will I. You'll make the rendezvous and pick up the tow, and transfer yourself to *Zoroaster*, while Willoughby takes your place. Or you could all pack in from the start, of course – save a bit of trouble. But the idea is to have those others crew the CMB as long as she's in tow. With the spare MM too – if you need a mechanic on board at all when she's in tow – d'you reckon?'

'Safer. Tow might part – boat lost – pitch dark, foul weather ...'

'All right. So you'll put Keane on board too. But you see, by making the trip in comfort *you* won't be played out when the time comes to make the run inshore. You and I and McNaught, plus the passenger, will swap round with the other three for that on the following night. And your passage crew get a square meal and a sleep while we're away.'

'I'll make one guess, Bob. Man we're landing's a Russian. Am I right?'

Glancing at him. It was so obvious: but he plainly did think he was being clever ... 'Think so, do you?'

'Well – after all – why else would *you* need to come along?'

He wagged his head. 'Brilliant, Johnny.'

It had been Count Solovyev's suggestion, that he should be able to communicate with the crew of whatever craft was running him in to the coast, right up to the moment of landing. There could be some snag or change of plan, reason to switch to some other landing place, for instance. Or a last-minute message to send back. And as he spoke no English other than 'How are you today?', and neither Pope nor Henderson had any Russian other than *Za vashi zdorovye* – which in this Caspian flotilla had largely replaced such phrases as 'Down the hatch' or 'God bless us' – an interpreter was obviously a must.

They'd turned back towards the boat now. Bob explaining, 'As for the pick-up — well, we've a bit of time yet for agreeing the details, but the best thing might be if *Allaverdi* stays with the patrol until we've put our man ashore and returned, then you and I embark in her, she takes the CMB in tow — with Henderson and Willoughby on the job again — and we steam back here. I'd thought of Petrovsk, earlier on, as it's so much closer, but most of the Russian flotilla's there now, could be a security risk. Anyway, from here we'd go up north again just the same way, with whichever of the flotilla's rejoining the patrol a week later.'

'Your man's going to take about a week, is he, doing whatever it is he's doing?'

'Could be longer. That second time, we may have to stay with the patrol, make a trip inshore every second day or so.'

'You'd *better* pray for your flat calm, then. I can tell you a CMB is neither designed nor in the least suited to long periods at sea. No, Bob . . .'

'Might have to hoist her inboard, then.' He thought about it — which ships had heavy lifts, which didn't . . . 'It's a good point, thank you.' He raised his voice. 'Sorry to keep you waiting, Chris.'

Chris Henderson, Sub-Lieutenant, touched his hat to them as they joined him. 'Secrets of State?'

'Wouldn't you know it.' Pope waved Bob ahead of him to the ladder. 'Age before beauty . . .'

They had the bow and stern lines rigged so that they could be cast off from down on the CMB, and Pope's mechanic already had the 340-horsepower engine ticking over, the deep throbbing of its exhaust pulsing across the quiet water. Bob climbed down the vertical iron ladder, stepped off it on to the boat's narrow side-decking and thence into the cockpit, where he crouched to peer in through the hatchway — in the cockpit's forward bulkhead, the engine-space being in the midships section of the boat — to say hello to the artificer. They already knew each other, of course: there was no one in the flotilla he didn't know, after the shared exertions of that overland haul from Basra.

'Zero' McNaught — hunched, craggy-faced, brilliantly blue eyes blazing in a lean, tanned face — was squatting on his wooden seat. An eyebrow rose: 'Com'n' out for a spin, sir?'

He nodded. 'Thought I should put in a bit of sea-time, you know.'

'Aye ... Sir — if you don't mind me asking — seeing as you might be in the know — is it true what they say, there's another six or twelve boats as'll be wi' us soon?'

It was true that there was such an intention — to give the flotilla a full set of sharp teeth, to counter the Bolsheviks' growing naval strength at Astrakhan. But those CMBs were in the Black Sea, waiting to be railed overland from Batoum to Baku when or if this Azerbaijani end of the railway could be secured against the Turks.

Not that any such development seemed exactly imminent, the way things had been going lately; rather the reverse, in fact. Bob confirmed, 'The boats are ear-marked for us, I gather. It's getting 'em here is the snag.'

McNaught and these others would be glad to have other CMB men here. They were a close-knit lot, many of them having served together in other theatres — notably in the Channel, out of Dover and Harwich. And Bob was quite used to seagoing officers and men asking him such questions; they knew that his interpreter's job made him privy to a lot of restricted information.

He was under instruction now, though. Pope telling him, 'Torpedo firing gear here, Bob. I know we won't be taking the fish with us, but I might as well give you a proper education ...'

They stayed out at sea for about an hour and a half, in the lee of the peninsula, in a sea that was choppy despite that shelter, and he learnt to handle the boat reasonably well. The point of doing so being that as he'd be taking Henderson's place later on, he should be able to do his share of the work. In fact since accidents can happen, especially on dark nights in unfamiliar waters in high-speed boats, he had to be capable of taking over, at a pinch, even if necessary of bringing the CMB back on his own. Pope, he guessed, would be taking this fact of life for granted.

'Want to take her in now, Bob?'

'All right ...'

'Just remember the engine can't be put astern. So if you're travelling too fast there's no way to slow her, your only hope is to have room to go round in circles while the way comes off her.'

He thought about it – about piling the CMB into some jetty, wrecking not only the boat but also their best way of putting Solovyev down on that coastline – and stood back from the wheel. 'Show us how, Johnny ...'

He was ashore in time to be only a few minutes late for his next appointment – with the flotilla navigating officer, in *President Kruger*'s charthouse at noon. The Commodore wouldn't have approved the navigational aspects of the plans without Lieutenant-Commander Snaith's imprimatur on them, and in any case Bob wanted the benefit of his advice in regard to that north coast, the local so-called 'charts' being notoriously unreliable.

Snaith, like Bob, was RNR, formerly a Merchant Navy officer. Red-faced over a pepper-and-salt beard, and with the reputation of having drunk a bunch of Cossack officers under the table – drinking vodka, their own tipple, at that ... He listened to Bob's outline of the plan, glanced at some notes he'd made, and shrugged. 'You're on a hiding to nothing, of course.'

'D'you think so?'

'For instance – we haven't a notion which channels are open, dredged or silted. Or the depths in any of 'em, or what kind of defences there may be – or where – guard-ships, offshore patrols ...'

Bob said – stonewalling, rather – 'Just have to feel our way in. Slowly and quietly. The CMB's silhouette being as low as it is—'

'Quietly?' Snaith jeered. 'They sound like aeroplanes,

those things! But anyway, d'you have some reason to think the eastern edge of the delta is a better bet than elsewhere?'

The mouths of the Volga extend over an east-west breadth of about eighty miles. A mass of channels and winding waterways, islands, lakes and swamps. The town of Astrakhan is at the delta's apex, more or less, some forty miles in from the open sea.

Bob said, answering Snaith's question, 'Only that it's the farthest from Astrakhan and the wider channels — which I'd have guessed might be the most heavily used and therefore guarded. And might they not be using these anchorages in the north-west corner? Unless the water's too shallow, of course ...'

'Float a rowing-boat, nothing much bigger.'

'Ah. Well ... But another point is that our man's got to make his way up-river. Way up, well north of Astrakhan. If we put him ashore in this area he'd have this vast area of water to get round. Add miles to his route.'

'*That*'s a valid point.' Snaith stroked his beard. 'You know what's to be done ashore, I don't ... But look here, now — as regards the eastern flank — we've heard of military activity in that area. Two Bolshevik armies, we're told, starting a deployment eastward to attack Guriev — here — presumably not before next spring because it's slow going. They're moving their stores in barges in tow of tugs, and the coast'll be iced-up solid before they're more than halfway. And if that is the case, you might well run into covering naval forces — torpedo boats or TBDs, for instance. The tugs might be armed, for that matter.'

It was worth being forewarned, obviously. But you could as well spin a coin, Bob thought, or shut your eyes and stab with the point of a pencil — there'd be uncertainties and risks whatever bit of coast one picked on, and Snaith's comments were so vague that it was obvious he was to some extent guessing. Also, there was the consideration of Solovyev's convenience — his route, and the distance he'd have to cover. It was a fact that the easier you could make it for him, the easier it would be for everyone else as well, the shorter the odds against success.

The odds *were* against it. In all the circumstances — especially after this length of time — they had to be. And meanwhile, here and now, time was leaking away: Bob had arranged to meet Solovyev at the Dunsterforce headquarters mess for lunch, and to report progress to the Commodore soon after.

'Unless you'd actually disagree, sir, I'd imagine the best place might be about — here. We'd be running in from the eastern end of the patrol line — hereabouts — so we'd have Ukatni island as a mark on our way in. Then we'd slip in here, between these islands, and put him in his skiff about — well, here. Subject to how it looks when we get in there, of course. Then it'd be up to him how far he can get by water from there on. But he'd have dry land to the east — even a road to follow. And — here, the railway — if he can make use of it. I don't know, I'll ask him ... But I'd creep in there very cautiously, watching for guardships, tugs etcetera, and if it didn't look too good we could sheer off to starboard, try again farther east.'

They settled on this, largely for the sake of having an outline plan on paper for the Commodore to approve. It could always be changed in detail later. Bob committed it to a signal-pad, in pencil and in note form, with a carbon under the top sheet, and Snaith appended his initials to both copies.

The blind leading the blind, Bob thought, heading up into town under the blinding midday sun. The truck wasn't in its usual place, unfortunately: so it was to be Shanks's pony all the way and he was going to be late getting to the headquarters. Sweating, carrying his cap because sunstroke seemed preferable to its weight and the clammy warmth of its leather headband. Running over in his mind as he hurried through the dockyard the things that would need to be done once this plan was approved. The CMB's torpedo to be landed, and a skiff of suitable size and weight to be found and requisitioned. Also — something he'd thought of during the session with Snaith — suggest to Pope that after landing the fish it might be an idea to go out and swing his compass: the accuracy of the landfall was, after all, going to be fairly vital.

What else ...? Well, the other MM to be drafted temporarily to HMS *Zoroaster.* Rations to be ordered for the passage crew. Orders to be drafted for the captains of *Zoroaster* and *Allaverdi.* And weapons — check whether Solovyev had a pistol of his own — he almost surely would have — and draw a revolver from Mr Dewhurst for himself. Pope and McNaught had better be issued with pistols too. And perhaps — one thought led to another — there ought to be a rifle and a few grenades in the boat. Just in case.

3

Bob, Nikolai Solovyev and Johnny Pope leant on *Zoroaster*'s white-painted rail at the after end of the promenade deck, gazing out over the ship's afterpart to where the CMB was towing fifty yards astern. Like staring into a fire: that kind of vague absorption ... *Zoroaster* was steaming at fifteen and a half knots, her wake a wide spread of churned sea in the centre of which, just where it began to smooth itself out again into the surrounding blue-black gloss, the CMB's bow-wave was a brilliant-white arrowhead, the boat's dark-grey shape distorted even from this distance and angle by the skiff which she was carrying piggy-back.

This was Thursday, mid-forenoon. They'd sailed as scheduled yesterday evening, pausing off Zhiloy island to pick up the tow at about 9 pm. There'd been no need for any transfer of personnel, as the passage crew had brought the CMB out, Pope and his mechanic being embarked in *Zoroaster* from the outset. Since then the old steamer had maintained her present speed and course — north fifteen degrees west — throughout the night. By early this afternoon she'd have Fort Alexandrovsk on the Mangyshlak Peninsula about fifty miles abeam to starboard, would then be entering the flotilla's patrol zone and looking for her rendezvous with *Allaverdi*.

Solovyev asked, 'If as you say the torpedo is carried behind the cockpit, and it's pointing in the same direction as the boat, how on earth is it discharged?'

Bob explained, 'It's launched backwards, by a hydraulic ram. You'll see it, of course, later on — but the ram has a cup-shaped end that fits over the torpedo's nose — the warhead — and shoves it back out of the boat's stern. As it's thrown back, the firing-lever on the torpedo's engine gets knocked forward, starting the engine so that the torpedo's own propellers are turning as it's launched. The CMB's doing nearly forty knots, and this man here —' he indicated Johnny Pope — 'is aiming his boat as if it's a torpedo itself. On a collision course with the target, in fact. Well, the torpedo's speed is also forty knots; so as soon as it's out of the stern he turns his boat out of its way and it just carries on — torpedo instead of CMB now on collision course with the target. D'you follow?'

A shrug. 'I suppose . . .'

Pope asked Bob, 'What was all that about?'

'He asked me how you fire your torpedo. I've just explained what you taught me on Tuesday.'

'Ah.' Pope looked sideways at the Russian. 'Tell *me* something. How's he going to get to wherever he's going? Won't be landing in that uniform, obviously . . .'

'Hardly.' In fact Solovyev was already working on his disguise, by not having shaved in the last two days. Bob told Pope, 'He's a Bolshy — wouldn't you know it? He'll be in scruffy clothes — name Ivan Snodgrassovich, and believe it or not he's on his way to Moscow to see Comrades Lenin and Trotsky — he's got advice for them.'

'You're pulling my leg.'

'Not at all. I agree with him — if you're going to tell lies, tell big ones. Much more likely to be believed. He's got advice for them which he's sure is vital to the success of the revolution. His story is that he was at Askhabad when the railway workers kicked out the Bolsheviks and hanged nine commissars in reprisal for Bolshy atrocities. There was a Cheka thug there by name Fralin — poisonous even by Cheka standards — they'd sent him down from Tashkent and he'd spent his days murdering and torturing and his nights in drunken orgies, he and his henchmen raping all the women and children, and so forth. This was what sparked the counter-revolution, the setting up of the Trans-Caspian Government — and our military missions installing themselves there . . . Anyway, Nick escaped, and he wants to describe it all to Lenin and persuade him to issue new directives to the Cheka — and to commissars, for that matter — to call a halt to all that counter-productive bestiality. Otherwise, he's convinced, the revolution's doomed to failure — as demonstrated, in Askhabad. Although Nick himself says the weakness of his case would be that men like Fralin are in fact the revolution's chosen tools, and the Cheka's fundamental policy is to terrorize.'

'He'd better not tell *them* what he's up to — right?'

The Cheka — secret police, corps of executioners, also known as the Red Terror — were the strong-arm of the revolution, empowered to destroy whatever stood in its way. Or in theirs. Pope was right: if the Count propounded his theory to *them*, they'd crush him like a beetle.

He nodded. 'He's counting on his acceptance of that risk as — well, proof of his *bona fides*. He's come on foot from Askhabad, he'll tell them, and he'll have gathered some intelligence for them *en route* — just to show willing — about the strength of the Cossack forces at Guriev. He'd have come through there, of course.' Bob glanced at Solovyev. 'He'll convince them, all right. He's pretty damn sharp, our Count.'

Another way of phrasing that would have been to say he'd bluff his way through just about anything. Which was a reminder of the distrust he — Bob — had begun to feel at that first meeting, at the Dunsterforce HQ. He'd thought about it quite a bit — that gleam of what had looked like triumph, then the way he'd so quickly smothered it . . .

But what the hell. Russians not being by nature undemonstrative, and Nikolai Solovyev being no stolid peasant, he'd been on the point of more or less whooping with delight, then seen the cold British eyes on him — and imposed self-control, the stiff upper lip. Something like that. In any case it wasn't easy to imagine what trickery could be involved: it was his own neck he was putting on the block, no one else's. He was a fairly intrepid character, in fact. And everyone seemed to like him.

He'd turned his back on the rail now: looking at Bob, and running the palm of one hand round his stubbled jawline. 'Well now, Robert Aleksand'ich — might be a good time for a glass of tea, d'you think?'

The mess-traps in *Zoroaster*'s wardroom were of Russian provenance. Very few items matched, few cups were unchipped or plates uncracked. But the tea glasses — tumblers, actually — were of fine thin glass, really quite elegant in their filigree coasters.

Solovyev put a lump of sugar in a spoon, dipped it in his tea, then sucked the tea through it rather noisily. If he'd done the same in a railway café in, say, Clapham — or Glasgow — Bob reflected, he'd have drawn critical stares if not comments. He smiled to himself as he put a sugar-lump in his own spoon. The appropriate naval expression would have been *Different ships, different long-splices*: the equivalent roughly of *When in Rome* ... The Count asked him, 'Would you tell me how your father came to make his life in Russia?'

The black, heavily sweetened tea was delicious. He nodded. 'Quite a story, really. Starts with my grandfather. He was a trawler skipper, on the west coast of Scotland. Lost his ship — literally had her sink under him, in one of those storms — well, you wouldn't know, but they do get them, on that coast ... Anyway — needing to earn a living, he'd taken some dockside job. In Argyllshire, this was — about 1860. Then he had a second stroke of bad luck — fell into a ship's hold and broke his back. So having lost his livelihood he'd then lost his capacity to work at all — at least for a while. And he had a wife and son — my father was ten years old at this time. So they moved down to Glasgow where a married sister had a room to spare, they could live in it for a while and my grandmother — father too — could get occasional work. Better than the workhouse for all three of them, anyway. And from Glasgow, my father ran away to sea.'

'He deserted his parents?'

'He stowed away. I suppose you could say he deserted them, but in the long run he couldn't have done anything better for them — as it turned out ... Anyway — his father had been a trawlerman, so he'd thought he'd try that too. Couldn't get a berth — or any other seagoing job, cabin-boy, anything — but he'd been hanging around the docks a lot, and eventually he stowed away, hid in a freighter's hold, and stayed hidden until they were off Kronstadt — they were taking the hatchcovers off, to be ready for when the lighters came alongside, and there he was. But the ship's master didn't want whatever complications were involved in those days with stowaways and the local regulations — fines, possibly, I don't know — and the simple answer was to throw him overboard.'

Visualizing the scene, seeing between the lines of his father's own terse description of it. The raggedly-dressed, half-starved urchin — *big as a middling-sized dog — and snarling like one, like as not* ... The seamen towering around him, gaunt giants in silhouette against grey moving sky. A growl from one — *Best get it done with, lads* — and the ring closing, long arms and calloused hands spread to catch him ...

'The ship was only about half a mile offshore, and he'd learnt to swim, after a fashion, so he got ashore all right. He was strongly made, incidentally. Short but stocky — weightlifter's build, you might say. Although just at that time he'd have been as scrawny as a rat ... Anyway, he had the luck — and nerve — to get himself a job in a merchant's warehouse, and pretty soon he was making himself so useful they couldn't do without him. He was good with figures, and he very quickly picked up enough Russian to get by, and before long he was this man's book-keeper, also interpreting for him with English-speaking ships' captains and supercargoes — oh, and correspondence with British shippers and importers — and you could say he'd fallen on his feet. Fluent in Russian soon enough, too. They had connections on the mainland, of course, in St Petersburg, and eventually — skipping a few years, obviously — he had his own business there.

Importing and exporting, ship's agency — insurance too, representing Lloyd's of London even. And he never looked back. By and large, he reckoned, those seamen who dropped him over the side had done him a good turn.'

'And his parents too, I suppose.'

'Oh yes.' Bob put another lump of sugar in his spoon. 'He looked after them financially for the rest of their lives.'

'And your mother was Russian, you said?'

'Yes. He didn't marry until he was over forty, and she wasn't quite twenty.'

Very pretty. Elizaveta. Liza, the old man called her. Quite tall, and slim: complete contrast to her husband, who was five feet six inches tall and not much less than that across the shoulders. 'Beauty and the Beast' had been his own description of himself and his young wife. Bob could see and hear him now — a thick forefinger tapping a sepia-toned wedding portrait and the hoarse voice grating 'How could she 'a done it? Tell me that? A lass wi' *her* looks, gettin' wedded to this *ape*?'

Solovyev asked him, 'Your parents are both dead now, I believe you said.'

'Yes. My mother died having a second child — in 1900. I was born in '91.'

'So you're only — twenty-seven?'

He nodded. He knew he looked at least thirty. His size contributed to the illusion — he stood six feet tall in his socks, and he'd inherited his father's broad shoulders. Not his mother's beauty, exactly — or fortunately — but he wasn't quite as square as a barn door, either. As he saw it, they'd each of them given him the best of themselves. But it was true that from early boyhood onwards he'd looked older than his real age. Johnny Pope's lighthearted 'age before beauty' jibe, a day or two ago, was typical — Johnny probably thought of him as an old man, but there were only four years between them. And the Count was murmuring now, 'I'd have sworn we were contemporaries. But — good Lord, I'm three years your senior ...' Glancing round, then, as a sailor knocked on the steel bulkhead beside the open doorway. One of *Zoroaster*'s Royal Navy contingent: Bob asked him, 'Want me, Gilchrist?'

'Captain does, sir. Said to tell you we have *Allaverdi* in visual communication, he'd be glad if you'd join him on the bridge.'

HMS *Allaverdi* had a single rather tall, slanting funnel just abaft her bridge, and a rather pretentious (Bob thought) clipper bow. Pretentions to elegance — to the kind of profile that would look all right on some millionaire's yacht. All that — and a White Ensign too ... She was moving out to take station on *Zoroaster*'s beam. Speed had been reduced to five knots, and Barker — he was senior to the other captain — had ordered a course of due west.

'We're here.' Leaning over the chart, he tapped a pencilled fix with the points of a pair of dividers. 'Course west, five knots. We have fifty miles of patrol-line to cover — that's this eastern third of it, *Babiabut* with *Emil Nobel* and *Venture* are covering the rest. So — at some point, allowing ourselves time to get to where we need to be this evening, I'll be turning back — or north-eastward — leaving *Allaverdi* to carry on alone. She'll turn about when she's at the end of our beat, at which time she'll be in signalling distance of one of the others. Meanwhile we'll be doing our stuff with you — including retrieving you in your CMB in the early hours — dawn or thereabouts — then meeting *Allaverdi* again so as to hand you and the tow over to her. She then departs with you for return to Baku. Correct, Bob?'

'Yes.' He gave the Count a quick translation of what Barker had been saying. Then nodded. 'Go on.'

'Well — what we have to establish now is the time and position for sending you away in the CMB tonight. It was to be roughly midnight and about fifty miles offshore: but nobody's mentioned which bit of shore yet. So, if we can have that settled now, I can plan our movements and inform *Allaverdi*, and she can tell the others what's going on when she's in sight of them ... All right?'

He nodded. 'If you'd give us just a minute ...'

Solovyev hadn't really been brought into it yet, in any detail. For one thing there hadn't been any good opportunity to get him to a chart, before departure from Baku. But there'd been no need to, either; and the principle of not letting the left hand know what the right hand's doing wasn't a bad one — not even when you were 100 per cent sure of the people you were dealing with ... Similarly, from a security point of view, passing information to the other ships by lamp was a lot safer than doing it by wireless.

Bob showed the Russian, 'Here — this is where we expect to land you — or rather where we'll transfer you to your rowing-boat. Pope wants to run in at twenty-five knots: so if we allow two hours for the trip, we can leave *Zoroaster* fifty miles offshore — here, say ... And if we start at midnight we'll have you in there at near enough 2 am, so you'd be on your way by about two-thirty. At the latest — touch wood — so you'll have a couple of hours of darkness for parking the boat — or whatever — and we have the same length of time for getting back out to this ship ... So — that's all right for us, but will the landing-place suit *you*?'

'The next thing we have to settle, Nikolai Petrovich, is picking you and the others up in a week's time — or longer, however long it's going to take you.'

Pacing the deck, side by side, *Allaverdi*'s profile four thousand yards abeam to starboard. There wasn't a lot of movement on the ship, only a gentle rolling as the long swells ran under her from slightly abaft the beam.

The Count agreed, 'It's *possible* that I could be back with them in one week.'

'So our first rendezvous will be seven nights from this coming one. Calling tonight night 1, it'll be night 8. Midnight, at the same place we leave you, wherever that turns out to be. All right?'

'Yes. Yes ...'

'But if you don't appear at midnight, we'll wait for one hour exactly, — until 1 am. All right?'

'And the next night —'

'No. Every second night. So counting from now it'd be nights 8, 10, 12, and so on.'

'It could take as long as two weeks, I suppose.'

'All right. Nights 14 and 16 as well.'

'Could you then leave a gap of one more week and try just one more time — night 23, say?'

'Very well. But you accept that that would be your last chance — as far as this way out is concerned?'

Putting his mind to it. Stroking his jaw — it had become a habit — and gazing out towards *Allaverdi*. Then he shrugged as he looked round at Bob. 'It's impossible to be at all certain, obviously. But I should guess if I don't get back to you in three weeks, Robert Aleksand'ich, you could forget it.'

Over lunch in the saloon-wardroom mess, listening to the Count in conversation with the *Zoroaster*'s Russian first lieutenant, and hearing him put some fairly pointed questions to him in the course of it, Bob remembered that Johnny Pope had asked him recently 'Do the Bolsheviks *have* clever spies?'

Suppose they did, he thought: and suppose Count Nikolai Petrovich Solovyev was one. Even using his real name and legitimate title: one had heard of cases of high-born Russians saving their skins or their children's by working as informers amongst their own kind. In point of fact the two he'd heard of had been women, but this didn't exclude the possibility of there being a few male aristos at it too.

That would justify one's earlier feeling of — uncertainty...

Sheer nonsense, probably, and grossly unfair to him. But — having started, think it through ... For instance, it was unquestionable that Bicherakov had sent Solovyev down to Baku from Petrovsk: and Bicherakov's loyalties weren't in question, even though he *had* got himself and his Cossacks to Baku initially by claiming to be pro-Bolshevik, so that the then Bolshevik government in Baku had appointed him commander-in-chief — realizing only later how completely they'd been fooled ... But had Bicherakov been shown any proof that the Count had come to him from General Denikin?

Probably not. He wouldn't have telegraphic communications with Denikin's headquarters either. Bicherakov would have taken Solovyev on his own assurances: just as Dunsterville in turn had accepted him on Bicherakov's. Dunsterville would certainly not have checked — in fact he'd told the Commodore that he didn't intend referring the business to Baghdad or London because of the security risks that might be involved in doing so. He'd added that in any case it came within his own brief, there was no need for any consultation; and behind this, Bob had guessed, he mightn't have been entirely disinterested in the prospect of coming up with such a brilliant *fait accompli* — the Tsar's daughters snatched to safety and now under the protection of the British flag.

Grintsev, this steamer's first lieutenant, was telling the Count, 'Four of our ships are on patrol at all times, yes. Across this narrower part — Cape Bryansk to Fort Aleksandrovsk — and from time to time we make a sweep farther to the north. You see, as long as we can hold the Caspian south of this line, we can prevent any movement towards the east and also protect the army's flank. As you'll appreciate, all the coastline between Petrovsk and Baku is open to bombardment from the sea.'

'What if Baku had to be evacuated?'

'Well — Johnny Turk would have his hands on the oil, for one thing. Or the Germans would — comes to the same thing. You'd have Germans in Baku within hours — they're just sitting in Astrakhan, our Bolshevik friends' honoured guests ... But we'd still have Petrovsk — and more importantly Krasnovodsk, which is an excellent port and base. And the British in Krasnovodsk are in greater strength — with no Turks besieging them either — so the position's secure enough, we'd hold on there and we'd still command this sea.'

'And Enzeli, you'd still have.'

'Certainly. But — on the subject of this patrol — yet another benefit is that we prevent the Bolsheviks making any effective use of the submarines which they have at Astrakhan. If they could operate south of us here, in deeper water, they could be a thorn in our flesh. But as the sea in the north is extremely shallow, they can't dive anywhere up there. Consequently if they tried to deploy southward we'd see them coming, and — well, blow them out of the water. On the surface a submarine's a clumsy thing; it has its torpedoes, of course, but it's slow and extremely vulnerable ...'

The Count nodding, taking it all in. Bob thinking, *We could be landing a spy tonight. Having wined and dined him and briefed him* ...

'Something troubling you, Robert Aleksand'ich?'

The green eyes had swung to meet his own sombre, thoughtful gaze. Almost as if reading those suspicions.

Not that one actually *believed* ...

He shrugged: 'Just listening to you. Kyril Ivan'ich is right about the submarines — where they are, they're useless.'

'How many are there? And for that matter, what *other* ships?'

Direct question — no subtlety at all. It would be of advantage to the Bolsheviks to know how accurate an assessment the Allies had of their naval strength. Bob shook his head. 'I haven't seen anything recently on that subject, come to think of it.' He added — before Grintsev might come up with a contradiction of this statement — 'With the Volga giving them a link to the Black Sea, ships come and go quite frequently, you see, it's hard to know from one day to another.'

'But their morale —' Grintsev's mouth bulged with mutton stew — 'is extremely low. We know this for certain.'

'What about the Russian Caspian flotilla? For instance, the gunboat that brought me down from Petrovsk?'

'That's another animal altogether.' Grintsev had begun to answer, and Bob left it to him. 'One has heard that some of those crews have Bolshevik sympathies. In particular amongst the engineroom personnel . . .'

Solovyev had come up with all the right questions, Bob thought. On the other hand, you could also say they were questions which might have occurred to any intelligent observer. And once you started on this kind of fantasy — well, you could very soon convince yourself.

Too late to start worrying about it now, anyway. If he *was* a Bolshevik agent, by this stage he'd be laughing up his sleeve. Maybe he'd laugh out loud, when he was rowing away into the darkness.

But he wasn't. *Couldn't* be . . .

It was mid-afternoon now. Bob was again at the rail at the after end of the promenade deck, smoking a cigarette and watching the CMB, which had more movement on her now as she slammed across the swell in *Zoroaster*'s wake. *Zoroaster* herself was rolling quite a bit. There'd be a change of course soon — at 4 pm, they'd be altering to north-east, the start of the transit up towards the coast; she'd be heading right into it then, which should actually be less uncomfortable for the CMB, better than all that rolling. He guessed that Messrs Henderson, Willoughby and Keane might by this time be quite eagerly looking forward to the midnight change-round.

So was he, for that matter. With nothing to do now except wait around . . . He'd been on the bridge with Eric Barker for a while, then found Pope down here and they'd chatted for a while — flotilla business, and the war, and so on. Johnny had gone below now for a nap — as good a way as any of killing time, and an example Bob thought he might follow, when he'd finished his cigarette.

Inhaling smoke slowly: and thinking about his father. Struggling to come to terms with the strangeness of there being empty space where all his life there'd been solid rock. Like one moment the certainty of a handhold if you reached out to it, and the next — thin air. *Nothing*. It was almost unbelievable — that the old man could be simply *not there*, not exist.

A hand fell on his shoulder. 'This is the second time I've caught you dreaming, Robert Aleksand'ich!'

Startled, he'd glanced round — at the green eyes and stubbled face.

'Nikolai Petrovich — I didn't hear you coming.' He flicked the stub of his cigarette away down-wind ... 'I suppose I *was* ... somewhat preoccupied ...'

'Dreaming of the young lady you left weeping in Baku?'

He was stumped again, for a moment — by the Count knowing of Leonide's existence, even ... Then realizing — getting the grey matter back into action — that he most likely *would* — especially with his habit of asking questions. He could have heard about her from someone in the Dunsterforce mess — or from Grintsev, after he'd left them in the saloon earlier on. There was a fair amount of gossip, he knew, about himself and Leonide Muromskaya, and it was largely because his colleagues failed to grasp the basic fact that he was half Russian, that it was perfectly natural for him to have social contacts ashore. They saw him as one of themselves — which he was too, of course — who happened to have spent some of his childhood in this benighted country and thus spoke the language: and the story that had been passed around was that 'old Kiss-'em-quick Cowan' had been 'chasing some girl in Krasnovodsk' and she'd since 'followed him to Baku'. This was the legend, and nothing he could say would change it — he hadn't much wanted to discuss it anyway — and the odds were that Solovyev with his sharp curiosity *would* have heard about it.

He'd shrugged ... 'I wasn't thinking about any young lady. Not at that moment ... How about you, d'you have any special — er — attachment — or attachments?'

'Attachment. Just one.' Grasping the rail: exerting pressure, by the look of it, tensing his muscles ... 'Except that at this wretched time we're unfortunately very much *de*tached, have been so for —' he shrugged — 'more than a year ... But I tell you, if she and I both come through all this — this mess we're in —'

'Hey.' He interrupted. '*When* — not *if*.'

'Yes.' The Count's expression was serious, earnest. 'You're right. We *have* to beat them, you're *absolutely* right.'

And he was completely genuine. Surely ... Bob felt a twinge of shame for his earlier suspicions. Although there *had* been grounds for them. Besides which, suspicion was a fairly standard attitude, seeing that in present circumstances virtually nobody could be trusted — without his hands tied and a pistol at his head ... But this fellow: he thought again, *surely* ...

He asked him, 'How will you get to Enotayevsk? On foot?'

'I think probably I'll go by train. Depending on — well, train as first choice. Coming back — that's something else ... These are matters I'm working at in *my* thoughts — while yours are on girls all the time.' He laughed — as if involuntarily, finding his own humour irresistible. 'No — the answer is I must take it as I find it. The major problem is of course the journey back, when I have them with me. But getting there's really not much problem at all. I'll just stick my chin out, and tell anyone who wants to know, "Here I am — I'm Anton Ivan'ich Vetrov, I'm from Askhabad, I have to get to Moscow." '

'Have you got papers?'

'Yes — new ones, fixed up for me in Baku. Came from a Bolshevik they had in the prison there — suitably altered, of course, but much better than straight forgeries.'

'Forgery's quite an industry, I'm told, in St Petersburg and Moscow now.'

He shrugged. 'Would be, wouldn't it.'

'Anyway — you make your way to Enotayevsk — by train, you say — and what then?'

'Oh.' He drew a long breath. 'I don't know. Until I —' he swung round, letting go of the rail and facing him: '— get there ... But that thought — arrival, what I may find there — it frightens me. Really. I have nightmares. Getting there, finding I've come too late, and then I find their bodies. I can't *describe* to you ...'

'Dreams are just dreams, Nikolai Petrovich. *Nick* — if I may ... Dreams don't have any bearing on reality.'

'I know. But it comes back so often that now I try to stay awake.' He turned away, looking out towards *Allaverdi* again. 'Ridiculous, I know — *weak* ...'

'I wouldn't call it either ridiculous *or* weak. After all, you've lived with it for — three months, is it, since you had the message? And your own mother and sister ...'

'You're — very kind.'

'One thing I'd advise — if you *want* advice, which you most likely don't ...'

'Please.'

'On the subject of sleep — if I were you I'd grab a few hours between now and midnight. Forget about nightmares, just get your head down.'

He nodded. 'Yes.'

'I'm going to, for sure. Right after supper — that's at seven. Tell you what, Nick — I'll arrange to be given a shake at, say, eleven o'clock, and I'll send the messenger on to make sure you and Johnny are awake too. Then we might all meet in the wardroom for a hot drink and a bite to eat — d'you think?'

'Yes. Yes. Excellent ...'

Formal tone. Grim expression. Nightmares still in his head ... Bob tried to take the man's mind off his nightmares — which might indeed be reflections of a grim reality — 'You said the house at Enotayevsk is in beautiful surroundings — riverside, of course ... Is it a big place?'

'Oh — not so big. Big enough that since '14 it's been a — well, convalescent home, for badly wounded officers. And — this might interest you — it was a summer cottage, belonged originally to a family — God, my memory's so bad ...' Banging his forehead ... 'Ah, Stukalin. Grigor Stukalin was a supporter of the rebel Pugachov, and allowed him the use of the house as a base for his operations. Do you know your Russian history?'

'You're talking about — 1790, thereabouts?'

'Not quite, but not far off. Late eighteenth century,

anyway. My' — he counted on the fingers of his left hand — 'great-great-great-grandfather led a force of Cossacks in the campaign which ended with Pugachov's capture and execution, and the Tsar in his gratitude made him a present of this house. Its former owner, as you can imagine, had no further use for it.'

'He was executed too, you mean?'

'He was pulled apart between Cossack horses — in the meadows between the house and the river. They say on a certain night of the year his screams are still to be heard. Not that I ever heard it — although as children we liked to pretend we did. My father, God rest him, used to joke that the poor fellow wasn't up to it any more — because his throat was sore from screaming every year since 1774.'

Bob laughed. 'Marvellous!'

'Yes ... And the house — well, it has — *I* think — considerable charm. And the setting truly is beautiful — the river and a huge lake, birchwoods and willows, meadows...'

'I'm sure you'll live there again. Eventually.'

'Thank you. It's a very happy thought. The *right* kind of dream — and it *could* come true — please God ...' He swung round — a look of excitement on his face as a new thought hit him — 'Robert Aleksand'ich — Bob — if it does, will you visit us — come and stay?'

Visit *us*...

He smiled. Inclined his head: formal acceptance of invitation. 'Thank you very much.' And wondering whether — despite his own insistence on *when, not if* — there could possibly be any happy outcome to this vast upheaval, wholesale slaughter and individual murder, the misery of man's incredible brutality to man: whether the Count didn't share his own suspicion that any thoughts of rainbows just around the corner could only be pretence, play-acting, whistling in pitch darkness.

Dark as sin ...

Zoroaster had stopped her engines and was under helm, turning to make a lee on her starboard side — some shelter in which the CMB, which by now would have cast off the tow, could come up alongside. Eleven-forty. Bob and Nick Solovyev were out on the side deck, getting their eyes used to the darkness after drinking mugs of cocoa and munching ships' biscuit in the saloon.

Solovyev had slept well, he'd said. No nightmares . . . He was wearing a leather herdsman's jacket that was shiny with age, riding breeches that didn't fit him properly, well-worn boots that did — desirable, if you were contemplating a walk of at least a hundred miles — and round his neck a red woollen scarf with its ends pushed inside his shirt. He'd told Bob, 'The red scarf is important. One red item clearly visible — they like to see it, eh?'

'You'll find it damned hot in daytime.'

'So I let it dangle loose, then.' He'd added, 'I've done this before, you know.'

The night air was noticeably cool. Leaning over the rail, above flickering torchlight where they were lowering the gangway and Johnny Pope was watching anxiously for his CMB to make her appearance from the darkness astern, Bob was glad of the thick sweater he'd put on under his reefer jacket. He wouldn't be back on board until about dawn, and the days didn't start warming up until the sun was well above the horizon and burnt the mist off the sea's surface. Then, it made up for lost time; but for now, this could have been an English autumn.

The deep rumble of the CMB's engine at low revs came throatily out of the darkness, over the shrill squeaking of the descending gangway. Then he could see her: the low bone in her teeth first, as she came pitching in from the quarter. It seemed to him an unnecessary risk, bringing her right alongside when there was this much movement on the sea; if he'd been in Pope's shoes he'd have had her lie off, asked Barker to lower a seaboat. But it was Pope's business, not his.

'Won't be long now, Nick. Better go down.'

'Good . . .'

The Count had no baggage, not even a haversack. Only half a loaf of bread and some apples in his pockets, and a knife, and a Browning automatic pistol inside his shirt. Bob envied him the little pistol — in comparison with the weight of a Service-issue .45 revolver on his own hip. On the other hand, for nipping in and out of boats he was much better off in his plimsolls than Solovyev was in those heavy boots.

The CMB was closing in towards the gangway by the time they got down to that lower deck. Two sailors were down on the gangway's lower platform with boathooks, ready to both hang on and fend off — Henderson would have put rope fenders over on his own account, of course — and from the wing of *Zoroaster*'s bridge an Aldis lamp was spotlighting the ship's side at that point.

'Starter's orders, Johnny?'

'Ah — there you are.' Pope hadn't been with them in the saloon, he'd been on the bridge with Barker, and this was his first sight of the Count in his shore-going rig. He murmured, 'Snakes alive …' and turned back to Bob. 'Mustn't forget to sling *that* aboard.' Pointing at a canvas holdall. 'Rations. Bit peckish already, actually … But look here — we'll have Keane inboard first, and McNaught into the boat in his place. Then Willoughby out, and the Count in. You too, Bob, better stay with him. And then I'll swap with Chris. But in that order, I don't want a buggers' rush.' Glancing at the Count's boots: 'And you'll look after *him* — huh?' He slapped his own .45 revolver in its webbing holster: 'Anyone'd think we were going on a Bolshy hunt, what?'

Eric Barker appeared then, bulky in a duffel-coat, Pope meanwhile using a megaphone to address Henderson in the CMB. Barker said, 'Best of luck, you chaps. And we'll see you and Pope in about four hours' time, Bob, right?'

He nodded. 'Don't forget to switch on your anchor lights, sir.'

'I won't. Don't worry.' He offered his hand to Solovyev. 'All the best, Count. Bring 'em back alive, eh?'

Solovyev glanced enquiringly at Bob, who translated, 'He wishes you success.' The Count smiled, shook the offered hand, then managed, '*Senk you very moch.*'

The transfer went more smoothly than it might have done. Three out, four in: within a matter of seconds, after the hours of waiting ... The CMB drew away from the ship's side slowly at first, then when she was clear of it Pope began to open up, the engine's mutter expanding into a roar and the bow beginning to lift, the boat heeling to port then as he edged her around on to her north-westerly course.

4

Committed, now. Whatever one might not have allowed for or foreseen was out there ahead, on the black Kirghiz coast.

Pope had said he'd take her as far as Ukatni island — nineteen miles from this starting point. Best part of an hour, therefore, at twenty-five knots, to which he'd adjusted the revs after settling her on north thirty-eight west. The night was cold, at sea-level and in the rush of wind, colder still with the salt spray in it, Solovyev huddling his leather coat around him and Bob turning up the collar of his reefer; Johnny was all right, he was dressed as Bob was but on top of that had a duffel which McNaught had handed up to him out of the engine-space where it was kept — even kept warm, for God's sake ... Bob had taken it from McNaught, and passed it on. 'Here. All right for some.'

'Right. Some aren't gormless ...'

To be heard, you had to shout. The wind and a smallish choppy sea were from ahead; there was still a low swell too although the short waves disguised it, the CMB hammering through the chop as well as slamming rhythmically, regular thudding impacts that jarred from your feet right up through your teeth.

The Count had declined an invitation to sit inside, where he'd be warm. Wise, probably: it was hellishly noisy in there, bearable only by mechanics with leather eardrums. And conducive to sea-sickness — noise, diesel stink, claustrophobically small space.

Bob ducked in there anyway, for a brief chat with McNaught.

Pointing at the thundering engine: 'All right?'

The MM raised an oily thumb, screamed, 'Had a good stand-off, didn't she!' During the tow up from Baku, he meant. And Jacko Keane would doubtless have started her up and run her for a minute or two now and again . . . 'You goin' ashore with the Russki, sir?'

'God, no!'

'Ah. So we shan't be getting the skiff back, then.'

'No, not this trip. He'll hide it somewhere — and come off in it when we come back for him.'

For obvious reasons: the Count might find he could get quite a long way inland before he beached himself, and the CMB wasn't going to hang around once he'd departed. He'd find some hiding-place for his boat — under the overhang of a river bank, for instance, and it had been suggested to him that he should remove the bung, let the boat fill or half-fill so she'd settle, be less visible and also less of a temptation to anyone who might find her. Then he'd have to bale her out — somehow, finding something to bale *with* . . . But he'd have the women — including a pair of young Grand Duchesses, please God — to help him with that labour.

Back in the cockpit — *Zoroaster* out of sight astern by this time — Bob slung Henderson's binoculars around his neck and settled down to the business of keeping a look-out. Pope was at the conning position needing his hands on the wheel and his eyes on the compass, and Solovyev leaning back in the angle between the after bulkhead and the fore end of the torpedo-trough, his boots jammed against the cylinder of the hydraulic ram to hold himself in place against the violent, thumping motion. He was out of the main blast of the wind there, too. Whereas Bob, propped against the forward bulkhead and up on the star-board-side step, was right in it, his head above the wind-screen and in the spray as well. Keeping binoculars dry was impossible — for more than a few seconds, on any forward bearing, and travelling at this speed meant that looking-out on anything *but* forward bearings didn't have much relevance . . .

Visibility was none too good horizontally — because of the spray, which created an aura of mist around the boat — but the sky overhead was clear, stars at elevations of more than a few degrees bright and glittering. There'd be a moon later, but not until they were well on their way back.
Binoculars were a waste of time, in these conditions. You spent longer drying their lenses than actually looking-out. Naked eye was the thing. Eyes slitted against the wind and flying salt water, and concentrating on the bow and about fifty degrees each side of it.

He picked up the low-lying shape of Ostrov Ukatni forty-five minutes after leaving *Zoroaster*'s side. Well out on the port bow but only about five thousand yards off the CMB's track, when he spotted it: not easily even then, so low to the sea that untrained eyes might not have known it was there at all.
Moving over, shouting into his ear — 'Thirty on the bow! Flat as a pancake!'
Pope used binoculars one-handed, standing back at arm's length from the wheel and then up on the side step, to see over the curve of salt-wet, by no means transparent windscreen. Glasses soaked immediately: cursing, letting them fall on their strap, then concentrating through narrowed eyes: 'Right . . .'
She'd drifted off by a few degrees. Adjusting course, he yelled at Bob to watch that bearing and take the time when the island was abeam. Conditions wouldn't have allowed for any chartwork, but they had the distances and courses memorized — knew for instance that after this they'd have a smaller island about the same distance to starboard after another twelve miles — at twenty-five knots, say thirty minutes — and then shallows around a nearer island close to port after another seven — from now, say forty-four minutes . . . So if forty-five passed and you hadn't picked it up, you'd start sweating . . . But in any case you'd be reducing speed by that stage, since you'd be nosing in among a whole lot of islands, most of which weren't shown on the chart. You'd be *feeling* the way in,

by then; and not many miles short of the sheltered water where the Count would be taking to his dinghy.

'Want a breather, Johnny?'

Sideways glance: then another at the compass. He nodded, made room for Bob to take over the wheel. 'Bite to eat, anyway. Sandwich. Where's—'

'In there.' Pointing — right-handed, left hand having taken over the wheel, and with his feet straddled against the boat's plunging motion — at the engine-space hatch ... 'If Zero hasn't already wolfed it all.'

McNaught did have a slightly wolfish look about him. Crouching in that lair of his, baring his teeth at intruders ... He had not only the food-bag in there with him, but also one Enfield .303 rifle and a few clips of ammunition for it, and a box of hand-grenades. Which — touch wood — would be returned to Mr Dewhurst's stores, unused, in a few days' time.

Coming up for 1.30 am ... Pope took over the wheel again and cut the revs, reducing to about fifteen knots. It was an earlier reduction of speed than the programme had allowed for, but there were low-lying islands all over the place — on both sides and ahead — and hardly any of them had been shown on the chart. They'd picked up the second island — which *was* charted — right on schedule, but then almost immediately some others which they hadn't known existed. Presumably the Russian hydrographer didn't either. But if one was right in assuming that the patch of salt-washed marsh on the port hand now was the island they all *had* known about — it was where one should have been, all right — then there'd be an extensive area of very shallow water to the south and west of it, and obviously one had to allow for the uncharted patches to have similar hazards around them.

In which case even fifteen knots was too fast for safety. But at twenty-five there'd still have been half an hour to go; and at this speed they were putting themselves twenty or thirty minutes behind schedule, which was already more time than one could afford to lose.

At least one could use binoculars now — at the lower revs, and with some shelter in here too. There was still a swell, but the gently rolling surface was barely ruffled.

'*Damn* it all ...'

Johnny was putting his wheel over — again — in order to stay middled between two land-patches. Although there was no way to be certain that the two visible areas of scrubby marshland weren't connected just below the surface. In which case, any minute now —

This had not, in fact, been the ideal choice of a place to put the Count ashore. And it was too late to rethink — or to pull out and try again farther east, for instance ... The Count was on his feet now, between Pope and Bob, all three of them straining their eyes into the dark. Wheel was amidships again, the land on either side seemingly in spitting distance, and nerves tight — waiting for the crash, catastrophe ...

The near-end of the patch to starboard looked higher: and sheer, steep-to. Bob was examining it through his glasses, guessing there might be deeper water there — the other side, the side they could have gone when they'd chosen this more westerly route instead. Not that there'd been anything in the choice, one could have spun a coin: with effectively no chart, no information or local knowledge whatsoever ... He heard Pope comment, 'Not quite as frantic as it looked, was it?' Because they were now through that gap and were still afloat, still moving in more or less the right direction, and with a prospect of open water ahead now.

Bob told him — fairly sure of it now — 'This is a deeper channel we've got into.'

'Looks like it.'

Dangerous words: a challenge to the Fates, last words before grounding ...

Not yet, though. The Fates playing cat-and-mouse. Engine throbbing steadily, the wake by now probably washing those last islands' fringes, the outspreading bow-wave constantly erasing stars' shimmering reflections from the smooth, dark surface. A gleam of phosphorescence where the white water curled away ... Pope waved an arm: 'This channel must be the main one — we'd have been in it already if we hadn't gone the wrong side of that little archipelago — d'you agree?'

'Yes. So on our way out—'

'Exactly.'

Shouting to each other, over the engine noise ... But that would be their route back out to sea, the way they would have come in if they'd diverged slightly to starboard instead of to port about a quarter of an hour ago. He turned his glasses that way: back over the quarter ... Caught his breath — held it, brain numbed by shock for about half a second — then: 'Johnny — slow down! Slow, Dead *slow* ...'

He'd done it: without knowing why. Engine only mumbling to itself now: water sounds audible under and around the CMB as she slowed. Bob's arm out pointing astern: 'Ship at anchor — destroyer. See that dim light — on her fo'c'sl?'

Anchored — as a guardship, possibly — in the channel they'd just agreed they should have come through. The destroyer's distinctive three-quarter profile — four idiosyncratically spaced funnels — told him she was Scottish-built — Yarrow-built — at about the turn of the century. There'd been four of that class in the Tsar's Black Sea fleet.

Pope had altered course by about ten degrees to point the CMB's stern directly at the destroyer, presenting any fo'c'sl sentry or bridge watchkeeper who might happen to be awake and sober with the smallest possible target. But a searchlight might still spring out, spearing them on its beam for the gunners then to do their worst. In which event — Bob guessed, instinctively seeking options — Pope's best move might be to open the throttle wide — forty knots — and backtrack around the way they'd just come. A second or two was long enough to decide this, and he knew Pope's thoughts would have been going the same way ... Pope remarking now — ordinary conversational tone, not much engine noise to beat — 'D'you know, I rather think we've got away with it?' Gentling the throttle open, just a little. The point of stopping — slowing right down — had been to reduce wake and bow-wave, but for a few minutes there'd been every possibility of the wake she'd already created getting there and alerting some dopey watchkeeper.

'What d'you think, Bob?'

'I think we picked the best side of those islands.'

A grunt ... 'We push on inshore, anyway — d'you agree?'

'I'm only wondering what she's guarding ... But yes — I do. And we go out the same way we came in.'

'Like the chap in the *Rubaiyat.*' Engine-noise rose as he gave her another knot or two. 'Should've brought my torpedo, shouldn't I?'

Except this was *not* what he'd called a 'Bolshy hunt'. The last thing one wanted was to cause explosions, announce one's presence; the aim was to creep in and then creep out again, leaving no sign of having been here.

The Count rested a hand on his shoulder. 'Is it all right?'

'It's fine. We were lucky, then.'

What seemed rather less than fine was the prospect of having to repeat this in a week's time and quite possibly every second night thereafter ... But then, on other nights there might well not be any guardship in that channel; also, one would be better off from the navigational point of view — having found a way in, knowing one *could* get in and out. Even knowing there had to be a minimum of eight feet of water in that channel, since eight feet was the draft of those Russian S-class, Yarrow-built TBDs.

Pope called over to them, 'We're running late now. Can't be helped, can it.' He gave her a few more revs, though: some *slight* help ... Stooping to the hatchway, enquiring, 'All right, McNaught?' and getting in reply a growl of something like 'Och, aye ...'

Low-lying land — whether islands or protrusions of the mainland was anyone's guess — was gradually closing in on both sides again. They'd come about two miles from where they'd seen the destroyer, and ahead now — although even with glasses it was hard to make it out — was what looked like a dead-end.

'Slower, Johnny?'

'Thinking of the time, as much as anything.' He cut the revs a bit. 'For your pal's sake, I mean.'

He was right, in this. Solovyev did need the two hours of darkness they'd allowed for, in which to cache his skiff and then either lie up for the daylight hours or transfer himself to some location where he'd be less conspicuous than he was going to be on about fifty thousand acres of empty marsh. Whereas for themselves it didn't matter much; they had the CMB's flat-out speed of forty knots to make use of, if they needed to make the trip out to *Zoroaster* in nearer one hour than two. There'd be a moon, admittedly, but they'd be well off the coast before it rose, and at least they'd beat the sunrise.

Meanwhile, the binocular-view of the head of this inlet was becoming clearer.

'I don't think it's a dead-end, Johnny. I think that's a gap near the left edge. Either for us or the skiff if we drop him off there.'

Pope put his own glasses up. Holding the boat on course with his belly against the wheel: then lowering them again, not having made much of it ... 'See how it looks when we get in there.'

Slowing again. The land on each side wasn't high but its edges were vertical — more or less — suggestive of deepish water. Not that the CMB needed much to float in, but other ships did — destroyers, for instance, an immediate concern being whether there might be more where that other came from — around the next corner, for instance. Alert, with a searchlight ready, and — well, twelve-pounders, those Yarrow ships had ... He was swivelling slowly, glasses up, as the entrance to a transverse channel opened up to starboard. It meant the land they'd had on their right hand was yet another island: but the northern side of that channel — and all the land abeam to starboard now —

might well be mainland.

Pope had ignored that junction: he'd seen it and evidently decided to hold straight on. Reducing revs again just slightly, a notch or two on the throttle.

Solovyev asked — from close on Bob's right — 'Are we near the place where I leave you?'

'Can't be far now. At least, I hope—' He'd checked — mouth still open ... Then, recovering: 'Hey, Johnny!'

'*Lights* in there!'

They'd both seen it — shouted at each other simultaneously ...

Some kind of — anchorage — base — camp ... Pope had pushed his throttle shut. There were three lights in a line, two others off to the left. In a place — the head of an inlet in an area of empty marshland — where you wouldn't expect there to be any electricity supply — or any need for it either ... And — Bob caught his breath — visible now against the background of starry sky — thin funnels, stubby masts. And a crane: he had it in his glasses, the head of it in slanting silhouette close to that pair of lights. He knew — well, guessed, but it had clicked suddenly, fitted into a slot in recent memory — what this must be, or be connected with ... Hearing Pope at his elbow — having cut the power he'd declutched but she was still running on and he couldn't leave the wheel — 'Tell McNaught I may want flat-out revs at the drop of a hat, will you?'

He passed the message. Remembering the flotilla navigator, Snaith, had mentioned that the Bolsheviks were preparing a deployment eastward against Guriev, and shipping their heavy equipment in barges in tow of tugs. So here was the loading base, the military depot: those were the masts of tugs and there'd be barges in there too, beyond doubt ... The engine's throb was down to nothing, barely more audible than the gurgle of sea around the CMB's timbers, its swirl and suck around her bow and under her stern as she continued to run on, still with steerage-way on her, Pope holding her on course for the centre of that gap between low banks of vegetation. It was all he *could* do — short of running her into one of those banks.

'I know what this is, Johnny. No need to look closer – if we can get where there's room to turn her—'

The bow struck some object. The CMB lurched, her forepart lifting as she jarred to a dead stop. A crash from inside the engine-space might have been McNaught falling off his stool: in the cockpit they'd all been holding on – Pope to the wheel, the other two to the coaming below the windscreen. There'd been a grating noise from for'ard, lasting about two seconds; it had stopped now and the stern was swinging, continuing under the impetus of her forward motion while the bow was held and slowly pivoting. The impact – thinking back on it in the immediate aftermath, needing to understand what had happened – had been solid but also – well, cushioned. Like a train hitting buffers, almost: not like grounding, or—

'Cable – chain cable. Boom across the bloody entrance. *Damn.*'

Bob moved: 'I'll get up for'ard with a boathook. Or over the side, if necessary. Where's—'

That same grating noise again. The rasp of chain against – under – the CMB's bow. Then a sideways lurch: and silence. Swinging, she'd slid off it. Touch wood . . . But you could feel the difference – that she was floating properly now, that rigidity gone out of her.

'How amazing . . .' Pope spoke detachedly, as if it was happening to someone else . . . He leant over the side, looking for'ard. Then over to the other side, crossing behind Bob and the Count. Straightening up, then . . . 'Boathook's a good idea, Bob. If you can get up on her nose and push us off a bit. Sooner be well clear before I use the screw – what?'

It would have been easy if one could have just backed off, but this craft couldn't be put astern. In point of fact, if she could have been they wouldn't have hit the cable in the first place, he'd have taken the way off her as soon as they'd seen those lights.

The boathook was stowed – like every other bit of loose gear on board, it seemed – in the engine-space. McNaught passed it out, and Bob went for'ard with it.

The timber roof of the engine-space, from the cockpit to the horizontal fore hatch, was flat, but the rest of the boat's sides and upperworks were curved — turtle-decked, was the term for it — with one protruding strake low down for toe-hold and a higher one to hold on by. He crabbed up towards the bow, concentrating on just getting there, anyway preferring not to see whatever reaction might be developing in or around that camp, depot, whatever this place was that they'd literally blundered into. If an alarm had been raised — could be the *raison d'être* of that cable, to set one off — the only hope was to get out of here before the Bolsheviks had rubbed the sleep out of their eyes …

Straddling the saddle-like stem then, with the bullring close in front of him as a convenient handhold, he leant over, peering into the dark, still water. At first he couldn't see the cable — or much else — but then about twenty feet towards one bank — and less than that distance towards the other — he spotted it, a ruler-straight black line with the tidal movement lapping around it where it emerged. Here in the middle it was under water: but right against the boat's forefoot, presumably …

Groping for it, with the boathook's ironclad working end. Contact … Working blind still, but getting the hook jammed into a link of cable so it would hold when he put some weight against it. As now … But achieving nothing — until after about a minute's perseverance he realized that the CMB's forepart was at last beginning to respond, swing away …

He shifted his grip: applied *all* his weight …

Pope's voice, then — after a few more minutes — 'Bravo, Bob. We can get at it here now. Hold her as she is, can you?'

He had a second boathook, presumably. Or he'd use one of the skiff's oars. Bob waited: holding the bow about three feet clear of the chain, everything more or less static for the moment, and no sounds or visible stirrings from the direction of the lights. Probably no one awake. One had heard that they drank a lot. But he knew why they had that destroyer anchored where she was — in the main channel, doubtless the tugs' entrance to and exit from this place. She'd be there either on defensive watch or as escort to barge convoys in daylight. This was first-class intelligence to take back to Baku, anyway; an extra dividend from Operation Nightingale.

Which was now well behind schedule.

'Ready, Bob? Together now — *heave* ...'

She barely responded at all, to start with, but then the gap between her and the chain began to widen.

'Right. Hang on now ...'

The engine's throb deepened and quickened. With a single screw you got a kick to starboard when you first put it ahead; Pope would have his wheel hard a-starboard, and that kick might be advantageous, insurance against swinging her stern into the cable as he turned her away from it.

Back in the cockpit: pushing the boathook inside. 'Here ...'

'Nice work, Bob.'

'Damn lucky, weren't we?'

They could so easily have got stuck there. If that chain had got itself involved with the propeller, for instance. Then what — hand-grenades at first light, Pope's Last Stand?

'Bob.' Motoring back the way they'd come, Pope pointed out over the port bow. 'I'd say our best bet is this eastward channel. Put your Count ashore somewhere there, and possibly get out that way ourselves — if we're really lucky?'

'Let's put him on his way first, uh?'

'Absolutely.' The side-channel's mouth was opening to them now. Pope began to ease his wheel over. 'Here we go ...'

Bob put a hand on the Count's shoulder: his leather coat was slippery-wet from spray or sea-dew. 'Sorry, Nick. Won't be long now, anyway. I'd guess this must be the eastern edge of the delta — so where we're heading now is pretty sure to be mainland — wouldn't you say?'

'Please God.'

'It *must* be, though. That's a military stores or loading depot, where we've just been. So there has to be a road to it — d'you see? Wouldn't have crossed water — needing a bridge, or—'

'Mainland in any case. Yes ...' Nodding — in the darkness lessened by a vague radiance from the engine-space. He'd added a cloth cap to his attire: must have had it in a pocket ... 'You're right, Bob. That's — capital ...'

They were in this new channel now. Remembering the chart — not its detail, which was so unreliable, but the general configuration of the delta — it was a reasonable guess that fairly soon they might be emerging into another of the north-south channels, and with any luck — as long as it didn't have any destroyers anchored in it, for instance — a direct exit to the sea. It would be marvellous if this proved to be the case, particularly from the point of view of having to get back in here in a week's time.

'Hey — Bob's your uncle!'

Here it was. A north-south channel.

'Well — for small mercies ...'

Solovyev's hand on his arm: 'Here?'

'Might as well take him a bit farther inland.' Pope was easing the wheel over to port. 'Couple of minutes for us, half an hour's hard pull for him — what?'

'Don't think so, Johnny.' Bob had the glasses at his eyes. 'No — no need. This isn't a river channel, it's the head of an inlet, a cul-de-sac ... Run up there for two minutes, you'd be on the putty.'

'Be damned.' Centring the wheel, cutting the revs, lifting his own glasses ... Bob told him, 'That's the mainland. Can't *not* be.' He added, 'Land of the Kirghizi. As cut-throat a bunch as you'd ever meet.'

It was past two-thirty by the time they had the lashings off the skiff — three of them working at it, while Pope kept his CMB in mid-channel with her long, slim bow pointing the way they'd be going in a minute. Which wasn't an unhappy thought at all ... Meanwhile, with the lashings off, Bob and the Count and McNaught were shoulder to shoulder on the starboard side of the torpedo-trough, with very little to hold on to except the skiff itself — which had now to be tilted up on to its port gunwale so it could then be toppled over into the water right-side-up.

'One-two-six — *heave*...'

Over, and — teetering, then — splashing in. Heavy, noisy, and drenching them all.

McNaught fetched crutches and oars out of the engine-space; Bob shook hands with the Count. 'We'll be saying prayers for you, Nick. See you in a week, or not much longer.'

'Yes.' Solovyev hung on to his hand for another moment. 'I'm more grateful to you than I can say, Bob.'

Pope called from the wheel, 'Tell him goodbye and good luck.'

The Count got into the boat then, shipped the crutches and settled the oars into them, while Bob lay more or less flat in the trough to hold the boat alongside and then push it off. He called again as they separated, 'See you, Nick.' Engine-noise already rising — Pope wasting no time, water already sluicing along the sides and swirling in a froth astern before he'd climbed back into the cockpit.

In less than a minute the Count and his skiff were out of sight in the darkness astern. The cockpit felt rather empty without its third occupant. Bob said, 'Home, James, and bugger the horses.'

'Before, or after?' He added, 'Channel may widen beyond that bend. I'll crack a few revs on then.'

Bob didn't think it did widen — not at that point, not that soon. The opening to the lateral channel, the one by which they'd arrived in this inlet, was visible from here, but the bulge of land beyond it might presage a bend — as Pope was assuming — might alternatively be indicative of a bottleneck.

Not that one cared, as long as it was navigable. Sooner or later you'd have clearer water; then it shouldn't be long before you'd be out of the delta altogether, in more or less open sea. Which, from the point of view of returning here next week ...

Wouldn't be bad from the point of view of getting back to *Zoroaster* and a hot bath and a comfortable bunk, either.

'Narrows a bit, doesn't it?'

He grunted. '*Quite* a bit.'

The CMB was making about twelve knots. It was the highest speed she could make without a breaking bow-wave or any wash to speak of. Pope had now seen the bottleneck — where the channel curved around that bulge — but he wasn't cutting the revs at all. Speaking again now — shouting — 'If there's a guardship or anything of that kind, I'll open her right up and dash past before they can say Jack Robinsonovich.'

'No — for God's sake ...'

'Huh?'

'Johnny — we have to be back here in seven days, and we don't want 'em on their guard. *If* we meet something — well, much better turn around, sneak out the way we came — don't you agree?'

A moment's silence ... Then: 'You've a point, I dare say.'

Colleagues surprised one, at times. They could make you feel as old as you looked, even, on occasion ... Pope had reduced speed now, anyway. And beyond the bottle-neck — they were coming up to it now — the fairway looked clear. Wide open, and empty. Touching wood — continually, with his elbows, needing both hands for the binoculars ... Hearing Pope begin, 'Anyway, once we're through this little hole, Bob old chap—'

The crash threw him backwards from the wheel. Bob had been knocked down too. With the thought — as the bow rose and he heard that now recognizable, ugly rasping — chain cable grating timber again — *Another bloody boom* ... Pope had got back to his controls and slammed the throttle shut; the scraping noise stopped before it had come more than a few feet aft from the bow. There was a bow-up angle. Could have ripped the bottom out of her

... Bob recognizing — checking in the engine-space whether she might be taking in water, but she didn't seem to be and McNaught was prospecting for damage now — that any ordinary kind of ship would have struck the cable with her forefoot, whereas the CMB with her small draft had ridden over it. In other words, that the chain-boom had not been rigged there with CMBs in mind.

Pope muttering — pointlessly — 'Should've damn well guessed ...'

He was right, he should have. Bob amended that to *we* should have. Where one channel had been barred, why not another? And they'd obviously have chosen a narrow spot like this — easier to rig it up, and only a comparatively short span of chain required; the chain on which the CMB was now well and truly stuck — having hit it a lot harder than she'd hit the first one.

For what purpose, though? Triggering some kind of alarm?

But the other one hadn't. That one, of course, had only been barring access to the inlet, might quite probably be shut at night and opened in daylight hours. It would be operated by a winch and when it was open the chain would lie slack on the bottom. While the purpose of this one would be — well, to leave only one way of coming from or going to the open sea — the route by which they happened to have come in by tonight. If this was the case, it would prescribe the action that needed to be taken now: get her off this chain — somehow — and then go back, take that same route, creeping past the anchored destroyer as before.

But — God almighty — same damn procedure in a week's time, then every second day!

Pope was musing aloud: 'Can't back off under power. Need to back off, though. If we still had the skiff, might have towed her off — one strong man on each oar. But we haven't ... Bob — you and McNaught over the side — if it's in your depth so you can stand, and keep a footing ...'

'I'll check. McNaught — got that boathook?'

He hung over the side with it, poking vertically

downward, eventually using its full length with his hands and its top end actually in the water and still not finding any bottom.

'Not in our depth, Johnny. Anyway the bottom's probably soft mud.' He asked the mechanic — giving him back the boathook — 'How about you and I swimming — each of us with a line to her?'

'Not a hope.' Pope was sure of it — probably right, at that. 'She's not a bloody skiff, you know.'

'So . . .'

'So we can't back off it. But we do have to *get* off. So — no option, Bob . . .' Turning to McNaught. 'Look, here's what. I'll give her a touch ahead — no more than a touch, just get her moving over the chain. She'll slide her keel over it all right, and we'll hear it, won't we. When it's right aft here, we get the boathook on it, try to push it down. While *you*, Bob — I'll want you right up on the stem, your weight up there — help bring her stern up.' Nodding to McNaught: 'Might actually hook on to it, drag it aft — drag ourselves forward, comes to the same thing . . . And failing all else, another little burst of engine-power — huh?'

'But Johnny — if you wipe your screw off, or bend a blade — or even just snag it in the cable . . .'

'There's a guard round it, old man. Sort of cage affair. Designed so things'll skid over it. Besides, if we're pushing the damn thing *down* . . .'

Bob looked at McNaught. 'What do you think?'

'Och . . .' A shake of the head. 'Lieutenant Pope's the skipper, sir.'

'No man e'er spoke a truer word. Let's get a wriggle on, now. Boathook handy? That's it . . . Bob, you stay here until we've manoeuvred the thing well aft — all right?'

It wasn't all right at all. He thought it was extremely likely that the chain would smash or damage the propeller or snag on its guard. Probably strip the screw of its blades and then snag between it and the rudder. But he wasn't a CMB man, he'd never seen one out of water, therefore knew nothing of its underwater construction — or the shape or strength of that propeller-guard, for instance. Whereas Pope did, presumably knew every square inch of his boat above and below the waterline. And McNaught was right — he *was* the skipper.

The first stage went as expected. One short burst of power that sent her rasping forward, brought the cable grating to a stop somewhere abaft the cockpit. Pope was quietly — giving him his due, *very* quietly — cock-a-hoop.

'So far, so good. Bob, may we have your not inconsiderable *avoirdupois* right up on the sharp end, please?'

He went up the starboard side and squatted on the bullring, facing aft. Fearing the worst, hoping for the best, hearing them splashing and banging around with the boathook, an occasional crash against the hull as it skidded off the cable. Thinking of the huge weight of that chain — that much iron, enough to stretch across this channel — and Johnny Pope actually believing he could push it this way or that *with a boathook*?

You could slide a boat — her keel — over it. As they had done. You could perhaps even lift the boat to a limited extent in the water — if you got her rocking, bouncing, the disturbance of the water itself assisting in the process ... From this thought, he hit on a way it might be done. One man each side, over the side but standing on the chain: and from that position manhandling the boat over, inch by inch.

He was about to stand up and call to Johnny, ask him to listen to this proposal. But at that moment Johnny threw in the clutch and opened the throttle for a short, sharp burst that was intended to drive her right over the obstruction by brute force. It snagged, as he'd known it would, on the propeller or the propeller-guard, the heavy chain was jerked bar-taut, and the mines attached to it were whipped up from the seabed on their steel-wire pendants, one of them right under the CMB's midships section — the cockpit, under the floor of which was the boat's petrol tank. The explosion was upward through the centre of the boat, a sheet of flame visible for miles, the sound of it audible in Astrakhan and Nikolsk let alone nearer settlements — Krasni-Yar, Seitovka . . .

All Bob was aware of — and all of it in one split second — was the shattering blast, blinding flash, intense heat instantly snuffed out in oblivion.

5

The voice in his skull beat all the surrounding noise: and it was warmly, supremely welcome — despite its serrated edge and harsh, overbearing tone — having just ordered him to get his head up, and now — harsher still, really hectoring — 'And *keep* it up! God's sake, a man can't breathe water!'

'Well — you'd know . . .'

'Hah! *Don't* I just!'

Twice. It was odd that one hadn't thought of it this way before — that they'd failed to drown him when he was a boy, made a proper job of it more recently. Properness of the job having been duly certified by that blue-pencil scrawl commencing *Their Lordships deeply regret to inform you . . .*

If it had been brought to the same conclusion when he'd been eleven nobody would have regretted anything at all.

'See her, lad?'

Seeing her, indeed. Sweet, oval face, soft dark hair falling as she bent over him, over the cot, and in the half-light — bedroom door half-open, light outside in the passage — a pale-yellow satin jacket open over a shimmery silver figure-hugging dress. And her perfume . . . Soft murmur then — her lips close to his face — 'Night, my darling, see you in the morning — *spokoinii noich, golubchik. Lyublyoo tebya . . .*' and his father's voice breaking in then, 'Did any other feller *ever* have such luck? Old roughneck like me, and — Christ, did you ever really *look* at her, boy?'

'Oh, yes . . .'

He thought — with a certainty of enduring happiness —

And all the time in the world to go on looking, now . . .

As soon as one could get through this. Whatever it was. Not a dream, it didn't feel like dreaming. Limbo? Halfway house? But the old man had intercepted that thought — or that preference, intention. Snarling at him — 'You'll do no such thing, boy! God, what a damn-fool way to—'

'But I *want*—'

'*Want*, bollocks!'

'*Vot, shto . . .*' Different voice entirely — thin, rather distant. As well as the switch of language. Not totally unfamiliar: but here and now only an intrusion. Discomfort too: he was aware of it now, of something tight round his chest, under his arms, cuttingly tight and getting tighter still . . . But the old man's voice again — less rough, the soothing tone he'd sometimes adopted when he'd been trying to put one over — 'You'll be all right now, lad. You'll see, you'll be fine . . .'

'Better for that, are we?'

Russian, again. Not his father's. His father seemed to have left him to this other chap. But they'd always spoken English to each other when they'd been alone, Russian at other times including those when his mother had been with them, as she'd had hardly any English. A little French and a smattering of German, but for some reason her parents hadn't bothered with an English teacher. The old man had been giving her lessons — sporadically, when he'd remembered and she'd had the inclination — with a view to eventual retirement to Scotland. At least to have that option, he'd explained, if when he got to be about a hundred they'd both wanted it.

Choking. Then — another gush . . .

Gagging: And more to come . . . The Russian was telling him something or other, his voice as muffled as if he might have been talking through a pillow. And meanwhile another memory as it were materializing — God, from so long ago, one he hadn't even known he possessed. He'd been a small boy then, eight or so, and his mother — swollen, big-bellied — pregnant, obviously, might have been the pregnancy that had killed her — he'd have been just nine, at that time — telling him in that sweet, quiet voice of hers, mellow, fluid Russian, 'He saved my life, Bobbie. I'd have done away with myself if it hadn't been for him. My own people were throwing me out — I can't explain it to you — not until you're older — but — oh, I'd been — *very* naughty ... Although even then — well, one day I'll tell you. When you're grown up — I promise. But now, I want you to know this much about — this man, your father — whom I love, Bobby darling, as deeply as any man was *ever* loved — I want you to know that if he hadn't come along — and saved me ...'

'Saved — me ...'

'Man's found his tongue!'

Memory fading, flickering out. Struggling to hold on to it ... Saved her how, and from what? Suicide, was the implication: her own people having — 'thrown her out'? For — well, for God's sake, what 'naughtiness' so-called could possibly have justified that kind of cruelty — and to someone so *gentle* ...

Crying ...

Aged — nine. Crying at the very *thought*—

'Hey! *Hey*! Hey, Bob! Listen, you're going to be all right now, you're ...'

'Nearly *killed* him ...'

'Nearly killed whom?'

Clinging to memory. While the Russian voice — low, but urgent — dragged at him like a grapnel. And the answer was of course his father — that was *whom.* When she died, he was — God, like a madman ...

'You're the only one it *didn't* kill!'

'What?'

'Ah — at last. Conscious ... Bob, *are* you conscious? Because — look, you *have* to be. *Now* ... Christ almighty ...'

'What's — *this*?'

Struggling up. *Cold* ... In long grass — reeds — with the Count's dark figure crouched beside him: a hand on his mouth, hissing some kind of warning ... He pushed the hand away. Freezing bloody cold. This thing he was picking at with numb fingers was a rope, a hemp line around his chest so tight it was embedded in the soaked material of his reefer jacket. 'Damn it, what's . . .'

'I had to tow you. Couldn't lift you into the boat, so . . .'

'Slip-knot . . . Might at least've used a bowline.' Peering, with a hand out, touching him: 'Nikolai Petrovich. How the hell . . .'

Thoughts all jumbled: a mess of confusions, conflicts, questions, the biggest of them being *What now*? In fact 'big' was hardly the word for it: it was so huge it was unanswerable, the utter lack of even the beginnings of an answer more than bewildering, actually frightening. He was aware of this and affected by the fear of it even without having any clear notion yet as to where he was or how he'd come to be here.

'Bob — now listen to me—'

'*Hey*, what's—'

Light flaring overhead. The Count pushed him down — he seemed frantic, with a sort of whinnying in his fast breathing. But it was dark again, the searchlight — that was what it was, had been — had moved on, sweeping the level surface of the land but perhaps in its operators' primary intention searching the water, the momentary overspill here quite unintentional. Bob was up on an elbow again, and the Count was kneeling, rather like a dog up on its hind legs to see over long grass, but with a hand on Bob's shoulder to keep him down where he was: then he crouched down, beside him. 'The searchlight's on the ship — over there, where I found you. Probably the one we saw earlier — destroyer, you said it was?'

'Did you know it was here?'

'Yes. I heard it coming — saw it too — not long after we got in here. But it was bound to, wasn't it — I was expecting it to come sooner — when I was towing you, I was thinking any *minute*, my God—'

'I'm — much obliged to you. But . . .'

'What was it that blew up?'

'A mine. Couldn't have been anything else. Connected

to the chain somehow. We hit this other chain, you see, then Johnny got a bit — well, desperate, I'm afraid ...'

He was putting it together as it came back to him. And that was the explanation of Johnny Pope's stupidity. He'd felt trapped: behind schedule already, they'd been caught once and got away with it and now again — only worse, and with time even shorter ... Bob focused on the Count again: 'How did *you*—'

'Wait.' His hand out again ... 'Quiet ...'

Actually they could have shouted to each other, nobody out there would have heard. A Russian was bawling orders: there was a squealing of sheaves in their blocks, more shouting, splashing, and a medley of thumping, clattering sounds carrying very clearly across the water and recognizable to a seaman's ear as oars banging down and a boat's falls being unhooked, even the clang of gear as it swung against a ship's steel side.

'How far from us?'

'Two hundred metres. Three hundred, perhaps. I brought you as far as I could — far as I dared. If I'd still been out there when they arrived, you see — and my God, rowing was so *slow*, with your weight. You should get your clothes off, by the way, and dry them out. After sunrise, maybe ... But I was worried I might have been drowning you, on this rope — if it had taken longer you *would* have drowned ... I'd rowed into that chain, too, you see, that's how it happened that I found you.'

'Chain still intact?'

'Yes. Surprising, I suppose ... Bob — do you understand, they may start searching for us?'

But the chain would stop them. Assuming they were the other side of it. Well, surely, from where that destroyer had been anchored ...

Must have had steam up all ready, to have got here this soon. Although — how long it might have been, God only knew ... One's last waking recollection could be a minute old, or a day ... Well — hardly that. Still dark, no sign of the dawn yet ... Another image then — from the thought of sunrise — *Zoroaster* out there, fifty miles south of here, lying stopped with her anchor-lights burning for himself and Johnny Pope to home-in on. Eric Barker beginning to wonder where the devil they'd got to — unless the sound of the explosion had carried that far out to sea, in which case he'd be making his own shrewd, unhappy guesses.

'Would they know — or have any reason to suspect . . .? He paused, struggling to get it together. Brain functioning, but in fits and starts, with foggy areas in between. Beginning again — different approach to the same question — 'Where's the skiff?'

'Here.' An arm in the dark, past his face. 'It's a sort of ditch, I rowed into it, then got out, dragged you in, then pulled the boat in farther. It can't be visible to them now, not the boat itself, but it's possible with the reeds all trampled — and anyway I found it in the dark, you see, so by daylight . . .'

Oars. Ragged stroke, clunking of looms in metal crutches, erratic splashings. The searchlight was still burning, but static. They'd have it pointing down at the water, he guessed, while they searched for wreckage, and so on. Debris would have been scattered over a wide radius, of course. They'd be examining the immediate area of the explosion now: then with daylight, and probably more help arriving . . .

But they'd have no reason, surely, to guess that anyone might have survived. Therefore, no reason to make any wider search. As they'd see it, there'd been an intrusion, their mine had done its job, here was the wreckage as evidence. And two bodies — or anyway the components of two bodies.

But then again — in daylight, if the place where Nick had dragged the skiff into the reeds looked obvious . . .

He thought, *Better move — while we* can *move* . . .

'Nick — once it's light, we're stuck.' Keeping his voice down. Voice none too strong yet anyway. 'We could crawl — put some distance behind us while we can?'

'I don't think so. I *did* consider it, but—'

'But if they see where you dragged the boat in . . .'

'It wouldn't make much difference. Also it's possible

there are many such — ditches, drains, and I only happened to notice this one because I was searching for some such place. But also, Bob — the reeds aren't so high, if they were moving and someone on the ship's bridge — high up, with binoculars ...'

'But we'd go slowly — carefully ...'

'No, Bob, listen. Suppose they find that place — or the boat. Then they'd be on our track anyway. And how far would we have gone — half a mile, a mile even?'

'So the alternative ...'

'Stay here. Sit it out. By tonight you'll be rested, strong again, and they will have gone — please God.'

'Well. I take your point, but — look, I'm right as rain now, and — we're too damn close to them. All right — I admit it scares me. If we *could* get as much as half a mile away—'

'*Listen* to me!' Hands grasped his arms: the Count's face was a dark blur close in front of his own. 'First — you damn near drowned, you're still shaking and you aren't thinking straight yet either. Second — we're not in one of your ships now, we're in *my* country — huh?'

Light growing from the East, and a light wind off the sea ruffling the tops of the reeds and chilling the pre-dawn air. Activity continuing out there in the channel: voices, and the searchlight shifting its beam from time to time.

The CMB's engine would be on the sea-bed somewhere. In deep mud, at that. They'd need a crane to get it up. If they wanted to ...

Shivering ... And having to convince himself, *This is real, it's not just a bad dream* ...

Then that unanswerable question again: *What now?*

He asked the Count — he'd thought he was dozing a minute ago, but he could see now that his eyes were open, the gleam of their whites — 'When you heard the explosion, were you still rowing or had you landed?'

'I was about to land. It was only a short distance, to the top of the inlet, and I'd just seen a place where I could haul the boat up.'

'So then you heard the bang, and — what made you decide to turn back?'

The Count moved — hunching over, drawing his knees up to rest his clasped hands on them ... 'I should like to say I came to save your life. The truth is that if I'd gone on I wouldn't have known what had happened. There was no certainty it was your CMB that had blown up. I didn't start back immediately — I thought about it, for some minutes, whether to carry on or go back. But then I thought — well, how do I know that when I get back here with the others there'll be anyone to meet us?'

He nodded. 'Very sensible.'

'So I had to find out, you see.'

'And now you know—' Some ducks passed over — low and loud, obviously quite close, but not visible — 'will you still go ahead?'

'D'you think I'd just leave them there?'

'So — you'll go to Enotayevsk — find them — get them out of that old house of yours — and then what?'

'I don't think there's much point even thinking about it at this stage. I've got to get there first, then find them and see what state they're in. Then see what options there may be. In other words — follow my nose and trust to luck ... But what about you, Bob, what will *you* ...'

He paused. Both of them listening to the regular thud-thud-thud of a powerful propeller churning shallow water at slow speed. Steamboat. As likely as not, a tug — out of that secret base of theirs. Bringing — one might guess — equipment of some kind. Heavy-lifting gear to recover the CMB's engine, maybe. Or divers with their pumps and so forth ... There'd be comings and goings all day, he supposed ... Unbuckling the flap on his webbing holster, he slid the revolver out. Might as well dry it out, to whatever extent one could. Its ammunition was the most important thing: and the firing-pin, to ensure it wasn't salted up or might rust later. Check that when the light came: and when he'd dried himself and his clothes out, a shirt-tail would serve as a cleaning rag. For now, going only by feel, he emptied the six .45 shells into his palm and rolled them around, getting the wet off them, then blew through the pistol's chambers and barrel before reloading. It felt quite oily still.

The newly-arrived ship — tug? — was passing close to where Nick must have dragged the boat into the reed-filled drainage-channel. No light was showing from that direction, and it was still dark enough; but it seemed crazy to be sitting here, this close to them — trusting to luck or to the Count's superior wisdom — and counting on none of them prospecting farther afield than just that patch of water. Their priority would be to identify the wreckage and the bodies, he imagined. Not difficult, Johnny Pope's being dressed in his uniform reefer jacket with RN stripes on the sleeves, brass buttons with anchors and laurels, naval cap. His own cap too —somewhere amongst it. But there'd be other identifying items too — bound to be, since neither capture nor destruction had been considered even as a possibility. The quick dash in and out, the master-stroke of a royal rescue — and nobody having publicly to admit to anything — was all that had ever been envisaged. Whereas now, the way it had turned out, it was likely to be a considerable embarrassment for the British government — seeing that official policy was not to interfere in Russia's internal affairs, that British soldiers and sailors were here solely to fight Turks and Germans.

Putting it crudely, the Foreign Office was likely to want the Commodore's guts for garters.

'Bob.' The Count's voice broke into his random thoughts. 'What will you do?'

Second time of asking. And more duck flying over — a big, high-speed rush of them, their wingbeats light and fast; he guessed they'd have been teal but again he'd failed to see them ... He had no answer to that question, not in the sense of having an answer that he could think of as the right one. The only course that he could see as open to him seemed to be in direct conflict with his duty — which was to get back to the flotilla, and report to the Commodore at the earliest possible moment on what had happened here.

But short of swimming several hundred miles ...

'Straight answer to that straight question, Nick — I'm damned if I know.'

'Come with me, then. Let's do it together.'

That was the obvious thing. Trouble was — no, troubles, plural, *were* — (a) his duty was plainly and simply to get back to the flotilla, (b) it was not legitimate for him to take any part in anti-Bolshevik activities ashore — or even afloat, for that matter — and (c) supposing he did go along with the Count and they found the women and children were still there — which didn't seem all that probable, after three months or more and with things as chaotic as they were — what options *could* there be, for God's sake?

His head was throbbing. It had been aching ever since he'd recovered consciousness but it was really hurting now. And the other prong of the dilemma was that if he told the Count no, he couldn't join him, the next question would be — again — 'So what *will* you do?'

Warmth came with the first rays of the sun, a fiery blaze flooding across the sea of reeds and grass, and the night's moisture beginning immediately to lift from the land like steam. He peeled his clothes off, spread them where the sun would get to them when it was higher, and began to think about mosquitoes, which were already whining around.

He hoped his gear wouldn't take long to dry. Not only mosquitoes: a whole crowd of Bolsheviks only a couple of hundred yards away. Not the ideal state in which to be taken prisoner.

'Well enough to feel hungry yet, Bob?'

The thought of food had occurred to him: he'd put it out of his mind. Now the Count was offering him a sandwich — explaining, 'There was so much food in that bag. Far more than the three of you could have needed. After all, you'd have been having breakfast by this time.'

He took it gratefully. 'Thanks.'

'I stole these from you, as well.'

Grenades. He'd put his sandwich in his mouth and was

holding out a grenade in each fist. 'Might have taken more than two, seeing the rest are under the water there now.' He shrugged. 'Not that I'm expecting to fight battles — please God.'

They'd recover that box, Bob realized. And the rifle. One Royal Navy vessel, with weapons and explosives on board, caught and destroyed when engaged on some clandestine mission into Bolshevik-held territory. They'd assume it to have been a mission directed against their new military stores depot. Must have anticipated the possibility of such intrusion — why else lay mines, and station a guardship on the only channel left open?

The Count said, 'I don't need these, anyway. Better without them.' Making a hole for the grenades, digging with his fingers. Bob told him, 'I think you're wise. I only brought them along in case we got stuck, had to fight our way out or something.'

'*Very* wise.'

'Not really. Considering we're supposed to be neutral in your civil war.'

'One's heard the theory, of course.' The Count shrugged. 'But it doesn't make much sense — when you have what you call Expeditionary Forces ashore at Archangel and Murmansk. *And* they've been fighting, as has your Royal Navy, up there . . .'

'Only to stop the Germans, Nick. If attacked, of course, one fights back, but—'

'What about the Far East too, then? You've landed men in Vladivostok. So have the Japanese — seventy thousand men, I heard — and a few Americans, and of course the French . . .'

'They're damn-all to do with *us*, Nick.'

'Royal Navy sailors and Marines manning armoured trains on the Trans-Siberian Railway, trains fitted with guns taken off one of your cruisers in Vladivostok?'

'Well . . . I *think* I heard that was in an effort to break through to the Czech Legion — so as to get them out, through Vladivostok I suppose.'

The Count chuckled, with his mouth full of sandwich.

'Except that we heard — General Denikin was *told* — that it had been decided the Czech Legion should be brought out through Archangel?'

'From Siberia — across the Urals . . .'

'They're concentrated in Western Siberia now — yes. They took Ekaterinburg quite recently, you know.'

Holding out another sandwich . . .

'Have you got enough?'

'As many as I could get into my pockets. Have it.'

'Thanks.'

'I need you with me, Bob. That's to say, I'd be immensely glad to have your company and help. Unless you *do* have other plans?'

Bob stared at him for a moment. Then: 'Ekaterinburg is where we heard they'd murdered the Imperial family. Including the four young Grand Duchesses — so the report maintained.'

'Rumour.' A shrug. 'Haven't there been dozens, and all different?' He bit into his own second sandwich. 'I think it's probable that there were murders committed at Ekaterinburg. But the message my young friend brought from Enotayevsk — well, you'll remember . . .'

'Yes, of course.'

'It satisfies me, for one, that not the whole family could have been slaughtered at that time. I was going to say, though — it's likely they murdered the Tsar, at least, at that time, because the Czechs were advancing on Ekaterinburg. They'd have been very unwilling to allow him and/or others of the Imperial family to be snatched out of their hands — by the Czechs especially.'

'I — suppose . . .'

'And another thing on the subject of foreigners being involved or not involved in our affairs, Bob — the Czech Legion have a whole crowd of French officers with them. Did you know?'

He shrugged. Thinking that the French would be grinding their own axes — as always . . . The Czech Legion, raised in Kiev by one Thomas Masaryk, consisted of former prisoners of war as well as pre-war Ukrainian settlers of Moravian and Bohemian origin. There were thirty thousand of them now operating along the Trans-Siberian Railway, of which they'd virtually taken control after Trotsky had made the mistake of ordering Bolshevik troops to disarm them. The Count was nodding — as if he thought he'd won a point here — 'French officers — openly, they're not disguising *their* involvement. I don't know why you British are so squeamish, Bob.'

'Possibly because we've got our hands full already, fighting Germans. Resources stretched pretty thin, at that.' He slapped at another mosquito. Thinking that as far as grinding axes was concerned this fellow might even be the equal of the French ... 'Politics aren't my line anyway — we get our orders, that's all. Ours not to reason why — all that.'

Two hundred yards away, Bolshevik voices were raised in song: *Volga, Volga, our natural mother/Volga, Russian river ...*

'But when you're on your own, as you are now —' the Count was looking in that direction, and he'd dropped his voice to a low murmur — 'surely you *have* to reason why. And *what* — such as, for instance, what you'll do if you don't come with me.'

'Yes. I'll have to work that out.'

'Would you like one of these?'

An apple. Bob took it from him. 'Thank you. But if we eat all your rations today ...'

'I have roubles, I can buy food — where there's any to be bought ... But tell me — what orders do you have that apply to you in the situation you're in now?'

'None except that it's my duty to get back to the flotilla. First, because that's where my job is, second because they need to know what's happened here.' He added, '*And* about that new supply base we found.'

'And how will you get back?'

He shrugged, munching apple. 'Small problem, there. But if I joined you, the problem would only be postponed — and trickier then, with women and children on our hands.'

'We'll find a way, Bob. Two heads are supposed to be better than one.'

'So let's put them together now. From here, Nick, *now*...'

'Easy. We'll go by way of Enotayevsk.'

'Well, naturally. First thing anyone would think of — go a hundred miles up-river. Then come floating down it again, I suppose?'

'That's a thought, isn't it?'

'In a punt? The girls reclining in the back end under parasols?'

'Bob — you know, you can joke as much as you like, but if you were with me the possibility — or alternative — of escape by sea does become more real. With your professional skills and—'

'And your daydreams, Nick. Down the Volga and out to sea past Astrakhan, Bolsheviks everywhere you look *and* half the Black Sea Fleet ... Seriously, if that's your reason for wanting me with you—'

'It's not. Although there could be something in it, you don't have to put it quite so baldly ... No, my reason is that I'd like your help, that I'd like to have you with me. Two heads *are* better than one: and in a tight spot it's not so bad to have someone you can trust to watch your back. But also — look —' he was whispering now — 'from your own point of view, first I can't see what other course is open to you, and second — well, you say your duty's to get back. All right, fine — but don't forget, your commodore and the General gave their approval to this mission. The General even mentioned that King George of England would be — gratified ... So, tell me this — which is better, to go back saying the boat and two lives are lost, I've left that damn Russian to look after himself — or mission accomplished?'

Like a hothouse. Jungle-type heat and humidity. No breath of wind, no movement permissible or safe, nothing to do but sit and sweat. He'd put his shirt and trousers back on; they weren't dry, only hot and damp, but they'd be like this again in minutes even if you'd put them on bone-dry, and anyway — protection against the mosquitoes *and* maintenance of morale . . .

Work was continuing, around the scene of the CMB's destruction. They could have had divers down: and a diesel-engined craft of some kind had visited, stayed an hour and gone away again. Voices were audible occasionally, but they were quieter — the excitement having worn off, he supposed — as well as the effect of this enervating heat.

The Count leant over, flipped up one of the sleeves of Bob's reefer, which was still steaming gently on the trampled reeds.

'Better pull those stripes off, hadn't you?'

'If I need it at all.'

'In the cold nights you will. Tonight anyway, crossing this marsh. We might find you something less conspicuous tomorrow.'

'Is it all that conspicuous?'

A nod. 'Obviously naval, and very good material. You could claim to have stolen it, but then it wouldn't fit you as it does.'

'Right.' He pulled it on to his lap, opened his seaman's knife — Admiralty issue, in naval parlance a 'pusser's dirk', worn on a lanyard around the waist — and began to slice the interwoven RNR gold-braid stripes off the thick, damp serge. Muttering, 'You seem to be assuming I'll be with you.'

'Not assuming. Hoping.' He slapped his neck and swore. 'We'll have malaria after this, for sure.'

'Wouldn't be at all surprised.'

Leonide's father suffered from malaria. So did a lot of the local people, of course, but she'd mentioned that he had very bad spells of it from time to time: she'd advanced this as an argument in favour of keeping shirt-sleeves buttoned at the wrist and never wearing short trousers. What she'd have said if she could have seen him sitting here stark naked, earlier on — well, one would never know . . . He frowned, wrenching the last inch of the second stripe off, and recognizing that she and her family would very soon be thinking he'd run out on her. He'd said — his last words to her — 'See you in a few days. Probably four or five.' But it would be weeks, not days. Even if he didn't go up-river with the Count, it would be weeks before he saw her. Not that this mattered, in terms of any great romance or thwarted love — the truth was that he'd been preparing to slide out of the relationship — in a friendly way, of course, and not expecting heartbreak on her side either — and still feeling a certain degree of responsibility for her safety, in that very uncertain Baku situation. He knew he was *not* 'responsible', had certainly had no idea that she'd been coming over from Krasnovodsk, but it wasn't inconceivable that in her own mind she'd been killing two birds with one stone when she'd decided to come to Uncle George's assistance, might have thought his interest in her was deeper than it ever had been.

Well — right at the start, perhaps — in that first week, he'd been fairly smitten . . .

Anyway, the last thing he'd want now was to have her think he'd been careless of her feelings.

Shutting his eyes, against heat and glare. Sweat streaming: he'd given up trying to mop it. No movement of air at all, down at this ground level . . . He remembered that the Count had reckoned on taking minimally seven days on this task but just as likely a fortnight and possibly as much as three weeks. And that had been just to get from here to Enotayevsk, get the women out of hiding and bring them back here. Whereas now one had probably to reckon on an overland trek — coastwise, perhaps, via Guriev.

From Guriev one could telegraph to Baku, perhaps. Or make contact by wireless. Establish a rendezvous, push off in a fishing-boat — or something . . .

Extraordinary to have only just thought of this! Brain half cooked, probably. First you half-drown, and then — he ripped the last inch of the last stripe off — damn well bake . . . From Enotayevsk to Guriev, though, would be something like — visualizing the map — well, three hundred miles, roughly. Across the Kirghiz Steppes. Best form of transport would surely be camel-back. If the Count had enough money to buy camels. But it might be crazy to think of crossing that particular stretch of country without a strong bodyguard: especially with women and girls in your caravan ...

'Bob. If you were to decide to join me, we'd need a new name for you. As you know, there's no such name as Robert or Bob — and we'd have to pass you off as a Russian, obviously.'

'What about my accent?'

'Well — it's very slight. More inflection than accent. I suppose it could become a bit of a problem, in certain circumstances. So we'd need a background for you that would explain it. I wonder ...'

'At a pinch, might I be a Persian?'

'Do you *talk* Persian?'

'No. But—'

'Talk any languages other than Russian and English?'

'Only schoolboy French.'

'Ah — *my* French isn't bad ... But—'

'Doesn't help us, does it. I was going to say — on our way up from the Gulf, when I wasn't shaving and wasn't obviously in uniform, I was mistaken for a Persian. And I wouldn't be meeting any others up there — would I?'

'Probably not. *Well*, now ...'

'Then if I needed a new name, as it happens there's a place called Robat, on the Afghan–Persian border. Oh — I think it's just inside Baluchistan. The three frontiers all meet at that point. But I could come from there. I'd be a man of mixed blood, but consider myself Persian and use the name Robat — wouldn't necessarily have been mine since birth, only what I've been known as — because that's been my stamping-ground. I may have been an outlaw — led guerrillas — d'you think?'

'Clever.' The Count nodded. 'Avoiding the risk of forgetting some other name at an awkward moment. And to have been a guerrilla leader — excellent, the Bolsheviks might see some use in you.' The green eyes smiled. 'What else, out of that fertile imagination?'

'Would anyone want more?'

'They might. And the more detail, if it's believable, the more you're — well, credible. So — for instance — how come you were in Askhabad?'

'Was I?'

'You and I must have met *somewhere* — huh?'

'Oh. I see.' He screwed his face up, thinking about it. Feeling his jaw, at the same time — quite a substantial first day's growth of stubble — and thinking about this mythical Persian guerrilla. Revolutionary — a Red now, if that was the side on which he believed his bread was buttered ...'

'I'm pro-Bolshevik, obviously. Keen to spread the gospel into Persia. That's the basic thing, and why you've brought me along with you — you being a deeply committed Bolshevik yourself ... What did you say your name is, by the way?'

'Vetrov, Anton Ivanovich. Better memorize it.'

'Anton.' Bob nodded. 'Anton of the winds.' He'd remember it now. The Russian word *veter* meaning wind, and as a memory-jogger the complete lack of any here ... Memory working well now anyway: throwing up the next idea ... 'Anton — my own recent history could be that I was with Kuchik Khan. Is that name familiar?'

'No, I don't—'

'Persian brigand. Guerrilla — like me. His last effort was trying to stop Bicherakov — and Dunsterville — getting from Kazvin to Enzeli, on their way to Baku. Kuchik was holding an all-important bridge at Menjil, on that road. In some strength, too. Bicherakov had only a thousand Cossacks with him, and Dunsterville had no more than a handful of Hussars and Hampshires. But he did have a couple of flying-machines with him, and they'd spotted a spur of mountain slope — untenanted at the time — from which artillery could dominate the Persian positions. Well, Kuchik Khan had a German so-called adviser, a Major von Passchen, and this Hun came along under a flag of truce to tell Bicherakov he was heavily outnumbered, didn't have a hope if it came to a fight, but they'd let him and his Cossacks through if they undertook to have nothing further to do with the British. So it's plain what *he* was there for. Anyway, Bicherakov's artillery had meanwhile occupied that key position, he told von Passchen to go and jump in the Caspian, opened the attack, Kuchik Khan's horde ran like riggers, and — well, that was it. Adding the fiction now, I'd have realized Kuchik wasn't worth bothering with — when I need a force down there I'd do better to raise it myself, from scratch — and this was when I moved up to Askhabad. Then Fralin the Cheka commander recruited me — and there you are.'

'And after the coup we escaped together.'

'Right. But talking of Fralin reminds me — your story, Anton ... You were working under him — but had you come down from Tashkent with him?'

'No. He took me on in Askhabad, too. I'm a Bolshevik but I'm not Cheka — never was.'

'That's fine. I'd wondered — how you'd explain not having gone back to Tashkent, if ...'

He'd stopped. Shook his head. 'Problem — no papers. Wouldn't even get off this bog without any — would I?'

'Into a Bolshevik prison, you would.'

'Exactly. So ...'

'They took your papers from you in Askhabad, during interrogation. They were going to hang you — you never got them back. I was cleverer, had mine in my socks — they look like it, too ... But I'd back you up on this, obviously — my God, you saved me from the gallows, I owe you my life!'

'It was a pleasure, Anton. Any time.'

The Count laughed. Reaching over, offering a handshake ...'Enotayevsk then, Robat. *Marvellous* ...'

6

Trekking north-westward — keeping the Pole star fine on the starboard bow, as it were ... By midnight it was getting easier, with less of the bogland and fewer streams and salt-lakes that had slowed their progress and forced them into detours earlier. Bob's shoes were still squelching wet, though. Tennis shoes, for God's sake. The Count had been absolutely right — Bob not having thought about it until he'd mentioned it — that the idea of a Persian guerrilla (or anyone else, for that matter) traversing this wild expanse of territory in English-made plimsolls was ludicrous. You'd be less conspicuous rigged up in a clown's outfit with a red nose and a ginger wig: and anyway — as he'd pointed out rather contemptuously — how could anyone have come all the way from Askhabad in *those*?

The intention was to go shopping at Seitovka. They'd be taking a train from there too. Heading north-west at this stage because according to the Count's mental map the village of Krasni-Yar would be to the west of where they'd landed — well inland, having made use of the skiff to start with, beaching it where the Count had been on the point of doing so when the mine had gone up. Bob had agreed it would be as well to keep clear of Krasni-Yar or any other villages or settlements during the dark hours — especially as they were coming from the direction of the sea, and every living soul for miles around would have heard last night's explosion. The idea was therefore to head north-west for about ten miles, circling around any inhabited places along the way, then west until they came to the road leading to Seitovka from Krasni-Yar, and follow that. With luck and no hold-ups they might average, say, three miles an hour, reaching Seitovka not long after dawn.

The criticism of Bob's footwear had come up at about the time the destroyer had been pushing off. About 4 pm, by the Count's watch — Bob's having stopped, and declining to start again despite efforts to dry out its works. As far as he remembered, that was when the subject had come up. Memory was somewhat vague: parts of it dream-like, reality and dream merging confusingly in retrospect, what with sleep and half-sleep, and the green-house heat, and the probably lingering effects of earlier trauma. He'd slept for about four hours — according to the Count's timing — from about noon to 4 pm, which had been the time when he'd woken to hear the destroyer's crew getting ready to pull out. Sleeping with his head among the reeds, in as much shade as existed, right in among their roots, and a smell like compost: then the tug's departure first, that slow, powerful thrashing northward, and soon afterwards the sounds of a boat being hoisted, then the loud, rhythmic clanking of the destroyer's steam capstan hauling in her cable. And the Count's murmur, 'I've been thinking, while you snored. You should have a more suitable jacket, Bob — anything, but not that one. And something red — like my scarf, or a shirt. You need a hat or a cap too — nobody goes bareheaded.'

He'd suggested facetiously, 'Bowler with a red feather in it?'

His head had stopped hurting, he'd realized. Thanks to the long sleep, no doubt. And thank God for large mercies . . .

'There must be a shop, in Seitovka. It's the only village of any size anywhere in that district, there'll be a store to serve the peasants' needs. Peasants and fishermen, I suppose . . . Not that the countryside's exactly crowded, in these regions.'

'Have we got enough money for all this?'

'Oh, yes.' A smile. 'Yes, we have, Robat.'

'For train tickets too?'

'Of course.'

'How often would trains go, from Seitovka?'

He'd shrugged. 'As frequently as they go from Astrakhan, probably. At least one a day, might be more. It's the first stop after Astrakhan. The line runs north to start with, then at Seitovka bends to the left and follows the river valley north-westward for — oh, three hundred versts or so.'

Geography lesson, then. This had been after the destroyer had gone; he remembered listening to all the sounds of its departure, therefore wouldn't have been listening to the Count as well. So probably it had been when they'd been watching the sun go down and the mosquitoes had been at their worst. They'd been eating the last of the Count's apples at that time, too — for thirst-quenching purposes that were essential, all the water here being so brackish as to be barely drinkable and, when you did drink any, counter-productive, increasing one's thirst more than satisfying it. It must have had a beneficial effect in replacing body-fluid lost through sweating, all the same, and it was easy enough to come by: all you had to do was dig a six-inch hole with a knife, and watch it fill. Then it was like taking medicine. Thirst in fact had been the greatest source of discomfort by late afternoon — worse than the mosquitoes, and flies, and the background anxiety which haunted one's fitful dreaming too — of having, in the long run, no way out of this . . .

The geography lesson, illustrated by scratchings in the mud, had started with the Volga: that it was now at its lowest, as much as forty feet lower than in the spring, so that at this time of year the main stream was only a mile or so in width — although deep enough to be navigable by quite large steamers, and recently of course by minor warships — with smaller streams winding in isolation through the rest of the twelve-mile-wide bottom-land. The main stream was on the valley's western side — the Enotayevsk side, that was.

'It rises somewhere north-west of Moscow — am I right?'

'At Tver. Quite small up there, of course. Three and a half thousand versts away — uh?'

'Two thousand miles . . . Some river!'

'As you say — some river . . . But the railway, now . . .'

Lesson continuing. This lower, widest part of the Volga came down from Tsarytsin, about three hundred miles north-west of Astrakhan, and the railway from here ran up the east side of the valley, leaving it at about the halfway mark where it slanted off northward towards Saratov. And down at this end of it, after Seitovka the next two stopping points were at Selitrenoe and Sasykolsk, respectively fifty and ninety miles from Seitovka. Enotayevsk lay roughly between those two places, but on the Volga's western bank, so they'd have to cross the river after leaving the train.

'I'll buy tickets to Sasykolsk. It's slightly closer to Enotayevsk — and in fact beyond it, and there's a fishing-station not far away, might get some boatman to take us across.'

'Just walk up and buy tickets, will you? Nobody'll ask questions?'

'If we're questioned — and if we have to answer — we can give them the stories we've worked out. No more than we have to — take care not to seem eager to tell all, Bob. It's a mistake people make — because they've prepared a story it's there on the tip of their tongues, they start spouting it all out. Whereas a man with nothing to hide's usually a bit reticent, he resents having to account for himself . . . But of course, if it's a Cheka agent, for instance — or any official — and if he insists — well, I'd tell him something about Askhabad, and you could touch on your activities in Persia, if you had to. Well, you *would* have to, as you don't have papers. That's — unfortunate . . . But even in those circumstances it's more believable if you're a bit — grudging, you know?'

'You sound like an expert.'

A shrug. 'I've had some experience. On the journey to Petrovsk, you know; and before I set off I talked with people who had advice to give.'

'I'll leave *our* talking to you, as far as possible.'

'The important thing is to act in character with the part

you're playing. You're a Persian, so *be* a Persian, think of yourself as one. Mind you, if we meet other Persians—'

'Didn't you agree it's unlikely?'

A nod. 'But it's still possible. Incidentally there's a goodish quota of Persian blood in the Astrakhan people. As well as Russian blood, Armenian, Kalmuck — and Tartar, of course, it was all Tartar land originally ... Anyway, just keep your eyes and ears open — you might have to be a Russian sometimes.'

Up to only an hour or so before they'd started they hadn't thought of using the boat. They'd been going to leave it where it was and set off on foot. Solovyev had said — watching the sun inching down towards the flat, heat-hazy green of the delta, 'We'd better let it get properly dark. Men on the move here in daylight would stand out like sore thumbs.'

'Who'd see them?'

'Maybe no one. It wouldn't be worth risking, anyway. For instance, fishermen might come down from Krasni-Yar to see if our friends might have left anything worth salvaging.'

'The boat, for instance.'

'Oh.' He'd put a hand to his head. 'Yes — *damn* it ...'

'It's not identifiable. We made sure of that, in case it was found wherever you'd have hidden it.'

'Well — that's something ... And I suppose there'd be no reason to connect it with the explosion. No *positive* reason?'

'No.' He thought about it. About some recent conclusion on the subject ... 'No — because as you said yourself, Nick — unless I dreamt this — they wouldn't believe anyone could've survived. So there'd be no question of any connection.'

'And it mightn't be found for a long time. If it was left here all summer — well, like everything else it'd be iced up for the winter months. Duck-hunters might find it, I suppose ... Then in the spring floods when the ice melts it'd be lifted off here, washed out to sea.' The green eyes narrowed and slid back to stare at Bob: 'You don't think we might want it? Later, to get away from this coast? If we took it now to where I was going to leave it?'

At first sight the notion was easy to dismiss. Two of them plus five female passengers, setting out to sea in a twelve-foot boat with one pair of oars, no sail . . .

On the other hand — when one had no assets — above all, no idea of any possible way out — why throw away the one thing you *did* have? However small its potential . . . And — beginning to think about it, consider it as even a remote possibility — a single night's hard rowing even with that load on board ought to get one out of this delta. Guardships permitting . . . Then — well, it would still be a longshot chance, but certainly on their way in in the CMB there'd seemed to be no kind of offshore surveillance or patrolling.

But — from this coast to the flotilla's patrol area — what, a hundred and fifty miles, or not much less? And no way of communicating, to arrange a rendezvous. Maybe a faint possibility — daydream, never-never land — that by that time Dunsterville might have his flying-machines up here and operational, 72 Squadron machines that were supposed to be coming up from Mesopotamia, with some idea of establishing an advanced base at Petrovsk. The airy-fairy picture in one's imagination being of some intrepid birdman winging out over the Caspian and spotting this small boat, crammed to the gunwales with young women.

Crazy. Could even be the effects of mild concussion . . .

Wagging his head: 'Good idea, Nick. Save us some time, too.'

It had. Half an hour's rowing to the head of the inlet must have saved about two hours of floundering over bog. And the skiff was now high and dry, hidden in thickish undergrowth under the bank of a stream that was only a trickle now but which in April would be a torrent.

Trekking on. Telling himself to forget the daydreams, that there were no miracles on the way, that getting out of this (a) was highly problematical, (b) if there was any chance at all, it rested in one's own hands and ingenuity —

not wishful thinking ... Thoughts none the less all over the place — from what lay ahead of them at Enotayevsk, and worry about his own lack of identity papers — this had been in his mind ever since the Count had mentioned it earlier in the day — to visions of two fuddy-duddy old men scratching their bald heads in Glasgow. They — McCrae and McCrae, Public Notaries — would presumably have had notification from the Admiralty of the death of Alexander Cowan. He'd have had them listed, as well as Bob as next of kin, on the 'blood chit' he'd have had to sign before being allowed to take passage in a warship. And in due course — maybe quite promptly — they'd write or would by now have written to Robert Cowan, their long-standing and highly-esteemed client's sole heir, expressing deep regret and also stating their intentions as regards winding up the estate and seeking probate, and as likely as not telling him what he knew already, that he *was* his father's heir, and now the head of Cowan Investments Ltd, which pending receipt of any instructions which he might care to give them they would of course continue to administer — or anyway, something along those lines. So it was going to knock the old boys sideways when in a day or two they received yet another communication from Their Lordships, this time informing them that Lieutenant Robert Cowan, RNR had been reported missing, presumed killed.

He wondered what happened to a large estate and profitable company, in these circumstances. Perhaps they'd dig out some very distant, hitherto unknown relative. Or anyway advertise for one, and spend a year or two checking through hundreds of phony claims.

Poor old devils. They were decent men, in their bumbling ways. When Bob had been a cadet in the Merchant Navy training ship, from age thirteen onwards, they'd doled out the fees and the money for his uniforms, and his pocket-money and other expenses, and reimbursed the families of fellow cadets with whom he'd spent his leaves, and so on. And if those short-term foster-parents had not been available or willing to act as such, the brothers McCrae had assured Bob's father they'd always see to it that the boy had a roof over his head and food in his belly — although after Bob at his father's urging had once visited them in Glasgow, he'd fervently prayed that no such contingency would ever arise. He could still shiver at the recollection of a cold and gloomy stone-built suburban house, the brothers who'd seemed old even then, their grim-faced women and shy, whispering children.

The McCrae brothers' father, old William McCrae, had looked after Bob's father's parents, right from the time when Alex Cowan as a young man had first realized he had more than a pound or two to send home and had been canny enough to set up an investment company and invite 'old Will' to administer it. After the old folks' deaths the company had remained in being, surviving William McCrae's decease as well; it had been very much a going concern by that time, virtually all the profits from the Russian company going back to it and some deals being negotiated through it — even the buying and later selling of a ship or two.

The McCrae 'boys' would be really stumped, Bob thought, when they did get notification of his own death. It would be worded 'missing, presumed killed', of course, but in the circumstances nobody could have much doubt about it.

'Hold on ...'

Stopping suddenly: then squatting down — becoming, at least as it seemed to oneself, invisible. Having seen — without as yet any notion as to what it might be — a wall of darkness darker than the night. The Count's hand on Bob's arm — as if he thought it necessary to restrain him — and both of them straining their eyes ...

No sounds, and no lights anywhere. It could have been a wall of some kind. But — in this wilderness, miles from anywhere?

Mentally picturing the map as sketched out earlier by the Count ... Krasni-Yar would be to the south of them now. Six, eight miles, roughly. Seitovka north-west, perhaps ten miles away, and the road linking those two places — and which they were intending to follow to Seitovka once they came to it — something like two or three miles ahead. He checked his bearings: using Polaris again, up there to their right, altitude about forty-five degrees. Their course up to now had been about west-north-west, and that dark barrier lay at a slight angle across this line of advance: north-west to south-east, say.

'Come on . . .'

As they approached it, he was guessing it might be a dike — a barrier against the spring flooding, built here to protect the road they were looking for, perhaps.

Or a levee, carrying the road.

'Couldn't be our road, could it?'

'I don't think so.'

Embankment. It *was* a levee. And it was new — no vegetation on it, only a thirty-degree slope packed with rock. Scrambling up it, hard edges making themselves felt through the soft rubber soles of his grossly unsuitable footwear . . . Crouching again, at the top, starshine glinting on steel rails running ruler-straight in the north-west/south-west direction.

'That way to Seitovka — right?'

And to the south-east — well, a fairly good guess was already forming in his mind. Initiating — at the moment rather vaguely, it had to be left until one had a chance to think it out — a whole strategic concept, starting with the proposition that this was a supply-line to the military base/stores depot where Johnny Pope had run his CMB on to the first cable.

The Count murmuring, 'Our road will be *that* way — about two miles. We could save ourselves that distance, follow this railway instead. It must connect Seitovka to that harbour place?'

'Exactly.'

Road access to it would be from Krasni-Yar. Because since there was an established road from Seitovka to Krasni-Yar, they'd only have had to build a fairly short extension to link it to the base. Whereas the only railway out of Seitovka slanted down to Astrakhan, so if they'd needed one they'd have had to build it from scratch.

An expensive undertaking — both in material and manpower. Indicating that the planned move eastwards against Guriev was of major importance in Bolshevik plans. Which made it even more imperative to get the intelligence out to Baku: and frustrating that at any rate in the foreseeable future there wasn't a hope in hell of doing so.

'Where will the moon rise, Bob?'

'There. Roughly.'

'So we'll walk *that* side.'

'All right. Won't be up for a while yet, mind you. Three-thirty. Sunrise about five ... Time now?'

'Two forty-five.' Stumbling down to the level ground on the embankment's far side. 'Might eat our last sandwiches now, d'you think?'

'*Well ...*'

Plodding on, then, with the embankment providing some feeling of security — cover from some of the starlight now and from the moon when it rose in an hour's time — as well as the certainty of a dead-straight line of march to Seitovka. Bob's thoughts meanwhile setting out again on their independent travels. Back via the McCraes and thoughts of his father's company and its assets which whatever they amounted to — it would be a substantial amount, he guessed — would now be his — *if* he got back there, ever — to recollections of that long train journey with his father fifteen years ago, from St Petersburg through Poland, Germany and France to Calais and the cross-Channel steamer on which he'd been violently sick, his father consoling him:

'It'll not be for a lifetime, laddie. Not unless you decide on your own it's what you want. Mind you, though — don't tell 'em this, don't ever let 'em guess you may *not* be spending your whole life ploughing yon ocean wave ... But it's an education, d'ye see. Education *as such*, to begin with — a damn sight more of it than *I* ever had, I'll tell ye! And beyond that, boy, you'll see the world and some of its people and what makes the whole mess tick. Four or five years o' that, and you'll be ready for dry land under your feet again; I hope ye'll join me, then, as likely as not in Scotland by that time — or London, maybe, I don't know — Russia's been kind enough to me, God knows, but the future — well . . .'

The old man had lived through the revolution of 1905, of course. Bob had been a cadet in his Merchant Navy training ship by then — having entered at thirteen, after a year's English schooling — but the old man had witnessed some of its horrors, then seen the scars and wounds patched up, glossed over, to all intents and purposes forgotten. Bob remembered that deep voice growling — to the McCraes, in that dim, cobwebby office of theirs, on a visit a year later, the old man explaining the reasons for his wanting to transfer as much of his reserves and profits as he could to investments outside Russia — 'I'm no seer, gentlemen, I may be shooting wide of the mark, but it seems to me that by no means all that particular lot of writing was ever washed off the wall.'

Bob wondered — his thoughts taking another jump — whether the Admiralty would have their records up to date and at their fingertips, or whether in the next day or two they'd be sending his own next-of-kin — Alexander Cowan, of the British Embassy currently at Vologda in North Russia — one of those sombre telegrams . . . Because by now the Commodore would have telegraphed a report to London. Eric Barker wouldn't have broken wireless silence until he'd had *Zoroaster* back on the patrol line; he'd have got back there by say eleven o'clock this morning, and by midday the Commodore would have conferred with Dunsterville. Supposing the signal had been despatched then: allowing for five hours' difference in time, London would have had the news — telegraphed via Baghdad — right at the start of their working day.

So the Popes would have had their telegram in Hampshire. And the McNaughts in Aberdeenshire. Poor souls . . .

Boots scraping on stone: and voices, a murmur of Russian, some way off. Bob and the Count already flat on their faces by this time, in deep shadow at the foot of the embankment. Stones scattering as the boots scrunched closer. More than one pair.

Forget Hampshire, and leave Aberdeen to the Aberdonians. *This* was the real world — the one that mattered, the world one was in oneself — without ever having volunteered to be here, for God's sake: and wishing to God one was *not* . . .

A Russian voice growled despondently, 'So when I'll get to see her again, Christ only knows.'

'Well, that's war for you, comrade!'

'Some fornicating *war* . . .'

Left, right, left, right . . . A slow march, though, and not in unison, heels dragging, nothing soldierly about it — more like a slow *slouch*, by the sound of it. The Count murmured, 'Guarding their new railway. Better sit tight a minute.'

Bob wondered what sort of treatment a British prisoner might get. Not being in uniform, might one legitimately be shot as a spy? Or did this not apply between countries that were not at war with each other?

Then again — might be better not to admit to being British. Having Russian birthright anyway.

They'd interrogate you, in any case. And if it was a Cheka interrogation . . .

Well. You'd tell them.

But — second thought — not about the Tsar's children, the young girls. At least one might *hope* one wouldn't . . . In fact you wouldn't be able to tell them anything — except lies, which might not fool them — because anything near the truth would lead them to that house.

What are you doing in our country? Why did you come here?

He'd left his reefer jacket in the delta — literally in it, holding it under to get it waterlogged. If it was ever fished up, it could have come from the CMB — which made this as good a place as any for dumping it. And it was too obviously naval — even without its stripes — and too well-fitting, and if he'd offered it as a trade-in any storekeeper might have been suspicious, wondering why he'd wanted to get rid of it. So the Count had said: and the night had been a warm one, he hadn't needed it.

'We can push on now, Bob.'

The Count was the boss. For one thing because this was, as he'd pointed out at some stage, his country, and for another because he was a soldier. As distinct — Bob told himself — from a fish out of water.

Quite a few miles from any water worthy of the name, too, by this time.

A thought then — sudden and so obvious one should have had it before. Although it hadn't apparently occurred to the Count yet either ... 'Nick. That foot patrol ...'

'Well?'

'*Foot* patrol. And we're still — what, eight or nine miles from Seitovka, eight from Krasni-Yar? What are they — marathon walkers, like us?'

They saw the answer less than an hour later. The land had been rising, the up-gradient never all that noticeable but tending upwards as they moved inland, and the levee, built to carry the railway line above the level of springtime floods, had become equivalently lower. By the time the moon rose, yellowish half-moon climbing out of the marshlands in the south-east, there was no cover from it whatsoever — and no natural feature in the north, either, to hide the military camp that sprawled beside the line a few hundred yards ahead.

Wooden huts, spaced out in lines of ten or twelve, the lines receding so that from this angle one couldn't count them. Perimeter fence — posts anyway, he could see this nearer corner. No lights anywhere ... It occurred to him that the inlet where they'd seen the tugs and the crane had to be an embarkation point as well as a storage depot.

'What do we do, Nick? Detour round it — or across country to the road, then follow that?'

'The road may be just the other side of this camp. So the camp has the railway this side of it, road access on the other.'

'Only if the road and the rail-line have converged quite

a bit in the last few miles.'

'They'd have to. At Seitovka they have to arrive at the same point, don't they.'

Dead right. Maybe the brain wasn't working at full power yet ... But they'd seen no transport using the road: and if the road was where they now guessed it was, you'd have seen and heard anything that had been on it, in the last hour or so. A conclusion might be that at night nothing *did* move.

But *they* had to — now. In moonlight and with no kind of cover, nothing anywhere to cast a shadow you could hide in. And coatless, with a bulky .45 revolver stuck in the waistband of an old pair of grey-flannel trousers bought years ago in Dover: and a damn great army camp within spitting distance ...

'Hear that?'

Train: coming from the direction of Seitovka. Its distant clatter: and a humming from the rails ... Putting the thought into Bob's mind that this was where it started, the point at which not having any papers began to feel like a noose around your neck. Strangely, it was quite different to facing action at sea. There, when you knew you'd soon be in action, you might feel the constriction in your gut, dry-mouth and so forth up to the moment when the first shot was fired, but after that you were too damn busy to think about being afraid. But here and now — well, he'd known since yesterday what he was walking into, but the reality of it — and the physical reactions — *now* he was beginning to sweat.

It was better at sea, he thought. *Much* better.

'Any ideas, Nick?'

'Well.' They'd been sitting, resting aching feet as well as reducing profile, but had both stood up now. Reacting similarly: accepting that they were now on stage and the curtain had as it were gone up ... 'You're Robat Khan, I'm Anton Ivan'ich Vetrov. From Astrakhan, on our way to Moscow — *if* it's anyone else's business.'

'Yes. Yes ...' He nodded. The train was in sight: like a nursery painting — Toy Train by Moonlight ... 'But that's a thought. Expensive one, rather. Destination Moscow, but you'll be getting tickets to — what's that place called, two stops up the line?'

'Sasykolsk.' The Count nodded. Watching the little train as it came puff-puffing towards them. 'I think I mentioned there's a fishing station not far from there. Well, believe it or not, my old aunt works there, she helps pack the caviar and *visigha.* And as we're passing this way and I haven't seen the old thing in years, I want to stop off and give her a hug, let her know I'm still alive — huh?'

Brilliant — one did believe him. But he'd have a better chance of *staying* alive, Bob thought, if he'd come on his own, hadn't burdened himself with the company of a man who had no papers.

7

The Count's cool nerve was as impressive — astonishing, really — as his genius as an actor. Perhaps it was *all* acting, perhaps he was racked up inside: in a perverse sort of way one almost hoped so. Here on the railway platform, for instance, sitting on crates full of clucking chickens, seemingly as relaxed as any ordinary, legitimate traveller although he knew at least as well as Bob did — Bob with his guts in knots from awareness of it — the the railway security official might show up at any moment and demand to see his non-existent papers.

In point of fact, if one had just seen this 'Anton Vetrov' here as a stranger — seen him behaving as he had in the clothing store for instance — one would have thought him fairly poisonous, and steered well clear. *That* good an actor. And why on earth he'd been so anxious to have one along, when he was so totally competent on his own ...

Well — the highly dubious possibility of an escape by sea, of course. Having had his escape route destroyed in that explosion, and still with the compulsion to push on and find his family and those others, and with no idea at all beyond that ... But meanwhile, nobody could have taken him for anything but a Bolshevik. His own view of one — and a fairly repulsive object at that. Switching to that role, his face actually changed — sort of loosened, and the intelligence drained out of the eyes. His voice coarsened, he walked with a swagger and adopted the jocular, bullying manner of a man who's used to getting his own way by one means or another. In the store, for instance — a shack with a tarpaulin stretched over its dilapidated roof and a haphazard assortment of clothing, tools and miscellaneous hardware spread on planks laid over upturned crates and piled against the walls — he'd taken charge completely, found his friend Robat a pair of boots that fitted — pocketing the plimsolls before the old Kalmuck proprietor had the chance of a close look at them — then sorting deftly through coats and jackets, coming up with this greenish, military-type tunic — badgeless, no emblems of rank on it, might have been Hungarian or Austrian.

Persian, even.

'How's this?'

It fitted quite well. Bob had nodded, grunted his acceptance of it — he wasn't opening his mouth more than he had to — and the Count had glanced at the Kalmuck — sixty-ish, with tufts of grey hair distributed sparsely over yellow skin, jutting cheekbones, flat nose, eyes that turned up at the corners — and told him, 'My friend's from Persia. Doesn't talk much Russian yet.'

'Ah, yes. He does have — as your honour says — a foreign look about him.'

'Your honour', instead of 'comrade' ... But it matched the Kalmuck's subservient manner. The only comrades he'd dare claim would be his own people — nomads who herded wild horses, carried their entire families, tents and household possessions on the backs of camels and got drunk on fermented mares' milk. Kalmucks were Buddhists, followers of the Dalai Lama, who'd settled on the Steppes west of the Volga even before Ivan the Terrible had seized these lands from the Tartars.

'What about this, now?'

Red-dyed calico. There was a bale of it, and on the Count's instructions the old man cut off a piece of the right size to make a sash or cummerbund. Dead right for a Persian, red for Bolshevism and it would hide the revolver too. A wink at the Kalmuck: 'So we know whose side he's on, eh?' Then after he'd found a cap — peaked, blue cloth, might have been a fisherman's — he'd rounded on him savagely: 'How much d'you hope to extort from us for this rubbish?'

Outside, he'd clapped Bob on the shoulder. 'Just what the doctor ordered. Every inch a Persian brigand. Incidentally, that's not a bad beard, for just two days' growth.'

'Well — thanks for your help.'

'Oh, my dear fellow . . .'

That smile, and the tone, had been pure Nikolai Solovyev. Forgetting his alias, in that moment, and one character succeeding the other so fast you might have wondered which was real, which the act. Bob had asked him, 'Station now, or breakfast?'

'Station. So we'll know how long we have.'

The first northbound train, the booking-clerk told him, would be one that was scheduled to leave Astrakhan at 10 am and to stop here at ten minutes to eleven.

'Or thereabouts. If it runs today. Doesn't always.' The booking-clerk was a small, grey-haired man with a squint and missing teeth. 'Where to, comrade?'

'Moscow, but—'

'Papers?'

Fumbling for them, the Count glanced at the security desk, which was unoccupied. Shrugging . . . 'Sleeping late, are they? Sleeping it off, I dare say. Pay you for doing their job, do they?' Turning back, pushing the papers at him. 'Here . . . Listen, comrade — I want to break the journey at Sasykolsk.'

'Through-ticket to Moscow, though.'

'No. Sasykolsk. And two, not one. My pal here —' looking round again . . . 'Oh. Pissed off, the bugger . . . Anyway, two to Sasykolsk. Else we might lose the bloody tickets. Might get drunk in Sasykolsk, who knows.' He jerked a thumb towards the security desk. 'They're not the only ones entitled to a drink — eh?'

'No reason you'd lose your tickets any more than you would your money, is there?'

'What if I dropped dead, then?'

'Huh?'

'Three thousand versts' worth of rail ticket's damn-all use to a corpse — right?'

'You look fit enough to me, comrade.'

'Sheer luck I'm alive this minute. That fellow —' a jerk of the head — 'saved my life . . . Anyway — 'nother story.' He took his papers, pushed them into an inside pocket, straightened out a dirty, crumpled ten-rouble note. 'How much, comrade?'

Breakfast hadn't been at all bad. Porridge, and fat bacon and black bread, washed down with two glasses of tea each. In Moscow and St Petersburg people were starving but in the country districts it wasn't so bad, except near fronts where the army or armies had taken everything that either grew or grunted.

The Count bought a packet of cigarettes, too, flipped one across the greasy table to Bob, fumbled for a match. 'So far so good, eh?'

'Where's all the money coming from — if anyone asks?'

'I was thinking about that —' compressing the cardboard tube twice, the dents at right-angles to each other so as to restrict the flow of smoke, putting it in his mouth, reaching over to light Bob's for him — 'when I was getting the tickets. The answer is you sold some sheep — down near the border. So you're the money-bags. Stole the sheep, did you?'

'Sounds like —' he coughed: it was like smoking old toe-rags — 'the sort of thing I *would* have done . . .'

'One thing occurred to me, Nick—'

'Anton.'

'Right. Anton . . .' They were back at the station, with the crates for seats, a long wait ahead of them, very few people about as yet and the security desk — as far as one knew, it wasn't in sight from here — still untended. He was finding it hard not to watch the corner around which the official would have to appear, some time . . . 'About those two we thought were a patrol on the railway line. They might not have been. Might have been from the new base — going back there, if they'd been visiting the camp, for instance?'

'Hell of a long walk.'

'Longer still if they were a patrol — all the way back again. And the railway's the direct route to the inlet, the new base — straight line, shortest distance between A and B — right? We know there was no traffic on the Krasni-Yar road — we'd have seen it if there had been. Heard it, seen lights ... So if they'd missed the last transport back, and no chance of a lift?'

'You could be right. Except we decided the camp was empty, didn't we — so why would they visit it?'

It had seemed empty. Not even guards on the entrances, either at the railway side or the other, where there was an access road leading to it from the Krasni-Yar—Seitovka road. They'd seen that side as well — admittedly from some distance, half or three-quarters of a mile — because after passing the camp along the railway they'd decided to cut across to the road, as this would seem like a more normal way of arriving in a village.

But there might be a care-and-maintenance party in the camp. Enjoying a quiet life, sleeping soundly — perhaps entertaining their friends from the base over a bottle of vodka earlier on — and no reason to have sentries posted or guards at the entrances when the place was otherwise quite empty, nothing there to be stolen except the huts themselves.

Empty until the spring, probably, then a transit camp for troops embarking at that new base for transport down-coast. He'd thought about the strategic angles, during the long night's walk.

Glancing at the Count. He'd been leaning back against the wall with his eyes shut, but they were open now.

'Nick, am I right in thinking that now General Denikin's taken Novorossisk, so we can supply him from the Black Sea, when he's ready and re-equipped he'll strike out in this direction?'

Blinking: letting the question sink in. Maybe he *had* been dozing. He nodded: 'That's the — expectation. Up the railway towards Tsaritsyn, and east and south-east to Petrovsk and Astrakhan. Linking up with Bicherakov, you see. And possibly with the Czech Legion, if they could fight their way down to join us.' A shrug. 'It's no secret. These swine would have to be very stupid not to expect it.'

'So in their plan for an attack on Guriev it makes sense for their main supply base to be well this side of Astrakhan. In case Denikin did reach the Volga?'

'Yes. Although the Bolsheviks have half a million men on the Volga — or so we're told.'

'So here's another thought — if they were hit good and hard here — this side of Astrakhan, that new base especially — perhaps by bombing from the air, but naval bombardment anyway — and perhaps a landing between here and Nikolsk — at the same time as Denikin's advancing from the west?'

'It *is* a thought.' Glancing round. Eyes pausing on that corner for a moment ... Looking back at Bob, then. 'But what's it leading to?'

'Well — it's fairly vital, isn't it. Seems to me we've *got* to get the information out to Baku — and *soon*.'

The Count had shut his eyes. A long intake of breath: an impression of trying to muster reserves of patience ... 'You're right — of course. But — I'd say one hardly needs any such imperative. There are — as far as *I'm* concerned, Bob — very much more personal reasons — flesh-and-blood reasons, for God's sake—'

'Oh, heavens, I *know*, I'm not ignoring—'

'*They* are all I'm thinking about. Anything else is — I'm sorry if it shocks you, but — the rest is trivial, to me. I'm sorry. But — well, I told you: and the closer we get to Enotayevsk — look, I'll admit this to you, Bob — it's a lot of the reason I'm so glad you're with me. If we find what I fear we *may* find — facing that alone ...'

'Well. I've wondered what use I could possibly be to you. More of a liability, I'd have thought. But — really and truly, there's no good reason to expect the worst, you know?'

'Not *expect* it, exactly, but—'

'Only minutes ago I was thinking how you didn't seem to have a care in the world. When you were getting the tickets, and—'

'They may come looking for us, you know. Speaking of tickets.' A nod towards that corner. 'Wanting to see your papers.'

'Don't I know it.' He reached behind his own right hip, touched the pistol. 'If they do — *when* they do — I'll give them the Askhabad story — papers taken from me prior to being strung up — right?'

'Yes, but it might be better if you'd let me tell them. They might permit it, if you seem not to talk much Russian. I could perhaps make a better job of it — I'm not boasting, but I believe I have a certain talent—'

'I'm damn sure you have!'

He shrugged. '*This* kind of situation, I can handle. But — what may have happened by now at *Riibachnaya Dacha*, that's — I told you, it freezes my brain, it's a nightmare even in broad daylight!'

'*Riibachnaya Dacha* ... Fisherman's Cottage. Did you say it's being used as a convalescent home?'

'Was. Maybe still is — but not by *us*, obviously. So how they could have survived there this long ...'

'Must be rather large, for a cottage?'

'It's called that because it's a place we only used for a month or two in the summers. And I believe it was quite small a few hundred years ago.'

'Right ... But one thing — while I think of it — if I get arrested, Nick — through not having papers — don't hang around. There'd be no point. Just go ahead, and good luck, leave me to take my chances — huh?'

'If they didn't arrest me too. Which they would, of course ...'

'Perhaps we should separate, then.'

'Too late. Even if it was a good idea — which I don't think it would be. If they come asking for your papers it'll be because that ticket idiot's put them on to us, they'll know we're together anyway.'

'I suppose you're right.'

They were silent for a while, then. Bob keeping an eye on that corner: there were a few other travellers around, now. A new lot just arriving, a whole gaggle of old peasant women shuffling on to the platform ... Thinking of the Solovyev women: 'Nick's mother and his sister — and another girl, sister of the boy who'd brought his mother's desperate appeal for help — and the two young Grand Duchesses ... Five of them, to be transported out of Bolshevik territory: when just sitting here on one's own was bloody terrifying! The prospect wasn't just daunting, it was appalling, just to think about it for a moment brought one out in a cold sweat ... Which was pointless. Self-destructive. The same as he'd been thinking about the Count and the nightmares he seemed almost to cherish, behind that bland actor's front.

'Nick — how about giving me a bit of background on your mother and sister — and the other girl — so I won't be entirely ignorant when I meet them?'

When I meet them ...

Crossing some fingers. Not at this stage sharing the Count's private anxieties, only the more immediate one as to whether they'd ever get on the train. Or at least whether he himself would ... The Count was telling him, '... The Dowager Countess Maria Ivanovna. And my sister's name is Irina. She's — twenty-one now. Her great friend, the sister of Boris Egorov who came with my mother's message, is Nadia Egorova. She's — er —' he'd looked away, as if embarrassed — 'my fiancée. As it happens.'

'The girl you were telling me about?'

'Are you so surprised?'

'You told me there was — well, *a* girl whom you were going to marry, but you didn't mention—'

'You can understand my — concern, perhaps. Exactly why I haven't wanted to talk about her. You think I'm worrying myself sick over nothing, Bob, but—'

He'd checked himself. Fists clenched, lips tight ... A shake of the head, then. 'I'm sorry.'

'No ... But your sister's name is — Irina, and your fiancée's Nadia —'

'The Princess Nadia Egorova.'

'Crikey!'

A smile. It was a relief to see it. Then: 'She's beautiful,

Bob. As well as charming. Truly, the most beautiful girl you ever saw.'

If one ever got out of this — alive — what a story for one's children. How we brought one dowager countess, two Grand Duchesses and a princess out of Russia ...

How, indeed.

Getting towards train time. He didn't know the exact time, but guessed it must be about ten-thirty. There was no clock in sight, and the Count was asleep — head back, mouth open, cloth cap pulled forward over his eyes — and his watch wasn't accessible without waking him.

Bob had dozed for a while too. But they weren't on the chicken-crates, the sun had moved over so that that area was no longer shaded, and they'd found this bench down at the other end. It was too close to the latrine, which stank, but after a whole night's walking a bad smell and a few more flies didn't count for much.

The platform was crowded now. Soldiers, peasants, Armenian-looking characters in suits, a pretty girl in a red dress and broad-brimmed hat, groups of Kalmucks, Kirghizi, others less easily identifiable ... The girl could have come straight off Piccadilly. She happened to turn her head his way when he was looking at her, held his interested gaze for a few seconds before looking away with a smile in her expression. He'd thought, *Any other time, my dear* ... Then abruptly getting his come-uppance for that thought — like a kick in the head, focusing suddenly on a thickset man in a white shirt, dark trousers, a red brassard on his right arm and a pistol worn openly on his belt: what made it chilling was the ticket-clerk was with him, both looking around at the milling crowd — and not idly, clearly looking *for someone* ... Bob looked away quickly, thinking *Here's where it starts* ... The only reason he didn't nudge the Count to wake him was that the security man might have spotted them by that time and have caught the Count in an unguarded state as he woke and reacted to the surveillance.

Must have spotted them. They — or the one with the

brassard — would be over here, any minute.

Comrade, I'm a Persian — did have papers, but—

So what's this?

.45 revolver. British-made, Admiralty-issue, British-made bullets in it . . .

Well — stole it, didn't I. From an Englishman in Askhabad, after those swine took over . . . He passed a hand around his jaw, the thickening stubble which wasn't bad for two days' growth but wasn't nearly close enough to an established beard yet either, and allowed his glance to drift back towards the source of danger.

Then wished he hadn't. The ticket-seller was pointing at him. At *them* . . . The little man's other hand grasping the security man's arm, and his lips in motion, gabbling. Then the other man nodded, said something curtly and started forward, shouldering his way through the crowd.

Bob nudged the Count. 'Trouble, Nick. Security man's on his way over.'

A groan: straightening himself up. And if *he* felt like that . . . 'Look, I'll do the talking.'

While I — sit and shake?

I'm a Persian. Speak some Russian but not all that much. Going to Moscow. Own plans — extending the Revolution into Persia, kicking the British out as stage one — and this Vetrov's ideas arising from the trouble at Askhabad — convince us we have a positive contribution to make to the ultimate triumph of the—

He saw the man coming, through a brief parting of the throng. Aggressive, swaggering. Lost to sight again now, but leaving one with the impression that he could easily be a brother to the character Nick had been playing. *Proletariat*, that was the word, *triumph of the proletariat* . . . Beside him, Nick was yawning, stretching, checking the time . . . 'Train should be in by now.'

'Don't even know it's left Astrakhan yet, do we.'

'Oh, God . . .'

Small-talk. Like ordinary people, nothing to worry them except the inconvenience of some slight delay. Although one of them, at least, had something more like a trip-hammer than a heartbeat banging in his chest. Yawning — catching that from Nick — and scratching at his stubble ...

'Hey — *you* there!'

The shout — close to them — was brutal in its tone and loudness. Crowd milling round — a lot who'd been sitting and lying on the paving were getting up, gathering bits of luggage — cloth bundles, cardboard boxes tied with string, sacks — getting ready to fight their way into the train, and for a few more moments the man in the red brassard was still not visible. Then he was: people nearby withdrawing, distancing themselves from whatever unpleasantness might be imminent.

'*You*, tovarischa!'

He was standing with his boots planted well apart, left hand on his hip and right arm extended, pointing — at the girl in red, the one Bob had been eyeing. She'd been walking away — as others had been — but now she'd stopped. Hesitating: then looking round over her shoulder at the threatening official.

He crooked a finger, beckoned.

The Count murmured, 'Wasn't us, anyway.'

Scared for *her*, now. With the wretchedness of knowing that whatever happened you couldn't lift a finger. Realizing that she might have been in the line of that pair's staring and pointing: probably had been, come to think of it now, he'd been looking at her only seconds before he'd seen *them* looking at *him*. Then his focus hadn't been on her or any other peripheries any more, he'd seen only those two and the booking-clerk pointing.

Unless the girl was only a chance distraction. If he *had* been coming to this bench ...

She'd walked back to him: he'd flicked his fingers for her papers. No one else near them, no one wanting to risk involvement. It had gone quiet at this end of the platform, there was only the gradually rising sound of the train's approach, otherwise this was the hush of a crowd's morbid interest in a fellow human's predicament.

'Patolicheva. Maria Patolicheva.' Studying the papers

she'd handed to him. 'Artiste, eh?' He sniggered: glancing round, an invitation to others to share his amusement. 'Artiste, indeed ...'

'I'm a singer.'

'Well, so am I, comrade, so am I! We might try a duet some time — huh?' She'd put her hand out for the papers but he wasn't surrendering them to her yet. 'Who've you been singing to in Seitovka, then?'

'Visiting my aunt. She's sick.'

Bob heard the train. The Count too: 'Here it comes. Look, if we move quickly ...'

Because there was still some space around the girl and her interrogator. It meant virtually rubbing shoulders with him, but if there was any threat from him they wouldn't avoid it by putting a few yards between them anyway.

'Next time you buy a railway ticket ...'

The Count slid eel-like between some women ... 'Excuse me, comrades ...' Bob circumnavigated them, to join him at the edge of the platform. Hearing the girl say, 'The comrade didn't ask me for them. I thought—'

Shriek of the train's whistle. The crowd all on the move now. The Count shouting that the odds were they'd get a goods van at this point ... Steam gushing loudly as the engine chuffed by: then brakes squealing, a few doors already open with passengers ready to alight.

'We're in luck — I think ...'

Bob thought that might have been something of an understatement, in the circumstances. Finding the girl close behind him, then; she looked more desperate than relieved — sagging, as if that encounter had used up all her reserves. Other travellers were crowding in ruthlessly as the train stopped with a jerk and the Count reached up to an opening door: sailors began emerging, jumping down. Bob shouted, 'Anton — help this comrade?' He'd put an arm behind her, more or less round her shoulders — protectively, saving her from being squeezed out by the encroaching throng of peasants. The Count — he was on the step now — reached down for her hand and hauled her up.

'Tovarischa.' He'd *almost* bowed.

'You're very kind. Thank you.' Bob was in by this time: she smiled at him from the corner seat as he flopped down beside the Count, facing her. 'Thank you *very* much.'

People crushing in, all seating space already filled. Oven-hot space, at that. Bob leant forward: 'I thought you were in for some trouble then.'

She grimaced – a wordless comment. She really was quite pretty: eye-pleasing figure, too, and the dress didn't hide much of it. Hearing an echo of his own words – that he'd thought *she'd* been in for some trouble ... But it had certainly helped him to forget his own predicament.

Dozing, on and off, as the train clattered northward. With all the windows open and air rushing through, the heat was just about bearable. One had known worse – and at least there were no flies or mosquitoes ... He'd asked the girl – out of politeness only, simply not wanting to ignore her – 'Long trip ahead of you?' and she'd told him no, only as far as Tsarytsin. You? 'Not even that far. Sasykolsk.' Even by that time they'd been getting glares from several large middle-aged women in shroud-like dresses and heavy boots. The girl had smiled at him, rolling her eyes expressively as she turned to look out of the window.

The Count had already fallen asleep. Cap over his eyes again, and the leather coat rolled on his lap. Bob recalling, in intervals of wakefulness, what the Count had told him about his mother, sister and fiancée, in their conversation on that platform.

He'd last seen the two girls just after Christmas, having run them to earth in a tiny, almost heatless two-roomed apartment which they'd shared in a requisitioned private house, its rooms allocated to lucky applicants by the local housing committee. He'd come from several hundred versts away, disguised as a Red Guard, from some place where he and others of his old regiment had joined a brigade of the Volunteer Army. This was about to march south to join up with the Cossacks in the Kuban – the western end of the Caucasus, the area around its capital,

Ekaterinodar. So this had been his last chance of seeing the girls for God only knew how long.

'Of seeing Nadia, especially. Irina too, of course, but you see I'd heard from my mother that she was shortly going to Petrograd to collect Irina and take her with her to the Crimea. My mother hadn't mentioned Nadia at all, and I wanted to be sure she'd go too, make her promise she would, and have Irina promise me they'd take her. My mother hadn't been with the Dowager Empress since the autumn of '17, she'd been in the country with other friends — and in the meantime Maria Feodorovna had moved down to the Crimea and now wanted my mother to rejoin her and to bring with her any of her family who might wish to come. This meant Irina only, of course. But Nadia is to all intents and purposes family — will be, for certain, as soon as circumstances permit. So that's why I made the long trip to find them. First time I'd ever travelled as you might say *incognito.* I was surprised how easy it was, to make oneself believed, accepted ... But I couldn't bear the thought of Nadia being left alone in Petrograd. She could vanish — literally — thousands already have ... All right, their life wasn't what you'd call ideal, to put it mildly, but they were comparatively secure — having this dreadful little hole of an apartment, and both having jobs, hardly any money, but at least they could eat — rations were part of the conditions of employment, that's the case more or less everywhere, now.'

'What work were they doing?'

'Irina qualified as a nurse in 1915. It began with my mother's decision to allow *Riibachnaya Dacha* to be used as a recuperative centre. Irina started by working there, then decided to enrol as an auxiliary — the army nursing service. Quite a lot of girls of her background did this. So, at the time of the October revolution she was nursing in the military hospital in Petrograd. Following the March revolution — well, as you know, the Menshevik government were continuing the war — nothing much changed in that respect, soldiers were still being brought back to be patched together, after a fashion ... Then under the

Bolshevik regime conditions became worse and worse, but the work was still there to be done, it wasn't exactly a joy-ride but it was — you could say, a way to stay alive. For Nadia, too, because through Irina's introduction she had an office job, patients' records, and so forth. She'd done clerical work — soldiers' welfare, actually — in the War Ministry until the Bolsheviks seized power, but in her own name and title of course, so then she had to disappear. Her family's town house was taken from them — luckily she wasn't there when it happened — that time at the height of the burning, raping, murdering. Her parents weren't there either — they were at their country house, expecting her to join them, but in fact her brother came for her and took her to stay with friends — Irina was there too, incidentally — and at the country house her parents were both murdered. So — luck, you see ... The brother I'm talking about was of course Boris Nikolai'ich, who—'

'I know.'

'Well. That's when I last saw them. Boris wasn't there, but it was he who'd told me where I could find them, and I saw him the next day, on my way out of Petrograd. He had false papers and a job in a slaughterhouse, carrying meat carcasses about. I suggested he should come with me, join the Volunteer Army — he'd started as a naval cadet, by the way, just before everything blew up — but he preferred to stay where he could look after his sister — a desire which of course I applauded — and he told me that if both girls left with my mother, and she'd permit it, he'd go with them and come to join us — if he could get to us on the Don or wherever we might be by then after he'd seen them to safety in the Crimea.' The Count had shrugged. 'He would have, too. He was a *molodyets*, young Boris.'

Molodyets meant a spunky young man, a go-er.

'The Cheka had arrested him at one time, they'd had him in the prison they call the *Gorochavaya*. If you're one of the unfortunate majority you're transferred from there to the *Shpalernaya* — that's the real torture house, where the experts really get down to it. Boris was either lucky or clever, they believed his story, false identity, and let him go. My God, if they knew they'd had their filthy hands on a real live prince they'd be kicking themselves now.'

'I take it the girls were never arrested?'

'No, thank God. Nadia had her employment paper, and residence permit, in the name of Nadia Schegorova. If she'd had bad luck, got into some trouble as Boris did, I suppose they might have rumbled her. Even worse with Irina, she used her real name — Nurse Irina Solovyeva. Luckily Solovyev's not such an uncommon name. But there were — are — hundreds and thousands like those two. A nurse and a secretary — undernourished, in old patched clothes ... But they were lucky — to have work and a place to live. Plenty don't — most either starve or steal or God knows what.'

'So then your mother joined them in — Petrograd.'

'Must have. But I had no word from them after that, not until Boris Nikolai'ich staggered into our lines. I'd assumed they'd all be in the Crimea by that time — assumed, prayed, made myself believe they *had* to be, that I hadn't heard from them only because they didn't know where I was. In any case communications were all to hell — still are, of course. When Boris arrived my first thought was that he'd have come from the Crimea. It's a mystery to me how they got to Enotayevsk instead.'

'Mystery that'll be answered soon enough.'

'Yes ...'

'But you and your *Dobrovoltsi* marched south to the Kuban. Clear across Russia, north to south — and in January, the worst of winter?'

A nod ... 'It was not — enjoyable.'

'Understatement's supposed to be a British characteristic.'

'So one has heard ... Well, I'll tell you. We were starving, frozen and under attack at every step. A lot of us didn't get there. Our commander was Alekseev — as you know — under the overall command of General Kornilov ... But you're right, it made me think about the French in 1812 — similar conditions, and the constant attacks — in our case by Bolshevik partisan bands. The same technique, you might say. And that wasn't the end of it, by any means. When we arrived in the Kuban we found the Cossacks whom we were going to join had been routed — scattered, leaderless — their leaders had all gone into hiding in the mountains. And Ekaterinodar had fallen to the Reds.'

'Since retaken by Denikin, though.'

'But there were some very hard times in the months between. First Kornilov tried to take it. Disaster — and he was killed himself, in that premature attack. Denikin had begged him to wait until he was stronger, but . . .' A shrug. 'Kornilov paid for his mistake, anyway. He and a lot of others. So then Denikin took over, and first established himself at Novocherkassk — regrouping, training, equipping. Mind you, it was a march of more than a thousand versts to get to Novocherkassk to start with, and there were only a few thousand of us. About five thousand . . . Now he has thirty thousand, and as you know he's turned the tables — Ekaterinodar and Novorossisk, God willing there'll be no stopping him.'

'God willing and the Royal Navy supplying — I hope . . . But you've had *your* share of the hard going, Nick.'

'Well.' He'd shrugged, spreading his hands. 'What else?'

The Count had woken again. Bob asked him quietly, close enough to him to talk under the train's noise, 'What's the programme when we get to Sasykolsk?'

Glancing round. Seeing the girl with her eyes shut and head nodding, old women with their shawled heads close together and eyes fixed on each other's faces as they whispered, one soldier asleep and the other gazing at the ceiling while he picked his nose . . . The Count murmured, 'There's a man and his wife who've worked for us as long as I can remember, and it seems they're still at the house. My mother mentioned them in the message: she didn't say we're at *Riibachnaya Dacha,* she said we're with old Maroussia. Maroussia Kamentseva. Husband's name is Ivan. We'll try to get in touch with them from the village.'

'Because you don't know who else might be in the house.'

'Exactly. If it's still being run as a hospital, there'll be Reds in charge. The saving grace — as far as my own sanity is concerned — has been those words in the message, *with Maroussia.* They — the Kamentsevs — lived above the stables, in their own flat. Other servants were in the house, in the attic rooms, but they were on their own. So, it's possible that …' He paused: and let it go … 'Any case, Irina and Nadia both worked in the Petrograd hospital after it came under Bolshevik administration. As I was telling you.' The Count glanced at him: and away again, taking a deep breath … Then: 'How Ivan and Maroussia have managed to survive is another mystery. All the loyal servants I've known about have been murdered with their masters and mistresses. All one can tell oneself is it's our good luck, as well as theirs … Hey, we're coming to Selitrenoe.'

The train was slowing: other passengers were also aware of it. The two women nearest to them were packing away their bits and pieces, and there was a general stirring. The girl's eyes opened: blinking for a few seconds as if wondering where she was, then recognizing Bob, touching her hair and returning his smile, tucking her feet under her so the looming women wouldn't trample on her. The train shrieked: they'd passed a signal-box and now, more slowly, a siding with another train waiting in it.

He asked the Count, 'How far's Sasykolsk from here?'

'About — seventy-five versts, I suppose.'

Forty miles. An hour, roughly. The train shuddered to a stop. Rush of released steam, passengers stumbling out, and the heat immediately oppressive now there was no through-draught. But there were fewer people boarding than leaving, the rush was quickly over and the compartment was much less crowded, the platform already clearing.

Imagining returning south by this line, with five women. If they had papers: as presumably they must have, to have got down here in the first place. Irina and Nadia had had their papers in St Petersburg, anyway ... Mentally correcting himself, then: he still thought of that great old city as St Petersburg, the name he'd known it by when he'd lived there, but it was Petrograd now, had been since the Tsar had renamed it in 1914, wanting to assert its Russianness.

Something was happening outside, on the platform. He'd seen the girl's expression change as she'd leant forward, and more or less simultaneously the Count's elbow jolted him in the ribs.

An elderly man — thin, grey-headed, grey-faced, in an overcoat with what looked like an astrakhan collar on it. Overcoat, in this heat ... Two men facing him: bully-boys in red brassards. He had his arms spread — as if inviting them to search him, but more likely only a gesture, protestation ... One of the men was shaking some paper or papers in the old man's face and shouting at him: open mouth, scarlet face, veins bulging in his thick neck — fury, barely restrained violence, and in the face of it the old man talking fast — arguing, pleading ... Doors were slamming as the train prepared to leave. The other security guard had drawn a pistol — revolver — a big, heavy-looking thing, probably a Nagant. He was aiming it at the old man's head. Shocked wide eyes fixed on it, mouth open, hands halfway up and open too — helpless, hopeless, drawing attention to that helplessness, imploring mercy ... The gun was out of sight then — the train had jerked forward, passengers without seats staggering, grabbing for handholds, and the broad back of the nearer of those two men hiding their victim from view for three or four seconds. Then he was in sight again — as the one with the pistol clubbed him with it, a vicious, smashing blow in the face, impact not audible of course but one imagined it, flinched at it, facial bones cracking as skin and flesh split open and blood flowed, the old man tottering backwards but caught by a fist closing on the front of his coat — or on his throat ...

'*Christ!*'

The Count murmured, 'Shush ...' The girl in the red

dress had her eyes shut and her lips moving — barely perceptibly but obviously in prayer. A woman who'd moved up this way when those other two had disembarked — face like a turnip, legs like a piano's, the rest a tub of lard — burst out loudly, 'You'd reckon they'd have accounted for the bastards by this time, wouldn't you. Still one or two in the long grass, eh?'

The Grand Duchesses, he thought, would surely have no papers. Unless some had been obtained for them. But in any case, how recognizable might they be, to the general populace? He was imagining that scene — with young girls in the old man's place.

And if that was the *public* performance, what might it be like when they had him — or her, or *them* — to themselves, in private?

An urge to talk, then. Shake it out of mind ...

'Anton.'

The Count's head turned — sleepily ... Since the train had left Selitrenoe neither of them had spoken, and opposite them the girl had continued hiding behind her closed eyes. Fingers moving now and then: she probably hadn't been aware of it ... 'Listen — Irina and Nadia did have papers, you said. Your mother must have had, too, to have got to them and then all the way to—'

'Probably.'

'Well — would they be valid now?' Moving his head — pointing back towards Selitrenoe. 'To pass *that* kind of—'

'Better not discuss it now.'

'I was only thinking ...'

'I know what you were thinking.'

The girl's eyes were open, watching them. He could guess at the kind of thoughts that might have been jumbling through *her* head, too. When she'd been stopped at Seitovka, for instance, how it *could* have been.

And my God, wasn't *I* damn lucky ...

Thanks entirely to the Count's bravado — or rather, to the nerve supporting that bravado. But again, picturing a return journey, the pair of them with one middle-aged woman and four young ones: even with forged papers, the plain fact of *who they were*, for God's sake ... Glancing round — needing distraction, an escape to some other kind of thinking — he met the eyes of the woman who'd made the comment about bastards in the long grass. They could have been glass eyes in a rubber face: you could imagine that if you poked your fingers into them they wouldn't flinch. The face, before he could look away again, split into a grin: 'Going far, comrade?'

Comrade ...

'No. Not far.' He tilted his head back, shut his eyes.

8

They got to Sasykolsk at about one-thirty, and lunched on black bread and goat cheese in a *traktir* near the station.

Facing the prospect of another long walk, now — in stiff old boots that didn't fit too well, and after an entire night spent walking . . .

Saying goodbye to the girl in the red dress, when the train had been pulling in and he'd been at the door ready for a quick exit, he'd told her — just to be friendly — 'Might look you up in Tsarytsin, one of these days.'

'Oh — that would be — *very* nice.' Under the brim of her hat her smile was warm, suggestive more of complicity than — well, streets ahead of the message he'd reacted to in that first exchange of glances at Seitovka. He *liked* her, now — and admired her, was seeing her again as she'd been a couple of hours earlier, facing that bully on the platform — utterly alone, at the bastard's mercy, and everyone else — himself included — standing back.

He'd leant down, whispered, 'I'll ask where do I find that smashing girl who wears a very becoming red dress and a hat *this* wide . . .'

'Robat — you're jamming up the works!'

'Goodbye . . .'

Her smile lingered in his memory — like an overlay, as it were, to the picture he had of Leonide — which emphasized that sort of dimpling at the corners of her mouth just as a smile was dawning . . .

But there'd have been a grin on his father's face, too. A derisive one. He thought, All *right*, all *right* . . . Accepting the unspoken comment — which would have been pithy and right to the point, if the old man had been here to make it — and switching his thoughts, via Leonide, to how things might be in Baku by this time. Three days and nights in those prevailing circumstances being a *long* time. It didn't seem possible that the Turks could be held off for ever, with so few reliable troops to defend the place against them.

Anyway, he'd warned her — and that slug Muromsky . . .

'Robat!' The Count — hurrying back from paying the old *babushka* at her table in the entrance. The food had been brought to them by a skinny, white-faced boy who'd seemed not quite all there, but he'd disappeared now, wasn't here at all. The Count told him excitedly, 'If we're quick we may get a lift. Come on!'

Pushing his chair back . . . 'Lift?'

'In a lorry. It brought a load to put on the train, last consignment of this season's catch.' He called a *spasibo* to the old woman as they hurried past her and out into the blaze of sunshine. 'Fellow that went out a minute ago is the driver. Somewhere along here, she said he'd be. Better run . . .'

The truck had been parked in shade under a big old beech just around the corner; its driver had started up, was grinding the old lorry out on to the dirt road when they came running, waving him down. He braked, stuck his head out. A bald, scrawny man, shoulder-muscles bulging the sleeves of a sweat-patched shirt.

'I'll take you if you want, comrades. But if you're fish-buyers, you're out of luck.'

'We're not buying anything.' The Count heaved himself up into the cab, slid over as far as he could to make room for Bob. 'Thanks, comrade, thanks a lot. Saves us a slog of — what, seven, eight versts?'

'Ten and a half.' He got going again, as Bob pulled the rattly door shut. Shifting gear, at the corner . . . 'What *is* your business there?'

'None. Old aunt of mine works there — or did. We're on our way north, thought I'd stop off and say hello.' He glanced at Bob and winked. 'Probably thinks I'm dead. Give the old bag a shock, eh?'

Turning off, on to a dirt road leading west towards the river. 'What's her name?'

'Vetrova. Lizaveta Vetrova.'

'Never heard of her. And if there was anyone of that name working there, I would have.'

'How long have you been on the job?'

'Couple of years. I've this slight — er — handicap. As you'll have noticed.' He jerked his bald head northwards. 'I was in the army, see. Got involved with a grenade, it didn't want to leave me.' He had no left hand: with the Count between them Bob hadn't seen it until now, but he was doing everything right-handed except for when he needed to change gear or use the handbrake, at which times he'd hold the wheel steady with the bound-up stump. 'I was lucky, at that ... Civvy jobs don't grow on trees round here — not for cripples, anyway. This one's only a few weeks' work twice a year, anyway.'

'What d'you do the rest of the time?'

'Part-time work. At Tsarytsin, where I live. I've a few openings ... But I do assure you, comrade, there's no Lizaveta Vetrova working at the station.'

'But she *was*. Maybe I'll find someone who'd know where she's gone. Must've been — well, just about the first month of the war I last heard from her. She was here then, all right.'

A quick glance: sardonic ...

'Been a few changes since, you know.'

'She's not the sort would be affected. Ordinary old bag earning a crust, that's all.'

The driver muttered a curse: avoiding a mule-cart ... 'You might be lucky. There's still a few women cleaning up, some of 'em have been working here since — well, God knows *how* long.' Glancing round at them, the wrist-stump taking the wheel's vibrations, right palm caressing his bald head ... 'Only thing is, you'll have to walk back, see. Once I get this old heap of junk back to its stable, there it stays.'

'Until the next season?'

'That's it exactly, comrade.'

The Count explained to Bob that there were two distinct fishing periods for the Beluga sturgeon. The first in the spring — that was the best one, when the fish come up-river to spawn — 'eggs pouring out of their ears ...'

'Gills, if anything.'

'Well — *some* damn orifice. They're full of eggs then, anyway. That season's March to early May — after the ice has melted, river's full of water and the fish are full of caviar. Then there's the summer season, July into August — the one that's just finished. They catch 'em on their way back to the sea.' He glanced at the driver's profile. 'Anyway — no chance of a lift back to Sasykolsk, eh?'

'None. The old bus hibernates now, you might say. Has to, there'd be no fuel for it. We get petrol just for the season, see?'

Conversation petered out, revived occasionally in short bursts, Bob leaving it all to the Count — hearing some of it, but mostly locked into his own thoughts, in particular the imperative of finding a way out of here. The further one got in, the more urgent that need became: and the mental effort still getting nowhere ...

Then they were at the fishing station: a colony of fishermen's huts and other buildings, a handful of men down by the water. Most of the fishermen had left, the driver said — leaving most of those forty-odd shacks empty, although a few would still be tenanted for a day or two. They already had a lot of boats high and dry, bottom-up. Planks drying out, Bob thought — and in a few months' time if they were still there they'd be frozen, snow-covered; maybe that would expand the dried-out, shrunken timbers. Otherwise you'd have to immerse them, leave them in the shallows sunk to their gunwales, soaking, so they'd get to be watertight again.

But there'd be quite a few boats still in the water, the driver had confirmed. They weren't visible from here because with the river as low as it was now the high banks shut off one's view of them.

He'd driven his lorry straight into a barn, parking it beside a smaller vehicle. Switching off, he patted the steering-wheel and muttered 'See you in March, you old she-goat.'

Bob asked him — on the ground, when he seemed to be just walking out of the barn with them — 'If you're leaving it all winter wouldn't you drain the radiator?'

'*That* comrade'll see to it.' A gesture towards the other vehicle — it was a van. 'Before the freeze-up, anyway. I've a notion he runs a little contraband, mind you, on the quiet.' A wink ... 'Well. What the eye don't see ... All got to live, eh?'

The Count had gone out into the sunshine ahead of them, was standing gazing at the river and across it to the green of its western bank. The driver strolled out to join him.

'Down there, comrade. That iron roof you see there — that's where you'll find 'em. Ask in there, one of 'em might have known your aunt, way back.'

'Yes. Thanks ...' Glancing at him. 'And many thanks for the lift ... How do you get yourself to Tsarytsin?'

'Train. How else ... Oh, there's another driver works here, he'll buzz me out to the station, I dare say.' A nod towards the huts. 'Not today, though. No rush, I haven't been paid yet anyway. We'll be having a bit of a cook-up tonight, a few of us — and I've got a bottle ...' His eyebrows lifted: 'How about you — you and your pal care to join us, comrade?'

'Thanks, but we won't hang around. Depending on what anyone can tell me about the old girl, of course ...' He turned, as Bob joined them. 'Robat — I was thinking — if we draw a blank here, we might persuade one of those boatmen to take us over to Enotayevsk. My aunt used to spend a lot of time there, I know. And having come this far ...'

'They'll row you across, all right.' The driver added, 'Don't let 'em know it was me that told you, but some of 'em live there, they'd be going over in any case. What I mean is, it shouldn't cost you a fortune — right?'

'You've been *very* helpful, comrade.'

'Oh, for nothing. Honoured to have met you. Good luck, comrades!'

He shook hands with them both and walked off towards the huts. Bob and the Count started towards the river and the iron-roofed building. Bob murmuring, 'He'll be giving his friends the Askhabad yarn before he's halfway into that bottle.'

'I dare say. No great harm in it, though.'

'Oh, none at all.' Referring to the fact that at one stage the Count had given the driver an outline of their fictional adventures. He hadn't *had* to, exactly, but he'd probably been wise, Bob thought. Better to divulge a little than to remain obstinately silent, inviting not only suspicion but probably hostility as well ... He changed the subject: 'Nick — nobody's going to know anything about anyone called Lizaveta Vetrova, obviously, but you'll still go through the motions?'

'Camouflage, that's all. So there's no talk about unexplained characters sniffing round ... Been darned lucky so far, don't want to spoil it — huh?'

'I'd say it's less a matter of good luck than you having done this sort of thing before.'

'It helps, certainly. But we've still been lucky, Robert Aleksand'ich.' Blinking into the heat-haze above the river. 'Almost *too* lucky.'

Thinking about *Riibachnaya Dacha* again, Bob guessed. As he had too, particularly in one respect. Nick's mention of the two girls having worked in a Bolshevik-run hospital: as if that set some precedent, made it conceivable that they might be getting away with the same thing here. Whereas it seemed to him utterly *in*conceivable, for a girl who'd lived in the place off and on throughout her life to have a hope in hell of getting away without being recognized by someone at some time: former servant, gardener, fisherman, villager — *someone* ... And with papers that were in her own name, for God's sake!

Well. The papers Nick had said she'd used in Petrograd, anyway. Might have had new ones forged since then. For all three of them, possibly, before they'd set out on their journey south.

It was the Count's business, anyway. And as likely as not he'd only been whistling in the dark when he'd said that. Beating his private demons back ... But as for the chance of being recognized, what about *him*? Even though he must have changed a lot in the years since he'd spent idle summers here, might there not be a family resemblance that some sharp-eyed old former retainer might spot?

'Eh, Bob?'

'What? Sorry ...'

'I asked how are the boots feeling now?'

He stopped, looking down at them. 'Actually, they're not at all a bad fit. Quite comfortable, in fact.'

'That's good. Lucky again, you see ... What were you so lost in thought about?'

'Oh, nothing special. This and that ... One thing — tell me about this fishing? You said they catch the sturgeon on unbaited hooks?'

'Yes.' Waving a hand towards the boats, the river. 'They line their boats up from bank to bank — across whichever channel they're fishing at that time. The hooks are slung on chains — well, rope at the top, chains below — at varying levels, say three hooks on different lengths of chain under each boat — so the whole water-space is full of hooks, if you see what I mean. The fish aren't necessarily caught by their mouths, therefore, they're simply hooked, there's no question of any bait.'

'Sounds pretty cruel, to me.'

A glint of amusement in the green eyes. 'It becomes *very* cruel. I'll show you. Mind you, you'd have to see the catch itself to really understand. It's a sight like no other.'

The smell of rotting fish was strong as they came down closer to the big shed with its tin roof. Imagining the heat in there, under that iron ... They were approaching the river at the shed's downstream end, following a cart-track, sunbaked dirt rutted by cartwheels and cut up by horses' hooves.

'See the piles there?'

Beyond a shed, a small inlet was barred off from the river by timber piles and staging. 'That's the slaughtering pen. After the fish are hooked the boats tow them in there. It becomes — a battlefield. They're big, you know, the Belugi, eight or ten feet long, weighing up to —' he made the calculation, from Russian *poods* into pounds — 'up to eight hundred pounds. You can imagine how such a fish can fight — and you might have a hundred or more in there, in a single hour of fishing. When they've got them in they bludgeon them then drag them up — there, see?'

At the other end of the shed, a slipway led up to it from the slaughtering pen.

'They split them open to remove all the eggs, the caviar. And the *visigha* — for that the backbone has to be wrenched out, they smash it to extract the marrow. And the fish isn't necessarily dead at this stage, some live another hour or so.'

Bob shook his head. 'Can't say I ever ate a lot of caviar, but — well, from now on . . .'

'The flesh comes last, of course, and when they butcher the fish its heart has probably only just stopped beating. Most of it's salted — as you know, salted-down in barrels, shipped all over Russia.'

'Going by the smell, they've left quite a lot *un*salted.'

'Residue. Bits and scraps. And guts of course. That'll be what they're clearing out now.' He stopped. 'Wait out here, Bob, if it's too much for you.'

'Would I be any help to you in there?'

'Not really. I'm going to ask does anyone know where I might find my aunt Lizaveta. After I've drawn blank, we'll go and talk to *those* comrades.'

The fishermen. They were hauling another boat out, three men each side lugging it up the slope on wooden rollers. Bob agreed, 'I'll wait here for you.'

He strolled towards the river — away from the stench of rotting fish-scraps. It was about three o'clock now: so just forty-eight hours ago he'd been on board *Zoroaster*, taking all those creature-comforts for granted and of course without the slightest inkling of what might lay ahead. Without much idea of what might lie ahead of the Count, even, only the feeling that he was a brave man to be taking it on, and behind that a touch of *sooner you than me, old chap* . . .

Those fishermen were trooping back down to the river. Old men, all of them. The lorry-driver had mentioned that with the Bolshevik army conscripting every able-bodied man of anything like military age into its ranks, the fishing stations were staffed entirely by women and old men. He'd added, referring to himself, 'And one cripple . . .' Then asked, perhaps a trifle over-casually, 'They haven't caught you two for soldiers yet, eh?'

'Oh, they caught me.' This was when Nick had given him the Askhabad yarn. 'I've been down in the south, though — on what you might call special service. This man here's from Persia. There was a local counter-revolution — in a place you probably wouldn't have heard of — they hanged nine of my colleagues, I was to have been the next but this good comrade cut a throat or two and got me out. Now we've a report to make, in Moscow.'

The driver had been visibly impressed. He'd asked — by the look of it making his own guesses — who they'd be making their report to. The Count had shaken his head. 'I've said too much already, comrade. And strictly speaking we shouldn't be breaking our journey here. So — keep it to yourself, would you?'

Knowing damn well he wouldn't.

The sight of boats reminded Bob of the skiff lying hidden in the delta; conjured up a vision of himself and the Count rowing, one at each oar, with a huddle of three women in the stern and another two in the bow. Trying to row quietly, expecting to find a guardship round every bend in the channel . . .

Hopeless, though. With that load, you'd get along at about two knots. Maybe three as long as the stream was with you. A night therefore to get clear of the delta — *if* you had the luck to make it that far anyway — and then a whole day and another night's rowing to get as much as fifty miles offshore, which in any case you could only contemplate in conditions approaching a glassy calm. So it amounted to hoping for a miracle. On the other hand, he didn't want to dismiss the notion altogether — partly because extraordinary feats of endurance had been achieved in recent years, by survivors of torpedoings, and so on — and also because as of this moment he'd had no other idea that worked. Except that earlier one of trekking across the Kirghiz Steppes to Guriev on camel-back — *if* one could get hold of camels, and manage them, and cope with other foreseeable hazards such as distance, desert terrain, Bolshevik forces in pursuit and *en route*, thirst, hunger, exhaustion, and Kirghizi who'd murder you for a rouble let alone for a group of nubile young women.

Sooner chance the skiff. Take an oar each until clear of the delta, then share the rowing . . .

'Hey, Robat!'

The Count was trotting down the long slope behind him. Trailing his leather coat, using the other hand to flap his shirt-front, to get air in . . . 'My God — nearest I've ever been to Hades itself . . . How those women *stand* it . . .'

'Warm inside there, is it?'

'Under that iron roof? And the *smell* . . .'

'Nobody heard of Aunt Liza, I suppose.'

'One old tough does remember her — believe it or not. I told her my aunt was here in '14, and she agreed, that would have been the year. But she didn't think I'd find her in Enotayevsk, her recollection is that Liza chased off to Murmansk after some sailor she'd met. My old aunt!'

'Runs in the family, does it?'

They were on the bank, thirty feet or so above the river. Mud-flats below them, and fifty yards to their left a moored landing-stage lying aslant on the mud, its outer edge in the water where four boats tugged at their painters. A fifth was just pushing off, with two greyheads in it and a heap of gear in the stern. The Count capped his hands to his mouth, bawled 'You comrades going to Enotayevsk, by any chance?'

His voice echoed across the water. The rowers paused;

then the one near the stern waved a hand negatively and pointed upstream. But from the tilted landing-stage another old-timer bellowed, 'Ready to go *now*?'

'*What* luck.' Glancing at Bob. They were together on the seat in the boat's stern, the gaunt old fisherman's deepset eyes on them as he rowed — seeming to exert very little effort but still sending the boat skidding along like a water-beetle. He was all bone, sinew and wrinkled hide, but in his younger days he must have been a giant of a man. The Count said again, 'Really, amazing luck.'

'Boats've been pushing off all day, comrade. And some still to follow. You picked the right day, that's all. Looking for an aunt, you said?'

The Count nodded. They'd had a half-hour's wait on the landing-stage, and he'd been obliged to trot out a few more lies. 'As I was telling your friends, I haven't seen her in years, just thought I'd say hello — if she's still around.'

'Lives in Enotayevsk, does she?'

He hedged: 'I suppose that's *your* home?'

'Yes. Well — off and on. All my life, off and on. Seasonal, you might say. Like the swallows or the snipe, eh?'

'Or the sturgeon . . .'

Bob's attention drifted away from their conversation. Making a mental note of having started from the fishing-station at a few minutes to four. He wished he still had his own watch and didn't have to keep asking the Count . . . But say four o'clock, easier to remember. And this leg downstream must be about a mile and a half, two miles . . .

Habit and training, all that emphasis on using one's powers of observation — underlined by the experience once or twice of having wished one *had* taken detailed notice, when one had failed to do so . . . The old fisherman was telling Nick, 'There's roadwork too. On that side the road's built up on a great bank. A levee, they call it — above the flood level, see. And that needs upkeep — year in, year out . . . What's your aunt's name?'

The hesitation lasted long enough for Bob to wonder

whether he was going to answer at all. Then: 'Her married name's Kamentseva. Husband's—'

'*Chyort* . . .'

'*Know* her, do you?'

He'd stopped rowing. Bolt upright, his great arms folded over the oars' looms, the blades slanting, dripping . . . 'Maroussia Kamentseva is your aunt?'

The current was carrying the boat on downstream. They were crossing this wide channel diagonally; there was an island of dried-out riverbed to starboard, half a mile away; they'd be rounding its lower end and then pulling upstream to a junction with the main deepwater channel. In spring, one might guess, there'd be no island, just the great river at this point ten or twelve miles wide.

Rate of flow about two knots, he guessed. On the next stretch the old man would be rowing *into* it.

'You actually do know her?'

A grunt . . . 'Told you — lived here all my life. And *that* goes back a bit. I knew Maroussia when she was — God, *this* high. Maroussia Biibochkina, she was . . . How does it happen she's your aunt?'

'Well — did you know her sister?'

'As I recall it, there were three girls in that family. One other I remember . . . Avdotya?'

'Elizaveta.'

He'd started rowing again. Getting the boat back on course. 'The family split up, didn't it, when the parents died. Typhus, wasn't it. Maroussia never left us, but — well, one of the other girls — I'll swear her name was Avdotya —'

'Maroussia was the only aunt I ever knew. Elizaveta was my mother's name. My father was a railwayman, we lived up near Saratov. Pokrovsk, to be exact. My parents are both dead now.'

'May they rest in peace.'

'Please God.'

'I'll tell you who else is dead.' Glancing over his shoulder, checking on his course, and adjusting slightly. Turning back. 'Ivan. Maroussia's husband. Died about a year ago — heart-failure, they said.'

'They?'

A shrug of the immensely broad shoulders. 'That's what was said. We don't see much of Maroussia these days. She's been into the village a few times but straight in, straight out. As if the devil's driving — so I've heard it said.' The deep eyes were sombre, in a face that might have been carved out of mahogany — if mahogany sprouted silver-grey stubble. The Count leaning towards him, listening avidly ... 'There's a house she works at — lives at — well, it must be all of fifty years she's been there. Outside the village ...'

'*Riibachnaya Dacha.*'

He'd stopped rowing again. Eyes on his passenger, and thoughtful ... Then: 'They call it *Krasnaya Dacha* now. Renamed since the revolution, of course — well, since they took it over. Belonged to the Solovyev family before that — as far back as anyone's grandparents could remember, even. Solovyevs spent all their summers here. They'd be mostly dead by now — shame, really, they were good to her, nobody around here had anything against them ... But of course, if Maroussia's your aunt you'd know about them.'

'She's mentioned them. Of course.' Hunched forward, hugging his knees, his eyes fixed on the gaunt, seamed face. Thinking about being one of a family who were mostly dead, Bob guessed. And whose former house was now called *Red* Cottage ... 'But this house — where you say Maroussia still works ...'

'Three versts outside the village. *Krasnaya Dacha.* That's where you'd find her.'

'You say it's been — requisitioned?'

'*Has* it!' Rowing again. Hands so big they made the oars look thin enough to snap like twigs. 'Headquarters of the Military Revolutionary Committee.'

Bob saw the Count's reaction: a small start, a tightening of muscles ... The green eyes slid his way, then returned to the old man. 'Are you sure she still works there?'

'Cooks, washes and scrubs for 'em. Same as she's done

all her life. But then, you see, the Solovyevs turned that place into a war hospital, back in '14. Place where badly wounded officers went to rest while they recovered. Well, *would* be for officers, a house like that one.'

'And now it's occupied by the Military Revolutionary Committee, you say?'

'And a bit more besides.'

'A bit more?'

The old man turned to face downwind, and spat heavily. A grunt, as he turned back then. 'As you say . . .'

Silence. The Count waiting for more, Bob realized, and not getting it. Only the regular thump and slither of the oars between the thole-pins, the small splash and suction of their blades . . . The Count cleared his throat, asked, 'How would I best get in touch with her, in present circumstances?'

More silence . . . Bob counted the strokes, while the old man thought about it. Four — five — six . . . Eyes hooded, in those deep hollows in his skull, but his gaze still resting on the Count. A brain at work in there, Bob guessed, while arms and oars moved like parts of a machine. But Nick might have made a bloomer, he thought. Having given his aunt's name as Lizaveta Vetrova to the people at the fishing-station, and now as Maroussia Kamentseva. One could see his reasoning, but if there was any social contact now between that side and this . . .

'I suppose you'd go out to the house, comrade. Go out there and ask for her.'

'Just walk up and knock on the door?'

'Well — there's a guard-post at the entrance. On both entrances, I should say. Would be, wouldn't there. You'd be required to identify yourself and state your business, I imagine.'

'Simple. Visiting my aunt Maroussia.'

'Papers in order, I suppose?'

'Certainly.'

'I should have asked to see them, I suppose, before—'

'They're in order. You have my word for it.'

'If they aren't — I'm not calling you a liar, I'm just

saying *if* they aren't — I'd ask you not to tell them it was me brought you across.'

'I've no intention of talking to them, *batushka*.'

'But they'll talk to *you*, lad.' A chuckle. '*And* by and by you'd be talking back to 'em!'

'I don't follow ...'

'Put it this way. If your papers are *not* in order, comrade — don't go *near* that house.'

'But why—'

'The Cheka, comrade. The Cheka. *That's* why.'

It had taken forty-five minutes for the boat to crab across that channel on the downstream leg. The boatman — he'd told them his name now, Leonid Mesyats — had spent his whole life at this, on this river, had made precisely the right amount of allowance for the current, so as to finish at the central island's downstream coastline without a yard or a pound of effort wasted. Then of course having rounded the bottom of the island he had the *hard* work ahead of him — a four-and-a-half- or five-mile struggle north-westward, butting upstream, needing all his weight and muscle and concentration against the Volga's power.

Low-water power, even though it was. What sort of a monster this must be in April when the ice and snow melted, throughout the two thousand miles of its journey across Russia.

There'd been a long silence after that bombshell-like reference to the Cheka. The Count had sat like a dummy — speechless, motionless. Bob watching him, guessing at the panic in his thoughts: having his own anyway, the core of them being that if the place now known as *Krasnaya Dacha* housed Cheka agents — as well as the Astrakhan district's military command — it couldn't possibly also contain those women. Girls ... Although obviously they must have been there at some time — when the Count's mother had sent off her message.

Before the Cheka had moved in, he guessed.

One way or another, they couldn't be there now.

A conclusion might be that he and the Count would

end up rowing that skiff out into the Caspian on their own.

'You said —' the Count had broken out of his reverie — 'that Maroussia does come into the village sometimes?'

'Yes. She's been known to. She brings a cart in for supplies sometimes. To fetch coal and logs in winter, for instance. Ivan used to do it, now she does. God knows why *they* don't, they have automobiles.'

'Probably got other uses for them.'

'I expect they have, but she's an old woman now, you know.'

'She'd be getting on a bit, that's a fact.' He nodded, with his eyes on the old man's. Then, after a pause: 'Is there any way that I could get a message to her, d'you think?'

'Message?'

'To let her know I'm here. I don't want to go — I mean, to get involved with — well, Cheka, for God's sake . . .'

'Why not?'

'Does it matter?'

'Might do. If you're a counter-revolutionary, or—'

'*Me* — counter-revolutionary!'

'Well, then . . .'

'Can I trust you? Explain it to you in strict confidence?'

'Depends on what you're going to tell me.'

'We're on our way to Moscow, with a report to deliver that's far from complimentary to certain members of the Cheka. Or to the basic principles of Cheka methods and objectives. Because — in a nutshell — they're working *against* us . . . There's *been* a counter-revolution, you see — a coup — down in the south, in the Persian border area, and it was Cheka methods that caused it. Nine of my comrades were hanged — by the counter-revolutionaries — and I'd have been the next, if this man hadn't got me away. He's Persian, incidentally. But d'you see the spot I'm in? How can I tell this to the Cheka?'

'Tell 'em something else, then.'

'Lying to them doesn't usually get much farther than having your fingernails pulled out, does it?'

The sun was edging down. Blazing off the water, and hot even in that reflection. Blinding . . . Bob thinking that the Count's story wasn't at all a bad one, in the present circumstances. Who could have come up with a yarn like that one just on the spur of the moment?

Well — he could, probably.

He was leaning forward: adopting a position virtually of supplication ... 'Can you think of any way I might get a message to her at the *Dacha*?'

Huge arms pumping away like pistons. Fast, powerful strokes, opposing the Volga's strength. He grunted: his eyes contemplative, resting on the Count ... 'I'll think about it. Leave me to row now.'

They'd turned on to the upstream leg at about a quarter to five, and it took the old man two solid hours of hard pulling to get up to the junction with the main channel. He hadn't missed a stroke since making the hairpin turn down there. Now, driving his boat around the point, the land on the boat's port side, the rower's right — he allowed his right arm its first rest in two hours, while giving two strong strokes with the other. Emitting a grunt — satisfaction, relief — as the boat spun, turning its bow downstream.

Bob said — the first words he'd spoken in hours — 'Congratulations. You're a fine oarsman.'

'Who says so?'

'I'm a seaman.'

'*Are* you, now ...'

Resting on his oars, gazing at him. The sun was colouring the western sky, blackening the land, silhouetting the top of the levee that supported the riverside road — all the way down to Astrakhan, Bob guessed — as flat-topped as a stone wall, jet-black against that brilliance ... The old man pointed that way with his jaw: 'Four miles downstream from here. One hour. Still be daylight when we get there. Not bad, though I say it myself.'

The Count agreed: 'I'm no seaman, but I'm impressed.'

'Well. It can help, to have your mind busy. You don't notice the work so much. I've been pondering your problem, comrade.'

'Yes?'

'I have a grandson. Andrei. Nine years old. Fine little lad, tough as old boots. Has a passion for raspberries.'

Silence. The last word — *malini* — hanging in the air . . . The Count laughed, snapped his fingers: 'Right!' A glance round at Bob: 'We always had *wonderful* raspberries at *Riibach*—'

He'd stopped dead. Open-mouthed: horror dawning. Old Mesyats resting on his oars, letting the current carry them along as he leant forward, peering at point-blank range into the Count's bearded face and shielding his own eyes against the blaze of the lowering sun.

Sitting back, then. Giant's hands resting on wide, bony knees, the oars trailing from leather strops that held them loosely to the pins. Sounds of the river, and the boat's timbers creaking . . .

'By all the saints. By all the saints in heaven, sir, you must be *raving mad*!'

9

Enotayevsk had a high stone-faced quay with room for the river steamers to berth on it, and stone steps leading down to a landing-stage for small boats. It was a long flight of steps because of the height of the land at this point, which of course explained the village having been sited here, connected to other villages by the levee road.

The land was black and silver now. Half an hour ago, when they'd been passing a smaller waterside village, the sky behind it had been scarlet. The Count had made some comment on the dramatic quality of the scene, and old Mesyats had growled, 'Reminds me ... Can you guess why they've changed the name of your house from *Riibachnaya* to *Krasnaya*?'

'Red's the colour of the revolution, isn't it?'

'That's not the reason. Fact is, it was the village people began calling it *Krasnaya Dacha.* Red being the colour of blood, that's why.'

'Blood ...' A pause. Splash of the oars' blades, and the regular thudding of their looms against the pins. Even the droplets flying from the blades were pink. The Count asked him, 'So what happened?'

'There were eleven officers recuperating from wounds in that house of yours, and a doctor and two nurses looking after them. I'm talking about October last.'

'I can guess now ...'

'Doesn't take much doing, does it? Seeing as it was the pattern all over — according to what one hears ... But this crowd — thirty or forty comrades, they say — came up from Astrakhan by boat. A little steamer, it's still there, some rich man's toy before this, the Cheka have it now ...

Well, there'd have been some of 'em in that mob, I dare say. And what they did was – look, this isn't a *nice* story ...'

'Go on.'

'As you wish. At least no kin of yours were there ... Isn't there a staircase that leads up to a gallery – musicians' gallery, is it? Looking down on your dining-hall?'

'Not *my* dining-hall exactly. But – yes.'

'So. What they did was they hung the officers by their feet – ropes tied to the ankles and then led round a gallery balustrade – if that's what you call it – so they could hoist 'em up like you'd hoist so many pigs. Then – taking their time about it, so each man had notice of what was coming to him – and setting out buckets below to catch the blood, d'you see – they slashed these fellows' throats, one by one. But of course the buckets—'

'May God have mercy ...'

'Well, one mercy for you is none of it could've been Solovyev blood.'

'Disappointing for them.'

'Perhaps. As I said, they weren't local men, what they'd come for was those officers. And as far as any of us knew, there wasn't even one of you still alive. Unless your mother was with – a certain person ... But not even Maroussia, she can't know, whatever news we'd get would be from her, d'you see, so it's clearly *her* belief you've all been – taken ... You had an older brother – Count Vladimir?'

'He was killed in March '16.'

'God rest him ... And a sister?'

'She was in Petrograd. No word from her or of her, so ...'

'I'm very sorry. Except – as far as your brother's concerned, much better killed in action than ...' He'd paused. An heroic, dramatic figure against that blood-red sunset. *Too* dramatic and the colour too apposite, Bob thought – watching them and listening, telling himself *It could be some dreadful nightmare tale, and this setting specially chosen for its telling, but it's the truth, it happened*

… The old man was telling Nick, 'The doctor and the nurses got the same treatment. Except the nurses — well, you can imagine, before they hung *them* up …'

'I can imagine.'

'I'm sorry. I warned you it wasn't — pretty … But there's a practical reason you should know about it — on account of poor Maroussia. She was called in to mop up, the day after, and she was still at it the *week* after, so people say … Old Ivan was dead by then, she was alone, and — it changed her. So I'm told. Haven't seen her myself, you see — well, I said, didn't I … But if it happens that you do see her — as well to be prepared …'

Approaching the quay at Enotayevsk, Mesyats pointed. 'The Swede's place is through there. There's an alley leads through, and where it gets to the road beyond those houses you'll find it on your left.'

'And we'll wait there until—'

'Until you get tired of waiting.' Shipping his oars, shifting round on the thwart to face the landing-stage as they glided in towards it. Getting there, Bob climbed out and took the painter to an eye-bolt.

'This one?'

'Good as any.' There were about a dozen other boats there. The old man told the Count, 'Remember, now. She'll get the message — if she's there to be given it — but then it's up to her what she does about it. If anything. You won't see the boy, and you won't see me again if I can help it.'

'Understood. But I want to say this, Leonid Timofeevich—'

'Better not, sir. There's no — sentiment.'

'What is there, then?'

'An old fool, that's all. And be warned — if my own kith and kin were endangered …'

'You'd inform on us.'

'Without thinking twice. Where's the sentiment in that?'

'In the fact that actions speak louder than words, *batushka*.'

'All right — so you can repay the favour ...'

'By sodding off.'

'Vanishing. *Please* ...'

The Swede's tavern — *Shvedski traktir* — was a long, narrow room entered directly from the road and containing four long tables with benches, and at one end of the room a stove big enough for a family of six to sleep on. In winter, of course. The Swede himself, Torkel Rasmussen, was a man in his late forties — smallish, with greying temples to his blond hair and grey streaks in his beard, and watery blue eyes. He'd been in Russia twelve years now, he told them, having come originally to set up a caviar-exporting business. The war had interrupted that, but in the interim he'd married a local girl and didn't want to leave, so he'd turned this place into a pub and — he explained — was hoping, please God, to be allowed to continue with it and also relaunch his caviar business before long.

'When things are settling down a little, huh?'

'Will it be allowed?'

A wide, white smile: 'Which?'

'Either.'

'I think. Because I am foreign. Also to bring in money. All right, maybe for the caviar we have a co-operative, some sort. But soon, I hope.'

'Well — good luck, comrade. There's certainly no doubt we're winning.'

'Oh — I'm sure. Are you comrades — passing through?'

'On our way to Moscow. But an aunt of mine used to live somewhere around here, we've stopped off to see if I can find her.'

'What is this lady's name, please?'

'Vetrova. Lizaveta.'

'No. No, I don't believe—'

'I've put certain enquiries in hand, we may have some news brought to us here later. If not, can we sleep here?'

'Of course.' He gestured: meaning sleep anywhere, just stretch out. They still didn't have beds in a lot of places of this kind. That toothy grin again: 'Not *grande luxe*, but ...'

'Fine. Now, some food, and beer?'

Fresh fish, baked in that stove, and turnip. And the Swede's beer wasn't bad. There were between a dozen and twenty other customers. Most of them were fishermen, the Swede had said. 'With money in their pockets — for a day or two, huh?'

The Count murmured, when he'd left them, 'The Bolsheviks won't allow private businesses to continue for long in areas they control. And the caviar'd certainly be State-owned, if they had the power. He must know that.'

'So he must be reckoning on *your* lot winning.'

'I suppose so. And when one hears stories of the kind we heard this evening — surely God can't allow such filth to prevail.' He shut his eyes. '*Christ* ...'

'I know. I feel the same. But here and now, Nick ...'

'We can only wait for Maroussia. Yes. And keep our voices down. You're quite right.'

'Also keep in mind that it was back in October they perpetrated that horror. When they were all really running mad. Well, weren't they — everywhere? Getting on for a year ago. And we know your mother and the others were with Maroussia when she sent you the message — just over *three* months ago, so—'

'So what?'

'Well — in detail, God knows, but—'

'Exactly. God knows. *Anything* ...'

'What'll we do if Maroussia doesn't respond?'

That, in the immediate situation, was the biggest and least answerable question. What to do if Maroussia got the message that the Count was here, and ignored it. Or wasn't able to respond to it, because of her own situation ... Bob thought that if this proved to be the case, and if he personally had then to make the decision, it would be to cut and run. Rather than throw away two *more* lives — get out, *now*.

That would be the logical, sane decision; and Leonid Timofeevich Mesyats would have agreed. But the Count wouldn't. He'd be outraged at the mere suggestion.

Understandably. His own flesh and blood, and the girl he loved . . .

'*Krasnaya Dacha* . . . To think that in the house where we spent such happy, carefree times — even in that big staircase hall, children's games . . .'

'Same must apply all over. In hundreds of homes, Nick. Thousands, even . . . Mesyats was right, it's been the pattern. You'll have heard about the Black Sea fleet mutineers, what they did to their officers — marching them off a jetty in chains with weights on them, and cracking their skulls under the lid of a grand piano in the sailors' club. It's the same . . . syndrome. Peasant bestiality. Not to mention the more deliberate brutality, all the poor wretches the Cheka have tortured to death or shot in the back of the head. It's a fact of these times, Nick — what I'm saying is this particular horror was perpetrated in your house, but — look, that was just one more drop in an *ocean* of blood, you should put it out of your mind just as you do with the other stories. As the old man pointed out, your family weren't there, thank God, so—'

'Yes. Thank God.'

'I'll admit there's one aspect of it I can't reconcile in my mind — the idea of a house in which the Cheka have set up shop, and in the same place —' he dropped his voice even further — 'two of the Tsar's daughters. That really does seem — so utterly incongruous.'

'Well, I—'

He'd started, then checked himself. Retreating into his own thoughts — fears, visions, whatever . . . Hands flat on the table, and staring down at them. It was a habit of his, Bob had noticed more than once, that when he didn't want to look someone in the eyes he picked another object on which to focus his attention. Instead of just looking away, he looked *at* something.

And here and now, anyway — in his shoes . . .

But in *anyone's*, Bob thought, who had any depth of feeling for this country. The Count shook his head: 'No more impossible, though, than that the others should be there. My mother, Irina, Nadia.'

'I suppose not.'

Sipping at his beer. Struggling to shut out awareness of the surrounding nightmare: shut his mind to it, concentrate not on the wood but on the trees — on the problems that had been nagging away in his own thoughts for two days and nights — how to get away from here, with or without the women: to get even the beginnings of a plan . . .

'Except for one thing.' The Count nodded slowly as he spoke. 'One thing I haven't mentioned. It may not make all that much difference, but . . .'

'What are you talking about?'

The green eyes dropped again.

'Bob, I think at this time I *won't* talk about it. If you don't mind. If it came to the very *worst* — if for instance you and I were arrested — well, the knowledge wouldn't be any use to you here and now — and if all goes well you'll see for yourself quite soon — so really there's no point — burdening you, with—'

'I agree.' He nodded. 'Whatever the deuce it is you're talking about . . . But incidentally, another thing you never told me was that you had a brother.'

'Vladimir. Three years older than me. He was killed in the fighting around Lake Narocz — in March '16, that was. You know where — on the Polish border? It was a very costly attack. We launched it primarily to take German and Austrian pressure off the French, who were in bad trouble at Verdun. Vlad was one of a whole list of good men killed.'

'Where were you at that time?'

'In the south-west. Brusilov's front. We were up against the Austrian Seventh Army, in the Bukovina. We smashed them, you know. And *this* was by way of helping the Italians — they'd begged us to do something to stop the Austrians reinforcing their Trentino front.' He shrugged. 'When you reckon it all up, I'd say we weren't so bad, while we were in it. Considering how inadequate our equipment was, and the supply problems.'

'Like shells that didn't fit the guns, we heard.'

He nodded. 'Must be quite a joke — if you don't happen to be there at the time.' He began nibbling at a thumbnail. 'I wonder how long we're going to have to wait here, Bob.'

'Well.' Glancing over at some men who were playing dominoes — slamming the pieces down, crashes like gunshots over the growl of conversation ... 'Might pass some time with a game — if the Swede has another set?'

'I don't think so. Unless you particularly—'

'No. I'm easy. But — could be hours, you know. Could be all night — and that wouldn't necessarily mean she isn't coming. We don't know what circumstances apply out at the house, when she can or can't get away, or—'

'I know. I know.' Hands flat on the table again: in an effort *not* to bite his nails, perhaps ... 'Unfortunately, patience is one of the virtues I don't have in abundance.'

The arrangement — the old man's scheme — was that he'd give his grandson Andrei a verbal message for Maroussia, simply *Nikki's waiting at the Swede's.* If the boy was unlucky enough to get caught, he'd say he'd sneaked in to see if there were any raspberries left on the canes; they'd believe him, knowing that he and his friends had been in the *Riibachnaya* gardens dozens of times before, had their own ways in, under or over the wall. If he was caught he might get his ears boxed, but no more than that; he'd risked that penalty often enough just for a hatful of fruit. And his task would be finished when he'd whispered those half-dozen words in the old woman's ear; after that he could go and pick berries, if he felt so inclined.

The Count said, after a long silence, 'That was a damn stupid mistake I made, wasn't it? Blurting that out, about our marvellous raspberries?'

'Easy to do, though. Relaxing, forgetting for a moment.'

'Exactly what we can't afford.'

'It's turned out well, anyway. What would you have done, without the old man and his grandson?'

'Well, I'd thought of getting a message out to her somehow, and the obvious way would have been by the hand of some child. Bunch of flowers for a supposed birthday — something of that sort. I'd have had to ask around first, that's all — how do I get hold of my aunt Maroussia, all that stuff. So there'd have been a certain risk, I grant you — if one had asked the wrong person ... For instance — in here, now, which one of these characters would you take a chance on?'

'Frankly, I wouldn't.'

'There you are, then. You're right, it's turned out well. If we're right to trust Mesyats, that is.'

'I'd say we're safe enough with him.'

'I agree. But — you can't be *certain* ... If his wife, for instance, didn't agree with what he's doing. Or suppose the boy gets caught and they don't believe he's come for raspberries. They'd get the truth out of him, all right. Or if they suspected he'd brought her a message — they're not stupid, they'd watch *her,* and —' he pointed at the door — 'it wouldn't be just my old aunt coming in there, would it.'

'Trying to work yourself up into a party mood, Nick, are you?'

'Trying to be realistic. Cigarette? Here ... You get fewer sudden shocks that way. Nothing like this is straightforward, ever ... Besides, Mesyats told us the old girl's a bit —' he touched his forehead — 'didn't he?'

'He said she'd changed. I took it to mean she may be slightly — you know, odd. If he thought she was actually *sumashedshaya,* I doubt he'd be risking his own neck, would he?'

'I hope you're right.'

'So do I.' Leaning down to the match in the Count's cupped hands. 'Thanks.'

'We should have pipes.' Looking round at the Swede's other customers. 'Be more in keeping, wouldn't it?'

'I don't smoke much. Cigar, when I'm offered one.'

'Well — if I'd known ...'

'You'd have brought some Cubans along, I know. You're a great disappointment to me, Nick.'

'I'll tell you one thing — seriously ...'

'Go on.'

'None of them will be here. When we talk to Maroussia — *if* we do — she'll tell us — well, either the worst you can imagine, what I've seen in nightmares for months now — or simply that they left, at some time or other ... She wouldn't know where, they wouldn't have told her ... I'm *certain* now, Bob.'

'One gets that kind of certainty sometimes, at crucial moments. Comes of having wanted a thing too much for too long. And being so close now — naturally you're scared.'

'It's simply not *possible* that they're here. Apart from the logical aspect — I mean, Cheka in the house, for God's sake ...'

'Main problem is we're both tired. We've only had catnaps, no proper sleep.' He put a hand on the Count's shoulder. 'And you're a touch overwrought. Just relax, *wait*.'

'For her to come walking in that door.' The Count nodded towards it. 'Look around you, Bob. No female gets to show even the tip of her nose in a place like this ... Why in hell didn't I think of this before? She *can't*—'

'She'll go to the side door and talk to the Swede, surely. She'd hardly *want* to show her face in here. I'd never imagined she would, to tell you the truth.'

'So then the Swede knows what's going on?'

'Not enough to be any danger to us. Anyway he's more likely to be anti-Bolshevik than for them.'

'For whichever side his bread's buttered, I'd say. And as this is Bolshevik country—'

'Nick ...'

Expelling pungent smoke ... 'Want me to shut up, do you?'

'Wouldn't do any harm. Oh, hang on, Nikolai Petrovich — stay more or less as you are, don't look up ... Leonid Mesyats just walked in.'

The old man was talking to the Swede. Standing, just inside the door — having to stoop slightly, under the low ceiling. The Count, despite the warning, had jerked his head up and was staring in that direction. Bob looked away, to reduce the degree of interest; being aware that any of these others could have been Cheka, or Cheka informers. He watched the domino players, who were still shouting like excited children as they crashed the pieces down.

'He wouldn't want us to know him, Nick.'

'Teach your grandmother.' Drawing hard on his *papirossa.* Glancing at Bob now. 'But we weren't going to see him again, were we? Let's hope it doesn't mean something's gone wrong. Like the grandson couldn't get in — or out — or she wouldn't come, or—'

'What's going on now?'

'Swede's gone through to the back. Mesyats is jawing with some other fishermen. Hasn't once looked our way.'

'Well.' Bob picked up the remains of his beer. 'Might as well finish this, it's too good to waste.'

'The Swede's back. He's brought a sack of — God knows . . . Could be turnips.'

'Yes.' Bob was allowing himself to watch too, now. 'I'd guess turnips.' The old man took the sack from the Swede, swung it on to his shoulder. He was glancing around the room, nodding to friends here and there. When his glance met the Count's and Bob's he moved his head slightly, a gesture towards the door.

He'd turned that way himself. Bob and the Count already on the move, calling goodnight to the Swede.

Very dark, and river-haze to thicken it; stars visible overhead, and the onion-shaped dome of the village church in vague silhouette against them. No moon: moonset would have been within about an hour of sunset.

'I'm here.' Mesyats — low-voiced, waiting for them at the corner where the alley ran through to the quayside, his big frame flattened against the wall and the sack of turnips at his feet. He muttered as they joined him, 'Coming now. Hear it?'

Iron-shod wheels on the hard-baked earth, and light trotting hoofbeats. From the alleyway, the soft, night-time murmur of the river. The old man growled, 'Don't waste time being sociable. When the *telega* stops, get in quick — under the tarpaulin. Then —' he pushed at the sack with his foot — 'mind your heads, I'll be dumping this on top.'

'Thought we weren't going to see you again.'

'You wouldn't have, if it hadn't become unavoidable. And you won't after this, don't worry ... Here she is.'

'Whoa-up.' Scratchy old voice ... The old woman was perched up on the front of the cart, which had a donkey in its shafts. 'Whoa-up ...' Addressing it in a whisper — which still carried well, in the quiet night. There was a very strong ammoniac reek of donkey.

'Leo?'

'Maroussia Sergeyevna, you're a marvel. In with you, comrades.'

'Nikolai Petrovich?'

'Maroussia — I'll embrace you later. Just tell me, though, quickly—'

'Holy Mother of God, it *is*—'

'No gassing — if you don't mind ...' The old man loomed over the Count. 'Get *in* ... Maroussia, listen — if you're wise, you'll send 'em on their way damn quick. Remember that, now. And here are your turnips — it's what you came for, the Swede promised you a free sackful and you suddenly remembered, got scared he might run out before you could take delivery — right?'

He dumped the sack on the tarpaulin that was stretched across the top of the cart; the middle of it sagged almost to the floor, under that weight. Bob was on one side, and the Count the other; there was just enough space for each of them to crouch down on his own side, with the tarpaulin pressing down between them.

The cart jerked, rolled forward — bouncing and crashing over rocks and ridges. With about three versts of this to come, Bob remembered from the Count's description. A mile and a half, say. Jolting and bouncing getting a lot worse, too, as the old woman whipped her donkey into a trot. Hard, splintery boards, acrid farmyard stench, the tarpaulin over his head unpleasantly slimy to the touch: better not to make any contact with it anyway, one didn't want any impression of a body or bodies to be visible from above. The patter of the donkey's hoofbeats was a soft drumming rhythm beyond the closer, harsher clatter of the wheels. Then — surprisingly — it was all slowing, getting easier. Cries of 'Whoa-up, whoa-up!' drifted down to him as Maroussia reined in, bringing the animal back to a walk after what couldn't have been more than a few hundred yards.

'Nikolai Petrovich?'

'*Yes*, Maroussia!'

'So you did come, at last!'

'Had a long way to come — and it wasn't simple. But listen—'

'That's not Boris Nikolai'ich with you.'

'No ...'

'I thought it would be. When he said two of you ...'

'Boris died — of wounds. He was dying when he reached me. I think they'd caught him at some stage and he'd got away somehow, but ... Maroussia, *please*, tell me about the others — my mother ...'

'Your sainted mother is with God, Nikolai Petrovich.'

A sound like a groan ...

'It was in His divine mercy that He took her. She'd been so *ill*. Poor lamb — such agony ... We did all we could, but — it was only three weeks ago ...'

'Nadia? Irina?'

'Irina's shaking with excitement that you've got here. We hardly dared believe that little boy.'

'Nadia?'

'She doesn't know yet. She may be back by now — in which case—'

'Back from where?'

'She works for them in the house, see. She's my—'

'For *them* ... D'you mean the Cheka?'

'— my niece, I tell them. Yes — them. What they believe is your mother was my sister and Nadia was her daughter. So they leave us be, and I get rations for her.'

'This is — astonishing ... What about Irina, where does she fit in?'

'They don't know she's with me. Doesn't show her face. We use the Hole, see, and—'

'The Hole? You mean—'

'The ice-cellar. They don't know it exists, so—'

'Irina *lives* in it?'

'She could be recognized, you see. She's a Solovyev, after all, there are plenty round about who'd know her – see the likeness ... What don't you understand?'

'I'm beginning to ... They knew my mother was with you – and ill – and that her daughter, so-called, but actually Nadia ...'

'That's right. And they think I'm mad. Suits me – I'm no danger to them, so they don't worry me – or mine, see ... I work for 'em too – have to, I'd be on the garbage-heap if I didn't ... I cook for 'em, launder clothes, clean the house, feed the prisoners ... Quick, get *down* – automobile ...'

Crouching, back in the noise and smell. Stifling, in contrast to the cool night air. Thinking – that last word, *prisoners* ... The two young girls? Bob was feeling the same surprise that he'd heard in the Count's voice, at the thought of his fiancée working for those – creatures ... He was hearing the motor now: the sound emerging from closer, surrounding noise and rising fast to a passing climax with light showing briefly between the *telega*'s planks: then it was dark again, and that racket dwindling away into the night.

'All clear, Maroussia?'

'All right now.'

'Was that some of them?'

'Cheka or military, yes. There's more military in the house than Cheka.' Bob was struggling up again: hearing as he got his head back into breathable air, 'Mother of God, how we've dreamt of you getting here. Your mother's last words, even –'

'What did she die of?'

'Some growth inside her. Some foul, malignant thing.'

'Did she have a doctor?'

'Yes – but once only, and—'

'You said something about prisoners?'

'The old storerooms are cells now. Bars on their windows. Czechoslovaks locked in there now – but they say they'll shoot them soon. Nikolai Petrovich, you'll take my darlings away with you now, will you?'

'As soon as we work out some way—'

'Excuse me.' Bob broke in. Seeing the shawled head jerk round, startled ... 'Nick, what about the children, the two young girls?'

'What's he say?' Her head turned back the other way. 'They're young girls, but he's wrong to call them children. What's he asking?' Bob could see the small, swathed figure above him against starry sky. Her hoarse voice putting another question on the heels of the first one: 'Who is he – if I may ask ...'

'A friend, Maroussia. I couldn't have got here without him. His name's Robat. It's not his real name but it's the one we'll use. He's a *good* friend.'

'What was it about children?'

Bob began again: 'The Tsar's daughters – aren't they with you too?'

'Tsar's daughters?' She flipped the reins: 'Come on, come on ... Did he say the Tsar's daughters – with *me*?'

'Nick ...'

'Maroussia – the message I had from Boris referred to "the two children" ...'

'Irina and the Princess Nadia.'

'No – as well as them. At least, I *thought* ... It sounded like a coded reference – and there did seem to be good reason to assume my mother had brought two of the Grand Duchesses here with her. I couldn't see what else—'

'I can tell you where you'd find the Tsar's children. At Ekaterinodar, that's where. Somewhere close by, anyway, is where you'd find their remains. All shot to pieces. I won't say it's common knowledge exactly, there've been denials and some choose to believe them, but my Czechs know all about it. Their Legion took Ekaterinodar from the Bolsheviks only five days after. No bodies – they'd hidden them or buried them somewhere, in the countryside nearby most likely. *They* didn't have to clear up like I did. Not that it would've been a mess like I had, not with bullets — although there was some stabbing too, my Czechs believe. Finishing them off — must be rotten shots, they say, there were dozens of shots fired in that room — revolver shots, the walls all pitted ... It was in a house belonging to a man called Ipatiev — he's back in it now already, would you credit that? They'd had the family imprisoned there for weeks — Cheka, I mean, not the Ipatievs — and that night they called them to the basement and shot them, all together. His Majesty and the Tsarina and the poor little sick Tsarevich, Aleksei Nikolaievich, and his four sisters, and their doctor and two footmen, and the Tsarina's maid — oh, and the little one's little dog — Anastasia's, she called it Jemmi — wasn't *that* cruel, now?'

'One might have thought — unnecessary.' The Count began, 'Bob ...'

'There were never any children. Am I right?'

'Seems so. But the message — I explained it to you — it was a matter of *interpretation*.'

'I'm sorry about your mother.'

'Thank you. But Bob, you must understand this ...'

'I think I understand it very well. But this is hardly a good time or circumstance—'

'Nikolai Petrovich — and you, sir — please get inside now. And keep still, don't speak, we'll be at the guard-post in a minute, don't move again until I tell you. They probably won't stop me, but—'

'All right.'

Bob wriggled down, manoeuvred the tarpaulin back into position above his head; they'd been passing through trees, he realized, as he crouched down on the boards where he'd been before. He'd barely noticed the trees, or any other features of their close surroundings. Meanwhile the old woman had forced her donkey back into a trot, whipping it and shouting imprecations at it, and the cart was careering along again quite fast. Less erratically than before — plenty of noise and vibration, but less of the earlier violence about it. Better surface to the road, obviously. Maroussia adding to the din now by bursting into song: while Bob recalled the compelling glint in the Count's green eyes as he'd explained — only six days ago, although it felt more like a month — *Personally I wouldn't have bet on any of them being alive, until this message . . . if the two children were anyone else, why would she* not *have named them? D'you take my point*? Then when he, Bob, had agreed with him that this interpretation seemed to hold water, he'd snapped, *Of course it does! This was also the view taken by General Denikin, I may tell you. We discussed it from all angles — what might be done and how, and by whom . . .*

By the Royal Navy, had been his — the Count's — answer. And persuading Denikin to fall for it must have been three-quarters of the battle. The rest of them — Bicherakov, the Commodore and Dunsterville — had gone over like toppling dominoes. Thus launching the attempted rescue of Count Nikolai Solovyev's mother, sister and fiancée. No one else.

Maroussia was still screeching out her song. The same old song that they'd heard Bolshevik sailors warbling a few days ago, down there in the delta: such a well-known, all-Russian ballad that it was almost an alternative to the national anthem, but it still belonged here on the Volga more than it did elsewhere. She was going full-blast at it now . . .

'*Volga, Volga, matts rodnaya,*
Volga, rooskaya reka!
Nye vidal reku takuyu —

A man's commanding shout, from somewhere up ahead: '*Stoi!*'

'Whoa-up. Whoa-up there, damn creature . . .'

Slowing, stopping.

'You're in great voice tonight, *babushka.*'

'My Ivan used to say I had a *lovely* voice. God rest his fine old soul . . . What's up, what d'you want?'

The cart rocked as the guard leant his weight against it, leaning over the top to get at the sack. Bob crouching on the stinking boards, thinking of the cost to date of the Count's single-minded devotion to his loved ones — two lives already lost, and a good chance he mightn't have much of a lease left on his own.

10

Lease of life of about thirty seconds at the outside, he'd reckoned at that moment . . .

The sentry had begun wrenching at the sack, dragging it towards his side of the cart, which was tilting that way under his weight as he leant over. If the sack had rolled on to the Count, there'd have been an instant investigation into what the obstruction might be.

'Turnips?' He'd got the sack open, evidently. 'Strange time of night for buying turnips, *babushka*?'

'Didn't buy 'em. Present. He'd promised, so I thought I'd get 'em before he changed his mind. Free sack of turnips is a free sack of turnips — eh?'

'Was when I was a boy.' The sack slumped back into the middle, and the cart levelled as that weight came off it. Sound of a heavy spit . . . 'Get along to bed then, granny . . .'

It must have been about five hundred yards, Bob guessed, from the guardpost to the house — or stables. Several things in mind, meanwhile, most notable among them being the Count's trickery that had fooled two generals — three, if Bicherakov was calling himself a general now — and one commodore and of course one's own dim-witted self. Because one *had* smelt some rat: and turned a blind eye . . .

Should have raised it with the Commodore. But raised what? Without even being sure there *was* any damn rat!

Rat with green eyes . . .

Justifiable — conceivable — from his point of view?

Putting oneself in his place: and searching for a parallel . . . Suppose for instance it had been the old man — one's father — who'd been trapped here but potentially within the scope of rescue ...

Motive enough?

Maybe. One wouldn't have had either the natural duplicity to have thought of it, or the sheer nerve to have put it into action. But apart from these factors, amounting to basic differences between Nikolai Solovyev's temperament and one's own, wouldn't there have been some sense of shame in *not* doing anything that *could* be done?

It was spilt milk now, anyway. Having been lured *in*, one had to accept the fact that one was in the trap, concentrate on getting *out* of it.

The iron wheel-rims were on cobbles suddenly, the clatter deafening in this enclosed space. Taking a corner: he could feel it, and hear wheels and hooves slither on the stone, the old woman's voice calling sharply 'Hold up, stupid, hold up ...'

There'd be only two girls to take along, now. That was something. Sad — tragic — but — less downright impossible than five, surely. But the move — *some* move — had to be made *now*: the old fisherman had been dead right when he'd told Maroussia *Send 'em on their way damn quick*. Delay would be tempting fate: lying up here for one day had to involve a certain quotient of danger, extending it to two must double that quotient.

'Whoa-up. Easy — whoa-up, old dear!'

Speaking *nicely* to the animal now ... Clattering to a stop. The Count hadn't stirred and Bob took his cue from him, continued to lie still and listen, wait ... Aware of the embryonic formation of some idea — or ideas, two in conjunction — in the back of his mind, but unable to concentrate on it for the moment ...

Maroussia's voice again: 'Ah, there you are, child!'

'Just a minute ...' Female voice: young, low, rather pleasant — as much as there'd been of it. Long creak of a hinge or hinges, heavy-sounding, and the same voice again, 'Is it true, *Tyotka dorogaya*? Have you got them there?'

A grunt from the old woman. Slap of reins on the

donkey's rump. *Tyotka* meaning aunt, that would have been Nadia, Nick's fiancée who was currently posing as Maroussia's niece. The cart rolled forward: stopped again. Maroussia called, 'Shut the doors, will you ... But listen, Nadia, *golubka* ...'

'Yes?'

A passing thought that maybe they were all natural tricksters, these people ... Maroussia was telling her, 'It's not your brother I've got here. You're going to have to be brave, my darling ...'

'Who are you?'

Irina stared at him. Lamplight between them, from the oil-lamp she was holding. Another lamp — on a step there — threw a pool of light around the foot of a flight of stairs that climbed the inner wall of this high-roofed coach-house. Yellowish lamplight and moving shadows patterning its cobbled floor, the back wall stacked with bales of hay, dark at the top where no light reached. Irina had only appeared after the other girl, Nadia, had dragged the heavy timber door shut. By that time Bob had been climbing out of the cart and the Count was already out — embracing his sister and this tall, dark girl more or less simultaneously, as that one came running from the door ... 'Oh, Nikki darling ...'

'Nadia, my sweet ...'

'*Quiet!*'

Maroussia — a gnarled forefinger to her bloodless lips. The Count nodding to her apologetically, and getting the worst over quickly, telling them about Boris; Bob feeling like an intruder, trying to act blind and deaf. The Count answering his sister's question then, over Nadia's shoulder — Nadia crying quietly, tears streaming down her cheeks — 'Friend of mine — *good* friend. I'll introduce you in a minute. Irina, dearest — Maroussia told me about our mother — only three weeks ago?'

Irina blinking at him: tears in her eyes too ... 'It's been — oh God, Nikki, it's been *dreadful*, you can't *imagine* ...'

Maroussia cut in again. She'd been unharnessing her

donkey but she left it now, went over and pulled at the Count's arm: 'Nikolai Petrovich — please — we're in danger here. Take them with you into the Hole. My darlings — all of you, *please* . . .'

'Yes. Of course—'

'And even in there, keep your voices down, for God's sake . . . I'll just give this animal a drink, and turn him out. Go on, now.'

'I'll give you a hand.' Bob went over to her. 'Join you presently, Nick.'

'Very well.' The Count nodded, and Irina smiled at him. Appreciating that he was giving them a few minutes to themselves, maybe. She bore a distinct resemblance to her brother, he thought. Even to the extravagance of green eyes: not that one could be sure of it in this light. But certainly the same kind of wavy brown hair and the same nose and forehead. Actually she looked a bit like a cat: which despite the family resemblance he hadn't noticed in her brother. They were moving away, their arms around each other, towards the back of the coachhouse where the hay was stacked: Bob asked Maroussia, 'Is that where this Hole is?'

'Yes. Used to be for ice. Filled in the winter, lasted right through summer.'

'For storing food — fish and—'

'Now there's a lot of stuff from the house down there. My Ivan hauled it over — before things got really bad. Heavy chests, Lord knows what — it's what killed him — did his heart in.'

'I'm very sorry.'

'Yes . . . Look — sir — kind of you to offer, but I can do this with my eyes shut. Almost do it for himself, this rogue . . . Although — well, since you're at it — if you'd mind filling that bucket — tap's in there . . .'

Through a small door, in a lean-to — wooden-walled, doubtless an addition tagged on in comparatively recent years — there was an iron cooking-stove and a wooden tub, above which was the tap, and another door led into a lavatory. Maroussia said when he came back with the filled bucket, 'Best to whisper. See, if one of 'em was prowling . . .'

'Do they prowl?'

'Oh yes. And see, might hear a man's voice in here . . .'

'Right.' The donkey was out of its harness; he pulled the cart back out of the way, up against an old dinghy that was propped on its beam-ends against the wall — about the size of old Mesyat's boat but a wreck, with some strakes missing and the rest rotten, crumbling. Firewood. He came back to her, patted the donkey's neck: 'Does this fellow get some hay now?'

'No, he does not. Much as he'd like it. There's plenty of grass out there for him, hay's for the winter. The place is walled and fenced, see, I let him wander . . . D'you expect you'll be here long?'

'We mustn't be. Sooner we clear out, the safer for all of us — including you.'

'So be it.' In precise translation from the Russian what she'd said was *What will be*, let *it be* . . . Gazing at him out of small brown eyes, round like a monkey's. Her face was a bit like a monkey's, too. She whispered, '*How* I'm gong to miss my darlings.'

They were facing each other, one each side of the donkey's head as he finished drinking. Lifting his dripping muzzle: big, soulful eyes glowing with reflected lamplight, gazing at his mistress almost as if he'd understood what she was feeling and felt sorry for her. As Bob did — recognizing, despite the old woman's stoic self-control, her barely-concealed despair at the prospect of being left alone.

He suggested: 'You could come with us?'

'Oh, bless you, *no* . . . Thank you sir, but—'

'So when we go — taking Nadia, whom they believe to be your niece — what happens to you?'

A shrug. 'I — stay here. Live — work . . .'

'But they'll know you must have known she was going, and where and how. So you'll be in trouble.'

'I don't believe so. They know I'm not right in the head, you see. And I'll be beside myself with grief. Easy performance, that, I *will* be ... I'll be angry, too, I'll want to know what *they've* done with her, I'll make a great song and dance ... Well, I'm potty, aren't I, I'm not *responsible* ... Now if you'd open that door — just pull it back a little, don't show yourself — we'll let this old *merzavets* out, eh?'

He had the impression, in his first minute after he'd joined them in the Hole, that something had gone wrong — some constraint between them now ... The Count tight-lipped, tight-faced inside his beard, eyes hard, resentful ... Nadia seemingly tense — watching him rather like a nurse with a patient who might be in imminent danger of relapse — and Irina more catlike than ever, her eyes definitely feline ... Then he'd arrived in their pool of lamplight — having come down brick steps from a trapdoor behind the hay bales — found them sitting on some old mattresses, an oil lamp throwing shadows that moved weirdly on the curve of brick walls and roof as Nick climbed to his feet, welcoming him, and the girls, no less welcoming, moved to make room for him. Whatever had been the problem, it wasn't any of his business.

Odd time to start quarrelling, though ... He was looking around, having to stoop under the low, arched roof. 'Must have taken a hell of a lot of ice, to fill this.'

'Dates from the Stukalins' time. I told you, remember?' Pointing into the dark behind him, the stack of furniture and packing-cases. 'Maroussia's husband moved all this stuff over, Irina's been telling me, soon after the start of the revolution, when the house was still a hospital. It was stored in rooms they weren't using. They should have got out while they could — but I suppose they had nowhere to go — and some couldn't anyway. And he was pretty frail himself by that time, Maroussia thinks it's what finished him.'

'She told me.' Bob nodded. 'And presumably they — Cheka and others — don't know there *is* a cellar here.'

'Thank God ... What's Maroussia doing now, d'you know?'

'She was going to make us some tea. But did she say about Czech prisoners in the house?'

Irina told him, 'In cells that were our old storerooms.' Glancing at her brother. 'Our *house*, Nikki, for God's sake. The cellar — the wine cellar — that's where the Cheka —' she crossed herself, shutting her eyes — 'Nikki, you can't *imagine* ...'

'The wine cellar —' Nadia said quietly — 'is where they conduct their interrogations.'

'You mean —' the Count was staring at her — 'torture?'

'Possibly.' She shrugged. 'Or — probably ...' Reacting to his stare, then, she flared suddenly: 'Not in my *presence*, if that's what's in your—'

'Please ...'

She'd glanced at Bob. Back at her fiancé now. 'I'm not in their confidence, Nikki. I do the work I'm given, but I'm no *part* of their damned—'

'But you're on good terms with this fellow?'

'I don't spit at him when I see him — I'm not stupid, or suicidal. And what's more, Irina's and Maroussia's safe existence here — your mother's, for that matter, while she lived ...'

'Yes — yes, I — I dare say ...' Staring at her: as if she'd shocked him ... Then he turned back to Bob. 'This cellar — Grigor Stukalin built it. It's said — I'd forgotten — they used it as a hiding-place even in those days. Now history repeats itself. Amazing ...'

Irina leaned across, put a hand on his arm: 'Remember the games we used to play — when Vlad would be Pugachov, and you and I—'

'Yes. Yes ...'

Bob broke a silence: 'The Czechs they've got locked up over there must be from the Czech Legion, I suppose.'

'Yes.' Nadia told him, 'They were trying to get away through the Bolshevik lines, but some Kirghizi caught them—'

'And handed them over —' the Count cut in — 'to your Cheka friends, huh?'

Bob looked from her to her fiancé ... 'Hardly *friends*, surely?'

'I work for them. For the head one, a man named

Viktor Lesechko. For the sole reason, Nikki, that I had no option. I have my own little room to work in, and I work for him only.'

Irina murmured, 'Nights too, sometimes.'

Nadia's eyes flashed at her: 'When *they* work at night — damn you, Irina—'

'Please.' The Count interrupted ... 'Bob doesn't want to hear this — squabbling ... Especially as we've enough *important* things to talk about. Although — well, really, it might be more sensible to get some sleep and talk in the morning.' He looked at Nadia. 'But I suppose you'll be —' he moved his head — 'with *them* all day.'

'You suppose wrongly, Nikolai Petrovich. Tomorrow's Sunday, and even with *them*, strangely enough, Sunday's still a day of rest.'

'Well, that's — convenient. And we can sleep late. All right, then ...' He nodded: leaving that subject, but with a glance at Nadia which suggested she hadn't heard the last of it ... 'Bob, may I introduce you properly, tell them who you are?'

'I don't know why you shouldn't.'

'Only that if things went wrong — if you or any of us were caught—'

'I'd tell them anyway. Long before they got me into their cellar.'

Nobody else smiled. If it had been a joke at all, it hadn't been in good taste.

'So — all right. With your permission, Bob ...' The Count said, rather formally, 'I'd like to present to you Lieutenant Robert Cowan, of His Britannic Majesty's Royal Navy.'

'Royal Naval Reserve, to be exact.'

He shrugged, and told his sister, 'What matters is that it's entirely through his help that I've been able to get here.'

Irina had clapped her hands. 'British navy — *here*! And speaking such good Russian! Lieutenant, we're honoured — as well as *extremely* grateful—'

'Lieutenant ...'

He turned to Nadia. 'Princess?'

'Having brought Nikki to us, are you now going to take us away with you?'

Reclining on the mattress: long-bodied and long-legged, attractive in an unobvious sort of way. Wide-spaced grey eyes, straight nose, and a full, appealing mouth. Dark, very soft-looking hair. He'd noticed earlier that even in heel-less slippers she was within about an inch of his own height. He told her — leaving her question unanswered for the moment — 'Believe it or not, I never met a princess before.'

The Count said rather brusquely, 'Although you lived in Petrograd — which used to be fairly littered with them?'

'I left when I was twelve, Nick. Maybe I played with a child princess or two, but—'

'Anyway — don't blame *me.*' Nadia shrugged. 'My father was a prince, that's all. For which crime incidentally he and my mother were literally torn to pieces.' She glanced at the Count. 'And you're mad enough to imagine I could — what, *like* one of them?' Staring at each other: then he'd looked away, and she asked him, 'How come the Royal Navy brought you, anyway?'

'That's — a long story . . .'

Bob cut in — to help him out, as much as anything — 'Part of the answer — to your other question as well, Princess, is that the boat we came in hit a mine. Nick saved my life — literally, I was in the water, unconscious and drowning, and he found me, pulled me out and pumped me dry. The unfortunate thing is that the same boat would have come back to pick you up — when Nick got you down to the coast, you see. But as the boat is now matchwood, and my own people don't even know any of us survived — and we've no way of contacting them — well, we have a problem.'

'But — you'll find a way round it, will you?'

'With a bit of help — yes. Got to, haven't we.' He looked at the Count. 'On that rather important subject, Nick, I've had what might be the beginnings of an idea. Depending on the outcome of some reconnaissance I need to do. Although there's one question Maroussia might answer, for a start.'

'D'you want to discuss it tonight?'

'I'd like to, yes. Amongst other things.' He looked for a reaction to that, and got it — almost a flinch ... He added, 'But of course, if the rest of you are tired ...'

'I'm not.' Nadia asked Irina, 'Are you?'

'No — oddly enough. Too excited, I suppose ... Oh — speak of the old devil ...'

Maroussia — coming slowly down the steps with a tray. Glasses of black tea, and—'

'Maroussia!' Nadia was kneeling, peering ... 'Is that a *cake*?'

'It is, my dears, it is. Little celebration. Surprise, eh?'

'Steamer, you say.'

'It's the word Leonid Mesyats used, yes. He said the Bolsheviks who came up from Astrakhan and murdered the officers in your house came in a — I think he said a "little steamer". And that it had been a rich man's toy before that, but had now been appropriated by the Cheka.'

'Well, there's a boat there, certainly, and the people I work for do make use of it, but I think it's the army's, really.'

'What matters is —' Bob explained — 'well, the first question — is it in fact a steamboat? That could have been just a word used loosely — he might call a petrol-engined cruiser a "steamer" — being strictly a rowing-boat man himself, you see.'

'How would one know the difference?'

'Well — it'd have a funnel, for instance. Like all the bigger ships.'

Maroussia shook her head. 'I know rowboats and sail-boats — and the other kind — but not them, sir.'

Nadia said, 'But if this man's a fisherman — surely he'd know?'

'Yes.' The Count nodded. 'Let's assume it's a steam-boat, Bob.'

'I'm afraid we have to.' He shrugged. 'Much rather not, actually ... anyway it leads to a second question — which Nadia *might* be able to answer. Not that I expect you will, Nadia. But — if you ever heard them talking about any river trip they were about to make, you might just possibly have a clue to it — whether they keep steam up or not?'

'I don't know what you mean. But anyway ...'

'You see — a steam engine needs a fire — furnace — coal-burning or wood-burning or even oil, if the rich owner converted it. Then to put power on the engine you need steam pressure; so the fire has to be lit and the boiler heated so as to convert water into steam. Otherwise, if the fire's out, everything's cold, dead, there's no possibility of just jumping aboard and pushing off — d'you see the point? To be any use to us, we'd need to be able to just — go ... Huh?'

'I take the point — but I work in my own little cell of an office, they don't discuss any plans or — well, *anything*, in my hearing.'

'So if they were going somewhere and had to give advance notice to the boat's crew, you wouldn't know it.'

'I wouldn't even be told anyone was going anywhere.'

'No. Right.' He turned to the Count. 'Only way to find out is to have a look. I'll have to sneak down there, in the dark.'

'But I'll go with you — naturally. Since I know my way around and you don't.'

'All right. Tomorrow night. We need to be on top form — it'd be silly to try it now.'

'Oh Lord, yes ...'

'So — we lie up all through tomorrow — or rather today, now — work out some plans and alternatives, perhaps — check the steamboat after dark — Sunday night, this'll be, it's Sunday now. And we start out from here, one way or another, on Monday night.'

'But if the steamboat's no good to us —'

'We've all tomorrow to work something else out.'

Irina asked him, 'Are you so confident?'

He shrugged. 'We can't stay here. One thing we know is we have a rowing-boat hidden down in the delta. At a pinch we might use that. As for getting to it — well, I do have some bits of ideas. Including the famous steamboat ... Incidentally — is that the only boat here? I mean apart from rowing-boats?'

'Other boats come sometimes. Come and go.' Nadia pointed southward with her head. 'Between here and Astrakhan — military headquarters here, naval command's down at the port, there's quite a bit of coming and going at times.'

'But no other craft — powered craft — actually kept here.'

'I don't think so.'

'So what's the idea, Bob?' The Count shifted from one elbow to the other. 'Jump on board and steam down the river, right through and out to sea?'

Bob looked at him, shook his head. 'Life isn't as simple as it was in Pugachov's day, Nick.'

'So what, then?'

'Down-river is Astrakhan town and port — a military garrison and quite a strong naval force. All right, they're Bolsheviks, but they can't all be asleep or drunk *all* the time. Besides, to the people here it would look like the obvious thing to do — since we're on the river — it's what they'd expect. And remember, Nadia will be missed — when she doesn't report for work they'll want to know where the hell she is.'

'So we must start out early in the night — right after dark ...'

'Of course.'

'And you need a boat, you say not down-river, so — we'd be going *up*-river?'

He'd smiled as if he thought he was suggesting something ridiculous; Irina echoed him — 'Up-river!' — and giggled. Bob ignored her, told her brother, 'That's why I want something better than a rowing-boat. If we were going south, anything would do — a raft even, you could drift down. But against the stream, with four people in a small boat — well, you saw how old Mesyats had to put his back into it?'

'Where would we be going?'

'Where we met Mesyats. The fishing-station. Where transport is still standing idle and unguarded — touch wood.'

'Oh — that lorry ...'

He nodded. 'The driver said they only get petrol for the fishing season, but there was a half-full drum at the back of the barn. I know he said he had a colleague who operates illegally, so it's conceivable we might get there and find it's gone. But that wouldn't be the end of the world, anyway — the railway's within walking distance, and if these girls have papers ...'

Nadia assured him, 'We do.'

'As it happens, I don't. So — we could walk, if we had to. Three or four nights — or five or six — walking all night and hiding in daylight. Nick could get food for us — he has papers and money.'

'How many versts of walking?'

'Don't ask, Irina. We'd just start walking, and say "Thank God" when we got there. With any luck we'll have motor transport and make the whole trip in one night. I'm only pointing out that we *would* have options.'

'Except for getting up-river as you said we'll have to.' Nadia's grey eyes held him. A calm, reasoning but somehow detachedly interested look: *warmly dispassionate* might have described it ... 'That is, if the steam-boat isn't usable.'

He agreed. 'There's some thinking to do. Dream up some alternatives — when the brain's a bit fresher than it is now — and make decisions after we've inspected the boat tomorrow.'

'Well. This may be a silly question. But — suppose it does need to have its furnace lit —' she was putting this to Bob as if the two of them were alone, hadn't glanced at either of the others — 'might it be feasible for you, or for you and Nikki together, to make a start on that soon after sunset, say, so that we could get away — I don't know, however much later it would have to be?'

'Yes. In theory. But I'd guess they'd have a guard or

guards on or near the boat. A crewman or two on board, and/or a sentry on the landing-stage. Any idea, Maroussia?'

The old woman came to: as if emerging from a day-dream ... 'I think — soldiers, on the river bank. Yes.'

'Might make it a bit awkward.' Still with his eyes on Nadia's, thinking about it but also aware of her. Glancing away, then — instinct suggesting it might be better if he did — at the Count ... 'Might be something in it, Nick. When we go down there tomorrow night: supposing it isn't guarded — or if there's just one man on board ... Two, even. If we could — well, deal with them ...'

Irina, sharply: 'D'you mean kill them?'

'Well. Probably ...' Addressing the Count again: 'Armed sentries on the bank might be something else. But in theory — if we *could* take control of the boat, flash-up the fire and all—'

'You could do that, could you?'

'Yes. And you'd come back here, Nick, bring the girls down, say, two hours later, by which time I'd have steam up.'

'What about the noise when you start up?'

'I'd let her drift out into the stream — some way down-stream, might even anchor for a while. There'd be some noise anyway — part of the risk, that's all. But if they're sloppy enough for this to be on the cards at all, it's quite likely the rest of them would sleep through it.'

'We'd have to steam up past the house, you realize.' The Count pondered this. 'River's easily visible from the house, of course, but the willows are all in leaf; in places the view would be quite well obstructed. And you could pass at some distance, well out into the river. Besides which, there must be some other night traffic ... Maroussia?'

'Yes. Yes, Nikolai Petrovich, I think there is.' She added vaguely, 'Sometimes ...'

'So it's — possible, Bob. We might get away tomorrow night.'

Irina purred, '*Isn't* Nadia clever?'

'Yes.' Bob looked at her again. 'She is. It might not work out, but it's certainly a chance.'

'Are you an engineer?'

'God, no. Just a plain sailor.'

'But all the business with the engine . . .'

'It's not very complicated. Mind you, Nick — as long as there's fuel on board — that's yet another full-sized *if* . . .'

'We met such a nice naval engineer on our way here from Petrograd.' Irina began telling her brother this. 'A man called Dherjakin. Quite old, middle forties or thereabouts, and — believe it or not — with only one leg. He'd been a captain, engineer captain in command of some dockyard in the north at one time, then in Petrograd where they'd arrested him, and he'd have been shot or something if he hadn't agreed to work for them. As he put it, how can a man with one leg run away? Anyway, he was *most* charming. We got into conversation with him on the train — all of us very cautious to start with, but then — we got on so naturally, you know, and — I think Mama really quite fell for him. He realized how things were with us, of course, he must have: and — *listen* to this, Nikki — he definitely saved our lives at one stage. Red Guards boarded the train, they weren't believing anything anyone said, even people with papers were being dragged off and—'

Maroussia whispered — trying not to interrupt the story — 'I'm off to my bed. All of you sleep well . . .'

'Maroussia.' The Count struggled to his feet. 'We've kept you up. I'm so sorry . . .'

'Happiest night for years.' Smiling, blinking her little round eyes at him in the lamplight; she was standing at her full height, the Count and Bob both stooped under the curve of the brick ceiling . . . 'Anyway, happiest night since these little ones arrived. And that was spoilt, with my darling Maria Ivanovna so ill . . .'

Bob said, 'Perhaps we should take Maroussia with us.'

'Oh *yes*!' Nadia was kneeling: Maroussia had just referred to her as a 'little one', but on her knees she was about the same height as the old woman was on her feet.

'Maroussia, *dorogaya*—'

'I shan't be going anywhere.' Smiling at Nadia. 'Bless you, but—'

'We might think about it again in the morning.' The Count put an arm round her shoulders. 'Might persuade you. I'm sorry we've kept you from your bed. And thank you — there's no adequate way I could ever repay all that you've—'

'Go on with you.' She patted his arm. Smiled at Bob. They were at the steps; she'd left another lamp at the top. 'Goodnight, all of you.'

They went back to the girls. Bob saying — to Irina — 'So you came on a train with a one-legged naval engineer. We came by truck with a one-handed driver.'

'It was very lucky for us that we did meet him.' Nadia confirmed Irina's story. 'It's a fact, we mightn't have got much further.'

'We *wouldn't* have.' Irina took over again. 'But he produced his own papers and official documents — he'd been given some very important job, and consequently this terrific sort of authority — little man with a wooden leg, for heaven's sake! He told them we were travelling with him, he took full responsibility for us — and in any case this comrade was ill, didn't they have eyes in their heads, etcetera ... I remember he said to them "Persecute the enemies of the revolution, not its friends!"'

The Count glanced at Bob. 'Sounds like the gospel according to Anton Vetrov and his accomplice Robat Khan.'

'Does, doesn't it.'

Nadia said, 'But isn't it extraordinary — a chance meeting like that, probably the difference between us all being alive or dead?'

'Actually — 'the Count was looking at Irina — 'it's dreadful. To inflict such terror ... And that we should become *used* to such — moral obscenity ...' He asked her, 'How did you finally get here — actually here to Maroussia, I mean? She couldn't have known you were coming?'

'Boris went ahead of us. We'd changed to the branch

line at Vladiminovka, and crossed from there on the ferry, then had the luck to get a lift in a farm-wagon. Not to Enotayevsk, Mama thought it would be too risky, someone that close to home would surely recognize her, or me. So we stopped at Fedorovka ...'

The place-name rang a bell in Bob's mind, which had begun to drift: he hadn't been far off dozing ... Fedorovka was the riverside village they'd been passing in old Mesyats' boat when the sun had been setting blood-red behind it and Mesyats had told them about the butchering of the wounded officers. Until this moment he'd forgotten its name — which Mesyats had mentioned — but he'd thought of it earlier in connection with possible escape routes.

The steamboat would be the answer, though. Gift from the gods — if one could work the trick ... Up past that place — Fedorovka — and switching channels where Mesyats had, taking that same route in reverse. Then at the fishing-station you'd turn the steamboat adrift, pray for the current to take it well downstream before it beached itself somewhere — and they'd never know where you'd landed. Maybe they'd work it out later, after the truck was reported stolen, but by that time you'd be — heaven knew where. But out of their reach, please God.

Irina's voice: 'Remember our rabbit-burrow, Nikki?'

The Count staring at her: frowning slightly. His bearded face dark on this side, away from the oil-lamp on his left. A hand up, fingers snapping: '*That* burrow. Not still there, surely?'

'How d'you think the boy got in here tonight, to tell us you were at the Swede's?'

'Now that's one I *didn't* think of. Should have, I suppose.' He looked round at Bob. 'There used to be — still is, apparently — a hole under the perimeter wall, back there.' A gesture, northward. Asking his sister, 'Did we make it, or—'

'Village boys did. Kids who'd be grown up now — or dead. I remember you and Vlad setting a sort of snare in it once. It didn't work, but—'

'Anyway, Boris found it, got in through it and came knocking on Maroussia's door here?'

'He got to her, anyway, and she came and fetched us in her donkey-cart. Same as she fetched you — same filthy old tarpaulin, with firewood on top of it ...'

'All the way to Fedorovka and back. Poor old donkey ... But my God, isn't Maroussia magnificent?'

'Oh.' Nadia hugging her knees, gently rocking, 'She's a saint.'

Someone was a saint. Bob nodded drowsily. Liking Nadia, happy to agree with her although he didn't know what they were on about, by this time. Half awake again now though — in spasms — and thinking about the plan for the following night — the steamboat. Tonight, not tomorrow night — today had now become tomorrow.

Sentries on the river bank, Maroussia had said. But only vaguely, she hadn't been sure. Crewmen in the boat was more than likely, they'd surely have at any rate one man sleeping on board. A mental echo of Irina's sharply-voiced question came on the heels of that conclusion: *D'you mean kill them?*

No shooting. One shot and you'd be finished. Leave the pistol here — then there'd be no such temptation. Persuade Nick to leave his Browning behind too. Knives would be the things. He thought, *When the devil drives* ... Hearing — distantly, as in the beginnings of a dream — the Count asking Irina to explain why they'd decided to come here to Enotayevsk instead of going to the Crimea as their mother had intended. She began, 'Because we were told — Boris was told — by the people from whom he was getting Mama's new papers — that it would be hopeless to try to get down there from Petrograd, people were being pulled off trains and shot almost without question. So if we came here first, we thought — as this part was supposed to be in White hands, until—' She broke off as Nadia interrupted in a whisper, reaching to touch her fiancé's knee, 'Your friend's asleep.'

11

Ready to go – except for the light out there. The sun had gone down but the moon wasn't going to set for another hour yet. At this time of year and latitude it was rising only a few minutes later each morning but setting later by more like half an hour.

It had been a day of rest, talk, preparation. With an element of wishful thinking. You had to be ready to leave this place tonight – which meant assuming that the steamboat would be there and usable and not too effectively guarded. It would be marvellous if it turned out like this, but . . .

But . . .

Waiting in the Hole now. They'd had supper up in the kitchen and spent several hours there off and on, but it was a pointless risk, really. If soldiers or Cheka came to the coachhouse door you'd have to pass through there to get to the trapdoor, and if the visitors were in a hurry – suspected there might be intruders, for instance – and forced that door . . .

And the women had been living like this for *months.*

He knew them a lot better now. He and the Count, too, probably understood each other better than they had before. He'd told him this morning, down in this Hole before breakfast – getting it over quickly because it did have to be stated and clear between them – that he had no doubt whatsoever that the story about the Tsar's daughters had been a lie invented solely for Nikolai Solovyev's own purposes.

'Bob – I think you should be careful what you say. The message I received—'

'No, Nick. Don't bother — please . . . Look, if you want to have this argument in public, up there with the others, I don't mind. But otherwise let's just have it understood between us, then forget it until we get back. Then, you'll have to answer for it — that's what I'm telling you. I might also tell you that personally I don't blame you all that much: I'm not sure that in your shoes I wouldn't have been inclined to do something like it. And I *am* sorry about your mother, Nick. But this has cost two lives already, and a ship, and — well, that's it, when we get back I'll be telling the truth as I see it . . . All right?'

He'd sulked for a while, pretending resentment at being called a liar, but seemed to have snapped out of it now. Might well have decided how he'd bluff his way through, when — or if — the time came.

As for the others: Irina was — well, complicated. But in some ways understandably so. And Maroussia was fantastic — shrewd as anything, apparently fearless and utterly dependable in her loyalty to — or love for — the Solovyevs. While Nadia — Nadia, he thought, was — well, something else again.

He was wearing a knife on his belt in a leather sheath which she'd cobbled together for him this morning. Maroussia's knife, actually, out of a kitchen drawer. He had his Admiralty-issue seaman's knife, but it was a heavy thing with a short folding blade — designed for cutting ropes not throats. There was a marlin-spike on it as well, but as a weapon it wouldn't have been much good. This kitchen knife, one of several that she'd offered, had a sharp, tough blade just under five inches long and a wooden haft that fitted his hand well; but the only way to carry it would be in a sheath, which Nadia had now made for him out of an old leather slipper.

The Count and Irina had been down in the Hole, raising a lot of dust while inspecting the family treasures which Maroussia's late husband Ivan had stored in there for them. Irina doubtless taking the chance of an intimate family conversation, too — if Bob's estimate of her was anything like accurate.

Sliding the knife into the sheath ... 'It's perfect, Nadia. Thank you very much.'

'Your belt will go through those slots.'

'Right.' He'd put it down and taken his belt off. 'No time like the present ...'

'Are you expecting to have to kill people — really?'

Maroussia had half-turned from the stove to hear his answer. She'd been stirring two pots of soup — one large and one smaller, contents of both mainly turnip — which they and also the Czech prisoners in the cells would be having for supper. Further rations — dried fish and cheese — were to be available either on their return from the reconnaissance, or if they were leaving tonight, to be taken along for consumption *en route.* The point being that if they were leaving tonight, Bob wouldn't be returning from the reconnaissance, he'd be staying down there to get steam up in the boat. Nick would be coming back to the coachhouse, but he wouldn't.

He'd answered Nadia's question. 'We're not setting out with that purpose. But if there's opposition — can't very well take prisoners, can we?'

'I suppose not. But are you so confident that it's you and Nick who'll do the killing — if there is any?'

He'd nodded. 'We have the advantage of what's called the element of surprise. We know we're coming, and they don't.'

'Yes. I see.' That same interested but oddly impersonal look, which he'd noticed last night.

And just as well — in all the circumstances.

'*Very* kind of you, Nadia.' Threading his belt through the slots she'd cut in the leather, then buckling it on again and slipping the knife back into the sheath. His Service revolver in its webbing holster lay on the table amongst pots and pans and cooking tools; he'd asked Nadia or Maroussia — either — 'Is there somewhere safe I can hide this pistol?'

'Aren't you taking it?'

'I'd say not! Might as well send up rockets ... Nick has a pistol, incidentally, he'd be wise to leave that behind too.'

'All right. I'll remind him, if you don't.' She picked up the revolver. 'Heavy ... Is it loaded?'

'No, I took the shells out. Here ...'

'You'll want it with you when we leave, I suppose?'

'Yes, definitely ... Could you bring it — or make sure Nick does?'

'Of course.'

'You're a very practical sort of person, aren't you?' Studying her: half-smiling, intrigued by her. Aware meanwhile of Maroussia's short, stocky figure just beyond her, at the stove, as motionless as if rooted there. A very intelligent and observant old woman, he reminded himself: and resourceful — as was this tall, dark girl, who was in her own way rather elegant, even in old, patched and in places threadbare clothes ... The grey eyes holding his: he'd wondered whether she might have been seeing him as he saw her — observing *his* detachment, a similarly friendly but distant interest, from precisely that same distance ... Distance, like beauty, being in the beholder's eye? Reduced by wishful thinking, increased by oversensitivity?

But like a sheet of thick glass between them. You could smash it — but you'd do so at your peril. The fact being that she was engaged to Nick, who seemed prone to jealousy to a fairly bizarre degree: and with that other bone of contention — in temporary abeyance but still there between them — and the fact you were going to have to work together, as likely as not *fight* together ...

Remembering those strained minutes last night: Nadia's contemptuous 'And you're mad enough to imagine I might — what, *like* one of them?'

Because she worked for the Cheka boss, and the work — as Irina had pointed out — sometimes extended into the late evenings. Crazy ... And — Bob guessed — he'd have to be aware of it, simply not able to help himself. With — a guess, this, Bob's own theory based on one or two small clues — Irina making the worst of it, preying on that weakness. The main clue being that little dig she hadn't been able to resist: *Nights too, sometimes* ... To which Nadia had reacted angrily but — clue number two — without surprise. Then there was the recollection of the Count having told him that he'd made his long and dangerous trip to Petrograd to see these girls and ensure that when his mother arrived to collect Irina they'd take Nadia along as well. The implication being that this wouldn't otherwise have been guaranteed, that Irina might have left with Mama, leaving her close friend and her brother's fiancée to the wolves.

One had also to remember that more recently the possessive sister had been cooped up for months on end, mostly underground and with a dying mother, while Nadia had been free to come and go. Not that 'free' would be the most apposite word for it.

'You only work for the head man, you said. In a small room all by yourself?'

'At the back of the house.' She nodded. 'Must have been a butler's pantry once.'

'And you only see this head man.'

'Normally, yes. He brings me the work, gives me any instructions there are to give, and comes to fetch it later. He's — all right. To me, anyway. The other two — Khitrov and Orudzhev — Khitrov's *loathsome.* A thug — that's a nice word for him. One time, he nearly ...'

She'd shaken her head.

'Nearly what?'

'It doesn't matter. Lesechko happened to arrive back at just that moment.'

'And — Lesechko himself ...'

'No.' Her dark hair swirled again. 'I don't believe he has any — ambitions of that sort. He's — I suppose the word's pragmatic. He needs my secretarial services — so I'm safe — as long as he does need them.'

Maroussia had clattered heavy lids on to the pots and turned away from the stove. 'I'll be upstairs, a minute or two.' Pausing, looking hard at Bob: 'Hear anyone at the door — down below quick as rabbits, eh?'

'I'd better go down anyway.'

A nod: as if she'd been thinking exactly that. Female

antennae quivering, no doubt ... She'd left them. He murmured, hearing her clumping up the stairs, 'Irina is rather possessive of her brother — am I right?'

She rolled her eyes: '*Rather* is an understatement.'

'Had a rough time, though. Stuck inside here — and her mother dying?'

'That's true. She's had a *dreadful* time ... You know the saying, no light at the end of the tunnel — there hasn't been even a glimmer. Except that after my brother Boris had left with the message, there was just the faint hope — hope, and faith — for as long as *those* sources of resilience can last in a hole like this one, and they were getting weaker all the time — you can imagine ... But for that same reason we couldn't leave — even if there'd been any way to leave or anywhere to go that could be any safer than we've been here. We've even wondered how long this could last — suppose we're still here when Maroussia dies? Imagine! And then last night — so *suddenly* — after so long with no hope at all ...'

'Bad enough for you, but in some way worse for Irina?'

'Yes.' A nod. 'Yes ... but — they're a little crazy, you know.' Her whisper was only just audible. 'I'd never realized, before.'

'But you're going to marry him?'

'*He* believes so. All I've ever promised is I won't marry anyone else until all these horrors are over.' She'd shrugged. 'In any case, what's going to happen to any of us — in five minutes even, let alone by tomorrow morning—'

'What's going to happen, Nadia, is we're going to get you out of here. But even if Nick's having his problems at the moment, you know, there's a lot to be said for him. For instance he's *here* — he's come for you — believe me, it took some doing. And he's had a hell of a war, one way or another. Even before the revolution, let alone this last year — well, that long march south, Alekseev's—'

'I'm sure of his — affection, and I've no doubt he's a fine soldier and a brave man, but—'

'Oh, *here* you are ...'

Irina, in the doorway. In her home-made felt slippers she'd come up from the Hole and across the coachhouse to this door as soundlessly as a ghost. Nadia rising to the occasion with considerable presence of mind, telling Bob — in the same low tone of voice and with only a glance towards Irina, as if not wanting to be interrupted in what she'd been telling him, 'It's not a Cheka headquarters as such, it's a military section, you see, with the function of maintaining close surveillance of all army units, especially of commanders and staffs. They have individuals and teams in the field, and these three here — the man I work for and his two assistants — administer the system, collect the reports and collate and analyse them, send weekly summaries to Moscow, and much the same the other way about — receiving and passing out Moscow's orders and pronouncements, and so forth. So yes, there's a *lot* of clerical work, and that's what they need me for. Whatever else they get up to — these Czechs Maroussia says they've got now, for instance — I don't get told and frankly I'd sooner not know. Ask Maroussia, if you're interested, she sees them twice a day.'

She'd looked up at Irina, finally. 'Hello, there. How are the Solovyev heirlooms? Gathering dust and cobwebs?'

Still waiting for the damn moon ... Remembering that he'd asked her later, when the others had been with them and they'd been planning tonight's excursion, what she knew about patrols or sentries around the house and grounds ... 'When you come and go between here and the house, for instance, d'you see any?'

'I never go near the front of the house. I use the back door, and the room I work in is at the back. There's always a sentry on that door, certainly ... The only ones I've seen on the move have been — I've assumed — going to or coming from the south gate.'

The Count had explained: 'The gate Maroussia *didn't* bring us in by.' Asking Maroussia then, 'Sentries at the front of the house — d'you know?'

'Oh.' She'd seemed to shiver ... 'Yes. Sentries there.

Two, I think. But I come and go by the back door — same as this one . . .'

This talk had been in the Hole — late forenoon, before a lunchtime snack of black bread and goat's cheese. Bob had asked Maroussia, 'Are there guards on the cells where the prisoners are?'

'Inside, in the cellar. One man always, sometimes two.'

'Cheka?'

'No. Soldiers, under the Cheka's orders. Oh, the Cheka swine show their faces sometimes. But not on the guard duty.'

'How about in the grounds — woods, the meadows, everywhere. When you go to get your donkey in, for instance, d'you see any?'

'Sometimes. I couldn't say where, or what times. But yes, sometimes.'

'They live in the house, do they?'

'The Cheka?' Her monkey eyes had shifted to Nadia for a moment . . . 'Yes. Soldiers too. They lie about on the floors, like pigs.'

'Perhaps because all the furniture's in this Hole?'

Irina had laughed; but the Count took the comment seriously. 'Not by any means all of it. Ivan only carried down what he thought were the best pieces.' He asked Maroussia, 'Must be quite a lot still in the house?'

'Not much that isn't smashed up. And what they've left intact is filthy from their boots and cigarettes and God knows what else.' The little eyes rolled upwards: 'My little flat's luxurious compared to the state of your house now, Nikolai Petrovich.'

Then over lunch — at the kitchen table — they'd had the story of the Dowager Countess Solovyeva and her one and only visit from a doctor. It had started from his asking Maroussia, 'Have the Bolsheviks *ever* been in here?'

'Only when these two and Maria Ivanovna were first here. Then, they came.'

'Cheka?'

'Lesechko — the head man, the one Nadia works for —

and a Red Army person with him. They went away after only a few minutes, and the next day Lesechko came back with the doctor.'

Irina murmured, 'The only time she saw *any* doctor.'

'They didn't see you, though, Irina?'

'No. I stayed in the Hole.' Solovyevski-green eyes flickered towards Nadia. 'I *lived* in it. Well — still do ... But they'd already seen Nadia, you see, she'd taken Mama outside for a breath of air, and — it was just bad luck. They'd gone out there at Mama's pleading, that's the truth ... Anyway, there'd have been no point in Nadia hiding, after that, and we *wanted* a doctor for Mama, so — Maroussia had this idea of saying Nadia was her daughter.'

'What about identification?'

Nadia had explained: 'I showed my papers. In the name of Nadia Schegorova — papers Boris had got for me in Petrograd. Maria Ivanovna was never asked for hers, it was enough that Maroussia told them she was her sister — nobody disbelieves Maroussia, you see, that honest face?'

Maroussia had shrugged. 'I'm the loony, see.'

'But also the doctor informed them that she hadn't long to live, so—'

'The doctor —' Irina had cut in, telling Bob — as she'd already described it to her brother, evidently, in one of the long private talks they'd had — 'this doctor knew us. Knew Mama, would have known me if he'd seen me, and knew full well that Nadia was *not* Mama's daughter. And of course that Mama wasn't Maroussia's sister either. Quite a young man, apparently; his name's Martynov. Face like a full moon, they said — round and white. May not have been quite so white before he saw Mama, of course.'

'He didn't say anything — obviously ... But was this Cheka person present?'

'Well, not when he was examining her!'

Nadia put in: 'He and I and Maroussia were here, in this kitchen. Maria Ivanovna was in Maroussia's bed upstairs. And this was when he suggested I should work for them — he'd checked my papers, and I'd told him I'd been doing secretarial work—'

'The doctor —' Irina again — 'Mama told us when they'd gone that he'd burst into floods of tears. He hadn't been our regular doctor or known us very long — he'd been called in once or twice for minor family emergencies — children's ailments, she said ... But he wept, all the time he was examining her the tears were running down his moon face and dripping on to her, she was getting so wet that it made her laugh — she made a funny story out of it, this little doctor crying and his patient giggling ...'

'So ...'

'He told her, 'Madame, I have to tell you the truth, which is that you're going to die. There's nothing I can do to save you, all I can offer is to leave you to die in peace. If it could be called peace ... That's to say, I must warn you that you'll be in pain. As you are already, I know, but — worse, worse than you've ever known. I'll give the young lady who calls herself your daughter some pills which you shouldn't take until it's too bad to stand without — well, *some* degree of alleviation ... But you know, Madame, I couldn't have you admitted to hospital here. Even if they could do anything to save you at this late stage: and believe me, they could not. While you'd be in a — well, a different kind of danger ...'

The Count had murmured, 'I can't say I remember him.'

'Nor did I.' Irina, shrugging. 'Neither the name nor the description. I suppose we were too little — he must have been only just qualified, if he's so young still ... But Mama told him she'd tell them she didn't want to see him or any other doctor again, that she only wanted to be left to die — as he'd said — in peace. This was as much as anything to save *him* from any further involvement, you see — in a way, returning the favour ... But — imagine it, that moment of mutual recognition, and with this Lesechko creature only yards away ...'

Getting near the time to start, now. Maroussia had gone out to see how the moon was doing. One would know which way to go — more or less — because when they'd finished lunch Nick had drawn a map — of sorts . . .

Nadia had teased him: turning it upside down, pretending she couldn't make sense of it. 'A map of *what*, is this?'

'You don't appreciate great art when you see it. Look here. Here — Bob . . .' He'd used the bottom of a cardboard box as his canvas. 'See here, now. River. Meadows. House. Two protruding wings on the river frontage — the house faces just about due south. Pillars along the carriage entrance here: then this is terrace, with a big half-circle of balustrade: the meadow, and the willows along the riverbank there. This isn't to an exact scale, of course . . . Here at the back of the house, now, this extension contains the storerooms which we're told have been made into cells.' He'd glanced at Maroussia. 'How many Czechs have they got in there?'

'Two. One's an officer and one's a sergeant. The officer looks like an orang-outan.'

'When did you ever see an orang-outan, Maroussia?'

She told Irina, pointing at the Count, 'Saw a picture — Nikolai Petrovich showed me, in a book he had, pictures of different animals.'

'What a memory . . .' He was smiling at her. 'But — as a matter of interest — are there any other prisoners besides the Czechs?'

'Not unless they're being starved.'

'Right . . . Now, Bob, the storerooms are reached through the upper part of the wine-cellar — this corner of the house, with the old kitchens and so on along the back here. But there's no door from the outside so there'll be no sentries in our view from here. This is where we are now — this rectangle is the coachhouse, with the stables along here. Between here and that corner — the storerooms — is about ninety metres. Gives you an idea of the distances — I'll admit this is *not* to scale . . . But now the drive — sweeps round the front of the house, comes also to the north-east corner here — tradesmen's entrance, used to be — and then on its way to the south entrance — where

Nadia's seen soldiers coming or going — it divides here, to pass on both sides of the coachhouse and stables. Behind us here, with beechwoods then all the way between it and the road — that's where the burrow under the wall used to be. Here, roughly, the road's along this edge, I haven't room to show it . . .'

'Why not concentrate on how we get to our steamboat?'

'All right . . . As I said — coachhouse here. Joined to the stables this side of us — under Maroussia's flat, right? Used mostly for firewood and stuff, Maroussia?'

'The first stable here is Don Juan's — in winter . . .'

Bob laughed. 'That the donkey's name?'

'With good reason.' The Count nodded solemnly. 'In his younger days, before he was castrated . . .'

Irina protested, 'Please, Nikki . . .'

'Bob, we come out here. Cobbled yard, grass area beyond it, and the other loop of the drive — the two parts link up down here — can't show it, isn't room, but about three hundred yards to the west. Birchwoods there. The point is, we have to cross it. So — out of the door, turn right, along the front of the stables to the end, then a quick dash across this open area to the trees. Southward then through that wood, and over the drive about here. Then we'll have willows for cover, the willows that fringe the lake. Lake's here, you see.'

'And the meadow where they pulled poor old Stukalin apart—'

'Here. Remember it's not to scale. Meadow's bounded by — here, the front of the house, the drive circling round . . . Willows all along the edge of the lake. And here — east and south-east, the river.'

'Where's our steamboat got to, in all this artistry?'

'Here. At the landing-stage. *This.*'

'So we'll get nearly all the way to it in the cover of those willows . . .'

Maroussia came back from checking on the light or lack of it; she told them, 'Moon's down. It won't get any darker.'

They got up. Well rested: they'd all slept during the

afternoon, in preparation for what might be a very long night. Bob said, 'Remember about your shoes. Might be doing a lot of walking.'

He hoped they would *not* have much walking to do. His daydream for this departure was of the lorry pounding southward through the latter part of this night, of locating the skiff in its hiding-place sometime around dawn, lying up in that marsh all day and — weather permitting — pushing off after sunset.

It was a gamble — the weather especially. The odds were long *against* it 'permitting'. He wasn't letting himself think about it. If you did, you'd sit and do nothing. The essential was to get out of here, *now*.

Nadia had kissed the Count, said with a glance at Bob as she made way for Irina, 'Good luck, both of you. Be careful.' Irina was embracing her brother: 'You'll be back here soon, I hope.' Bob meanwhile holding old Maroussia's hands: 'I may be back. In case I'm not — well, I can't thank you enough, and — I wish you *would* come with us.'

'Don't worry about me. Worry about *them*. Are you ready now?'

In the coachhouse she unfastened the door, pushed it open and stepped out, stood outside it for a minute ostensibly enjoying the cool night air while her small, quick eyes probed the shadows. Bob and the Count waiting inside, behind the door. The girls had stayed down in the Hole.

A whisper: 'It's all clear.'

The Count led, Bob following a few yards behind, walking slowly, carefully, along the front of the stables to their right. Pitch black: to start with you were blind.

They stopped at the end of the line of stables. Scents of grass, trees, river. The river's nearest point from here would be about five or six hundred yards away, but even over that distance you could hear it, the soft but carrying night-time murmur of moving water. And from this angle the side of the house was a high, black cut-out against the eastern sky, with ornate chimney shapes decorating the higher rooftop. The low part, single-storey, to the left —

the back of the house — was the extension containing what were now prison cells. All dark there; but there were lights in other windows — big sash windows at two levels, much smaller ones above them, the attic floor which would have been servants' sleeping quarters.

The Count held Bob's arm, pointed at a black density of woods about two hundred yards south-west. 'That way now.'

Taking it slowly, as they'd agreed, treating the darkness like water in a pool across which one had to swim with as little disturbance of its surface as might be possible. Following the Count's quietly moving figure — knowing that if there were sentries for instance in the edge of those woods they'd be watching you come and you wouldn't have even a glimpse of them until it was too late.

Off the cobbles now: in ankle-deep grass or weed. He could see the curve of the drive over to his left, where it came after circling the front of the house and led away around the far side of the spinney which they were approaching now. That was where they'd be crossing it, beyond that birchwood spinney. But at this point the drive ran along the edge of the meadow where Grigor Stukalin had had his grisly come-uppance.

One could imagine that scream: hear it in imagination — howl of agony splitting the quiet night ...

Christ!

He'd stopped: baffled as to which had come first, the thought or the sound, but realizing in the next second as the breath unlocked in his throat, *Owl, not howl* ... The Count had stopped too, glancing back — no doubt with a grin on his face ... Starting off again now but changing direction slightly, aiming for the left-hand edge of the wood as if to skirt around it. It would be a strange experience for him, this clandestine intrusion in a place in which he'd spent so much of his childhood. One could imagine that if it had been one's own, one's father's and forefathers', there'd be little doubt in one's mind that a day would come when one would repossess, conceivably live happily ever after.

With Princess Nadia as chatelaine. And Robert Cowan as a guest, in some glorious, peaceful summer.

A guest with an unseemly interest in his hostess.

Trees. The streaky patterns of silver birch.

A whisper: 'All right, Bob?'

'Thought that owl was Stukalin.'

'That owl does it on purpose. Then it falls off the branch laughing ... This way now.'

Through the edge of the wood, circling to the left. Better than going straight through — you could see where you were, more or less where you were going. The drive — not visible yet — would be closing in from the left, and you'd follow the curve of it until you had the lake — or rather its fringe of willows — right opposite you, on the drive's other side. There was hard ground and a crackle of dead leaves underfoot, a breeze stirring the branches. The breeze came from behind — from the north — would be against one, therefore, on the way up-river. Wind and current: he hoped to God the steamboat would be usable. Would be *there*, to start with.

'We'll cross here, Bob.'

The blur of trees over there had to be the willows ...

'Hey—'

Engine-noise — from the right. A motor, and a flicker of light through the trees. And voices ...

'*Down!*'

Light — headlights, yellowish, flickery beams — with the birch-trunks jet-black verticals against it as it grew. Rattly engine reminiscent of the fishing-station's lorry, and the lights coming up brighter, closer. Passing *now* ... With drunken voices singing, that and the engine-noise in a peak of sound that was falling and the tail-lights fading, pink sparks finally invisible as the truck bore right around the edge of the meadow. A military truck, its canvas-covered rear section doubtless crowded with the comrades back from their weekend junketing in Astrakhan.

Gone now, anyway. And no more coming, nothing moving, except branches and foliage in the breeze ...

'Come on.' Trotting: over hard, dry ground, then a turf

bank, and stopping again with the willows' twisted shapes all round them and a glitter of star-reflecting water just beyond. The lake — which Nick had said teemed with mallard ... Lights in the north-east — at the house. That truck had stopped at its front, headlights yellowing the Palladian-style frontage, pillars extending from one protruding wing to the other and supporting a stone balcony. There'd be a splendid view from there, over miles of winding river.

'Some cottage, you have there.'

'Oh.' Pausing beside him. 'Not bad, huh?'

'Remember I'll be coming as your guest. Yours and Nadia's.'

'Damn sure you will.' A fist thumped his shoulder. 'Damn *sure*!'

'Let's get on.'

Slightly uneasy: with a sense of one's own treachery. The mention of Nadia, and the doubt — from as much as she'd said herself — that she had any real intention of marrying her 'Nikki', whom one was following now through the erratically wandering belt of willows. Stukalin's meadow was open to the left and the house in view across it, the truck's engine audible again as it drove on and round the house's south-eastern corner: it was dark again there now, and quiet.

But for heaven's sake, *he* was devious enough ...

He'd stopped. Pointing ahead, as Bob came up beside him.

That sheen was straight on the Volga's moving surface. The riverbank sloped down at this point; when the river was high the water would be right up here, the landing-stage hauled in closer, between two lines of timber piles driven into the river-bed, one such barrier at each end of it. You'd need them too, he guessed — when the river was in spate ... And that was a steamboat, all right. Not unlike one of the Royal Navy's steam picket-boats. A tall, thin funnel with a belled top to it. Small wheelhouse, engine-room casing abaft it, where the funnel was — engineroom hatchway would be somewhere there, probably immediately abaft the wheelhouse — then coach-top, and a cabin down there that would be accessible from the open stern. You didn't have to be any closer to be certain of that layout: a glance from this distance, with a sailor's eye, was all it took.

No movement, and no lights. He felt for the knife on his belt — ensuring that he could free it quickly when he needed it.

'Nick, listen ... I'll be quieter on my own. You keep lookout here, give me a whistle if there's any problem — like people or other boats coming.'

'All right. And if you need help—'

'I'll whistle.'

The timber piles, running like exceptionally large, wide-spaced fenceposts down the slope of bank and into the river, made for good cover *en route* to the landing-stage. The Count saw Bob's crouching form melt into invisibility against the farther — downstream — line of them; the steamboat was nearer that end of the stage than this. He turned, went back into the cover of the willows and picked his way along through them, parallel to the bank and the landing-stage, to wait opposite that end of it.

Squatting down, he could still see the top of the funnel and the short, stubby mast above the wheelhouse. And the shine of the river beyond it, some distance out. River noise was loud here: from where it flowed between those piles, swirling around the timbers ... This was the main channel, the deepwater one which all the larger ships would use when the river was at its lowest as it was now. On its far side you'd come to a big expanse of currently high-and-dry middle ground and then some other, narrower channels, and beyond them — back on mainland now — Selitrenoe, the railway halt where they'd seen the old man being pistol-whipped.

He started: froze ... Then stood up slowly, listening hard ...

Movement: rustling movement in the trees behind him — between his present position and the lakeside. Turning to face in that direction: his right shoulder against a willow's trunk, hand sliding down to the haft of his knife, unsheathing it.

Louder movement: and heavy breathing. A slab of the darkness moved. *Big* slab ...

Puzzled: but knife in hand, crouching, muscles taut ...

Then he straightened — in a gust of stifled laughter ... 'Hey — Don Juan! Here, old fellow ...'

The animal was motionless again. End-on. Having given him that scare ... Could have ended up with a punctured hide — and what might Maroussia have said to *that* ... The knife was back in its sheath now; he left his tree, approached the donkey. 'It's me, Don Juan, your old pal Nikolai Petrovich.' Reaching to pat him. Don Juan had a white streak on his forehead, and it was visible through the darkness at this close range: although one would never have seen his drab-grey bulk if he hadn't moved. And of course they'd come along the edge of the trees, the meadow edge — maybe fifty feet away, with a lot of willows in between. 'There, old fellow — have to leave you now ...'

The darkness filled. What had seemed like a void was — was *not.* Bewildering — as if one was hallucinating — like the ground itself rising, humping, here and there: then a man's voice growled 'What the devil ... Igor, you awake? What's — who's *that*?'

'You — stay where you are!'

Only the donkey hadn't moved. Nick Solovyev motionless too now, though. He'd begun to move — with two men in front of him coming up as if materializing out of the roots of trees, he'd sidestepped away, instinctively to put the donkey between himself and them: and now found a third — diminutive, gnome-like — but with a rifle-barrel practically touching his face and a hoarse voice demanding 'Where'd *you* spring from, comrade?'

'Bugger'd have robbed us while we slept. Cut our throats, maybe.' This one had a heavy local accent. 'If it hadn't been for the moke here — trod on my bloody foot ...'

'Where've you come from — *you*?'

Backing away, with his hands halfway up: the attitude of a man willing to surrender but sure he wouldn't have to once they realized he was a friend, meant them no harm … One of them muttering something about lighting the fornicating lamp, and this other one poking at him with the rifle: 'Well? *Where*?'

'Came in a boat. Only looking for a place to doss down for the night. Why — what's the fuss, comrades?'

He hadn't thought about Bob in that moment. His priority had been not to say anything that could possibly point them at the coachhouse.

'Boat, eh … Where from? Where you headed?'

'Igor — see if there's a boat there.' Crouching over the lamp. '*Bloody* thing …'

Bob had boarded the steamboat right aft, into the wide stern. There was a gangplank further forward, abreast the wheelhouse, but that was all it was, a narrow plank, liable to shift and bang around when weight came on it. In any case access to the cabin would be aft here: and the cabin, which might be inhabited, came first, engineroom second.

Crouching, he crept slowly, as soundlessly as possible, to where the companionway door or doors would be. Finding when he got there that it was a pair of doors, one shut and the other latched open. So there *was* someone below.

He leant in, listened with his head inside the opening.

Someone was snoring.

He waited. One man snoring didn't guarantee there weren't two or three of them on board. Thinking about this, while continuing to listen in the hope of learning more, it occurred to him that the best thing might be to go back, collect Nick and bring him down here. As far as the landing-stage, anyway. *Then* go down inside. One man would be easy, two should present no great problem, but if there were more than that it might be as well to have some back-up.

Should have brought him down here in the first place.

He'd swung one leg over the side, pausing there for a moment just to check that the crewman was still snoring, when he heard a voice raised — not a shout, not loud, but on a note of alarm. Could only have been Nick calling to him — as agreed, and trying to make him hear but no louder than he had to …

Another voice: low-toned but again urgent-sounding. Bob by this time halfway up the slope of the riverbank, with the timber piles — thick as railway sleepers — on his left. Pausing at the top to listen: then forward again, cautiously … 'Nick?'

A shout, 'No, Bob, *run*.'

'Hey, *you*!'

A light had flared in there, farther inside the trees, in about the same moment that he'd heard and recognized Nick's voice. Then in an overlapping second while his hand was still going to his knife, this voice on his right — close — and the expanding aura of lamplight exposing a dwarflike creature crouching five or six feet to the side with a rifle aimed at his head … 'Move one inch, comrade, it'll be your last … Hey, lads, we've got another one!' Bob squinting at the rifle's unwavering foresight and thinking dazedly that this could not be happening: but then, *No sense getting dead — however bloody stupid …*

12

Incredibly stupid. Blundering, incompetent ... He'd read the same self-criticism in the Count's expression, when proximity of the lamp had allowed them a sight of each other. A look of shock, as well as shame ... Bob recalling the complacency of his response to Nadia, about having the advantage of surprise: *We know we're coming, and they don't* ... Those words of spurious wisdom echoing in his apology for a brain while in the lamplight he saw one of the three men gathering up fishing-rods, a home-made gaff and a landing-net, then other bits of gear which he tossed into a basket. A fishing party — off-duty Bolshevik soldiers — camping here, probably after sea-trout, getting their heads down early in order to be up and on the river in the dawn ...

But why they'd have had Maroussia's donkey with them — unless he'd just decided to join them, seeking company ... Standing there watching it all now, twitching his ears, an interested spectator ... Nick began — low-voiced and speaking quickly — 'I've told 'em we just landed here, looking for a place to spend the night—'

'Quiet, you!'

The little one: with the rifle on them from about six feet away, eyes like a rat's over its sights, waiting for the gear to be packed away. Bob asked — dully, which was how he felt — 'What d'you want with us, comrades? What are we supposed to've done?'

'Creeping about at night where you don't belong, that's what ... We're going that way now — go on, *move* — and keep your hands up!'

Out through the willows and across Stukalin's meadow,

heading for the house. Thinking about Nadia and Irina who'd be expecting to get their 'Nikki' back quite soon now, would doubtless be counting minutes — and then hours — by which time they'd be frantic ...

He thought, *Crouch, turn and charge* ...

At least one of them would be flattened. And one of them, incidentally, was a midget anyway. Vicious little swine, but still only half-size ... He turned his head: 'Anton—'

'*Silence*, you!'

Then a muttering from one of them to Igor to keep his gun on 'that one' ... 'And spread out a bit, comrades, watch 'em, they may try something ...' Odds thus shifting against success: they'd shoot as you began to move. Another point being that lives didn't count for much in this country and this year of grace. And with the house there — Maroussia had said there'd be sentries at the front of it — all it would take would be a rifle-shot and a shout or two: and even if you did flatten these three and grab their guns — what then? With the whole place up in arms — and one certainly couldn't go near the coachhouse ...

This trio might have seen action together, he guessed. They acted like a team and like men who knew the score, knew what they were doing. Unfortunately. The wrong kind of fishermen to run into.

Dew-wet, knee-high meadow grass, a meadow that had already been the scene of one spectacular execution. And right ahead of them, the house, with quite a few of its rooms lit up at the ground-floor level, and two glowing rectangles on the first floor. Cheka burning the night oil, maybe ... Bob aware that the story about escape from the hanging in Askhabad was shortly to be put to the test, and suspecting that it might not stand up too well to Cheka-style examination.

Two minutes, near enough, with the sentry at the front of the house — there was only one on duty, not two — and then about five with a balding character who might have been an NCO, sergeant of the guard or somesuch. By this second stage, still with the rifles pointing at their heads, they were up on the marbled portico, between two of the graceful columns.

'So you're Anton Vetrov.'

'Right. And this—'

'This, we're expected to believe, is a Persian with no papers.'

'Right again: but you *can* believe it . . .'

'You landed — from what kind of boat, by the way?'

'Rowing-boat — ordinary . . .'

'So it's still there, is it?'

'I suppose so. Unless someone's—'

'Stole it, did you?'

'Borrowed it, comrade. Out of necessity and—'

'Where from?'

'Little way downstream, I think it's called Kosika.'

'So you were rowing upstream — with the intention of crossing to Selitrenoe, on your way to Moscow in the service of the Revolution.'

'Yes. And we hadn't realized how strong the current was, which was the reason for landing. And if you could put us up for the night—'

'You know, I expect we'll do that.' He grinned. 'I'd say it's very likely.' Nodding to the others — the three fishermen and the sentry, who'd left his steps unguarded now — 'Keep them here. I'm reporting to the duty officer. Or Comrade Lesechko, maybe, could be *his* pigeon.'

Lesechko. Nadia's boss . . . Bob met the Count's glance. He shrugged, commented loudly, 'Why don't they believe us? What do they think we are?'

'Shut your face, you!'

Bob glared at the tiny man. 'Listen. We work for the Revolution. In Askhabad the SRs were about to hang us.' A nod towards the Count. 'Him first. They'd hanged nine of our comrades, he was next. I broke a door down—'

The little man demanded, 'What are SRs, for shit's sake?'

'Social Revolutionaries. Mensheviks.'

'Oh — *those* traitors!'

'— as I was saying—'

'*I'd* say you're a bloody liar, comrade!'

'Right, then.' The bald sergeant, accompanied by four men with pistols, came back out into the portico. 'We'll take care of 'em now. You lads cut along. You've done well, very well. Goodnight, comrades ... You two — in here. Haul 'em in, comrades ...'

Cavernous staircase hall. Oil-lamps here and there — one on a deal table, one at the foot of each of the two branches of a double staircase — and one at the top, on the gallery there. Bob's eyes riveted, though, on the ropes. Ropes dangling — ten or twelve of them, dark-stained at their frayed lower ends ... He'd shambled to a halt with a guard each side of him, hands grasping his arms, and he was seeing the ropes like props in a carefully staged nightmare, hearing in recent memory — from only yesterday, but it could have been a year ago, or more — old Leonid Mesyats' growling monotone, *What they did was they hung 'em by their feet — ropes tied to the gallery balustrade — so they could hoist 'em up like so many pigs — and setting out buckets below to catch the blood, d'you see ...*

No buckets now. Only the ropes ... But Mesyats had added something to the effect that none of it could have been Solovyev blood. Glancing round, Bob focused on the Solovyev features, the green eyes directed upward to the balustrade: unaware of the close proximity to him of a burly, unshaven character — field shirt, khaki breeches — staring at him from a range of about three feet.

Bob asked — blurting it out suddenly, loudly, breaking that concentration because he'd had to, having conceived a vision that was an extension of the nightmare and might for all he knew be a true picture of what was coming next — 'You the duty officer?'

The close-cropped head turned. 'What if I am?'

'I want to complain of this treatment. Comrade Vetrov here and I are dedicated servants of the Revolution. I'm a Persian: I have influence and armed followers in my own country, I'm here to offer my people's co-operation—'

'What's all this now, comrade Captain?'

The question had been put to him by a small middle-aged man who was coming down the left-hand branch of the stairs. Taking it carefully, not hurrying: he was tubby, with thin grey hair, and wearing some sort of dressing-gown.

Lesechko, obviously.

'Eh? Got problems, have we?' These two — *these* problems?'

'Comrade — we aren't sure yet. They were caught prowling — over near the landing, there. Some comrades on a night fishing expedition rounded them up — and one of 'em has no papers, see — *and* such a cock-and-bull story as you never heard ...'

'Well, I think I'd *better* hear it.' A quiet smile: 'I'm a bit of a specialist in cock-and-bull stories, Captain. Heard so many, you see ...' He'd picked the lamp up from the table, was holding it up to throw light on the Count's face — since he was the nearer. The duty officer muttering, 'I'd swear that's a face I've seen before', and Lesechko glancing at him politely, interestedly ... 'Is that so? Well, we'll have his beard off, then, and you can look again. Beards are like masks, sometimes.' Moving to Bob: the captain stating flatly, 'This is the one that doesn't have papers. Says he's a Persian, comrade *polkovnik*. Oh, he had this knife, by the way.' A shrug. 'Or this one — they both had knives.'

So Lesechko was a colonel: Nadia hadn't mentioned this. Not that it made any difference: Cheka didn't need ranks, could do as they pleased — with powers of life and death, no answerability to any authority other than their own ... Eyebrows hooping as he peered upward into Bob's face. 'Well, well. No papers, *and* yet another beard ... You know, when people think about taking a beard off, what they mean is *shaving* it off. It's the usual way, of course. But another way is with pincers, ripping it out in lumps. I've seen men admit to false identities almost before it's started, even. I'll admit it's not a *pleasant* sight, a certain amount of skin and flesh comes with it ... What's your name, comrade?'

'Robat. What's yours?'

'Lesechko. Viktor Lesechko. But yours is more unusual, so we'll talk about you, not me ... For instance, if you're a Persian —' He paused, thinking this over; then changed his mind, looked back at the Count. 'No. You can wait.' A hand out to the captain: 'Let's see this one's papers. Since he's gone to the trouble and expense of equipping himself with such rubbish.' A smile: 'Didn't pay too much for them, I hope?'

Nadia's voice, in memory: *I don't spit at him when I see him, I'm not suicidal ...*

Meaning he was lethal? The adjective she'd used was 'pragmatic' — and he very likely *was* pragmatic, as well as lethal, but here and now pragmatism was hardly the issue. Lethality was, lethality was in the very air.

Bob looked away from the gleam of sweat on Nick's forehead — wishing he hadn't seen it. As the Cheka colonel most surely had; watching him, you could see he was — well, not revelling, exactly, but very much *involved*, now, absolutely in his own element. Nadia had expressed her loathing of this man's underling, describing him as a thug or worse, but Lesechko — Bob thought, watching and listening, drawing impressions from his reactions, expressions, tones of voice — this mild-mannered little man was more frightening than any thug could be. Frighteningly intuitive — homing in on his victim's visible fear and probing for its roots, with an easy confidence that seemed to imply certainty of getting to them — and sooner rather than later ... Nick had repeated his name — Anton Vetrov — and Lesechko had glanced at the papers to confirm it, muttering 'As good a name as any, I suppose. Let's hear the cock-and-bull story, then', and Nick had launched himself into it immediately — stumbling over the words — floored by each swift, knife-like interruption — and with his glance constantly returning to those ropes as if they were having some mesmeric effect on him, impairing his usually nimble brain, those remarkable powers of invention and prevarication ... Lesechko interrupted again: 'Wait.' Glancing round ... 'Bring me a chair.'

Nick staring at the ropes — again. Maybe seeing the bodies of the wounded officers — or his own, even — hanging by the ankles. It wasn't easy *not* to think about it, reanimate that scene: even in Bob's memory the old fisherman's voice was still as it were on tap, against the remembered backdrop of a blood-red sunset — *but of course the buckets* . . .

You wouldn't catch much in a bucket — from a hanging, swaying body. It — they — would be swaying, swinging around. Green eyes shut — or open? Face a sheet of blood, in place of sweat . . .

Imagination — nightmare, arising from one's own fear, dread, the certainty that when he — Lesechko — did get to the roots — or even could make a good enough guess to satisfy himself that he was close enough to them — there'd be no deliberation or consideration of a just verdict. Ultimately there'd be nothing but plain murder.

'You say nine of your comrades were hanged. Close friends, no doubt, men you knew well?'

'Oh — yes . . .'

'You'll be able to give me their names, then. Names, family names and patronymics. Write them all down for me — and no mistakes, uh?'

'Yes. Yes . . .'

Bob broke in — under compulsion again, *driven* to — to give him a chance to get himself together — 'What *is* this place?' Jutting his beard towards the ropes: 'Gymnasium?'

Lesechko smiled. Genuinely amused, almost but not quite laughing. Taking the chair from the man who'd brought it, and throwing a glance over his shoulder at the ropes as he seated himself, adjusting the dressing-gown over narrow, bony knees. 'Gymnasium.' Nodding, as if savouring the word . . . 'A Bolshevik *gymnasium* . . . Yes, you might call it that.'

The smile faded as he turned back to the Count. 'Now — Anton Vetrov. *If* that's your name — which we'll know soon enough, don't worry . . . Describe to me, Comrade Vetrov, the details of your journey here from Askhabad.'

*

Irina's eyes were damp. Murmuring, 'Something's gone wrong. *Must* have.'

'It's still possible he could have stayed to help. Bob might have found he couldn't do it on his own.'

It was about the fourth time she'd said it — or something like it. They were in the coachhouse — at the back, where the hay was. Maroussia had to be up here anyway, close to the door and ready to open it to Nikki when he got here — she'd been there for more than an hour now, waiting and listening for his knock — and the girls felt a need to be up here too — where they'd see him arrive . . .

It would take only seconds for Irina to do a disappearing act into the Hole, if she had to, and for Nadia to shift some bales across the trapdoor. There'd always been the possibility of such an emergency arising, they'd practised it about forty thousand times.

Nadia said, 'He'll come. They knew the dangers, they've got eyes and ears, and they're both big, strong men.'

'What if they don't?'

'What d'you mean?'

'Well. If they were taken prisoner — or killed — which would amount to the same thing anyway . . .'

'Irina — please — have *faith*—'

'Faith!' A laugh like a snort . . . 'If *you'd* spent the past four months in that hole—'

'Look —' she'd begun sharply, loudly: making Maroussia jump, over by the door . . . Adding more quietly, 'Irina dear, I know how bad it was for you, you've told us over and over. D'you mind if we *don't* start on it all over again?'

'I'm — worried for my brother. That's all.'

'D'you imagine I'm not worried for him?'

'Since you mention it — I wouldn't know . . . *Are* you?'

'I don't know if you realize it, but you have a tendency, when you're feeling sorry for yourself for any reason, to become rude to other people. It's not a very appealing trait, Irina.'

Silence. Then a soft murmur of Maroussia praying: and more silence. Five minutes. Ten . . .

'Maroussia darling.' Irina had gone over to her, crouched beside her. 'Couldn't you go out looking for Don Juan?'

'Why should I do that?'

'Well, to see what's happening — *if* anything's happening or has happened.'

Nadia said, 'It would be an idiotic thing to do.'

'Oh, would it?'

'Look — if anything's gone wrong, all she'd achieve would be to draw attention to us here — make them think we knew something was happening. And if nothing's wrong — well, to start with, why bother, and also if Nikki comes and she's out there ...'

'Well, for God's sake, *we'd* be here to let him in ...'

Maroussia patted Irina's shoulder. 'Be patient. Nadia Nikolaievna is right. We have to wait. Be patient and just wait.'

Lesechko had broken off his interrogation of Nick Solovyev to point at Bob with his chin and tell the captain, 'Put this one in a cell. Then come back here.'

'Very well, comrade Colonel.' He'd nodded to the two guards who were waiting behind Bob. 'Bring him along.' One of them on each arm, and the captain leading — through a doorway in the panelled west wall into a marble-floored hallway where men were asleep on straw pallets, ornamental double doors leading to what would be the main apartments of the house — formerly the drawing-room, morning room, library and so forth — then these people's guardroom — a door standing open and a few men inside — including the bald sergeant — playing cards. That might have been the young Solovyevs' schoolroom, Bob thought, glancing in as he passed the door; it had that sort of look about it. They were coming to a swing-door now; the passageway beyond it was narrower and doors smaller, plainer. Kitchen, then. He'd been taking note of his surroundings more or less automatically, out of habit, none of it being even of passing interest when one was reeling under such a crushing weight of hopelessness. Lesechko had cut Nick's story to ribbons, reduced it to absurdity while Nick had still clung to it — stammeringly repetitive, clinging to it for the sole reason that he had nothing else to cling to.

Presumably Lesechko had separated them with some clear purpose in mind. Possibly in the hope that when he was on his own Nick's rather futile resistance might crumble altogether. He might make him an offer: we'll go easy on you if you'll rat on your friend. This wouldn't of course get them anywhere, since the one and only secret that was of value, basic to the whole business, was simply Nick's identity. Nick therefore couldn't bargain: but this Robat character, this Persian, he could.

And probably walk free.

But he wouldn't. So it would come down to torture.

Here — in this cellar. A bleary-eyed guard on his feet, reaching to take a large iron key off a hook on the wall: growling at the captain over his shoulder, as the latter tossed the two sheath-knives on to a table, 'Place getting crowded ...'

'*And* another to come. Well — maybe ...' Bob glanced round: at a heavy oak chair with straps hanging from its arms and legs, and an iron bedstead also with straps fitted and a heap of whips, clubs and ropes on it. A small, black stove, free-standing, with fire-irons near it — poker, tongs ... The cellar was on two levels: this higher part against the outside wall, really a passage through from the door they'd just come in by to another facing it, and five or six steps down to the larger area where all that junk was.

Smell of sewage. Short passages leading out of that lower part — alcoves with empty wine-racks in them. Against the outside wall, an enormous heap of coal. Far more than they'd want for that little stove, more likely a supply for all the fireplaces in the house. The stove was surely there for heating the irons in: branding irons, effectively ... He wondered whether Nick Solovyev would be capable of standing up to torture.

How much he himself would stand, for that matter.

Those looked like dental tools, on a bench near the chair that had straps on its arms and legs. And — he caught on to this suddenly, having been mesmerized by this scene for perhaps a minute, perhaps two — that the captain had deliberately given him time to take note of it. Glancing round at him in an effort to look unimpressed, as the turnkey asked 'What's this one, then?' and the captain shrugged: 'Dunno. Soon will, though — soon as Khitrov's back, eh?'

Khitrov was a name one had heard before. Recently...

Nadia. Nadia had said, 'Khitrov's *loathsome*...'

He'd be the cellar boss, presumably. It made sense. Lesechko had talked about pulling beards out with pincers, but he'd be out of his depth in that cellar. He'd want the results that came out of it, that was all; Khitrov would bring them to him, and if what he'd left behind wasn't nice to look at — well, Lesechko wouldn't have to look at it.

But perhaps he watched. Just didn't like getting his hands dirty.

Time, Bob thought, would tell. One had wondered, occasionally. When one had heard or read of others being tortured and either standing up to it or failing to. Not only in the present war, but in history — the rack, for instance, accounts of King Henry VIII's torturers extracting confessions, true or false, from his wives' alleged lovers. And of course the Inquisition, which so many English seamen had encountered, three or four hundred years ago. One had wondered: just as, before one had ever been in action at sea, one hadn't known whether one would stand up to *that* as well as one should.

But Nick Solovyev and torture or the threat of torture was a particular and immediate worry; one felt less sure of him even than of oneself. The main issue at stake, of course, being the two girls, and old Maroussia. Before, one would have sworn he'd hold out. When he'd been through so much: and displayed such cool nerve more than once. Only *now* ... Remembering the sweat, the stammering: and the suspicion that his nerve had gone — broken by the sight of those dangling ropes. Whether Lesechko could have caught on to the fact that the breakdown was of such recent origin . . .

If he did — and if he was as clever as one suspected — he could be on the right path to the truth.

But why, Bob asked himself, would they have left the ropes hanging there all this time?

Commemoration of their own bloodlust? Bolshevik sentiment?

Or, more simply, *pour encourager les autres*?

If intimidation was the purpose of it, it had worked with N. P. Solovyev, all right. Hadn't exactly missed the target on R. Cowan. Except that R. Cowan was less personally involved and in that sense less vulnerable — neither an aristocrat nor the rightful owner of this house.

One *hell* of a difference, actually . . .

Better not count chickens. Who could possibly know how well or how badly they'd react?

'Here y'are, then.'

The guard had picked up a lamp, come up the steps and gone to the other door. Pulling it open: no lock on that one. Stone passage — narrow, unlit except for the lamp the guard was carrying. The captain followed him, constantly looking back at Bob, and behind Bob the two guards who'd brought him through the house. The revolvers they carried were Nagants, he'd noticed. Big, heavy things, clumsier than his own .45 which he'd left with Nadia.

He wondered what they'd do, those girls. What they'd be guessing could have happened. How long it might be before they realized . . .

And *then* what?

Well, for one thing, Irina would probably go mad, in time.

Passing a second door: he supposed the Czech prisoners would be in those first two cells. In solitary confinement and total darkness — as he'd be too, in a moment. The fact that this in itself would be a form of torture only began to dawn on him at that moment. Third door: stopping here. Pushing the key into the hole, but it wasn't locked, it opened when the man turned the latch and pushed it.

The door was made of timber about four inches thick, he noted.

'In you go, comrade.'

The two behind him had let go of his arms, allowing him to walk in on his own. The lamp's rays very briefly lighting the stone-floored cell — about ten feet by six, with a damp, lavatorial odour, nothing in it except a bucket in one corner, and with one very small window, high up and barred, less a window as such than what Russians called a *fortochka.* Then he was inside and the door had thudded shut; he heard the clash of the heavy lock as the key turned. Pitch black, not even a glimmer of starlight from that tiny window.

13

Faint light in that small, barred rectangle. Daybreak — by which time as he'd envisaged it they'd have been down there in the delta, locating the skiff and settling down for a day with the mosquitoes.

He thought he'd dozed a bit. Off and on . . . Awake now, though, sitting with his back against the wall, as far away from the bucket as he could get, with his eyes on that minute section of dawn sky and thoughts of Khitrov in mind. Those words *as soon as Khitrov's back* could imply a wait of hours, or days . . . But he'd thought about the girls as well: for one thing, that at some time during the day Maroussia might be bringing a ration of bread and soup, so that after that they'd know the worst.

Nadia facing a life-sentence in the service of the Cheka, for instance, and with Irina to keep hidden. For how long — with Irina already less stable than she might be? Then — Nadia's eyes, in close-up, as they focused on those ropes. Nadia and Khitrov . . .

In half-sleep, he'd indulged in conversations with his father, who'd had no advice to offer other than to stick it out, try to stay sane, hope for a miracle and grab any chance that was offered. His own advice to himself, of course, since in these dialogues he took both parts, deriving comfort from *pretending* to have the old man in communication. Also trying to exercise his mind by recalling bits and pieces of poetry which in years gone by he'd had to memorize at school; not much of it had stuck, and he'd found himself coming back time and time again to Macaulay's epic about Lars Porsena of Clusium holding some damn bridge or other, and the rhetorical *How shall man die better than facing fearful odds?*

Not by facing Khitrov. That was for sure.

Nadia woke with a start: and Irina's hand on her shoulder, shaking her.

'Nadia — you were *sleeping*!'

'Huh? Well, of course I . . .'

It hit her, then. Why Irina would *not* have slept, and why she seemed outraged that she, Nadia, *had*. Rolling on to her back, seeing Irina's rather small head black against the dawn-lit window. Irina complaining, 'I haven't had one moment's sleep. Maroussia's down there snoring her head off, too . . . God help us, what are we going to *do*?'

'Nothing.' Getting her mind to it. 'Nothing we *can* do. I'm afraid it looks as if they must have caught them. And if so . . .'

'What?'

'Oh — nothing . . .'

'They'd torture them, wouldn't they? To find out who they are and what they've come here for?'

'I — suppose . . .' She shook her head. 'I don't *know* — any more than you do . . . But there's nothing we can do except carry on as usual — I'll go to work, you stay in the Hole . . .'

'Christ.' A small whimper. 'You've no *idea*—'

'Yes, I have. I've a very good idea, I've spent quite a bit of time down there myself . . . But listen — those two men could be hiding somewhere. Might have not been able to get back here, for some reason. There could be all sorts of explanations. We don't *know*, so let's hope for the best, say our prayers and not despair before there's any need to — eh?'

Maroussia had spent the night on a blanket close to the door, where she'd have been woken if they'd turned up during the small hours. While Nadia had gone to bed up here in the flat telling herself *When I wake up, they'll be here . . .*

She wondered if they could have come, knocked, and Maroussia *not* woken?

*

During breakfast — tea and bread in the kitchen — Maroussia's eyes were on Irina a lot of the time, and with spasms of the rapid blinking which Nadia had come to recognize as a sign of internal stress, about the only symptom of it the old girl ever showed.

Probably thinking Irina ought to be in the Hole. Nadia thought so too — that in the circumstances — after all, *something* must have happened — a surprise visit by soldiers and/or Cheka had to be on the cards. On the other hand Irina was so strung up, seemed so close to hysteria, that it seemed wise to handle her gently, for fear of nudging her into a full-scale nervous breakdown.

'I was thinking —' speaking to Maroussia, but aiming the message at Irina — 'that if they'd got themselves stuck last night — had to hide in that boat, for instance—'

'How could that happen?'

'Could've got trapped somehow, couldn't they? If they were on it and then its crew came along or something.' Glancing at Maroussia again: 'Anything like that, they'd have to sit it out — wherever they are — until it's dark enough to come back to us tonight. Then I suppose they'd — I don't know, start all over again, perhaps ... And if they *were* on the boat — well, it could be they'd have done all the technical things Bob said were necessary. So then *tonight*—'

'And pigs might fly.'

Maroussia glared at her: 'Irina Petrovna!' Irina looked shocked: like a naughty child. Nadia holding her mental breath, waiting for the floods, the screams ... Maroussia telling her, 'That was a rude and stupid thing to say!'

'Well, I'm sorry, but—'

'No, you must control yourself. Nadia's perfectly right and sensible, we have to have faith and courage, Irina. Remember your darling mother, my precious Maria Ivanovna, the courage *she* showed us all ...'

The sentry on duty at the *Dacha*'s former tradesmen's

entrance eyed her as she came walking quickly across the cobbles. In his mid-twenties, with a narrow, foxy face, forage cap on a shaven head, green field shirt, red brassard, khaki trousers pushed into high boots. Looking her up and down — as they always did, and she always ignored it, trying to look as if she didn't notice.

She did, though. And inside, in the stone hallway, where a few men were still asleep, others rolling their blankets or in the slow process of waking up, she was again the target of lewd interest and muttered comments. She was aware — heard it quite often — that they called her 'the Cheka's whore'. She went on quickly; through the hall and down a short passage, where the third door on the left — with Lesechko's notice on the door reading PRIVATE, NO ENTRY — was her office. Former pantry, about eight feet by ten with an oak dresser at the far end and a small table on which stood her typewriting machine with a piece of old curtain material over it as a dust-cover. She had a kitchen chair behind the table, and her first work of the day — continuation of Saturday evening's, when Lesechko had finally told her she could go, get down to it again first thing Monday — was stacked beside the machine just as she'd left it.

She pulled the chair out, and the cover off the machine, and sat down. It occurred to her that when she'd last sat on this chair she hadn't known that Nikki was alive: or that any Scotsman by the name of Bob Cowan even existed.

Maybe he didn't now. Maybe neither of them did. In which case . . .

She sat still for a few moments with her eyes shut and her hands pressed flat together, fingertips in contact with her chin . . . Then started work.

Maroussia leant sideways like a sailing ship in a hard blow, to counter the weight of the full bucket she was carrying. Scrubbing-brush and a wad of cloth in the other hand, that arm stuck out almost horizontally. She was on her way to the office of the chairman of the Military Revolutionary Committee — it had been the Solovyevs' library in former days — as she was supposed to get that one done first. She'd come in by the back door, collecting this gear from the scullery which led off from the kitchen; now she'd turned into the passage that led through to the west wing of the house. Through the swing door — opening it with her left shoulder — and she was passing the guardroom when a voice called sharply. 'Oy! Kamentseva!'

They all used her family name. Or on occasion just *Babushka*, grandmother. The family name was all right, in fact she preferred it, wouldn't have wanted to be on closer terms with any of this riff-raff — and certainly not with this one, a scowling Kirghiz sergeant by name of Lyashko.

'What d'you want?'

'Message for you. You've got two more mouths to feed today. See to it, eh?'

Blinking at him. *Rapid* blinking . . .

'In the cells *now*, d'you mean? That I've got to feed *today*?'

'What did I just tell you, woman?'

'But —' she made an effort to control the blinking — 'I won't have enough bread. The Czechs would've finished up Saturday's. But if it's *four* now—'

'Better go bake some fresh, hadn't you?'

Irina lounged on hay-bales near the trapdoor. They'd begged her to stay inside the Hole, but she'd argued that if Nikki came and she was down there she wouldn't hear him.

'But he won't, Irina dear.' Nadia with an arm round her shoulders, talking in what Irina called her 'nanny' voice. 'Not in daylight. You *know* he wouldn't!'

She wondered if he was dead.

If he was — well — thirteen years ago, their father. Then just the other day, Mama. Now Nikki. Leaving, in logical progression — and inevitably, because if he were gone — how in the name of Christ—

The door rattled. She jerked upright: glancing to the open trapdoor and half rising — ready to climb quickly down inside there and pull the trap shut over her head. Remembering Nadia's nagging: 'But if you're inside before we leave we can cover the trapdoor with hay. When you're on your own you *can't*. . .'

'Irina?'

Maroussia's voice, as the door creaked shut. Irina let out the breath she'd been holding . . . 'What brings you back – is there news, have you heard . . .?'

'You should be in the Hole.' A shake of the grey head. 'No. I've heard nothing. I dare say Nadia's right and they're in hiding, we'll see them later . . . I have to make more bread, that's all, I'd forgotten . . .'

She'd fastened the outside door. Murmuring as she went into the kitchen that she'd just get this lot into the oven, then go and get on with her cleaning, come back later . . . Scooping the coarse brown flour from the barrel into her big mixing-bowl: aware of Irina's presence somewhere behind her. No point burdening the child with secrets she didn't need to have: if it turned out well, it would turn out well, and if it didn't – she crossed herself, murmured in her mind *Into Thy hands, oh Lord* . . . She heard the scrape of a chair then, as Irina sat down at the table: like a dog or a cat, always following one around. Turning the leaves of some old book Nadia had been reading. Occupied, anyway . . . Maroussia knelt down, began to grope at the back of the stove, at floor level. Careful of the hot metal: but still having to feel for it, you couldn't see into that narrow gap and she didn't remember *exactly* where she'd hidden the thing. On a ledge of sorts, a flange of the cast-iron base . . .

Her fingertips touched it, felt it move. Eyes watering – blinking like mad – scared that if she pushed it too far in she'd *never* –

Got it. Rolling it with a conjuror's deftness into her apron. Ready to tell Irina that it was a spoon she'd dropped.

The bread now. Mixing, then pounding the heavy dough with her small, work-hardened fists; deciding while she thumped and muttered at it that the stranger who'd brought Nikolai Petrovich here was the stronger of the two, that he'd be the one to entrust with this.

Bob heard the clash of the lock in his cell door. He began to get up, thinking *Here it is now – Khitrov*...

Two guards: one in the doorway and the other behind him. There wasn't a lot of light out there, but compared to the gloom in the cell it was dazzling.

'*Parasha.*'

He hadn't understood.

'*Parasha!*' Pointing at the bucket. Bob getting it then: very much a prison word, dictionary interpretation something like *close-stool.* The guard ordered, 'Bring it out!'

He picked it up carefully. It had an iron lid on it and it wasn't anything like full, but it stank and he was wary of it. Wary of the guard too, who had a club in his right hand and was pointing with the other: 'Along there.'

The backup guard was carrying a Nagant. It wasn't cocked, Bob noticed. They were both smaller than he was; he had the impression that they were aware of it.

At the end of the stone passage — after passing the fourth and last cell, in which he supposed Nick would be — was an open drain in the cemented floor, a channel that led away under the wall close to the corner. And a tap on the wall above it. He put the bucket down, removed its lid and put that down beside it, tipped the bucket's contents into the drain and then re-covered it: managing not to breathe in, meanwhile.

'Drink.'

A gesture with the club, towards the tap. Bob moved closer to it, turned it on, rinsed his hands in its thin stream and then cupped them, drank...

'All right. Back in your kennel, sonny boy.'

He looked at him as he passed him: thinking, *I'll know you again – sonny boy*... Asking himself then, as he went obediently into his cell and they slammed its door shut, what point there could be in thinking anything of the sort. Mere bravado: wishful thinking...

Should have asked them *When does Khitrov get back?*

He stood now, leaning against the wall with his face in the patch of light projected through the little window. Thinking about the blundering that had put him here: that it had been more bad luck than bad planning or execution. Just hadn't paid off, that was all. And remembering the run of luck they'd had earlier — getting through the train journey and the platform checks without papers, getting a lift in the truck, and finding old Mesyats available with his boat — might have realized, with any foresight, that you'd been getting more than your fair share of it.

Then: *Shouldn't have come on this hopeless expedition in the first place . . .*

Absolutely true. Incontrovertible fact. Starting with Nikolai Solovyev's barefaced lies at Baku and compounded by one's own decision down there on the marsh to accompany him up-river. Should have got in that bloody skiff, waved goodbye and rowed out to sea.

No notion of time. Might be noon — or later, could be mid-afternoon. And for all one knew, Khitrov might be back. Taking his cue from the boss, dealing with Anton Vetrov first.

Remember: whether Nick broke or didn't, they'd try to convince you they'd got it out of him . . .

His situation was a lot worse than one's own. If he broke, told them who he was — and *maybe* he could do so without mentioning the girls — they'd still kill him in the end, and probably very nastily. Whereas if 'Robat Khan' confessed to being Robert Cowan, RNR — well, it was a toss-up, but by no means inconceivable that one might survive.

Except they'd still want to know what one had come here *for*. Which Nick — touch wood — would *not* have told them. So they probably wouldn't give up, without having extracted that information.

Key in the door . . .

His heart banged: pulses began to race . . . Some delay now: Khitrov fumbling it, not getting the key in properly . . . Then it clicked over, and the door swung open.

The figure standing there peering in at him was about half the size of the one he'd been expecting. This was Maroussia. There was a guard behind her, leaning against the wall on the other side of the passage. She had a tin mug in one hand and a brick-sized lump of black bread in the other. He'd moved towards her — to make sure she could see him properly, recognize him. Accepting the mug, muttering *'Spasibo, bolshoi spasibo . . .'*

'Turnip soup and good fresh bread.' Then in a barely audible murmur, 'Don't bite into the bread too hard.' Louder again: 'Got good strong teeth, have you?'

'Come on, grandma.' The guard pushed himself off the wall. Signalling to her with his club to move on. 'Another one here, let's get on with it . . .'

She backed out, and he swung the door shut.

The bread was heavy: even for the solid, yeastless black bread that she made in that old stove of hers, it was a hell of a weight for its size. And — *not to bite into it too hard* . . . He crouched, put the mug down, pulled the bread apart with his fingers.

An iron key, and a kitchen knife.

A jingle in his mind, derived from the nursery-days plea for fine weather: *Khitrov, Khitrov, stay away/Come to play another day . . .*

Before the old girl's visit he'd almost have opted to get it over. Now, his prayer was for the hours to pass, the sky to darken.

There'd be no waiting for the moon to set, tonight. It would be up there for about half an hour longer than it had been last night, and that would make it just too damn late. Have to risk the moonlight, therefore. Risk everything on this one chance.

Even though it could only land one back on that marsh. Better there than here . . .

Ideas churning: forming, some then discarded as impractical or too risky, others sticking but needing change, adjustment to fit in with the concept as a whole. Also, one had learnt a lesson — namely that when up against an enemy who was completely without scruple or mercy, one's only hope of winning was to adopt the same rules — or lack of them. Down on the boat last night, for instance — he suspected that it had been partly his aversion to the idea of killing in cold blood that had made him delay it by going to fetch the Count.

There'd be no such hesitation now.

The key and the knife were under the *parasha.* So if they hauled him out now for questioning or other processing, they wouldn't find it. Suppose Khitrov came for him now, for instance. From as much as one had ever heard or read, torture sessions tended to be of limited duration — often terminating with the prisoner unconscious, but usually lasting only an hour or two. It might be easier to hold out, too, he guessed, knowing those precious items were lying there under the stinking bucket.

Dark enough now. Anyway it would be darker still in ten minutes, and the preliminaries were bound to take at least that long.

He went to the bucket, tilted it, fingered the knife and the key out, pocketed the knife and went to the door.

This bit might be as chancy as any. No sounds carried through the heavy timber, you might be opening it in the surprised faces of half a dozen Khitrovs.

One way to find out — *if* the key fitted ...

It did. He heard the now familiar *clack* as the lock turned. Withdrew the key, put it in that pocket in place of the knife, which was transferred to his right hand.

One of the decisions he'd made was to take care of whatever guard or guards were around *before* he let Nick out. Preferable to rely on oneself alone, he'd decided, particularly as one didn't know what sort of shape Nick might be in.

He crept past the other two cells, paused to listen for a moment at the door into the cellar, then slowly turned its handle, edging it open.

One guard: sitting at the table with his back this way — reading a newspaper, smoke curling from a cigarette. In the last few inches of the door's opening its hinges groaned: the guard jerked upright on his chair, was pushing himself up, swivelling, as Bob burst in with the door crashing back, launching himself in a running jump and landing more or less on top of him, left arm locking round the man's neck and tightening, and the table collapsing under their combined weight. Kneeling then, wrenching the guard's body up and backwards and stabbing from the front, driving the knife in upwards under the ribs on the left side of the arched torso. The body thrashed in a climactic spasm, then went limp, and he let it drop.

First time ever ... And now — the door, the one into the house. Quickly back up the steps ... The door had bolts top and bottom, and he slid them home. As Khitrov would have done, no doubt, before starting work ... Then back to the cellar below to check that the guard was dead: and finding his other knife, in the sheath Nadia had made for it, amongst the wreckage of the table. Nick's ought to be here too — they both had been ...

And a Nagant revolver. Must have been lying on the table. Six rounds in its cylinder: he snapped it shut, stuck it inside his belt. Nick, now — and the question of whether this key fitted the other cells as well — or had Maroussia given Nick *his* key ... He looked to where a key had hung, on the wall. It was there, all right ... And it matched this one, they were twins. So — one to take away, and one to leave in the outside of Nick's cell door: so there'd be nothing to tell them that either prisoner had had a key, they'd have to believe that the dead guard, for some unexplainable reason of his own, had let one of them out.

Blood was leaking from the body. He stepped over it, ran up the steps and past three cell doors to the one at the end. Minutes counted — even seconds — to get out of here and away before another guard came to relieve this one. The bolted door wouldn't hold him for long — once they caught on. There might be hours to go before a relief was due — or even all night, if the dead man would have slept here — but on the other hand there could be — well, no time at all . . .

The key did fit. He pushed the door open, swinging back into the dark cell . . . 'Nick?'

A gasp . . . Then: 'Holy Mother of God . . .'

'You all right, Nick?'

'I'm —' staring, crazed-looking: in the doorway, his arms out like a blind man's . . . 'Bob? Am I dreaming — is this *real*?'

'Didn't Maroussia tell you?'

He seemed to be — intact. Just as well: since one was counting on his thinking straight now. Giving him a minute first — half a minute anyway — to get over the shock . . .

'Maroussia said — she said to have courage, it was going to be all right . . . But — *how*—'

'Talk later, Nick. Sorry to rush you — here, come on, this way —' pulling him along — 'we've a lot to do, long way to go . . . Hey, what's the time?'

Blank . . . Then a bare wrist exposed . . . 'They took it. I don't know — no idea, what . . .'

'Doesn't matter.' Only to have known how many hours they might have, hours of darkness . . . 'Nick, listen — this first bit's up to you — we need a way through the house that does *not* pass that guardroom. Maybe to a window we can get out of? Otherwise the back door'll be our best bet — a sentry there, I know, but only one, we could—'

'Oh, Christ . . .' He'd stopped, pulling free: like a horse shying, at the body. '*God* . . . *You* do that?'

'Yes. Here's your knife, by the way.'

Staring at it, as he took it . . . 'With *this*, you—'

'No, no . . . Come on now, Nick — which way through the house?'

Dull green eyes blinking . . . 'Through the house — no . . .'

'Look — I just explained—'

'Uh-huh.' Taking his eyes off the dead guard, at last. Glancing at the door, shaking his head. 'Not possible. Not a hope.'

'What are you saying?'

'They flop everywhere. All over. Every room, corridor, the hallways. On the stairs — the kitchens, even. Maroussia was telling us — yesterday, was it? Honestly, we'd be mad, even to—'

Even to try. Going on, driving the point home ...

But one *had* to try. All the thinking and planning of the last few hours had taken this bit in its stride, hadn't taken it into account as any problem. Partly because he couldn't have worked it out on his own, knowing so little of the house's layout — beyond the fact one certainly couldn't go through to the front past that guardroom — and Nick obviously knew every square foot of it.

Pointing at the door: 'Is it locked?'

'Bolted. But listen — we've no option. Except to stay here — which personally —' He stopped, shook his head. Conscious of wasting precious time. And the driving *need* ... 'Look, there's no other—'

'There.' Pointing again — down across the cellar, at the coal-heap. 'That's a way. There's a chute somewhere behind that. They dump the coal from a cart outside and it slides down. So if we clear it ...' Pausing, looking round: he seemed dazed, still: 'See? If we could clear it — then crawl out?'

But how long might it take ... There was a shovel — one only, and not up to much either, by the looks of it. One man shovelling, though — as long as the thing held together — and the other using his hands ... But there was no way of guessing how much coal — how many tons of it, for God's sake — might be piled against the wall outside, to keep filling the chute as fast as one could shift the stuff down into the cellar.

Could take hours ...

But Nick was probably right about the house. Hundreds of Bolsheviks lying around — and some of them quite sharp, like those fishermen. It would only take one challenge — then you'd be back where you'd started — worse, with this guard killed ... Staring at the mass of coal: imagining the two of them toiling away at it — hour after hour. *Might* work out, but . . .

New idea, then. He considered it for a moment, then rejected it. On the grounds that it would create — well, at least exacerbate certain later problems, and quite possibly create new ones.

But — what *else*?

And standing here talking about it didn't get one anywhere — except back into a cell, if you waited long enough . . .

He put a hand on the Count's shoulder. 'Look here. Two of us, shifting that lot could take all night. But what if there were four of us at it — if we let the Czechs out . . .'

So they'd got them out. Two bewildered — at first scared and suspicious, therefore hostile, Czechs . . . Both odd-looking — anyway at first sight: like strange beasts emerging uncertainly from their cages . . . But at least not maimed, as he'd guessed they might be if Khitrov had been at them during their stay here.

This was probably a mistake, he realized. Especially in relation to questions of weight and space in a small boat. *Two* small boats: one on the river, then the skiff down in the delta. Except perhaps by that time they'd have gone their own way . . . In any case this was the answer *now*: even if it meant signing a blank cheque for payment later. During the hours of waiting this evening he'd thought about letting the Czechs out anyway, for plain humanitarian reasons — Maroussia having mentioned that they were going to be shot — eventually, or soon, anyway *something* about their being shot — so to free them had been a natural impulse. He'd decided against it because it would complicate his own escape plans and the priority of saving the girls' lives — on which he'd no right to compromise. Now, therefore, *if* it worked out, they'd owe their lives to a heap of coal.

The first problem had been how to explain the basics of the situation to the one who looked like an orang-outan — Maroussia had been right when she'd said the officer looked like one — as he spoke practically no Russian, and certainly no English. Bob wasn't getting anywhere with him until the other Czech, a young sergeant who spoke Russian quite well, was let out of *his* cage. He was quick to pick up the essentials and passed them on in German to his captain — Captain Franz Majerle, the orang-outan — orange hair and beard, receding forehead, deep-sunk eyes, wide shoulders and long arms ... The sergeant, who'd said his name was Joseph Krebst, was also of distinctive appearance — Germanic-blond, only about five-six or five-seven but stocky, built like a small bull — dead right for the job of shifting a few tons of coal. Could have been his own father's son, in fact, Bob thought as they started work ... All four looking like coal-miners within minutes. Three anyway — he assumed he'd be no different. Majerle — the orang-outan — plastered in sweat and coal-dust, deepset eyes gleaming under the ridged forehead as they held Krebst's for a moment — pausing, shaking sweat off, grunting a few words in German. The sergeant grinned: an easy-going character, seemingly quite relaxed, taking this abrupt change in circumstances for granted — telling Bob, 'Captain say not believing — dying, he say, gone to hell!'

'Could be right.' Coal came sliding in a long, tumbling avalanche ... He left them at it for a moment. Noticing as he moved away that Nick looked like some creature out of a story by Jules Verne ... He stooped, got a hold on the legs of the dead guard and dragged him up into the area of the spreading coal-heap. The body left a wide, smeared trail of blood, but coal-dust would effectively disguise that soon enough. It seemed like a good idea to have it out of sight — burial being so easy, in the black flood piling behind them as they worked in towards its source. It might be some days before the Bolsheviks' noses detected it: meanwhile a guard as well as four prisoners would seem to have vanished.

Seeing the body, when they'd come through from the cells, had delighted both the Czechs. It had served as visible proof of *bona fides*: whoever had killed that Bolshevik was their ally — had his heart in the right place, so to speak. Much the same as they'd accepted *this* move now — he'd seen their interest, then comprehension and approval; lumps of coal were already landing on the body as he restarted work. Krebst and Nick Solovyev were so to speak at the coalface, Bob now joining the orang-outan behind them, clearing away the coal as the other two shifted it back. Bob stopped again: another thought sending him back to the corpse — before it disappeared — in the hope the guard might have had a watch. Should have thought of this before ... But no wristwatch anyway: in fact he'd only have had one if he'd stolen it. Pockets — nothing ... Except possibly — last chance ...

One battered timepiece. Rather more than battered — smashed. Its glass was gone and the metal casing had been squashed in. Hands still on the dial, stopped at five minutes to nine ... Glancing up, at a shout from Krebst: seeing him snatch at the Count's arm, pulling him back out of the way of a sudden rush of coal pouring in from where the mouth of the chute would be — must have cleared a blockage, and this was an influx from the heap outside, thundering in like black lava; its dust filled the cellar in a choking cloud.

Like fate itself, taunting them ...

Slowing, now: and stopped. A lump or two bouncing down: dust partially settling. A contortion of the Count's nigger-minstrel features, as if he might have been about to burst into tears ... Bob said to the orang-outan, 'You and me now.' Their turn at the face, the other two clearing behind them — and starting more or less from scratch. In fact there was *more* than there'd been to start with. And it could happen again — and again. With, incidentally, the risk of noise from the outside coalheap's subsidence attracting interference — from the back-door sentry, for instance.

Thinking, as he worked — that if that watch had been smashed when he'd killed the guard, that would have been, say, thirty-five or forty minutes ago, and the time now would be about a quarter to ten.

He'd expected to be out of here half an hour ago, at least. Sunset would have been at about eight o'clock, eight-fifteen. Moonset might not be more than half an hour off now. And this mining operation could be ended abruptly by the night shift coming on duty — or by that outside sentry hearing something ... Working like this, making a lot of noise because it couldn't be done quietly, you wouldn't have heard even if they'd been battering at the door ... But — controlling imagination, and assuming the chute *was* going to be cleared before any such disaster struck — think about revised timing for the rest of it ...

His own solo job might take about half an hour. Concurrent with the others' preparations, which he guessed would probably take longer — depending to a large extent on how long it might take Maroussia to locate her donkey and get him back to the coachhouse.

Another five minutes gone. Coal-dust, sweat, no obvious progress ...

'*Hunh!*'

Deep grunt from the orang-outan. Name — Franz, Franz Majerle ... Gibbering, and pointing into the black void. It did seem to be a void — a hollow, as if there was nothing there now to gush through. Although a couple of times before it had seemed to be like this and each time it had only been congestion which had then been cleared, starting a new inflow.

But this time — *perhaps* ...

Bob had pushed up beside him: peering into the black hole.

Through it. At night sky — still moon-washed — and a glitter of stars ... Nick's voice in a croak: 'Is it clear?'

'Looks like it.' Turning back to them: relief already overtaken by the need to get on with it — get *out* of here. But Nick had to be briefed first. And meanwhile for the orang-outan's benefit a finger to his lips: explaining to Krebst, 'Sentries — might hear us, and then —' miming, pointing outside, touching his ears for hearing, then a forefinger cutting his own throat. Understanding, translation, the orang-outan — Majerle — nodding his ridged, sloping forehead, ape's eyes gleaming white from the black surround. Ready-camouflaged, in fact, for the next stage ... He told the Count — the other two crowding in as well, Krebst visibly concentrating on what was being said — 'Nick — take these two to the coachhouse now. Don't leave a trail — when you're clear, stop and take your boots off, carry them. But there's a moon, so use the shadows, go *very* carefully.'

'What will you be doing?'

'Laying a false trail. I've thought it through, I know how to do it. Should take me about half an hour. But if I don't make it, Nick, when the rest of you are ready to go, just *go*, don't wait for me — huh?'

'Go where?'

'I'm about to explain that. But this is important — on no account wait for me, just go ahead — d'you understand?'

'Why don't we both take these two to the coachhouse, then you and I together—'

'No. We'll do it the way I'm telling you — please.' He was talking fast, urgently ... 'I've planned this out, it stands a good chance if we do it right — but the plain fact — you've *got* to accept this, Nick — is that *if* I don't make it there'd be no point waiting, it wouldn't help me, or anyone else either. What matters is getting the girls out of here, and this is the only chance we're likely to get. Here's the scheme now — it's up to you to explain it to them and get them started, so you *have* to go with these two to the coachhouse — sooner the better ... First — Maroussia — while you three are getting cleaned up and the girls are getting ready — ask them to get some food together, whatever can be spared — Maroussia must get her donkey in and harness him to the *telega.* Now there's the remains of an old boat in the coachhouse. Get that on the cart — with the tarpaulin over it. Lash the boat keel-up across the top of the cart — keel up, upside down, in other words ... And tell Maroussia — she's supposed to be barmy — right? — that although that boat's timbers are all holed and rotten she's got to have this crazy notion that she can sell it or barter it for food. And if they ask her why she's setting out in the middle of the night, she can say they make her work all day, what other time does she have, etcetera. She'll be going north, incidentally . . .'

'And we'll be in the cart?'

'No — we won't. Listen . . .'

He'd given Nick the revolver. 'Here. I won't be doing any shooting. Don't you, either. But we might need it in the next day or two. Go on now, Nick.'

'But what if we can't find that—'

'Just bloody well *have* to. Now go *on*!'

The Count went first, worming out through the chute. Then the orang-outan, and last the sergeant, with a farewell grin and a nod to Bob over his shoulder before he began to wriggle through.

Keys: one in a cell door, the other — he checked — in his pocket. Knife on his belt, in Nadia's sheath. Nick had got his own knife back . . . Hesitating, whether or not to douse the oil-lamp. He decided to leave it: in an hour or two it would burn out anyway, meanwhile better to leave things looking as they had been.

The others would be knocking on the coachhouse door by now. Please God. He climbed up the slope of coal, pushed his top half into the aperture, used elbows and knees to force himself through.

Into clean night air. Silent, moonlit, apparently empty night. A little breeze, and the distant thrumming of the river. The side of the coachhouse — actually of the lean-to kitchen — was directly across from here, across open ground that was palely moonlit until you got over there where there was shadow from the stable block. They'd be inside by now: the girls probably fainting with shock at the sight of them.

Not Nadia, though. He thought she wasn't the fainting type. But he was going to put them at some risk now by passing close to them, using that shadow: pass close by the coachhouse and along the stable block frontage — the way he and Nick had gone last night. Starting now, and hoping *not* to run slap into Maroussia ...

Boots off. Then running — doubled, head down, trying to do it soundlessly. Thinking meanwhile that it would probably be more sensible to walk — upright, even whistling ...

Into the welcome shadow. Bare feet — well, shreds of socks adhered to them still — on cool, smooth cobbles. Same route now, exactly, as last night when he'd followed Nick. Same destination too. Trusting there'd be no fishing-party around: last night having been Sunday, the end of the weekend, with any luck Monday wouldn't be a fishing night.

Behind him, as he left the western end of the stables, starting towards the birchwoods, he heard Maroussia calling 'Don Juan! Hey hey, Don Juan! *Gdye tiy*, Don Juan?'

The old darling. God bless her. And save her from what might otherwise be — he guessed — inevitable. Work some miracle for her? He thought, If ever a miracle was deserved ... In the thick grass now, where they'd been last night when the owl had hooted. He was ready for that tonight ... But only Maroussia calling again, somewhere behind him: she might even have spotted him, if those small, round eyes of hers were busy searching for Don Juan ... *Bloody* moon. Best get into cover before stopping to put boots back on.

Except — this wet grass — ideal ... He stopped, squatting down to wipe them clean of coal-dust. What had been important was not to lead them to the coachhouse, but here they could pick his trail up if they liked, they were supposed to believe escapers had come this way. A thought arose from that: to come back over the *same* tracks. Just in case they lasted, into the light of day — even the early morning dew ... He had his boots on, was trotting on: a minute later he was in the cover of the birches.

And around them, in the spinney's edge, as last night. If he ran into Stukalin's ghost looking as he was now the poor thing would probably let out a worse yell than ever

... There'd been no more yells from Maroussia. Presumably she'd found her donkey. He halted, short of the driveway and looking up and down it, listening. Nothing ... He went on across it: glancing left across Stukalin's meadow at the glowing front of *Rïibachnaya Dacha* — which last night he'd also seen from here; this same view but little guessing when he'd been gazing at it that very shortly afterwards he'd be marching in there with his hands up.

A lesson learnt the hard way. But it could have been harder still. And it wasn't only luck — this was part of the same lesson — you needed some luck but mostly it was doing the thing *right.*

Like killing, when you had to.

He could see the river. The moon lighting its surface like polished silver a hundred or a hundred and fifty yards out, while closer to this bank the shadows from the trees reached out, their reach extending further as the moon slid down. The steamboat was in sight too now, funnel and superstructure silhouetted against the bright water out beyond.

At about this point last night he'd told Nick he didn't need him, that he'd go on alone.

Assume there were no fishermen. There surely wouldn't be, two nights running: and to check it out you'd be taking the risk Nick hadn't realized *was* a risk — groping through the trees, with sticks and dead leaves scrunching underfoot. Job for a Red Indian ...

Riverbank, then, no reconnaissance of the willow groves. As quietly as possible, but also bearing in mind that you didn't have any time to waste.

The steamboat was berthed precisely where it had been. He backed into the trees' cover, then moved quietly along towards the downstream barrier of timber piles. It was all in shadow there, the deepest shadow being around and between the piles themselves. He'd come far enough. Pausing to listen — for parties bivouacked in the woods, first. But the river's sounds would cover most of any other, when you were this close to it ... He was near-enough certain of total invisibility, right close to the piles, rubbing shoulders with them.

Cigarette smell . . .

Searching — and finding it. Red pinpoint, down on the landing-stage. And the dark shape of a man sitting or squatting on the stage, more or less abreast the steamboat's stern . . . He cleared his throat, and spat. He — not Bob . . . Bob standing as still as the timber pile beside him, examining the landing-stage, riverbank and the steamboat's deck and stern for any other human presence.

Just that one. As far as he could tell.

Knife — accessible, loose in its sheath. He left it there, lowered himself to his hands and knees and started crawling down towards the stage. Grateful for the noise the river made where it sluiced between the timbers and between the stage and the steamboat's hull. That crewman — watchman, whatever he was — was facing the river. Would be, obviously. Gazing out past the boat's stern at the silvered midstream flow of Russia's beloved mother-river . . .

Creeping on down, getting close now. Keeping to the deep shadow and his eyes on the as yet unsuspecting smoker. Deciding against using the knife: if it could be done without it. He'd been lucky with the guard in the cellar; he was no knife-man, had no experience of knife-fighting and knew very little about anatomy. But probably more important here was the question of blood. Not out of squeamishness — he'd put that kind of weakness behind him — but with a half-formed thought that it might be better if there was not any mess on the landing-stage.

Actually that thought wasn't only *half*-formed . . . He was close enough now. Pausing . . . The thought had been temporarily obscured, that was all, but it was sound enough, it surely *would* be better not to leave signs of a killing here.

He went at him in a crouching run, not directly from behind but from the right flank. Crashing into him, hands grabbing at his throat and crushing, the crewman jack-knifed over on to his face by the impact — he'd had no chance, had been taken completely by surprise, the breath knocked out of him and no breath or sound getting in or out thereafter: neck broken, probably — it had felt like it, through his hands — and throat crushed flat.

Holding on. Making sure of it. Panting: heart going like a piston ... Thoughts going back to the girls waiting in the coachhouse, remembering the panic he'd felt for them during the long hours when there'd seemed to be no hope. And of the ropes dangling, those *disgusting* mementoes of appalling bestiality ... And himself in that pitch-dark cell — *shaking*, in anticipation of Khitrov. Facing it: nothing one could have done *but* face it: but still shaking, in the dark. The river's thrum and its gurgling flow between the timber piles were the only sounds outside his own hard, short breathing ... A minute: might have been ninety seconds by now: and his father's voice out of memory, the old man warning him about deficiencies which in the pursuit of a career at sea he might find it advantageous to overcome: *You're a bit of an old softie, you know...*

He let go slowly. The body slumped down and he pulled back, taking his weight off it.

There was a holstered pistol. He took it, pushed it inside his own belt, leaving the holster because there wasn't time for that. Having to check the steamer now. And boots off, first: then into her stern, boarding just where he had the previous night. Stern and side-decks were empty: a glance up each side was all that took. Wheelhouse, then — also empty: so back to the stern.

He crouched, listening: heart still thumping ...

No snores, tonight.

But a sleeper didn't have to snore. And seconds, not minutes, counting now: with a body lying in the open and even chances of other crewmen coming back aboard for the night. Not to mention the half-hour he'd allowed himself, the fact Nick *might* do as he'd been told ... He stooped into the companionway, crept down inside.

Empty cabin: lit by moonlight reflected from the river through ports on the outboard — starboard — side ... Relief was — considerable ... But now, get on with it —

while the luck held. He went up, and forward, found the engineroom hatch — boiler-space, then engine-space abaft it, and in there two iron deckplates giving access to the bilges. Up on deck again and back over the stern to the landing-stage: hoisting the body across his shoulders, carrying it on board and below, finally sliding it into the bilge-space head-first; he had to fold the legs in before he could get the cover properly reseated.

They wouldn't check in there immediately. The little steamer would be found somewhere down-river — with good luck, a long way down. They'd find her deserted, and assume that whoever had taken her — escaped prisoners, surely — had either been content to let the river carry them downstream, or so ignorant of the principles of steam propulsion that they'd boarded and cast off in the belief there'd be some way to start the engine. When they'd realized their error — or grounded on some bend or mudbank — they'd abandoned her.

But that would be the way they'd gone. Even if she was only carried a few hundred yards before she stuck. Not even Lesechko would doubt it — for a day or two.

On the landing-stage he cast off the bow mooring rope first, then leant his weight against her stem to start her swinging out. A start was all it needed: the stream took charge then, pivoting her on her stern, which was against the stage, held by the after breast. Then judging his moment, he threw the turns off that bollard too, lobbed the coils of line into her stern, and watched her go.

14

He knocked on the door — panting, having jogged all the way back from the river — and his double rap was answered immediately with a whisper of 'Who's there?'

'Bob.'

'Glory to God ...' Nadia's hissed murmur, as the door creaked open; then he was inside and she was pushing it shut and fastening it behind him. Bob taking in the lamplit scene: Don Juan standing between the *telega*'s shafts, that wreck of a boat on top of it, Nick and Krebst looking up from securing the tarpaulin over it with rotten-looking twine. He checked the time — on Nadia's little watch: ten forty-two ... Maroussia beaming at him, her old fingers working at the donkey's cheek-strap, Irina coming from the kitchen with a bundle wrapped in cloth — food, no doubt. Both the girls were wearing trousers and wool jackets. Nadia whispered, brushing at herself where he'd touched her when getting at her watch, 'You're *filthy*!'

'No time to wash, either.' Smiling as he turned to her. 'Sorry. Later, I'll—'

'You're also brilliant. Truly.' Irina pushed in between them, similarly welcoming, and Bob smiled at her: 'Irina. Sorry we gave you an anxious time.' Nadia continuing, across this, 'Nick's told us all about it, Bob. We owe you — *everything* ...'

'Owe Maroussia, not me.' But he wasn't thinking much about who owed what to whom: for the moment there wasn't time to think about anything except the essentials of this evacuation. Although as it were in the same short breath he was conscious of a surge of — well, *elation* — astonishment in it too — at what he'd read — was *still* reading — in her face.

Lovely face. Having then to wrench his eyes off it, and using Maroussia as an excuse — although he meant this anyway — 'Maroussia, how can I thank you? There aren't words . . .'

'Who *wants* words?'

'But I think you'll have to come with us now. They're sure to guess — in time.'

'In time, I'll be dead. What did you do with the key?'

'Here.'

'Would you get rid of it? A long way off?'

'Right.' Glancing round. 'You ready, Nick?'

The Count nodded. He'd washed most of the coal-dust off; his head and beard were dripping wet still. 'Did you fix the steamboat?'

'It's on its way down-river.'

'No trouble?'

He shrugged. 'Not much.' Asking Krebst, 'All set, Sergeant?'

'Very good — thank you!' Krebst laughed. He was the sort of man who laughs easily. Nadia murmured, 'The other one talks French, Bob.' Nodding towards Majerle, the orang-outan, as he came out of the kitchen shaking water off himself. Nadia added, '*Good* French.' Bob's eyes held hers again — for about two seconds that might have been two minutes . . . Then: '*That's* worth knowing. Not that mine's up to much.' He tried some of it, all the same, on the orang-outan: '*Très bon! On peut causer en Francais, uh?*'

'*Mais oui! Et je veux vous remercier, Monsieur . . .*'

'*Robat. Je m'appelle Robat. Mais — pas nécessaire — du tout.*'

Krebst didn't talk French, Nick told him — drawing him aside, wanting a private word. But the rest of them did, of course . . . 'Bob — we do have to take the Czechs along with us, I suppose?'

'Unless they choose to go off on their own. That would

be fine. But we need to get 'em well away from here first, don't you agree?'

'You mean in case they were recaptured, and—'

'Exactly. And for the same reason let's stick to Anton Vetrov and Robat, and not a word about princesses.'

Not that one had positive reason to distrust them. But when time and circumstances allowed, one might enquire into their background, probe a little: it seemed strange that Khitrov didn't seem to have done them any harm. 'Nick — on the same subject — I acquired another pistol down there. I want mine, by the way — wherever Nadia or Maroussia put it ... But we have four between us now — what d'you think about arming the Czechs?'

'I don't know ...'

'Let's not, then. What about the tunnel under the wall?'

'Nobody's sure. But we have a rope, we could get over it, if—'

'Right. Make sure you bring it. And it's up to you to take us to the right spot. Next question is where should Maroussia pick us up? Cutting the corner, if we get to the road a hundred metres north of the gate, as you said — how far from there, with cover we can wait in?'

'Four, five hundred metres, from where we rejoin the road. There's a bend before that, and we could wait down on the river side of the levee.'

'Fine. And Maroussia — when you get to us, don't stop. If you did they might hear it from the gate. Keep Don Juan down to a walk, we'll pile in one at a time while you're on the move, then you can give him his head. All right?'

She'd nodded. Don Juan moving his ears about as if to hear better. Bob said, 'Then the big decision — how far north can you take us?'

'Not to Fedorovka?'

Fedorovka, of the blood-red sunset, had been the place in his mind when he'd briefed Nick an hour earlier. Knowing that she and the donkey had been that far, to collect Nick's mother and the two girls, that it was a distance they could manage. But he'd been having second thoughts: had been reminded, when he'd cast the steam-boat adrift, of this river's strength.

'Fedorovka would do, Maroussia. A long way for you and this fellow anyway. But — look ...' He sketched it with a forefinger on the donkey's grey hide. 'Here's the river. Here on the other bank, Sasykolsk. We need to fetch up somewhere near there — actually just *above*—'

'Where you met Leonid Mesyats.'

'Exactly! But you see — six of us in a boat, with one man rowing ...'

'Kopanovka would be the best place. You'd have a channel right across, and all downstream.' Glancing at the Count. 'For me, ten or twelve versts farther, that's all.'

'Could you really make that distance?'

'*He* could.' She ruffled Don Juan's ears. 'Take a bit longer, that's all.'

The Count led, with Nadia next behind him, then Majerle, Krebst, Irina, and Bob bringing up the rear. Single file and about six paces apart, slipping out of the door and turning right along the front of the stable-block and around its end, then northward towards the road. The moon was down, but the night was windless now and every sound the others made ahead of him seemed dangerously loud.

The vital thing was to be gone before a relief guard found the cellar door bolted, got no response from inside and started yelling. But not just for *them* to be gone — Maroussia too. These few minutes now would be the worst time of all for the alarms to sound. The plan was that she'd give them time to get clear before she started out, so when she was stopped at the gate she'd have nothing on board except the remains of the old dinghy, and they'd be waiting for her to pick them up just down the road: they'd have got out either through the old bolt-hole which Leonid Mesyats' grandson was thought to have made use of a few days ago, or if Nick couldn't find it, over the wall.

These were beeches. Fine old trees, their great canopies shutting out the sky. Sounds as of a small army blundering through the night ahead of him.

Irina, suddenly close . . .

'All right?'

Her pale face as she turned . . . 'Having trouble finding it, I expect.'

'Might as well close up. You might help him.'

'Yes . . .'

Bunching up. Krebst — Majerle, then . . . 'Nadia?'

'Yes, I'm here.' Her whisper. 'But — just a minute . . .'

'This way.' Nick's voice, from the right. 'I've found it. Nadia?'

'Coming.' From behind them, the direction of the house, an owl hooted. Possibly *the* owl . . . They were advancing in a group now, a few paces behind Nadia. Then the wall loomed black, with the trees' great branches overhanging it. Nadia had stopped. 'Nikki?'

'I don't think it's any use.' His voice came from ground-level. 'Too narrow. All right for a child, perhaps, but—'

'Didn't Boris use it?'

'We don't know for sure. Might have partly filled in since then, anyway. Bob?'

'Over the top.' He came up beside Nadia. 'Where's the rope?'

He took the coil from Nick: it felt like *rotten* rope . . . Get over without it, maybe. Up one of these trees, out along a branch to the wall, haul the girls up . . . Looking up at the branches, he decided to try the rope anyway: not that this would be a good time for breaking legs.

'Give me some room. I'll chuck it over that one.'

The third throw made it. He reached up for the dangling end, hauled it down so that the rope was doubled over the branch, close enough to the wall.

'I'll go up first — if this doesn't break — then haul the girls up. Then you, Nick, and you go over the other side and I'll lower them down to you. I'll get the Czechs up after you three are over. All right?'

Nadia muttered, '*Will* it take your weight?'

'Soon find out . . .'

Luckily, it did. Which meant it would take the others'

weight too. It didn't have to take the whole weight anyway, except at some brief moments, a lot of it was on the wall through one's feet as one scrambled up: but if it *had* broken he'd have come down on his back. He made it, though, digging the toes of his boots into crevices between the bricks, then transferring — not easy — from the branch to the top of the wall ...

'All right. Girls now ...'

Nadia, then Irina. Then the Count, then the orang-outan and Krebst. He pulled the ends of the rope up, threw them down on the other side. 'Down you go, Nick.' The Count slid down into the darkness on that side, and when he whispered up that he was ready Bob lowered Irina into his arms. Then Nadia. The Czechs went over, using the rope, and he followed.

Landing in long grass and bushes: he hauled the rope down by jerking it around the branch. Maroussia might need it, but in any case the last thing one wanted was to leave a marker here. Coiling it between hand and elbow as he ran, following the others across the road — which curved concavely at this point, following the edge of the high ground which had justified Stukalin or his predecessors building a house here. The curve's concavity was eastward: and the intention now was to cut across that area of low ground — bog, presumably — and rejoin the road well above the north gate, out of which Maroussia and Don Juan would be clattering in about ten minutes' time. Where you rejoined the road you'd be climbing up on to the levee, artificial banking that carried the road above the level of spring floods.

Nick led again — over the road and down a steep, uneven slope. Even in mid-summer the dead-flat ground was soft underfoot. The long grass would keep it so, Bob supposed. Soft, but firm enough to walk on. Getting an idea from it, an alternative approach to the river crossing. Wishing he had Leonid Mesyats here to consult ... Up ahead, Nick had Irina with him, and the Czechs were close behind them; looking round for Nadia, Bob found her close on his left.

Putting out a hand: 'All right?'

'Need to hurry, don't we?'

'Yes . . .'

Otherwise Maroussia might be driving out on to the road ahead of them, and have to stop, not knowing where they'd got to. Then the man or men on the north gate would hear her stop: and later, when all hell broke loose, might remember . . .

What might happen to Maroussia was a major worry. The other big one was what to do when — assuming the right word was *when*, not *if* — what to do when one got down to the delta, with only one small boat at one's disposal and six grown people to be transported in it. Even in a flat calm — and as the days passed the odds against getting many more flat calms on the Caspian were lengthening.

Nadia panted, 'Ought to *just* make it . . .'

Nick whispered back to them, 'I can make out the levee now. Not far to go.'

They all heard it then: the cart's iron-rimmed wheels on cobbles. On a still night like this you'd just about hear it in Enotayevsk . . . It had stopped now. Nadia had begun, 'Oh Lord, that's —' and then checked, in the silence. Bob imagining the cart stopped, Don Juan flexing his ears while Maroussia went to shut the coachhouse door. She'd be climbing back up now, flipping the reins . . .

At exactly that moment the wheels began to grind again. He called, 'Nick — better *run*?'

Maroussia said crossly, 'Told you, didn't I? It's a boat. My late husband, God bless him, used to catch fish from it. None of *your* business, anyway.'

'You wouldn't catch many fish from it now, *babushka*, I'll tell you that for nothing!'

'It can be mended. Look, cover that end up, put it back as it was before!'

'I'd sell it under the cover, if I were you. Best chance you'd have. What d'you reckon you'll get for it?'

She sniffed. 'Sack of turnips, maybe.'

'You and your turnips.' The soldier laughed. 'On you go, then, *babushka*. Let me know how you get on, eh?'

She flipped the reins. '*Po-idyom* ...'

Plodding out through the gateway and turning right, northward. Iron wheel-rims clattering on the ridged surface. After about a hundred yards, just around the bend, she saw a figure on the road ahead: with four or five hundred metres still to cover before she'd been supposed to see anyone ...

'Maroussia.' Low-voiced, but audible enough — the Count. Other figures appearing behind him now, seeming to rise out of the ground like apparitions ... She clicked her tongue at Don Juan, to keep him going, guessing he'd take this meeting as a good excuse to stop if he was given half a chance ... 'Thought you'd be farther on than this.'

'Only just made it.' Panting. 'Had to run ...'

'Put my darlings in first, eh?'

'Of course.' The Count was loosening the twine and pulling back the leading edge of the tarpaulin. The cart having an escort of pedestrians now — stumbling along beside it, puffing and blowing ... He had the front uncovered, room for anyone to get in on either side of the boat's bow and then duck under and sit down. There'd be plenty of headroom, anyway ... 'Nadia — here, I'll give you a leg up ...'

Trundling northwards. Don Juan was doing well, having maintained a reasonably fast trot for — well, more than an hour now, probably — Maroussia keeping him up to scratch with an occasional crack across the rump — using the loose end of the reins, leaning forward from her perch to reach him with it — while the *telega* banged and clattered over ruts and potholes, swayed around the bends.

Under the boat's stern were the two girls and the Count — they'd been the first to board — while the Czechs and Bob were in the front, the thwart across the midships section of the boat dividing the head-space into these two halves. The tendency was to sit with the feet drawn in, hugging one's knees. Noise and vibration kept verbal exchanges to a minimum; although Bob was using his advantageous position in the bow to spend periods on his feet, leaning beside Maroussia for sporadic conversation.

Some of this was useful. For instance she was sure about there being a transverse deepwater channel that would take them across from Kopanovka to the fishing-station a few miles downstream. It linked the two main, roughly parallel channels, ran — he gathered, putting his own interpretation on to her sketchy description of it — from north-west to south-east, starting about two miles below Kopanovka where you'd take a left fork into it. When she'd last been on the river up there — with her husband, years ago — there used always to be a small island high and dry in about the middle of it, and after the island a branch southward which was not a main channel but into which the current was always very strong. So you'd hug the left bank, keep to it, and finally emerge into the main channel only about a mile above the fishing-station. Which, she warned him, would be deserted now, Leonid Mesyats and his like having all dispersed to their own villages. Her Ivan had been a keen fisherman in his day, and in her own younger days she'd spent a lot of time on the river with him. All their friends had been fishing people; from childhood onwards the river had been initially their livelihood, later their recreation and still an appreciable source of food.

'So when the Solovyev family weren't here . . .'

'Spring and autumn — yes.'

Then later he'd broached another subject . . . 'Maroussia. This very long trip you're making for us. You aren't likely to be back at the *Dacha* much before sunrise, are you?'

'About then.' She cackled. 'In time for work.' A flip of the reins . . . 'All right for this old devil, he can sleep all day. Sleep and eat, is all he does!'

'Will you take the boat back with you?'

'Suppose so. I'll say they wouldn't buy it. Mean pigs . . .'

'Then you'll find Nadia missing, and you'll want to know what they've done with her.'

'I'll say she went out with me to find Don Juan, and the

night was beautiful so she decided to stay out for a little while. That was the last I saw her. They might believe the prisoners caught her and took her with them.' A shrug of the bent, shawled figure ... 'Give them *something* to believe. But I'll say their filthy soldiers must have — taken her, or—'

'You'd be desperate, wouldn't you — *mad* with worry.'

'I'll be mad, all right!'

'But as regards this boat — couldn't you stop in Enotayevsk, at the *Shvedski traktir*, persuade the Swede to give you some turnips for it? Half a sack, say?'

'Maybe. Wake him up. Tell him I was there earlier looking for him. And I've been out all night looking for a buyer. Went to Fedorovka, maybe ...'

'That's good. You'd have at least *some* support for your story, then. If you needed any. And if anyone had seen you passing through Enotayevsk earlier — seen or heard you ...'

'Yes. Yes ...'

They'd been coming up to Fedorovka. He'd got back inside, feeling a bit better about the old girl, that she might get away with it. Being allegedly crazy, she'd be hard to trap. Only if there was physical evidence — coal-dust for instance. Even in this cart: and notably from himself, the only one of them who hadn't cleaned himself up. He made a mental note to tell her this: so she'd throw a bucket or two of water over it. But the mess in her kitchen, too, around the tap where the others had rinsed themselves. And she ought to check the Hole very carefully for any evidence of its having been made use of; then shift all that hay back over the trapdoor.

The orang-outan asked him in French, 'Are we doing all right?'

'Doing fine.' Over the internal noise, you had to yell. 'But we're about to go through a village. So — need to stay quiet.' He leant back to warn the others: 'Fedorovka coming up.'

'Maroussia and Don Juan all right?'

'Both doing well.'

'But —' Nick, leaning forward past Irina — 'Are we — up to schedule?'

'God knows.' There wasn't any schedule. The hope, as he saw their present situation, was simply to get to the other side of the river, to that transport, before daylight. At *least* before daylight . . . 'Nadia, can you see the time by your watch?'

'No, but it must be — twelve-thirty?'

He grunted, sitting back. Noise and motion changing as the condition of the road surface changed, in the approach to the village. Clock-watching wouldn't help anyway, he thought, all you could do was push on as fast as possible; you couldn't estimate how long any particular stage of the journey might take. How long to get to Kopanovka, then to find and take a boat; then the crossing, landing, doing something or other about the boat — covering of tracks being vitally important . . .

More distantly — but getting less so as time passed — the real spectre was the looming problem of one small skiff, six people, and the Caspian, which could be as treacherous as any other sea.

The three women were in tears when the time came to say goodbye, on the levee road a few hundred yards short of Kopanovka. Even the Count's voice had sounded a bit strangled. Bob meanwhile resisting the urge to hug the old woman, for fear of impregnating her clothes with coal-dust. Frightening thought, that just a few grammes of coal-dust might put her into Khitrov's hands . . . She'd been turning the cart, Nick leading the donkey round; Bob had told her, 'We all owe you our lives. I'm sure none of us will ever forget you.' Nadia sobbed, 'We'll be praying for you, Maroussia darling.'

'More sense to pray for yourselves. Nobody's going to do an old crow like me any harm. Go with God, may He protect you and bless you with happy lives, my children.' She'd whacked Don Juan into a trot, mercifully cutting the bad moment short, and they'd scrambled down the side of the levee, so as to approach the village along the river and as invisibly as possible.

Irina whispered, 'It's *dreadful*, to think we'll never see her again!'

'I know.' Nadia was still snuffling too. 'It's *wrong*. If only we could have persuaded her to come with us . . .'

Then there'd have been *seven* in the skiff, Bob thought. Although he had tried to persuade her, and was far from happy at the thought of her going back to *Krasnaya Dacha* . . . He was leading the party now, feeling his way carefully over uneven ground, hearing the girls' whispers behind him and an occasional exchange of mutters from the Czechs, and with the village in sight ahead, roofs and chimneys clear-cut against the stars. Destination the waterfront, village quay — and either one boat or two.

The disadvantage of using two would be the risk of the boats getting separated and losing each other. Imagining the Czechs on their own in one boat being swept into the downstream channel that Maroussia had mentioned: he personally wouldn't have been exactly distraught at losing them now, but an extension of the scenario was to see them stranded somewhere, arrested, and talking to save their own skins. Even if the rest of them had got clear by then, Maroussia would be — to put it mildly, vulnerable . . .

The village was very close now. Very small, too: a hamlet more than a village. Waiting for the others to catch up, he was looking down at the river, at its swift bubbling flow a few yards out from the bank. Closer in, the bank hid it. But a path led down: fishermen's access, he guessed, perhaps the village boys. String and bent pins . . . An idea forming: why not make use of that current, let it work for us?

Once he had a boat he'd every intention of doing exactly that. But now — the business of *getting* a boat . . .

Brand new idea hatching. Hell of a lot better than one he'd toyed with earlier. That one had been to avoid any upstream work with a heavily-loaded boat by rowing straight across and landing on the central island or islands, the dried-out land in the middle of the river, hauling the boat across and relaunching it. Not impossible, with four men to do the *portage*. But the going might have been too difficult — swampy areas, for instance.

'Hang on a minute, Nick?'

He wanted to check on how accessible or otherwise the river might be, down there where the path led. It might lead right down to the water, or the bank lower down might be sheer and so high above the present water-level that you'd need a ladder.

It was steep, anyway. He sat, went down feet first, using his heels and his bottom, hands flat on the dew-damp, slippery ground.

The path did take one right down to the water. Although — well, fishermen *might* use it, but not as much as cattle did. Cattle used it a lot.

And this was viable. A lot better than six people trooping into a tiny, dead-quiet village and probably waking them all up.

On the point of returning to the others he paused, groped in his pocket for Maroussia's key and lobbed it into the darkness above the river. Hearing no splash, over the river's continuous murmur. She'd told him, in the *telega*, that the key had been her husband's, the Bolsheviks had never changed those locks when they'd converted store-rooms into cells; she'd hung on to it, just in case a day might come when she'd have need of it.

As indeed it had. And again, thank God for her.

He climbed on up. His thought until this moment having been to go on his own into the village, get hold of a boat and bring it, embark them down there where the cattle drank. But — rethinking it now — swimming to the boats' moorings would be far better. Or wading, or crawling along in the shallows — depending on how one found it. That short distance, even against a current of two or as much as four knots, would present no problems. And however small this place was there'd surely be boats — or at least *a* boat — at the quay.

Landing-stage below the quay, probably. As at Enota-yevsk. The system would be universal, meeting the needs of fishermen and other river users.

'Nick — no need to go into the village. The river's accessible, at the bottom of this path. I'm going to swim from there, bring a boat back.' He pointed downstream. 'Going that way — don't even have to *pass* the village.'

'Brilliant ... But I'll go with you.'

'Much better if you stayed with the girls. Suppose I got into trouble?'

'Well ...'

'*I* go with you?'

Krebst ...

'Can you swim well?'

A nod ... 'Swim good. Row boat good, too.'

'All right ... Irina, is that a white shirt you're wearing, under your coat?'

'Yes. Why?'

'When you're waiting down there, take your coat off? The white'll show up, give me a mark ... Nick, the path's steep, and slippery, best go down on your bums. And watch out for bloody cowpats, I put my hand in one ... Oh, look, if you wouldn't mind — hang on to this lot for me?'

One jacket, assorted weaponry, boots ...

Nadia was whispering in French to the other Czech, explaining what was happening. Bob led the sergeant down, and explained to him before they went into the river that he'd take one boat if it was big enough to hold them all, or two if they were all the smaller type of dinghy. Also, to save time and noise and be less visible, instead of getting into the boat or boats they'd stay in the water, swim with them.

'Let's go, then.'

Slithering in: the river's flow immediately very noticeable. As well as cleansing: recalling Nadia's critical remark ... Soft mud bottom: easier to swim than wade. He looked back, waiting to be sure that Krebst could cope all right: and he could, was doing so, using a powerful breaststroke that was ideal for the purpose — producing no splash, only a little bow-wave as he forged into the current, face low in the water. Riverbank on the left darkly visible ... Bob used breaststroke too, swimming a few yards ahead of him.

He could see the quay, its vertical stone-faced wall replacing the curve of riverbank and bushes. Houses' roofs behind it. The post of a derrick, gibbet-like against the sky. River steamers would load farm produce here, he guessed.

Boats — Mesyats-type boats — ahead and to his left, more or less end-on, noticeable in the first place through movement — the flow of the current past them, the surface breaking where it lapped noisily around their timbers — and the boats jostling each other as they moved to it. Three — four ... And that *was* a timber landing-stage. He glanced back, saw Krebst close to him, turned and swam to this near-end of the stage, almost under the first boat's stern.

Irina whispered, crouching on the bank between Nadia and the Count, 'Be awful if our food got wet. When they come with the boat, Nikki ...'

'I'll take it from you and pass it over when you're in. Don't worry.'

Nadia said, after a pause, 'Isn't Bob absolutely *splendid*?'

'He's a good fellow.' The Count added, 'But of course this stuff —' pointing at the water — 'is his natural element. And boats and so forth, it's his trade, that's why he's here. So — what's the saying, if you keep a dog why do your own barking?'

From the direction of the village, a dog began to bark.

'Speak of the devil ...'

Majerle, the orang-outan, muttered in French, 'They've woken them up.'

A man's voice — shouting. Words indistinguishable, but in a tone of alarm. More than one dog was barking now: it sounded very close. Irina hugged her brother's arm: 'Oh, *God*..'

'Steady on ...'

The barking was all one dog's again, and even that one's frenzy seemed to have passed its peak. Then, over the river's thrum, what might have been a door slamming — or, in retrospect now, a shot. The orang-outan growled, 'They've run into trouble, *that's* for sure.'

He was a fool, Nadia thought. As well as highly unprepossessing. She muttered in French, 'I see no reason to believe so. Just because some dogs start barking.'

'You're right, Nadia.' The Count — clutching at the straw. 'Absolutely right.' He had his arm round Irina, who was whispering 'Come on, come *on* . . .'

The boat virtually sprang at them out of the dark at that moment. Swerving sharply into the bank out of empty blackness and the river's passing flood, a large figure materializing out of the shallows at its bow end and then another near the stern. Bob called quietly, 'Nick — take this line?'

He did the rowing himself until he'd got them into the channel that branched off eastward. Then Krebst took over, with Bob navigating, making sure he stayed close to the left-hand bank, circling even farther northward when about an hour later the channel divided around the central island. The island in fact was barely visible — wouldn't have been identifiable as such if one hadn't known of it and been looking for it. The southward drag of current was very strong at that stage, and for about half an hour it was necessary to aim off by as much as twenty or thirty degrees — aiming the boat at the bank in order to crab along parallel to it. Things got easier after they'd passed the island; Nick took a spell at the oars, and Bob relieved him after another half-hour, by which time they'd been entering the main channel.

Two hours, roughly, since departure from Kopanovka.

He was the only one of them who hadn't slept. He'd forced himself to stay awake — several times catching himself on the point of nodding off — because he'd realized that it was all being left to him now, Nick Solovyev having apparently — effectively — become a passenger.

As if he'd expended all his energies. Or had the stuffing knocked out of him, during those minutes facing Lesechko in his own ancestral home.

But maybe he was just exhausted. Bob himself didn't remember ever feeling quite this tired. Not even in his year and a half in the Dover Patrol — in an ancient destroyer, wild days and nights often in force 8 gales playing hide-and-seek with German destroyers in and around the minefields, with hardly any rest even in harbour — repairing, refuelling, ammunitioning, maybe a few hours at anchor in the destroyer lines where it was about as rough as it was outside the breakwaters ... Chaotic memories returning now because this state of exhaustion *was* comparable: and in present circumstances alarming, raising doubts as to whether one could trust one's own judgement, or reactions in any new emergency.

He'd thought an emergency had been developing at Kopanovka, when the dog had started giving tongue. He'd been on the landing-stage, casting off the boat's painter from an iron ring, and the ring had toppled, clanged against the iron plate securing it to the timber. That was all it had taken to rouse the dog — one clink ... It had started barking, then a window had scraped up in one of the cottages and an old man had shouted angrily at it. Quavery old voice ... Another dog had joined in for a while: Bob had thought the whole village would have been roused, that maybe he and Krebst were going to have to run — or rather swim — for it ... Frightening prospect: without a boat they'd have been done for. Working fast, getting the stern line off — not all that simple in the dark, one had first to trace that line from the boat to another ring with other boats' lines on it as well. Then — enormous relief — back in the water, towing the boat out from the stage: barks diminishing, the dog getting no support for its efforts and giving up, and finally the old man had slammed his window shut.

'Bob — isn't that the processing shed?'

Nick — in the stern with the girls, all three of them had been slumbering — was leaning forward, pointing. Bob rested on his oars, and looked round. Knowing they *would* come to that iron-roofed shed first . . .

That was it, all right. The shed's long iron roof was a low slab of blackness against lighter sky.

Definitely lighter sky. He hadn't realized it until this moment: but the stars were fading, in that eastern sector.

So in an hour, hour and a half at most, you'd have something like daylight here. And the emergency, therefore, was *now*. Having anticipated getting down into the delta by sunrise: now having it thrust into one's sluggish mind that no such thing was possible. Roughly a hundred miles to go: having first to (a) get ashore (b) hide the boat somehow (c) get to the barn — hoping to God the truck would be there — unguarded, and with petrol in its tank . . .

And then — *if* all that worked out — you'd be making the journey south in daylight. In order to end up on that marsh with your small skiff and six people to take out to sea in it.

Bloody nightmare. And a head that felt as if it might have been full of lead . . . He told himself, *Don't try to think. Just get on with it.*

Rowing, anyway . . . And asking Nick, 'Tell me when you see the landing-stage. About a hundred yards beyond the shed, wasn't it?' He adjusted his course, edging the boat round to close in nearer the bank. At the same time, visualizing the landing place and the slope beyond it where he'd watched fishermen hauling their boats up, he realized that the obvious thing to do with this boat was exactly that, the same as they'd done with theirs. There'd be no counting of boats, it might lie there for months — at least for the few days they needed now with no one on their trail.

'Nick, listen. We'll land the girls at the stage. Then the four of us can pull this boat up and park it with the others. The girls can keep lookout while we're doing it. And — listen . . .'

The brain did still work, after a fashion and at about half speed. Remembering now that those fishermen had wooden rollers on which they'd hauled their boats up, and guessing that the rollers would be up at the top of the slope, left there when the last boat had been taken up. So Nick could go up there, take a precautionary look around, leave the girls there and bring the rollers down. While the Czechs also disembarked here at the tilted landing-stage, to meet him when he brought the boat to the bottom of the slip.

Nick commented, about ten minutes later when they'd done it. 'That was good thinking, Bob.'

He looked at him through the darkness. Finding himself short of words as well as sleep. He managed, 'Let's see if the truck's there now.' A hand on Nadia's arm: 'This way.'

Until they got up there, their only cover was the darkness. No trees, bushes, anything. Leading them uphill, with Nadia beside him and the Count somewhere on his left with Irina, the Czechs following, he forced himself to the effort of putting the immediate problems into words: less for anyone's information than in the hope that someone — meaning Nick, primarily — might come up with answers, or comments that might lead to answers. The main points being that it would be light in about an hour, that if they set off in the truck now most of the journey would be made in daylight, and it wasn't beyond the bounds of possibility that the Cheka might have put out a general alert — anti-Bolshevik prisoners on the run. They'd use the telephones at railway stations, probably. Another point was that in daylight the truck — or lorry — might be recognized. And — finally — they'd arrive on the marsh in daylight, and for obvious reasons they'd want to put some distance between themselves and wherever they dumped the truck: so you'd have six people on the move, on foot, in daylight — *possibly* with an alert out for them.

His voice tailed off. It had been a major effort, trying to put it into words.

He could see the barn now. And then the huts too: it was spotting the barn that had led his eye to them. But in any case it was, clearly, getting lighter.

'Any ideas, Nick?'

'Only — I suppose — push on ...'

'Not lie up here until it's dark again, *then* push on?'

'Oh, God — another day ...'

Irina said, 'I think Nikki's right. Another day for them to send out descriptions, and have everyone looking for us.'

'Well.' Bob yawned. 'You have a point. But I think the false trail I laid should hold them for a day or two. Before they start looking on this side, I mean.'

Nadia asked quietly. 'You'd wait for tonight, Bob, would you?'

'I — suppose ...'

Looking at her dark profile, close to him. Thinking this *had* to be the right decision — if only because it would be dangerous to press on without getting some sleep first. But also, suppressing an inclination to put his arm round that tall, lithe figure: or better still — thinking about it now — to stop and use both arms, crush her body against his ... Astonishing. Dead on one's feet, a brain that felt like river-mud, and *still* ... He thought, *Survival of the species* ... Telling the others over his shoulder, 'Let's see if the truck's here, anyway.'

15

He'd left them among the huts, at the end nearest to the barn — the fishermen's huts which by now should all have been vacated and which might come in handy if one decided to sit the day out here. Or rather, sleep it out. Prior to deciding this he needed to prospect the barn — whether the lorry was in there, and petrol — and wanted to do it on his own, so in this rapidly thinning darkness it had seemed a good idea to leave them where there was some cover.

The business of the skiff was a bigger weight on his mind than the more immediate questions such as availability of transport and whether they moved on now or later. Even the prospect of having to explain it to them: for instance that the Caspian was no lake — or river — and that a small boat with six people in it had very little freeboard, would be shipping water in even a moderate breeze. With such a distance to be covered: and the fact that at this time of year — *any* time, but now especially with the summer on its way out — you could have a calm for breakfast and a full gale by lunch ... And this was to think only of the weather hazards: disregarding the Bolshevik naval presence.

And they'd hold him responsible. Crazy though it was, he could see this coming. He'd been instrumental in getting them away from the *dacha*: now their attitude would be *Well — where do we go from here?*

The dawn sky was on his left, and the end wall of the barn in front of him. Deep shadow there. This place *might* be uninhabited now, but out in the open like this one still felt exposed and vulnerable. Stooped, sort of loping up the incline, anxious to get into that shadow. Glancing back: seeing no movement around the huts: glad of that, but allowing himself the unworthy thought *Probably all flat out* . . . Into the shadow now — at last — against the barn's wooden wall, and moving to his right then — to what would be its front right-hand corner, if you were inside and looking out through its doors.

Before, they'd been standing open. Now they were shut and locked. Internal lock, too, not a padlock. A padlock would have been easy.

Have to force it. And this was an old building, heavy-timbered. And one had no tools except knives.

Check the hinges. If external, they might be unscrewable. He'd got as far as discovering that they were *not* external when he heard the lorry coming. Petrol engine anyway — up on the road. And quite likely just passing . . . He stood still, listening: willing it to drive on by but hearing it slow down, and then the shift of gear: turning in here . . .

He was back around that corner: moving back farther still. Thankful for the spark of sense that had made him leave the others at a distance and out of sight. The lorry — truck, van, whatever it was — *had* turned off the road, and now from the back corner of the barn he saw its headlight beams jerking up and down as it bounced and rocked over the descending, winding track. Passing behind some other farm-type buildings: then in sight again, headlights swinging this way as it negotiated the last curve.

Returning to its garage, surely. The one-handed driver — who'd be in Tsarytsin by now — had mentioned that his colleague dealt in contraband of some kind; the odds were that he *would* aim to have his illicitly-used transport back under cover before daylight . . . Headlights lit the track this side of the bend, scythed across the open hillside between here and the shacks, then swept over the front of the barn. Then there was only the overspill of light beyond and to the right as the vehicle slowed and stopped — out of one's sight but very close.

Dead still, listening. Hearing the driver get out —

engine still ticking over — and a key being pushed into the door. Long creak of the door opening outwards. They were double doors, but only one had been standing open to receive the lorry, on that previous occasion. Now the driver was back on board: his door pulled loosely shut, and a blip on the accelerator, all the spill of light snuffed out as the truck nosed into the barn. Brake on: engine off: it coughed to itself a couple of times, then fell silent.

Door slamming shut. No light anywhere now ... Creak of the barn door again: he'd be locking it now. Missed opportunity, maybe. Except that one wasn't looking for confrontations at this stage. For one thing it was vitally important not to leave any tracks or traces this side of the river, and for another — well, for that same reason, if there *was* any confrontation it would have to be another killing, another body hidden. Here — this far from *Krasnaya Dacha* — he hoped that might be avoidable. There, the rule had been kill or be killed: whereas here — well, life wasn't exactly back to normal, but—

But what?

Killer instincts — if any — now dormant. *That* was what.

Just about *every* instinct near-enough bloody dormant ...

He was at the front corner of the barn again, and non-dormant enough — just — to know he had to see which way the driver went ... Catching sight of him now. Bulky figure, in a coat that reached to the ground. About ten yards away at this moment, near enough to see the coat's skirts swinging as he walked. A rolling, lumbering walk: a heavily-built man, probably a big belly on him. He was heading towards the fishermen's huts: lost to sight now, the darkness swallowing his dark-clothed bulk, but he'd been right on course for those nearer huts — where one might hope the others would *not* be all flat out, snoring ...

They'd been edging back. The huts were laid out in more or less a crescent formation, five or six huts deep in the centre but thinning out — at this southern end anyway —

into a thinner straggle, with the last hut out on its own. Nick and the others had been between about the third and fourth from that end, up front where they could see across to the barn; now they'd retreated, were among the second rank — hard-baked earth, patches of weeds, and a smell of which the predominant ingredients seemed to be fish-residue and urine.

Nadia whispered, 'He's going to the one at the end.'

The Czechs had been muttering in German; now the orang-outan whispered in French from Nick's right, 'We might move away — *this* way?'

'Let him get inside first, Captain.'

Nadia's hand closed on Nick's arm: 'See him?'

He was just arriving at the hut that was out on its own. Opening its door — no pause there, no lock — and leaving it open as he disappeared inside.

Which suggested, Nick guessed, that he'd be coming out again quite soon. Holding Nadia's hand now, squeezing it ... Behind them Irina whispered too loudly, 'We're going to be stuck here, aren't we—'

'*Quiet*...'

A match flared, in that hut, the flare of it visible through the open door. Then a softer glow, expanding, as a lamp was lit. Sounds of movement, heavy treads on the board floor. Nick whispered to Irina, 'No, we won't be stuck. If he's staying there we can sneak off *that* way.'

'But the lorry...'

Nadia murmured, 'Leave in it tonight, surely. What Bob was proposing anyway. Rest here today, then—'

'Hush.' Nick's hand tightened again on hers. 'He's coming out.'

Carrying the lamp. And something different about him...

No coat — that was it, he'd left it in the hut, appeared less bulky than he had before. Pushing the door shut: and turning, setting off towards the barn again, with the oil-lamp swinging in one hand.

Bob watched him — watched the lamp — going up the

track to the road, and when he was sure he wasn't coming back he first checked the barn door — in case the key had been left in it — then trotted over to join the others. Hearing, just as he reached them, some other vehicle on the road. It was stopping ... Then a door slammed and it drove on again.

And good riddance ...

He said as he joined them, 'Gone home to his breakfast. Left the barn locked, unfortunately, took the key with him. We'll have to force that lock, Nick.'

'When? Now?'

'I think in daylight. After we've had a sleep. Then leave it until sundown, get away in the lorry then. Must have *some* petrol in it.'

Irina asked him, 'Spend the day here, you mean.'

'We don't have much option, really. Look at that.'

The sky. Dawn's left hand. Light flushing up from the east faintly pink, no stars left now in the spreading gloss. Nick agreed: 'We could use one of these huts — or two — and eat some of our food now, d'you think?'

'Why not. If anyone can stay awake long enough.'

'Bob.' Nadia touched him, getting his attention. 'He went into that hut at the end, and he left his long coat in there.'

'So?'

'The key could be in its pocket?'

'Oh.' Blinking at her. 'You're right. It *could*.'

Contrabandist's night-driving coat ...

Nadia said, 'You're tired out. *I'll* go and look.'

'Well — come with me.' He pushed himself off the wall where he'd been leaning. Sagging ... 'If it's there I'll go back to the barn. We'd all sleep better for knowing what's what.'

It was getting pinker overhead. And no wind at all, not a breath. The weather might hold, might not. What one needed was a miracle — like a couple of days and nights of flat calm. Nadia said, 'I never saw a man more tired.'

'Cracking up. Poor material, I suppose.'

'I'm sure.' She smiled at him. Dawn's pink light in her

face. He thought, as they set off together between the lines of huts, *I could spend my life with that face.*

'I don't think it can be locked. He walked straight in and out.'

She was right. And the hut was only thirty yards away. Inside, it seemed to be just one room. Interior detail not visible in the dark, no more than a faint radiance penetrating the open doorway. But she found the man's coat almost immediately. It was on a peg behind the door: she'd found it by common sense and then by feel ... Muttering 'Ugh. Smelly ...' Groping in its pockets: Bob standing watching, waiting for the verdict, with nothing much in mind except to go back to the others in a minute, then lie down and fall asleep. Then she was laughing, and dangling something in front of his face: putting it in his hand then — one large key, on a twist of wire. 'How's *that*?'

'I'd call it genius.' A small spark of genius of his own, then: 'But hang on a minute ...'

If one made a hole in the lining of that pocket, when the driver didn't find his key he'd think he knew what must have happened to it, might spend an hour or two on his hands and knees out there unaware that anything was missing from the barn. Like a truck, for instance ... Bob used the point of his knife — Maroussia's knife out of Nadia's sheath — and then the barn key, to make it look less like a cut.

'Nadia, you are — stupendous. Brilliant. As well as *very* nice to look at.'

'H'm. In the dark — that's some compliment.'

'I've got cat's eyes. But you're terrific in any light.' He paused. 'Look, I'll do the barn on my own now ... Easier — if some other local comes along ...'

Easier, too, to do it now before full daylight. Jogging over towards the barn while she went back to the others, he began thinking about the delta again, another aspect of it that had been fermenting in the back of his mind — namely that the risk of drowning might be acceptable, if the alternative was to be rounded up and shipped back to

Krasnaya Dacha — to Lesechko and Khitrov — which might well be the procedure if they were caught ... But if it wasn't just a *risk* of drowning, more like a certainty — if the weather looked really dangerous — what then?

As a seaman one's answer would have to be no — definitely *no*, not even if conditions looked reasonably good when you were starting out. But — having seen that cellar, and the ropes — imagining *Nadia* — for God's sake — and Lesechko's fury that she'd tricked him ...

The key turned easily. Inside, he shut the door and relocked it. Locking himself in in near-total darkness with one lorry, and one van. And at the back of the barn — groping for it and then finding it — a drum of petrol. He'd seen one here the other day. He tilted it, heard liquid sloshing, put his nose to it. Petrol, all right.

The van might be the best, for their purposes. If it started; which one might try now. From the closed barn there'd be very little leakage of noise.

Get some light first — using the lorry's lights, because one knew that battery had some juice in it. And — got it ... Yellowish light flooded the barn's interior. He slid out of the lorry and into the van — it was an Austin, and looked as if it had been worked very hard for a very long time. Checking over its dashboard ... Ignition switch — on. Spark — he slid the knob right over, to retard it fully. Better than getting a broken wrist ... Hand-throttle: he opened it just a little. Then out, round to the front, the crank-handle, feeling it for compression first and then swinging good and hard ... To his surprise, the engine fired. He tried the headlights then, found that they worked, switched them and the engine off and tried the feel of the steering and gear-change. Then he got out, went all round peering at and running his hands over the tyres. Not all of them were completely bald.

He told them, 'All is well. Thanks to Nadia, we have access. Choice of vehicles — the lorry or a van. I think the van, but either'd do. And there's petrol.'

He'd found them in one of the huts — or rather, Nick

had met him and shown him where they were. It would be daylight very soon, you needed to be under cover. Nadia asked him — glancing at Nick as well, tactfully including him in the question — 'What if that man comes back before we leave?'

'What we have to do — *I* have to, anyway — is sleep. Then —' he was letting himself down to sit with his back against the wall — 'well, wouldn't matter. We'll start off when it's dark. Talk again before that.'

'But if he comes during the day?'

'If he stayed around, when we're ready to move we'd have to deal with him. Kill him, I suppose. But if he comes and goes — well, he'll have problems with keys, but whichever truck he does *not* take —' he'd swung round parallel to the wall, to lie flat with his hands behind his head — 'that'll be ours.'

'Bob, dear.' Nadia crouched beside him. 'Irina's dividing up some of the food. Don't you think you should eat something before you—'

'No.' Smiling at her, although she probably couldn't see it. 'Thank you, but—'

'We brought cold tea, too.'

'Wonderful.' A long sigh. 'Absolutely wonderful ...'

Waking, and clear-headed, his first thought was that he had to tell them, explain about the boat, get it across to them so they'd know what they were facing and he wouldn't have to go on struggling with it as if the situation was of *his* making.

Nadia's voice — quiet, indicative of others being still asleep nearby — 'The man's awake ... Ready for your breakfast, Bob?'

He sat up. 'Yes. Please ... You been awake long?'

'About an hour. Some of the others woke too, but they've dropped off again.'

'And the time now?'

'About noon.' She checked her watch. 'Twenty past. You've been unconscious for eight hours.'

'Feel a lot better for it, too.' He got up, went to the

door. 'I'll be back in a minute. Have you had anything to eat?'

'Before I went to sleep. We all did, except you. We thought we might eat again before we start tonight.'

And that, presumably, would use up all the food they'd brought. So there'd be no rations to take with them in the boat. So — *if* sea conditions allowed one to put out — and then to stay afloat — amongst other evils one would be facing two or three foodless days and nights ... Then, pushing the door shut behind him, he saw that they were not likely to have anything *like* tolerable sea conditions. The sky was about four-fifths cloud, and there was a wind of force 3 or 4 pushing it over from the north.

So there you were. Outlook a stage or two bleaker than it had been when you'd got your head down. A phrase came into his mind while he was walking away between the huts: *between the devil and the deep blue sea.* Or even shallow blue sea — which the Caspian was, in its northern reaches, one of its characteristics being that on that shallow water even a very moderate blow threw up a choppy sea very quickly. Bugbear of the CMB fraternity.

Which took one's thoughts back to poor old Johnny Pope, and Zero McNaught ...

When he got back, he found that Nadia had put his rations out for him: bread, dried fish, and an enamel mug of cold tea.

'It's what we all had. Fish now, cheese tonight.'

'Couldn't be better.'

'Couldn't it?'

'Well ...'

It would have been a relief to have been able to talk to her about the skiff and the delta; but it wouldn't have been fair — they had *all* to hear it, not just poor Nadia to be burdened with it so as to lighten his own load. He drank some tea, spread fish on the bread and began to eat. Looking around now — seeing Irina's high-hipped figure on one of two wooden bunks, and Nick Solovyev sprawled on the floor at the back of the room. A small stove was fixed to the wall there; that and the bunks were the only furnishings. One small, square window near the door: and that was it. Eyes back to Nadia, who was sitting near him.

'Czechs in another hut, I suppose?'

'Next door ... Bob, did Nick say you were brought up in Petrograd?'

He nodded. 'Except it was then St Petersburg.'

'Of course. And your mother was Russian.'

'Looked a bit like you. Anyway — similarities ... But like you, *very* pretty.'

'I'm not pretty!'

'Well, I'd say you were.'

'Better not say it too loudly, anyway.'

'Ah — right ... But another thing too — I wanted to say this earlier on — how dreadfully sorry I am that we had to bring you such news about your brother. On top of losing your parents not long before. I do think you're *extremely* brave — the way you've simply carried on, and—'

'There hasn't been all that much alternative, really. And I'd already convinced myself that Boris must have been killed. So I was already over the shock, I'd — reconciled myself to it. But —' she shook her head — 'don't imagine I don't cry inside. We *all* do — don't we? Probably ever after? And I feel surprise too — that I'm alive, that it should be *me* who's survived this far ... That's something else about it — it often feels as if it might be just — you know, a postponement.'

'Postponed a hell of a long time, I hope.'

'Well — thanks to *you*.'

'I'd say thanks to all of us. First and foremost to old Maroussia. And to Nick. And what about your own effort, bluffing it out with Lesechko all this time?'

She shrugged. 'I had no choice. Really, none ... But we got off the track, somehow, I was asking about your upbringing in Petrograd. St Petersburg if you like. How did your father come to be there, and to marry a Russian woman?'

It was a question that took some time to answer. Trawlerman's grandson, trader's son, explaining his origins to a princess whose family and ancestors would never have had anything to do with trade in any shape or form. But taking pleasure in the description of his father: the old man's warmth, and the strength behind that warmth.

She'd smiled. 'That's where it comes from, then.'

'Oh, no. I may be a chip off the old block, but no more than a chip.'

'I'd have liked to have known him.'

'I wish you had. He'd have loved you.'

The statement — low-pitched, they'd been talking quietly so as not to disturb the others — hung in the air between them, in a silence. Nadia's wide, grey eyes on his: as intent as if she was trying to read his mind. Leaning over, then, a hand for balance on his shoulder as she touched his lips with hers and whispered 'Meeting *you* was the next best thing.'

Waking, talking, going back to sleep. Sleep was as good a use of the time as anything, Bob thought. The Czechs came from the next-door hut, chatted, crept away again. He would have liked to have talked more with Nadia, but Nick's presence inhibited it. While Irina's chatter in turn embarrassed Nick: it was so clearly aimed at establishing her possession of him as *her* brother — constant references to childhood experiences, their parents, mutual friends — invariably subjects that excluded Nadia. Bob of course was right out of all this; he dozed off from time to time, and even in sleep or half-sleep was thinking constantly about the skiff, and their lack of options.

With this change in the weather, *total* lack.

He broke in — into a pause in Irina's gabbling — 'Nick — all of you, really — there's something we have to talk about very seriously. I'm sorry, but—'

'Of course —' Irina had glanced at him very briefly, and decided to ignore the interruption. Looking back at her brother, picking up the threads of whatever she'd been on about ... '— until she came to find me in Petrograd — as you know, intending to take me to the Crimea — Mama hardly knew Nadia at all. You'd met her once, I think — and she knew your parents, of course, but —'

'You're right, we hardly knew each other.' Nadia looked at Bob. 'What's this serious thing?'

'But you did become great friends, by the end ... Oh, that *dreadful* train journey!'

'Yes. Yes, it was ...'

'Wasn't it the most terrific luck that we met that charming Captain Dherjakin?' A glance at Bob. 'I'm not sure if I told you about him, Bob. I know I was going to — he's a naval captain, you see.'

'You did mention him, I think. A naval engineer captain with only one leg.'

'Nadia, wasn't he an angel in disguise?'

'He certainly got us out of an awkward spot.' Nadia was looking at Bob apologetically. But it was easier to get this over, let Irina talk while she felt she had to. She'd mentioned some such individual on the night that he and Nick had got to them. But that wasn't stopping her telling them again now: 'Engineer Captain Sergei Dherjakin. He was coming down here from Moscow, to some new command, somewhere near — did he say it was near Krasni-Yar, Nadia?'

'Yes. Now you mention it.'

Bob put in — a bell ringing at the name of that village, Krasni-Yar, but sticking to what he'd been about to say — 'Didn't you tell us he was in charge of some dockyard up there?'

'Yes — he *had* been—'

'There aren't any dockyards in Moscow. And those in the north — Archangelsk and Murmansk — are in White hands. British forces there now too.'

'Well — the fact remains, he'd been sent down from Moscow to take command of this new base. Military supply base, I think he called it. And he was so *kind* to us. Quite extraordinary, really, this senior officer — he'd had this high rank in the Imperial Navy, obviously — working for the Bolsheviks now because they'd somehow forced him to, and using his position to befriend *us*! I think he had an eye for Mama, to be absolutely frank ... Well, he'd be — you know, middle forties, that sort of age. But honestly, when the train was stopped by Red Guards, and they were demanding everyone's papers, dragging people off — God, we were *terrified* — *I* was, anyway . . .'

'This Dherjakin person vouched for us.' Nadia told Bob, cutting the story short, 'He showed the commander of the Red Guards his own papers, and whatever his background he certainly had — influence . . . What were you going to say, Bob?'

He nodded. Getting it together in his mind. In its briefest, most brutal form it would have been *We have no way out.*

But there *had* to be. Hesitating, he looked back at Irina. 'You did say a military supply base, and near Krasni-Yar?'

'Yes. And that dockyard business — all I can say for certain is he was no Bolshevik — *definitely* not. But they needed his technical ability and experience, I suppose they don't have many such highly qualified men, and — I don't know, I guessed at either blackmail or his family held hostage — he made a joke, that a man with a wooden leg couldn't run away.'

'I remember, you told us. But you didn't mention any military supply base — or Krasni-Yar . . .' Looking at the Count. 'Are you thinking what I'm thinking, Nick?'

'That place where we ran into the chain?'

'Exactly!'

There was a silence. The three of them watching him. Nick said, looking mystified, 'It's confirmation of what you guessed, I see that. You thought it might be a military stores depot — in support of their move against Guriev . . .'

'Bob — if there's something we have to hear about . . .'

'Yes. Sorry. Thing is, this might — change it, rather.' Gazing at her: with the idea forming. A hope, a long-shot chance. Probably madness even to consider it: giving it even this much consideration was — straw-clutching . . . But *what* a straw — coming at just this moment, you might call it God-given.

And that was the nature of floating straws, surely, what the concept of straws to clutch at was *about.* When there was nothing else — except a dead-end, and worse. And —

this much looked like sound reasoning — that it was highly unlikely there could be more than one new military supply base near Krasni-Yar ...

'Listen. I'll tell you what I was *going* to tell you, first. What it boils down to is we don't have any way off that coast once we get there. Really — *none*, we're stuck. Take a look out there, Nick — and imagine six of us in that skiff. In good weather it'd be bad enough—'

Nadia chipped in, 'What exactly is a skiff?'

'Rowing-boat — about the size of the boat we came across in, but a bit narrower.'

'But — Bob, the weather *might*- -'

'And might not. Listen — up to about three minutes ago the skiff was all we had. The only reason for even considering it was we didn't have any alternative. You know that, you've known it all along, so don't pretend I'm springing anything new on you ... But that's how it *was.* Until — well, look, I know this is as chancy as hell. But we know where that base is — right? And there are ships there — tugs, I saw them — that we could get away in, if we could steal one ...'

16

Trundling eastward – approaching Sasykolsk. It couldn't be by-passed, one had to take the risk of the van being recognized.

The up-gradient eased to more level going, and he changed down – not exactly adept yet with the rather quirky gearbox, but getting some relief then, less of a scream from the straining engine. Should have taken the lorry, maybe ... Yellow headlamp beams quivered on the pitted road, and the wheel in his hands felt like a steam-hammer. Entering the village now. A few lights here and there ... Corner coming up: then there'd be a second turn where the shade-tree was, where the lorry had been parked.

Nick Solovyev was beside him, nursing fears. Getting over them, please God. He hadn't spoken since they'd left the fishing-station a quarter of an hour ago. Bob had been backing the van out of the barn – no lights on, hadn't switched them on until they'd got up to the road – and the Czech sergeant had been waiting to shut and lock the door before joining the orang-outan and the two girls in the back; Nick had burst out with 'This is *mad*, Bob, there's no *chance* we'll get away with it!'

'Then we're all dead.' He'd put his hand out of the window, taking the barn key from Krebst. 'Well done. Hop in.' Then, up on the road and switching the lights on, relieved at having got that far without any confrontation with the lorry-driver, he'd turned to him: 'Come on, Nick. You were all right an hour ago ... Look, remember how you lectured me, down on that bog, about playing a part, believing in the role you're playing, *being* it? Nick – I'm not being rude, you were offended last time I mentioned it but it's just plain fact — you've had your nerve shaken. But you're the same man and you're more than capable of this. Look how brilliantly you acted at the shop where we bought my gear — and on that platform ...'

Silence.

Or rather, no response. The word *silence* hardly applied, crashing and clattering along in this old conveyance. Heading south, with about forty miles to Selitrenoe: then fifty to Seitovka. Names evocative of what by now could have been a distant past ... In the back, the girls had the option of sitting on empty wooden crates that had been in the back of the barn, or on the metal floor and using them as backrests. Neither position would be exactly comfortable, those surfaces were all extremely hard. But the pair of them were better together than apart, there wouldn't have been room for both of them *and* Nick in this cab, and he'd wanted to have Nick with him so they could talk, perhaps make adjustments to the plan — which couldn't be detailed anyway, you were going to have to adjust to circumstances as you found them — and also so he, Bob, could try to keep him up to the mark.

Earlier, they'd almost come to blows. Bob having challenged him with 'Your nerve's gone, has it?'

One furious Count ... Probably all the more so for knowing it was the truth. But he was the only one of them who'd stand any chance of pulling this off: and on his old form, he'd have walked it ... He'd blustered, this afternoon, 'I'm not *stupid*, that's all!'

'So what d'you suggest we do? Wait for the ice to form so we can *walk* home?'

'You're so amusing ... And frankly, so *idiotic*, Bob, to think you could force your way into a guarded military base — naval, whatever it is — just because you happen to know the name of the commanding officer!'

'You can't have been listening, Nick. That name is the password, that's all, it's what will — should — open the gate for us. God, I've explained all this ...'

He'd explained it all several times over. A general *idea*

more than a plan as such. Nick accepting it at times, then finding new reasons to reject it. Which hadn't been so bad, had been productive in a way, elements of a plan emerging from the argument ... For instance, the central issue of Captain Dherjakin, whether one could realistically expect to get to him personally...

'He *will* respond, Nick. Because you'll make it a personal issue — for his eyes only. And it's not a very large establishment — you know, you saw it.'

'Hardly. Very little.'

'Well, *I* saw enough. And it only becomes operational in the spring — that's not guesswork, with several months of ice ahead it's useless until the thaw. So meanwhile it's in being but at half-cock — minimal staffing, you can bet ... All right, so they have a boom on the entrance and a guardship out in that channel — *did* have, anyway — and that mine-barrier — but those are obvious precautions. They know we could have got wind of it, and that there could be an attack on it from the sea, our own flotilla's on their doorstep night and day and there's also the Russian flotilla, the gunboats — anyone in his right mind would set up some defences. But what they would *not* be expecting is a ring on the front-door bell, so to speak.'

'All speculation, Bob!'

'*Informed* speculation. Probability. As far as the naval angles are concerned, I *am* a professional, you know.'

'I thought you were a reservist.'

'Professional seaman, with several years of war experience. Anyway — we aren't talking about me — or you — we're talking about all of us, including Nadia and your sister, and the point is we have to get *out*, get *them* out — what we're here for, isn't it? Unless you know any other way of doing it ...'

'The skiff—'

'Christ, I've *told* you—'

The surface wasn't too bad, along this stretch. The road followed the course of the river, which was in sight all the time and beautiful in the moonlight. Moon dipping down in the south-west, very close to setting, with a linked reflection of itself in the veil of thin cloud racing past it, a double-image creating the illusion of an elliptical moon, a teardrop moving at high speed.

A lot more than one could say for this van. Not that one would have wanted to drive all that fast. For one thing, a vehicle being driven hard would tend to attract attention, and for another the van might have shaken itself apart.

'All right, Nick?'

He'd grunted. Then: 'I'll take a turn at the wheel, when you want a break.'

'Ah . . . Well, how about after Selitrenoe?'

'Whenever you like.'

'It's no Rolls-Royce, I'll tell you that . . . Hope the girls aren't *too* uncomfortable back there . . .'

Nadia's reaction, when she'd climbed into the back of this thing and tried out the seating arrangements — and noticed Irina's expression of dismay — had been to murmur 'My God!' and then add, 'Better than walking, anyway.'

Some princess, that was, back there . . .

She'd warned him — privately, when the Solovyevs had been talking to the Czechs — not to trust Engineer Captain Sergei Dherjakin.

'Although he saved your lives?'

'Well, as to that — you see, he must have recognized us as his own kind. Although we'd gone to some trouble *not* to be recognizable as anything of the sort — and not that we could have looked quite as extraordinary as you do now, Bob . . .'

'Well, *thanks*.'

'If you ask me nicely I'll trim your beard for you. I've got some scissors. I'd better do Nikki's too. Not even Bolsheviks have to look like scarecrows . . . But — Dherjakin's no fool, he'd sized up our situation — and Maria Ivanovna was so obviously a sick woman . . .'

'So he's a decent sort of fellow. Why not trust him?'

'Because — *decent* or not, the inclination to help us would have been natural, wouldn't it? — I mean to a man of his background. And — fine, thank God for it and that he acted as he did, but — the plain fact is, Bob, he's working for the Bolsheviks. That silly joke he made — that a man with a wooden leg can't run away — it *is* silly, isn't it, it's meaningless. Irina swallowed it, of course—'

'Yes.'

'— and Maria Ivanovna was too sick — and frightened — to be thinking much at all ... Well, I grant you, there could be reasons such as blackmail, or his family held as hostages — if they're so short of men of his calibre and experience — they're capable of *anything*, I know. But apart from that — this is a senior officer of the Imperial Navy, and he's serving that crowd of murderers. That's *fact* — and why I say — take care.'

He would, of course. But Dherjakin was the key to this — or should be.

They were getting close to Selitrenoe when two cars passed, going fast in the opposite direction, headlights blazing. Better lights than the old van had. Neither Bob nor the Count said a word until the second car's tail-lights had gone out of sight astern: then Bob muttered, 'Keep your fingers crossed. They may find a place to turn, and come after us.'

'The possibility had occurred to me.'

They could have come from Selitrenoe, which was half a mile ahead, or Seitovka, or from that big camp, or the village of Krasni-Yar, or from the supply base. Dherjakin might have been in one of them. Being dragged back to Moscow for the privilege of receiving a bullet in the back of the head, for instance — if he'd made too much of a habit of being kind to enemies of the Revolution.

That was what Nadia had been warning him against, Bob realized. When the gallant captain had helped them on the train he'd been putting himself at no risk at all, he'd obviously had a very high degree of protection from the papers he was carrying. But if he was in a position where yielding to gentlemanly instincts *might* endanger him: and being, as she'd also said, no fool ...

'They don't seem to be coming after us.'

'Might have thought this truck was military. It could be, at a glance.'

Nick said, after another half-mile, 'There'll be a search going on by now, won't there?'

'On the other side of the river, yes. And in Astrakhan itself, I'd guess.'

'What if the owner of the boat we took from Kopanovka has reported it as stolen?'

'Yes — that's a risk, I know. But — trust to luck, really. Mind you, he can't fish *every* day ... And when he does report it, it mightn't be linked to us. The steamboat's pretty solid evidence of an escape down-river, you know, down that main western channel. If you were Lesechko, would you guess at anyone doing what I did?'

'Not as long as I didn't suspect Maroussia — and then hear she'd gone north on such a pointless errand.'

'Not pointless by Maroussia's standards. I admit Nadia's disappearance *could* point at her, but I'd back the old girl to bluff that one out. And the steamboat thing won't look to them like some little dodge just to put them off the scent — not when they find one of its crewmen in the engine-space bilge with a broken neck.'

'*Oh* ...'

'May not find him until some time after they get the boat back. But to be worth doing at all it had to look as if whoever did it really meant business. In any case he was *there* — poor bastard ...' They were rumbling through the village now. 'Stop the other side, shall I — d'you still want to take over?'

'Yes.' Shifting in his seat, looking at a group of men standing on a corner. The local *soviet*, maybe ... 'Yes, Bob. Surely.'

'We might change back again after Seitovka. Fifty miles, roughly — if that suits you ... Are you feeling better about all this, Nick?'

'Not really.' He let out a long, hard breath. 'But it's happening, isn't it.'

*

At the second stop — south of Seitovka, for Bob to take over the driving again — they'd been on the road about four hours. He climbed out and went to the back to tell Krebst to open up. The sergeant had a piece of wood that he could hold in place to jam the door mechanism, and the arrangement was that he'd hold it there until he knew it was all right, no emergency.

'Not even a flat tyre. Incredible — if you had a close look at them. How are you two? All bruises?'

'Oh, we'll survive ...'

Irina said, 'I'm black and blue ... Hello, Nikki.'

The Czechs helped Bob to get the petrol drum out of the back and top up the van's tank. Without a funnel it was a tricky job in the dark, the moon having gone down hours ago.

The orang-outan asked him while they were doing it — Bob himself and the sergeant doing most of it — 'Will it be much longer?'

'About fifteen miles — twenty-five kilometres, say — to the village of Krasni-Yar, and then three or four more. I'd guess another hour.'

The Czechs were both armed now, with the pistols taken from dead Bolsheviks. Bob had given these to them this afternoon, when he'd also outlined the plan for tonight and sketched out his idea of the inlet's shape and a possible layout of harbour installations. Having only a visual memory of the little he'd seen from the CMB — some lights, a crane, masts and funnels. And of course the location of the chain boom — which, depending on how Dherjakin reacted, might well be a major problem ... At the same time, having the Czechs to himself for a while, he'd elicited — mostly from Krebst — that they were deserters from their Czech Legion, had been captured by Kirghizi tribesmen and transferred to *Krasnaya Dacha* for interrogation, but hadn't been tortured for the simple reason that they'd answered every question that had been put to them. Krebst had been guided entirely by the orang-outan, who'd told him that their war was over, so what the hell ... Neither of them had guessed that having been pumped of all useful intelligence they were to have been shot.

Bob told Krebst now, 'Remember — and tell *him* — that from now on you — and he — will take orders directly from me. In other words, when I give you an order you don't have to refer it to him. Translate that to him now, please.'

He left them to it. The girls had been on the other side of the van, and coming back now they were talking more loudly than was necessary, doubtless as a warning to the men. Bob looking round at the dark, flat, featureless landscape. Thinking of this and that: including his feeling that he could probably rely on Krebst's reactions in a tight corner, but much less so on the orang-utan's. So — watch your back ... The wind had come up a bit, he thought; there'd have been no question of using the skiff.

He turned back towards the others. 'We ready?'

Four into the back ... The Count helped the girls up — having embraced them both, murmuring farewells of which the details weren't audible from where Bob stood. He walked round to his side of the cab, heaved himself in behind the wheel. Waiting for Nick to do the cranking; wondering suddenly, *This* time, will it start?

It did. For better, or for worse. Or — putting that another way — for want of anything better. This was — he knew it as well as Nick did — a *hell* of a gamble.

They passed the military camp which they'd seen when they'd been following the new railway line towards Seitovka. There was an entrance to it from this road, and two — *three* lights burning, in that quite large acreage of hutments.

'Someone's in residence, Nick.'

'Yes. Caretakers. Remember we thought those soldiers on the railway line might have been visiting here. Women, maybe.'

'*Could* be.'

The camp fell away behind them. Empty road, flat and empty-seeming land, Krasni-Yar about ten miles ahead.

*

'Nick, one thing. Precautionary, only. Assuming we get some suitable craft — and assuming that between you you can drive it — Nadia knows a bit about boats, I gather.'

'So does Irina and so do I. We've all sailed. But *you're* the—'

'What I'm saying, Nick, is if I happened to get knocked off in the process, would you know which way to steer?'

'Only — away from the land, I suppose. And anyway, none of us knows anything about — well, engines, for instance. You'd just better *not* get — knocked off.'

'I'll try not to be. But your course to steer would be south-south-east. Assuming there'll be a compass in whatever you're in. Due south would take you across the approaches to Astrakhan — likely to be patrolled, even if ships aren't out hunting for you — and if your course was too westerly you'd hit the Mangyshlak Peninsula. Whereas south-south-east takes you clear of Fort Aleksandrovsk, and across our flotilla's patrol line. Better than evens you'd be spotted and picked up.'

'Fifty-fifty, uh?'

'Well — if the weather's a bit murky . . .'

'You'd better be with us, Bob.'

Krasni-Yar coming up ahead. This was high ground now — comparatively speaking — the delta as such all to the west, between here and Astrakhan. But you could smell the sea.

One dim light, in one cottage window. Midnight oil being burned. The local Cheka man, it could be, on duty beside the village's only telephone. There'd surely be a telephone here, because the line from Astrakhan to Dherjakin's base — where there *had* to be one — would pass through here, and they'd surely take advantage of that. Telephones and telegraphs being few and far between, confined mostly to the larger centres and railway stations.

There wasn't much of Krasni-Yar. A dozen cottages, probably a general store and *traktir.* He guessed that fishermen would live here: and/or the odd shepherd or goatherd. About as odd as you'd find anywhere, probably . . .

'There.' A left fork, still new-looking, earthworks still visible. He was having to slow down, anyway, as the headlights washed over a shawled, stooped figure crossing the road at snail's pace, near the house that had a light in it. He muttered, 'Past your bedtime, grandma.' Easing the wheel over, taking the corner gently for the sake of the girls in the back. Irina had said something about being flung around, on bends. That smooth metal floor, and nothing to hold on to . . . The old woman had stopped in the middle of the road, was shuffling round to get a look at the van as it turned, a few yards short of her.

Heading west now, and picking up speed again . . . 'Any telephone wires visible that side?'

'Yes. Strung along on beanpoles . . . I hope I'm not going to let you down, Bob.'

'We'll put about a mile between us and the village, then stop and I'll cut it.' He caught on to what Nick had said then, told him sharply 'Of *course* you aren't!' And then softened it: 'Nick – stop worrying. Once you're so to speak on stage . . .'

As if he was going to be the *only* one on stage, for God's sake!

Cutting the wire took only a minute. He did it himself, and used a short piece of twine to link the two severed ends, so that at any rate in the dark and without close inspection the break wouldn't be noticeable.

Driving on again now. Despite being of recent construction, the road-surface was of the washboard, bone-shaking type.

'This base will have a wireless, of course. For talking to ships at sea – including the guardship, if there's still one out there, we'd better remember *that* . . .'

Any minute now, they'd be there. There was a wire fence on the right: beyond it, invisible in the dark and at varying distances, would be numerous inlets such as they'd nosed in and out of in the CMB. Probably the biggest and deepest of them being Dherjakin's.

Another half-mile ... Then a glimpse of lights: hidden immediately by a rise. But — lights, glittering on water. And this was a *high* fence, now.

'There it is — guardhouse ...'

'Papers!'

'Here you are. But let's not waste time, comrade, I have to see your commander — Comrade Captain Dherjakin. It's urgent — send word that I'm here, would you?'

'This time of night? Why should he —' squinting at Anton Vetrov's papers, shrugging, pushing them back at him — 'want *you* waking him up?'

'Tell him I'm here on the orders of Comrade Vasilii Bugayev. And that it's *urgent*, damn it!'

'Who's Bugayev?'

'God help us ... Vasilii Bugayev — chairman of the Military Revolutionary Committee, Astrakhan District. And you could add for good measure the name of Commandant Aleksei Karasyov — who commands *you* and this base, comrade! Your commander can verify it for himself by telephone, if he cares to. But *now*, not in an hour's time!'

'Wait.'

Bob murmured, 'Marvellous. You're back on form.'

'*Hell* I am ...'

There were two other sentries out now, one in the guardhouse entrance and one on Bob's side of the van. The first one had pushed in past his colleague, who was slouching this way with one hand on a holstered revolver. Behind him, the first one was cranking the handle of a field telephone.

'Come far, comrade?'

Bob glanced at him. Keeping the engine running: even idling, it was noisy. The aim was to have it understood that they weren't expecting to be kept waiting here for long. He told him casually, 'Far enough.'

'Where from, then?'

He shouted, over the engine-noise, 'Confidential

business, comrade. We've orders to speak only to your CO.'

'That so.' Moving his head to spit. Then turning, strolling towards the back of the van. 'What's inside there?'

'Communications equipment.' He opened his own door so he could lean out and keep him in sight. To get out would be a mistake, a first step towards losing the initiative. 'That's secret too. And the doors are locked. All right?'

Rather like liar dice — declaring a full house when you didn't even have a pair. Except that playing liars didn't make one sweat. The sentry was near the back now, gazing at the double doors; inside them, Krcbst would be holding his two-foot piece of four-by-two jammed under the rod that secured one door to the other. It would feel as if it was locked, if the handle was tried from the outside, but you'd also know from the feel of it that one good wrench would have it open.

He'd gone out of sight, around the back. Bob pulled his driving door shut. Wishing to God the other one would get a move on. Then Nick was leaning out on his side: 'You've been warned, comrade!'

'Yah. And you can stuff it.' He'd circled round the back: was strolling towards the guardhouse when the first one finished his call and came out.

'You two — you're to escort these comrades to the CO's office. Wait there until he comes out to you.' He stopped at the window, and told Nick, 'He's not pleased.'

'Never mind. He will be.'

Bob muttered, 'Well done, Nick.' He blipped the engine and pushed the old contraption into gear. One of those two, slinging his rifle, stepped on to the running-board on Nick's side, while the one who'd expressed interest in the van's contents came back to this side and got up beside Bob. Number one was meanwhile pushing up the barrier. The man at Bob's elbow told him, 'Drive through and fork right.'

Water ahead — after about fifty yards of roadway — with reflected lights flashing on its wind-ruffled surface.

And across the water — about the same distance again — this was the head of the inlet — tugs lay alongside a wooden pier. There was a lamp-post on the quay near the pier, and a long two-storied building backing the quay.

'Left at the corner here.'

You'd have had to take the right fork to get to that pier where the tugs were berthed. Four of them, two each side of it. Then a dark conglomeration low on the water in the angle between pier and quayside: barges, or lighters. Couldn't look that way any longer, had to make this turn — with the water ahead and a brick building on the left, the corner. Turning now ... There was another building beyond this corner one, and a lamp-post between them lighting the fronts of both buildings and this part of the waterfront. Then farther along — a hundred yards, roughly, but there was a bend before it, road and waterfront angling about thirty degrees right — beyond that bend was a long straight quayside backed by sheds. Cargo sheds. And that was where the crane was, on that long quay: also three more lamp-posts. He remembered those three lights: from the entrance, the angle of view he'd had that night, the line of them would be almost end-on, so they'd seemed a lot closer to each other than in fact they were.

'Stop there.' Pointing, with a hand outside the windscreen. 'That doorway, see?'

'Right.'

There was a light in one first-floor window: it went out of his sight as he slowed, pulling in where he'd been told. Guessing that Dherjakin might be in that lit room, getting dressed ... The external light — the lamp-post between the two buildings — threw the van's shadow forward along the roadway, the shadow of the man on Nick's side separating from it as he jumped off, running a few steps as the van came to a halt. The one this side got off too then, and walked round to join his colleague.

Sitting, waiting, scanning as much of the inlet and the quays as was visible from here. And a sense of disaster growing. With no sight of any ship or boat that could be any damn use at all . . .

The girls would be sitting or lying behind the crates, so that if the door was wrenched open they wouldn't be immediately in sight. The Czechs, with guns in their hands, would be between the crates and whoever had forced the door. The idea being that if this happened, the shooting would have to start there and then: because it would mean the initiative had been taken by the Bolsheviks, you'd have lost any chance of making a quiet departure, with or without Dherjakin. Shooting would *have* to start, therefore, but by that time — this had been the theory — you'd have decided on whichever tug or other craft you were going to take. You'd take it — with Dherjakin possibly as hostage — and land somewhere near the chain-boom to get it open — fighting off however much opposition there might be by then — which might not be much, if you'd killed a few of them in the first few minutes and there weren't many of them anyway.

One knew the way out, of course — where the guardship had been last week and where *a* guardship presumably would be tonight: and the way past it — the way Pope had brought the CMB in.

But the reality didn't match the theory. The one essential, which one had taken for granted, was — well, conspicuous by its absence. The tugs on the other side, at that pier, were lying quiet and dark, obviously didn't have steam up. And nearer at hand — on that long quay — from here the view of it was across water again, because of the elbow-bend in the shoreline between here and there — there was a boat of some kind — unlit and in the shadow of the quay, but only small — in terms of present requirements no more use than the skiff would have been. And that was all there was. Last week there'd been a lot of stuff afloat: he'd seen dozens of masts and funnels, and this had remained as his mental picture of the place — ships coming and going, some with steam up and ready to go — if necessary with pistols at the engineers' or stokers' heads, as well as at Dherjakin's . . .

But this place was dead. Dead-end — again. No

improvement on the skiff. Nick had been right, with his 'There's no *chance*...'

Hold on, now. Steady...

One of those tugs. Two hours, say, to get steam up. Starting out, then – if it all went, well, *reasonably* smoothly – at about dawn, instead of having several hours of dark, in which to get well clear of the coast. One would have to accept this: longer exposure both here and after departure...

If there was going to be any departure anyway. This wasn't panic – despite the cold sweat – unfortunately it was a matter of facing facts. Main fact being that it wasn't going to be at all easy – especially with the girls to look after while you were at it. You might even say – facing it squarely – that it was probably impossible.

He felt sick. *He'd* brought them all here, forced his own optimism on Nick, and—

'Now what the devil's this about?'

Nick muttered. 'Come on' and pushed his door open, slid out. 'Comrade Engineer Captain Dherjakin? My name's Vetrov. I'm here on the orders of the Military Revolutionary Committee – a matter of extreme urgency, and—'

'Of what nature, comrade?'

Bob came round the front of the van. Getting his first look at Irina's hero, Nadia's villain. He was in the doorway – on the step, giving himself a bit of extra height: a short, stocky figure in naval reefer, baggy trousers tucked into boots. No stripes or other insignia. An aggressive, cocky stance, hands thrust into the reefer's pockets: it was an attitude that reminded one of photographs of Admiral David Beatty, C-in-C of the Grand Fleet ... The jutting jaw was aimed at *him* now. 'Who's this?'

'Technical adviser, sir.' Nick indicated the van. 'We've special equipment in there. But if we could have a word with you – in private, please, my orders are that it's strictly for your ears only, at this stage.'

'Well. God knows why it has to be in the middle of the night. But – I suppose ...' He'd begun to turn away, then glanced back at his own men. 'One of you comrades can go back to the gate. The other stay and guard this thing.' He seemd to notice the van's decrepit state for the first time. 'My God. Where did you find it — on a rubbish tip?'

Nick shrugged. 'It goes, that's the main thing. And we needed that much cargo space.' The two guards were arguing over which should go back to the gate and which should stay; Dherjakin stared at them disapprovingly for a moment, then turned and went inside. 'Shut the door behind you.' Following him into the building, Bob was thinking that this part, which might have been the trickiest, was turning out to be dead easy. One might have been feeling pretty good about things generally, at this stage. *Might* have ... Dherjakin opened the first door on the right. 'Come in here. But let's make it quick, comrades.'

Bob followed Nick in, and shut the door. It was an office — Dherjakin's own, presumably — containing chairs, a table, shelving, a roll-top desk, chart tacked to the wall. And a window to the front, unfortunately — uncurtained, the goldfish-bowl effect, with that sentry outside. The light was an unshaded overhead bulb: power from that generator, of course ... Nick was murmuring, '— apologize for our appearance, Captain—'

'Never mind *that*.' A double-take, then: 'Well — I see what you mean. Where the devil have you—'

'It's quite a long story, sir.' Bob took over. Getting a closer look at him now. About five-nine, solidly built, with a square jaw and the pinkish complexion that often goes with ginger hair. Ginger stubble on it glistening in the hard light. 'May I ask, first, what tugs or other seagoing craft you have immediately available?'

'None. Nice short answer, eh? No — most of 'em left us in the last two or three days. I've half a dozen tugs here — four on the pier, two at moorings — that we'll be working on through the winter, plus whatever else they send me before we ice-up — but ...'

'You say "working on" — but d'you mean there isn't one of them that could get steam up tonight?'

'Well — if it was a matter of life and death — and given a few hours — I'd have to turn out the maintenance crew — and I'd need an order from naval headquarters — which I can tell you I'd much rather *not* have ...'

Shock, in Nick Solovyev's expression ... Bob looked back at Dherjakin — struggling to find a way around the impasse, looming disaster — recalling that during the long day they'd spent on the marsh some diesel craft had visited the scene of the explosion — which in any case it was now time to mention, as justification for this visit ... 'Captain — aren't I right in thinking you have a diesel-powered boat of some kind here?'

'Diesel launch, yes. You're well-informed, my friend ... But you said seagoing, didn't you?'

'Well — what length and beam—'

'Twenty feet long, beam eight and a half ... Why, what would you want her for?'

Gazing at him. Thinking: better than absolutely nothing. A lot better than the skiff, anyway. Still *highly* dangerous. But — a way out, of sorts.

'Just one more question, sir. So you'll know we aren't interrupting your night's rest to no good purpose. As you know, there was an explosion out there, one night last week. A British coastal motorboat went up on your mine barrier in the channel there.'

'How do *you* know that's what it was?'

'We also know where it came from and who was in it and what it was here for. And the idea now is — well, you might say to forestall another attempt of the same kind.'

'I'll be damned ...'

Reaching for a chair. And believing this, accepting them now. Bob adding, 'So perhaps you can understand the urgency.' He himself could understand, meanwhile, Dherjakin's acceptance of this charade. It was going just as one had hoped it might. Basically, because it was easier to believe than to *dis*believe. Even if Dherjakin had been tipped off about escapers on the run: escapers wouldn't invade a military base, it was the last thing they'd risk. In fact the Cheka probably wouldn't bother to tip off a commander in Dherjakin's position. Everything at this point was *right*: just as he'd assured Nick it would be. Except for the boat question. And even there — well, all right, it was yet another gamble, but if the wind dropped, as it *might* . . .

Nick had reached to help Dherjakin with the chair, and the captain was fending him off: 'Damn it, man, I'm not helpless!'

'Sorry — sorry . . .'

'Told you I was a cripple, did they?'

Bob excused himself, turned to look at the chart. This inlet and the base area had been outlined in red ink. The chain-boom was a dotted red line across the bottleneck entrance, and the small red square beside it on the east bank would be the winch-gear for raising and lowering it. He spoke over his shoulder, interrupting Dherjakin telling Nick that he'd lost his foot — only the foot, cut off at the ankle by a steel-wire rope on the deck of the battlecruiser *Petropavlovsk* — at Revel in '15 . . . 'You do have a guard-ship on station here, comrade Captain?' He touched the chart: the position where that destroyer had been lying that night was marked, also in red. 'Here?'

'Where you see. I've put a buoy there now, a permanent mooring.'

'Keep a sharp lookout, do they?'

'Of course. They'd be in trouble if they didn't — since the incident last week?'

He nodded. Studying the chart . . . The destroyer hadn't been keeping much of a lookout *that* night. But obviously they'd have learnt a lesson, might be a real danger now. If one needed any more dangers — more than the sea outside there . . . But one advantage of using the diesel launch was you'd have some chance of sneaking by — a lot more than you'd have had in anything like a tug. In one of those tugs you could have counted on the guardship giving chase; this had been in his earlier calculations, the fact he'd need to box clever, evade the bastard, be out of visibility range of him by sunrise.

So maybe there was something to be said for this

launch. Except chances were you'd founder . . .

Have to damn well *not* founder, that was all. It would be touch-and-go, but possibly one's seamanship would be up to it.

He turned from the chart. 'Captain — do you have a wireless transmitter here?'

Dherjakin pointed with his chin. 'End of the passage there. Why?'

'Well — I'll explain it all in a minute, as I say, but we'll need to pay a visit to your guardship — to take that gear out to her. Might be as well — I think you'll agree, sir — to warn her CO that we're coming. So if I could get a signal off — *then* give you the explanation to which you're fully entitled?'

'Want me to send you out there in the launch, that it?'

'Well, yes. If you'd be so kind. But — if we could talk about that in a minute — visit your wireless room first?'

To put the set out of action, which was obviously a priority.

Out into the passage. Away from that bare window — which was a step forward, in itself. Wrecking the wireless transmitter was of course going to involve breaking the bad news to Dherjakin now, an end to the pretence — which anyway might not have been easy to maintain for much longer. But getting on with it now: having — once again — no alternative . . .

'Comrade Captain — this diesel launch of yours — is she berthed on the quay farther along there, forty or fifty yards from us here?'

A nod . . . 'This end of the loading quay.'

'And could you drive her — get her started, and—'

'*Me?*'

Turning — with his hand on the door — having begun to open it. Bob explaining, 'I only thought — if you'd come with us — we could handle her between the three of us, you wouldn't need to turn a crew out — and you see, your authority with the CO of the guardship—'

'What I *see* is that — that you have a bloody cheek, comrade!'

He'd stopped with his hand on the door: looking back at them, anger and suspicion mounting. Bob leant past him, opened the door and pushed on in, pushing Dherjakin in ahead of him more or less sideways, the three of them in a block, squeezing into this small, narrow room — windowless, airless, with the characteristic W/T-shack smell of electrics and a reek of cigarettes. Saucer full of crushed cardboard ends, beside the transmitter key. The set was on a table-height bench built across the end of the room, and a telegraphist was swinging round on his chair: middle-aged, bald, fat, unshaven, bulging out of a dirty singlet . . . 'Comrade Captain!'

'Get on that telephone — call the guard!'

There was a Nagant revolver on the end of the bench, in a holster on a belt which the telegraphist had taken off presumably for comfort, to allow his paunch to expand. Bob was close up against Dherjakin, his hand was on the butt of his .45 but with no elbow-room at all, in that instant and the confined space. He'd told Nick, 'Shut the door!' and Nick had rammed it shut with his shoulder: Dherjakin swinging round aggressively, gasping as he saw Bob's pistol by this time halfway up, while the slobbish-looking telegraphist — not as slow in the uptake as you'd have thought he might be, but rash — was reaching not for the telephone but for the belt, the gun on it. Nick shot him. The Browning's single cracking bark was loud in the enclosed space, as well as shocking. The fat man slumped, blood beginning to seep from the side of his head behind the ear: he slumped across the W/T bench with one pudgy arm still extended towards his pistol, and then slid down, bringing the chair over on top of him. Dherjakin frozen, petrified — mouth open, blue eyes wide with shock.

Bob picked up the chair, set it against the wall and gestured with the .45 in his other hand: 'Sit down, Captain. I'll tell you all about it now. Nick, pull all the wires out — wreck it. And the telephone. Captain, is anyone likely to have heard that shot?'

'I — don't know . . .'

'Anyone else sleep in this building?'

'No.' He looked like a man about to have heart failure. 'No. But—'

'The sentry he left outside, Bob. Look, I'm sorry, I—'

'God almighty, who *are* you, you—'

'Captain – shut up. Please.' He pointed at the body, with his gun. 'You can see we aren't playing games. I'll kill *you*, if I have to. If the sentry comes along now, tell him a door slammed. I promise you, if you don't do exactly what I tell you, I *will* kill you. I'd rather not, I'd like your help, like you with us — I mean *really* with us . . .'

17

Bob locked the door of the wireless room behind them, and pocketed the key. Nick had taken the dead telegraphist's revolver. Dherjakin was still half-stunned.

'And what then?'

'You'll see. Very soon.' The news he hadn't broken to him was that they were going to try to cross about a hundred and fifty miles of possibly rough sea in that open launch. He gestured with his .45 ... 'Go on. Remember what you're going to tell him?'

'Yes. Yes ...'

Nick had him by the arm, with the Browning in his other hand not far from his ribs. Nick seemed to be the real bogeyman, to Dherjakin, the one who killed without a moment's hesitation. Bob told him, 'Before long, Captain, you'll realize we're doing you a favour.'

'*Favour!*'

'Believe me. As long as you do what you're told. Starting *now*.'

Nick opened the door to the roadway, ushered the stocky Captain out ahead of them. The rumble of the generator seemed louder than it had before. And the wind was more noticeable too. Either it was still increasing, or one had become more wind-conscious, with pictures in mind of what the Caspian might be like, down there below the delta. Possibly both factors applied ... The van stood as they'd left it — rear doors still shut, was the first thing one looked for — in the light from the street lamp back there. The sentry rose up now into that light: he'd been sitting on the running-board on this near side, in shadow. The one with the rifle, this was. Dherjakin told him hoarsely, 'You can — go back to your duty on the gate now, comrade. Tell — tell the guard commander all's well here.'

'Very well, comrade Captain.' Slinging his rifle . . . Bob said — as if to Dherjakin — 'We'll move our van down to the other quay — with your permission, Captain.'

He'd said it for the sentry's benefit. Otherwise when they heard the engine start they might wonder what was happening. The sentry muttered, slouching off, 'Night, comrades.'

'Goodnight. Thank you.'

So far, so good. For the moment . . . Bob moved up beside Dherjakin, told him quietly, 'That was good. But listen now. As I've said — if you try anything, you're dead. But you'd be silly to. You're not the Bolshevik type, Captain. I don't know how you got caught up with them, but you're out of your element with this crowd. Remember a few months ago on your way here, you saved three ladies from Red Guards on a train?'

'Ladies?' Staring, open-mouthed; then recollection dawning . . . 'I don't — oh God, *yes* — as it happens, but how—'

'You'll be meeting two of the ladies before long. That's how. And it's why I've no wish to harm you. But also, think of this — we asked for you at the gate by name. And you've just dismissed that sentry. As far as they're concerned, you're in this with us. If we left you behind now, d'you think the Cheka would accept your explanation?'

Laboured breathing . . . Then: 'What d'you want me to do?'

'First answer a question. That chain-boom — is there a watch on it, or any alarm system?'

'No. Physical barrier only.'

'I thought so. So — we get in this van. Drive to your diesel launch. Some of us embark in her, and you get her started up. While two of us — there are more of us in the van here, you see — drive on to the entrance and winch the boom open. Hand-operated winch, is it?'

'Yes.'

'Nick, you might do that job. Take one of the Czechs with you. Captain Dherjakin will explain the gear to you — now, as we drive along. Then you either drive back to us here, in which case we wait, or if we can pick you up *at* the entrance — Captain?'

'Better to land from the launch and do it,' said Dherjakin. 'Two men to do the winching — I'll show them. I'll show you where we can land, just inside the boom.'

'Even better. Still, might as well take the van as far as the launch . . . Get in, please, Captain. Nick . . .'

'All right.'

He thought that in Dherjakin's position *he'd* do what he was told . . . Dherjakin was in now, Nick having encouraged him in and now going on round to the front to wind the handle. Bob got in too, called back from behind the wheel, 'You people all right? Nadia, Irina?' Chorus of questions and a lot of scrabbling around, a spouting of French from the orang-utan, and Nadia's 'Have you done it, Bob, have you actually *done* it?'

'Not quite. But we're driving along to a boat now — stay where you are, only a minute.'

It seemed Dherjakin *was* going to co-operate — at this stage, anyway. His suggestion about landing from the boat, the offer to help personally . . . But he was a sailor as well as an engineer. When he heard it all — about putting out to sea — he was going to scream blue murder. And there was the guardship to get past, before one faced the sea: he might envisage the possibility of losing out at that stage, and what the Cheka might do to him thereafter. So — as advised by Nadia — don't take him for granted yet. Even though he didn't have all that many options either — the danger would be panic, unreasoning desperation . . . The engine fired: for a moment he'd thought it had shot its bolt and wouldn't. Not that that would have mattered much, the old wreck had served its purpose . . . Nick climbing in, squashing Dherjakin over against Bob. He told him — needing his wholehearted co-operation, seeking therefore to strengthen his morale — 'Plenty of jobs for experienced engineer officers, in and around our Royal Navy flotilla.'

'Royal – Navy? *English?*'

'I'm a Scot, as it happens. My name's Cowan – Robert Cowan, Lieutenant, Royal Naval Reserve. I was in the CMB you blew up. This man here saved my life ... But that's the truth – you'd have a choice of good jobs ashore or afloat. And you'd be among friends, what's more ... By the way, there's fuel in the launch's tank, I hope?'

'For how long a trip?'

'You tell me – fuel for how far, how long? And what speed?'

'Best speed about six knots. And the tank's kept full. You've another of your Royal navy ships coming, is that it?'

They'd rounded the elbow in the quay; he stopped the van thirty yards beyond it. Agreeing with Dherjakin – to keep him happy for the moment – 'We'll be meeting one of our flotilla, yes.'

'Close in here, huh?'

'Well – not all *that* close ...'

But a full tank of diesel would be plenty.

Disembarkation, then: all scrambling out of the back, milling around, stretching cramped limbs, asking questions, inspecting the surroundings, and Nadia – embarrassingly, in this well-lit area – trying to embrace him under the eyes of her fiancé. Whether he was or wasn't, *he* thought he was. Bob held her off: reaching for Irina with the other arm, presenting Dherjakin with these two clownishly-dressed females: 'This is Captain Sergei Dherjakin – he's coming with us. Nadia – Irina – the man who saved you on the train.'

'Captain – we've blessed you ever since that day!'

'Talk in the boat, Irina. Or later. All aboard now ...'

There were iron rungs set in the stone facing of the quay. Dherjakin pulling at his arm: 'How far out d'you have to go? See for yourself – even as a harbour launch she's small. So—'

'Tell you the truth, Captain, our first problem isn't the sea-state, it's to sneak out past your guardship without being spotted. We managed it before, but as you said, they might be more awake now ... Go on down, please, start up?'

He watched for a moment to see how he managed the ladder, with only one foot. But it was all right. And the launch looked sturdy enough, in her present setting. Broad-beamed, with the engine set more or less amidships — and enclosed, in a sort of box about the size of a large dog-kennel, wheel and controls at its after end. If there'd been any kind of canopy up forward to keep lopping seas out of her it mightn't have been so bad; but there wasn't, in any noticeable sea you'd be shipping water all the time.

Krebst was cranking for Dherjakin. Bob shouting into the Captain's ear — as the engine finally spluttered and growled into life — 'Do we have a bilge-pump, Captain?'

'Hand-pump. There.'

You'd be baling too, he guessed. If there was a baler, for God's sake ...

Chugging out. Van deserted on the quayside above them. Finder's keepers ... He wondered how accurately and how soon the Cheka would reconstruct the details of this escape. If one *did* escape. Might claim success when one was standing on the deck of one of the RN flotilla's ships, with all these others present: but not before, and that moment was still a long way off.

Hugging the quayside — and then the bank — on their port hand. With the end of the loading quay astern, a bend to port now. Chugging along at about three knots. Nobody talking much — probably pondering what he'd said about problems still to come.

In the straight now — the neck of the bottle ...

'There. Forty metres. Throttle down a bit.'

The wind was gusting from astern, the north. You'd have no shelter from it over the flat land, none at all. The best hope was that by dawn it might be dropping. At this moment he guessed it was about force 4, twelve or fifteen knots. Come up just a little, to twenty, you'd be calling it force 5. Still classified as breeze, not wind. Even force 6 was technically only 'strong breeze'. And force 6, in this launch in open sea — well, to put it mildly, the girls weren't going to enjoy it much.

Not that anyone's comfort was such a major consideration. What mattered was to get them through it alive.

'Two lengths to go. On the bow there. See the place?'

He throttled right down. Gear lever into neutral. 'Nick — Krebst ...' Bank sliding by quite fast still, and the wind astern would be helping; he put her slow astern and revved up a little. Then as the way came off her, back into neutral with the engine idling, as the boat's forepart nudged the bank. Majerle — the orang-utan — jumped ashore with the bow line; he'd stay on the bank, holding the boat in, until they were ready to shove off again. Nick had been instructing him in this *en route*; as well to make *some* use of him. Dherjakin called, 'One of you out first, give me a hand?'

So there were *some* limitations, from the peg-leg. Bob looked round, into the stern: 'You two all right?'

'So far.' Nadia ... 'But will it be very rough on the sea, Bob?'

'May be a *little* bumpy.'

'It's rather a small boat to go to sea in, isn't it?'

'Bigger than the one we thought we'd be using. And an engine's a lot better than a pair of oars.'

'Yes. Of course ...'

Irina chipped in: 'It *is* going to be bad, though? I mean *really* bad?'

'Unless the wind drops — yes. But—'

'Nick said —' Nadia again — 'there was no bigger boat there to take.'

'Unfortunately, there wasn't. Isn't. But — we'll make it, don't worry.'

Hearing himself say it: wondering, *will* we, though ...

And just waiting now. The winch hut was a cube against dark sky up there ahead as the boat drifted round on the wind, held only by her bow. Without someone like Dherjakin who knew his way around they'd have needed some sort of light in there; but they were doing all right, he could hear the iron cogs squeaking round, and visualize that heavy chain sagging towards the mud.

And remember the collision. The secondary crash which had been McNaught falling of his stool in the engine-space, and Johnny's calm 'Boom across the bloody entrance. *Damn.*'

Nick's voice instead, though, from the shore: 'It's done, Bob, we're coming down to you.'

No longer any boom across the bloody entrance, then. Only a guardship sitting out there like a cat beside a mousehole. This was the fence you had to square up to now. The one after that, the last — unless one ran into the Bolshevik navy, of course — would be the most difficult and the longest-lasting, but it was better not to think too much about it now, much better to concentrate on getting past the destroyer. Have everyone squat down in the bottom of the launch, he thought, when the time comes. And creep out at no more than two or three knots, round that corner into the other channel. Holding one's breath, and saying prayers.

Dherjakin was helped over the side. Nick and Krebst close behind him. Bob called, 'Well done. And thank you, Captain.' He raised his voice: 'Shove off for'ard!' Then remembered, switched to French: 'Push off at the front!'

He backed her off, with port rudder on to turn her. Then they were gliding out, the banks close on either side.

'How much water over the chain when it's lowered, Captain?'

'Plenty. Twelve feet, easy.'

'So you could get a destroyer in there, if you needed to.'

'Certainly. Let alone the little Schichau that's sitting out there now.' He'd waved a hand into the darkness ahead. 'I've had that one in — converted him to oil. I'll be getting a whole clutch of 'em in the spring. That is — I *would* have had.'

Bob hesitated. Listening to the echoes of what Dherjakin had just said, and wary of clutching at straws that turned out to have no substance. It was possible that he was misunderstanding this — straw-clutching out of wishful thinking . . . He asked the Captain, 'Are you talking about a Schichau destroyer, or Schichau torpedo-boat?'

'Torpedo-boat. I said — middling *little* feller.'

'Schichau torpedo-boat. The guardship on station there *now*?'

'Should I try to put it into English for you?'

'No. That — won't be necessary.'

Irascible old sod . . .

But — Christ almighty . . . He'd pushed the throttle to nearly shut. Needing time to think now. To think *hard* . . . Having assumed — not unnaturally — that the guardship would be a destroyer. And it could have been a Schichau destroyer — fairly antique, but full-sized, more or less. About one's own age, roughly; they and the tiddlers, the torpedo-boats, had been built in Germany between — oh, 1886 to about '98. But a Schichau torpedo-boat was small — with a correspondingly small ship's company. She'd probably have a displacement of only about a hundred and fifty tons, two torpedo-tubes in her turtle-decked fo'c'sl, and a gun of some kind on her stern. Designed speed might have been about twenty knots or better — thirty years ago, of course.

The launch still had way on, the banks of the inlet falling back on her quarters, but the engine only muttering, screw barely turning . . . He looked at Dherjakin again. 'What sort of complement would this Schichau have?'

'H.256 is her pennant number. Complement — fully manned, twenty-four. But we're short-handed everywhere, she's down to about — oh, fifteen or sixteen. Three fourteen-inch tubes, displacement a hundred and seventy tons — what else d'you want to know?'

Nick came aft, stepping over the midships thwart. 'Are we stopping for any particular reason?'

'Just — marking time. New development. Hang on.' He swung back to Dherjakin . . . 'She's not one of the really midget Schichaus, then.'

'No. Effectively, you could say she's a very small, lightly-armed destroyer.'

'Two officers?'

'If you can call 'em officers. The CO was a Leading Torpedoman until a year ago. The number two – God knows . . .'

'Hear that, Nick? The guardship, we're talking about . . .' Back to Dherjakin – and excited now, finding excitement difficult to contain . . . 'Captain – one very important question for you. And please let me have an absolutely straight answer – even if you have to think about it for a minute first . . . Are you with us? *Seriously* with us, now?'

About two miles to go. Having the chart in mind, also recollections of one's previous visit here. He had the throttle wide open and the launch was making her six knots, possibly a little better, with the wind's help. They'd just passed the opening to port which was the channel they'd taken in the CMB. Johnny Pope had ignored it on the way in, held straight on and shortly afterwards hit the boom. If he hadn't – well, you wouldn't have known the new base existed. You'd still have hit the mine-barrier – without any way of guessing what it was there for – and your only way out now would have been the skiff. And you *would* have drowned.

Even in this launch . . . Five minutes ago he'd had to endure Dherjakin's scorn, after having to admit that he'd planned on taking her out into the open sea.

But now – two miles at six knots or better – twenty minutes, maximum. Easing her over to stay close to the starboard-side bank, so you'd see that fork off to starboard when you came to it.

'Any ideas, Nick?'

'Only to remind the Czechs they have just six bullets each – as we have – so not to go wasting shots.'

'Might not have to shoot at all . . .'

If it went really neatly. Of the crew of sixteen, at least two and possibly four might be on deck; and there'd be no attempt to take them by surprise. Dherjakin's co-operation here was crucial: the surprise would come after you'd boarded. By that time the watch on deck would have called the CO, so there might be say half a dozen men to deal with initially. But there'd be five armed men boarding. Five because he'd given Dherjakin the pistol from the wireless room — trusting him (a) because he thought it was safe to do so, and (b) because if you were going to use him at all, you had to.

Some questions for him, now . . .

'Is it a four-pounder on her stern?'

'Yes. And there's a machine-gun — one of yours, water-cooled Lewis — abaft the funnel.'

'Nick — you're a soldier, you must know all about machine-guns?'

'Yes. I'll take care of it.'

'Better than that — we'll have about sixteen crewmen to handle, we might muster them where you can cover them with it. You could show Krebst how to handle it, perhaps.'

'And then what?'

He'd turned back to Dherjakin . . . 'What's the CO's name?'

'Bakin. Calls himself a lieutenant.'

'And is he any good?'

'In his way, and by their standards. The ship remains afloat and functioning, his men obey him, more or less . . .'

A mile to go. He gave Dherjakin the wheel while he had a chat with the girls. Feeling *able* to talk with them now: until just minutes ago he'd felt an estrangement, sense of treachery almost, in his intention of subjecting them to that ordeal. Now, it was a sense of enormous relief: at close range and in the dark he could actually look Nadia in the face — and hold her hands . . . She asked him, 'What are the chances, really?'

'Good. *Very* good.'

'Are you telling us the truth, this time?'

'I *always* tell the truth.' There was some dispute on this, and when he took over the wheel again the launch had covered about another half-mile. Estimates of distanc were approximate, since there were no landmarks to by, only the high bank — comparatively high, in terms of local topography — receding steadily into the darkness, monotonously the same, minute after minute.

'Captain — mind telling me how you came to be working for the Bolsheviks?'

'It's — a long story, Lieutenant.'

'Just the bare bones of it?'

'Well. When I lost this foot, the Navy I'd served all my life threw me on the scrap-heap. After half a lifetime. And I'm good at my job, I had — *have* — a record to be proud of. Understand me?'

'Of course.'

'No *of course* about it. But it was actually said to my face — *What use is a damn cripple to us, Dherjakin?* Huh?'

'So when the revolution came—'

'I was needed again!'

'By the wrong side ...'

'Who the hell are *you* to say what's wrong, right—'

'Well — surely—'

'*Nothing's* sure. *Nothing.*' He flung an arm out; 'Reduce speed, uh?'

'Yes ... You were able to — turn a blind eye to the murders, bloody massacres even ...'

'No. I wasn't there, I'd been forced into retirement before all that. In any case — what comes first, the chicken or the egg — ever hear *that*, did you?' The arm flapped again: 'Slower!'

So as not to give them longer notice of this visit than one had to. A minute or two — making a point of announcing the comrade Base Commander's arrival — so they'd have no inkling of any threat ... He cut the revs: less bow-wave, and less noise.

'If you have to tell them who you're bringing with you ...'

'Military Revolutionary Committee's planning sub-committee, checking on defensive capability.'

'Perfect.' Whatever his politics, he seemed to know which side his bread was buttered *now*.

*

Down to two knots now. The other channel was visible, leading off to starboard. He'd lost sight of the nearer bank, then picked up the low, black hump of the other. The guardship would be somewhere to the left of that, out in the stream and only two or three hundred yards from them now. It occurred to him that they'd have got past, easily enough; with the sky clouded as it was now, the night was a lot darker than the last time they'd been here.

Glimmer of light ...

Dherjakin had seen it too. 'Lieutenant—'

'Yes, I'm on it.' No masthead light, though, as there should have been. If there'd been one you'd have seen it a long time ago, across the low intervening land. But they'd probably be aiming at near-invisibility, hoping to catch intruders — intruding CMBs, for instance — unawares. That light would be at upper-deck level: or from a scuttle that shouldn't have been left open. He adjusted the course. Thinking about the actual boarding, now that it was only minutes away. He'd have liked to have been the next man on deck behind Dherjakin; but someone had to put this launch alongside, and it had to be done properly — not bungled, waking them all up too soon ... He called, 'Heads down, now.' Because they might switch on a searchlight, and it would be better if to start with they only saw himself and Dherjakin — two figures rather than five — or even seven. The girls would *stay* down out of sight ... He could see the outlines of the Schichau now — bow-on, at an angle of about forty-five degrees. That light was on her upper deck right aft — about where you'd expect them to lower a gangway or drop a ladder over, for the convenience of their visitors.

They weren't keeping much of a lookout, meanwhile.

'Give 'em a hail, Captain?'

Dherjakin cupped his hands to his mouth, bellowed, 'Two-five-six, ahoy? Ahoy there, two-five-six!'

Waiting. Echoes floating across the gently heaving water. Bob had the launch under helm, circling to come in on the torpedo-boat's quarter . . . The answering hail came out of the night like a seagull's screech: 'Boat ahoy! Who are you?'

'Dherjakin! Captain Dherjakin visiting comrade Lieutenant Bakin!'

One could imagine the surprise. The Base Commander — middle of the night . . . A figure had crossed in front of that light, more lights came on, another man was hurrying for'ard. To the searchlight, the Lewis? But surely the name Dherjakin . . . They'd be too late with the gun anyway — the launch was sweeping in close to her and it wouldn't depress that far.

Dherjakin said, 'They're putting a ladder over.'

A shout: 'Comrade Engineer Captain Dherjakin?'

'Yes!'

Voices — a medley of them, carrying but confused, across the water . . . Then another hail: 'Come aboard, comrade Captain!'

Dherjakin growled, 'What the hell d'you *think* I'm doing . . .'

Bob called, 'As soon as there's room on the ladder, Nick . . .'

'All right.'

'I'll be behind you. Krebst — if they don't take the bow line—'

'He knows, Bob.'

The orang-utan knew too, presumably. Bob hoped so: he couldn't have managed much French at this moment. Gear into neutral, then astern, and a touch of power, wheel hard a-port: a bump as she scraped alongside. Dherjakin moving quickly to the ladder, Krebst throwing a coil of the bow line up to someone on the Schichau's deck. Gear back into neutral, wheel amidships, engine just muttering to itself. Nick threw a quick look behind him, saw the girls crouching in the stern, Nadia's face turned up, watching him, pale in the thin shedding of light from up there on the deck. He turned back: she — they — had only to stay put, keep out of the way and out of danger . . . Dherjakin was on board, Nick Solovyev was in the act of boarding and the orang-utan was hauling itself up the ladder behind him. Krebst standing back, making way for Bob ... He flung himself up the ladder — wooden slats between double chains — and on to the Schichau's deck.

Dherjakin was right in front of him, facing inboard — that cocky stance of his, but no gun in his hand yet as he faced two surprised-looking crewmen. Nick had just pushed past them, rushing for'ard with the orang-utan on his heels — both of them bearded, piratical, wild-looking even to the eyes of Bolsheviks — and the CO arrived at this moment, a thickset youngish man with his shirt hanging outside his trousers, coming in a hurry from the open screen-door in the side of the superstructure: 'Captain Dherjakin!'

'Ah.' A gesture towards him as he told Bob, 'Lieutenant Bakin.'

Bob had his gun out. 'Put your hands up, Lieutenant. And you two — hands up!' A glance at Dherjakin: 'Captain, for God's sake!'

Dherjakin drew his pistol, then. The three obeying now, raising their hands — incredulous ... Bob said, 'Come with me, Lieutenant Bakin. I want you to tell your crew to surrender without making any trouble. They're under arrest, you all are, and you'll be shot dead if you resist ... Captain, keep those two here for the moment. Krebst ...'

The orang-utan had stopped to help Nick Solovyev get the cover off the Lewis gun and then a pan of ammunition on to it from the ready-use locker, but Bob, on his way for'ard with Krebst and the Schichau's CO to draw fuzes in the wireless shack, then rout crew out of the fo'c'sl, yelled at him in French to go down and clear the engine-spaces — access to engineroom and boiler-room being via the little hutch on which the Lewis was mounted.

The hatch inside there was standing open, air sucking in, sucked down by the fans, and a steel ladder led down vertically into a glare of brilliance, warmth, the fans' roar ... The orang-utan paused in the hatchway, gazing down:

seeing a steel grid about three-quarters of the way down — across the front of the oil-fired furnace — and a stoker with a cloth tied round his head, bare-chested, just leaving it, expertly skimming down an extension of the ladder to the lowest level. He wouldn't have heard a shout over the noise the fans made. The orang-utan swung himself on to the ladder and started down — one-handed, pistol in the other, the steel sides of the ladder sliding through that palm silver-bright and oil-coated, slippery — same as the rungs, and he'd missed his footing, grabbing to save himself but somehow failing to make contact — probably part-blinded by the glare, over-confident initially and then in panic as he fell backwards. The stoker heard the crash above him, saw the body sprawled on its back on the narrow gridded platform which he — the stoker — had been standing on only seconds earlier. He dashed up the short ladder fast, a wheel-spanner still clutched in one hand . . .

Muttering 'What the flaming hell . . .' And in the same breath then — swinging himself on to the platform — 'Oh, *Christ*. . .'

Aghast: staring down at the prone figure of the orang-utan. It did look like one — or like something maybe *semi*-human — or out of hell except he'd come crashing down from up *there* . . . The creature's eyes opened, focused momentarily on the figure looming over him with what might have been a weapon in one hand: getting its own hand up slowly — a dying insect raising its sting — and the pistol jumping as he fired with no aim but point-blank: his eyes were shutting, but he'd fired again, then a third time absolutely blind.

Nick had the Lewis loaded and cocked, trained on the Schichau's crewmen lined up on the ship's port side. They'd been arriving in small groups escorted by Krebst, who'd been parking them here then going back to Bob and the ship's CO for more. But this was the whole crew now, and they were all back here now — Bob, Krebst, Dher-jakin, and Bakin.

'All right, Lieutenant — over there with the others.'

Bakin appealed to Dherjakin: 'Comrade Captain — I can't believe you'd permit this — *outrage*.'

Bob cut in, 'Shut up, Lieutenant. Do what you're told.'

He counted them: sixteen in all — and now realized the orang-utan wasn't present. Looking round ... 'Where's Majerle?'

'Went down here.' Nick pointed downward. 'You told him to check out the engineroom.'

'God — engineroom watchkeepers!' He'd thought of them earlier, then forgotten ... At immediate notice for sea, fires would be lit, they'd have been maintaining a head of steam, there'd have to be watchkeepers below — and the Czech shouldn't have needed more than a few minutes to hunt them out. He turned towards the shelter: glancing up at Nick as he went inside: 'Bloody hell ...'

Not an inappropriate comment: with a bird's-eye view of the debris on that steel shelving — two bodies, the orang-utan's and another sprawled on top of it, a lot of blood ...

'Krebst!'

A movement amongst the machinery even further down: human but like a crab scuttling into shelter — not that there was much of it, you could still see him through the web of steel. Small, wizened, terrified. Mechanician, stoker, whatever ... Bob shouted and beckoned, but he only stood staring up — open-mouthed, shaking with fright. Bob and Krebst went down and herded him up, then carried the bodies up between them — the stoker's first, with three bullet-holes in its torso, then the orang-utan's with the back of its skull a bloody pulp. It seemed obvious what had happened — more or less ...

So there'd been eighteen of them, not sixteen. Seventeen now, bunched along the port-side guardrail with Nick Solovyev facing them, crouched behind the Lewis, one hand fondling the trigger-guard, his green eyes flickering towards Bob with a question in them.

A question like *Is this the lot now?* Or possibly a request: *May I?*

Bakin began — wrenching his eyes off the stoker's body, obviously in no doubt of what was about to happen — 'If you please — comrades — comrade Engineer Captain — *please*, hear me out? We've done no wrong — I and my crew are loyal servants of the Revolution — we know you are also, comrade Captain, so . . .'

Dherjakin turned away. Washing his hands . . .

'Krebst — here, a minute.'

Krebst stood up. He'd been squatting on the iron deck, pulling off the orang-utan's boots. Bob glanced back at the Count: 'Don't shoot unless they make real trouble, Nick.'

The green eyes blinked at him. Surprise — anger — and hesitation: he might have been asking himself why he should accept this outsider's orders. A lot of eyes were fixed on him and on the gun; the Schichau pitching slightly, a gentle rocking to the surge, metallic sounds from for'ard as she tugged intermittently at her mooring.

'Nick — it'd be plain murder. *Their* speciality, not yours.'

No reaction, other than that green stare, no relaxation of the tension in him. Harbouring recollections perhaps of ropes, buckets, cellars, his own humiliation, Red Guards dragging young women off trains . . .

Then he'd seemed to relax; he'd nodded. Bob said, 'Good man. Hang on a minute now.' He hurried aft, with Krebst behind him, and called down, 'Come up here? The ship's ours now.' The launch's bow line had been secured to a cleat near the ladder; he crouched, taking the turns off, then handed the line to Krebst. 'Lead the boat round the stern and up that side, so the crew can embark from where they are now. Understand?'

'*Ponimayu, ponimayu . . .*'

But not liking it all that much. By his manner, as disconcerted as the Count had seemed. Bob turned back to the ladder as the girls came up — Nadia first. He reached to her, helped her over on to the deck: then she'd taken him completely by surprise — her arms round his neck, voice breathless in his ear — 'Bob, oh *Bob*, my darling, how *wonderful*!'

Her arms tight, her lips, body...

'*Nadia!*'

Irina — shocked, a squawk of protest. And having had to climb aboard unaided ... He'd been freeing himself from that hot embrace, in any case, was dreading the sudden clatter of the Lewis opening fire if he didn't get back there fast. Telling them both in a rush as he broke away, 'Wait here, would you — right *here* — just a minute?'

He could still feel her arms: and her lips — soft, open, leaving no shred of doubt — even right under that kid's shocked eyes. On his way for'ard, trotting, his mind was reeling, dizzy ... Despite knowing damn well this was neither the time nor place, that there were new and pressing problems facing him now, and a lot of hard work: and even shorter-handed now than he'd expected ... Nadia, though — *Nadia!* Incredible ... if she'd display her inclinations so openly in front of Nick's sister, she'd make no bones about them to Nick himself. So then — all right, he'd have Nick to deal with. And — *all right.* Nadia was a lifetime's happiness at stake — he didn't even have to think about it, he *knew* it, felt certain she did too.

Nadia filling his mind in one second, wiped from it in the next ... Catching the look the Count threw in his direction as he got back to them — the intention he'd had before, and — it was plain in that moment — decision to do it *now*...

'Hey — Nick!'

'Where are they?'

'*Uh?*'

Then he caught on: the question had been where were the girls — whom he'd left back there to be out of harm's way until he'd got Bakin and company off the ship.

Wanting an audience? What he'd been waiting for?

'This is *Russian* business, Bob!'

'Makes it half mine, then.' He put himself in front of the Lewis — between it and the Schichau's crew. Close-up, masking it — the gun, and the eyes glaring at him over its sights ... 'Think you'd get this ship away without me, Nick?'

A second's pause ... Then the barrel swung up. He turned his back on it.

'Lieutenant Bakin.' A gesture with the .45 ... 'The boat's being brought round. Over the side, all of you. Then the hell out ...'

18

It was a good moment when he had the armed merchantman HMS *Slava*'s tall-funnelled, rather elegant shape in focus in Lieutenant Bakin's binoculars. No surprise — he'd been looking for her, searching the grey, tumbling sea ahead for half an hour before he picked her up. He rang down to Dherjakin in the engineroom for a reduction to half speed, woke the Count for about the sixth time since departure from the delta and cajoled him once again into taking the wheel, then got up in the raised wing of the control position — you could hardly call it a bridge — to talk to *Slava*, or rather Jimmy Roebuck, RNR, her captain, by signal lamp.

Slava had been sent north from the patrol line to meet them. At first light, by which time they'd covered fifty miles by log since leaving the delta, he'd first made a careful inspection of the surroundings to make sure there were no Bolshevik ships around, then broken wireless silence on the RN flotilla's frequency to announce his identity and the capture of the Schichau, his estimated position, course and speed, the names of his passengers — the girls had been prostrate with seasickness even before they'd been out of the delta, and the Count had surrendered to it soon afterwards — and details of what might laughably have been called his ship's company — a one-legged Russian engineer captain running the machinery with the help of a deserter from the Czech Legion, and Lieutenant Robert Cowan, RNR, as captain, navigator, quartermaster and telegraphist.

Receipt of this signal had been acknowledged by HMS *Emil Nobel*, on the patrol line, and shortly afterwards

SNO Caspian — the Commodore — had come on the air, calling for a preliminary report of proceedings commencing midnight 11th September to be wirelessed forthwith. This meant giving him an outline of everything that had happened since Johnny Pope's CMB had left *Zoroaster* that night. Bob acknowledged the signal, spent half an hour putting the briefest possible account together while also supervising Nick Solovyev's helmsmanship, then about ten minutes tapping it out. The Schichau meanwhile standing on her nose and then her tail, plunging around like a marlin on a hook. In fact it had been getting easier by then — from about sunrise onward. But the skiff wouldn't have lasted ten minutes in the wind and sea they'd had in the preceding hours. Gusts of up to about force 7 had forced a reduction in speed, since with that amount of pitching the screw had a tendency to lift out of the water and race, with a danger of stripping the shaft bearing. Dherjakin had expected to deliver seventeen knots but they'd been down to twelve at the worst time, and were making fifteen at the time of this rendezvous with *Slava*.

A light blossomed on *Slava*'s bridge, answering his call, and he flashed to Roebuck, *Good morning. Both women and one male passenger still sick, also Engineer Captain Dherjakin complaining of heat exhaustion. Will you swap them for the spare hands already requested please?*

The answer was affirmative. Also, informative. Transfer of passengers would have been necessary in any case. *Slava* would be taking them to Enzeli, while the Schichau was to proceed to Krasnovodsk. So — parting of the ways; he'd dumped his lamp back into its bracket and was wondering what arrangements he could make privately with Nadia for getting in touch later, here in Russia or elsewhere: his dream of course was that she might come to England, as so many of the aristos were doing, in which case if she had the address of Messrs McCrae and McCrae she could let him know where he'd find her when he himself got home — eventually ... Then the flashing had started up again, and Roebuck's signalman had morsed to him, *For your information, Dunsterforce evacuated to Enzeli fourteenth September, Turks now in Baku town and port.*

Bob flashed an acknowledgement. Adding, as an afterthought, a request for an ensign to be sent over in *Slava*'s boat. But with a thought to the Muromskys — remembering in particular Leonide's Uncle George's certainty that they had nothing at all to fear. And maybe he *would* have had ample warning and got away: or at least got poor little Leonide away.

Slava made a lee in which to launch her boat, and Bob brought the Schichau up to within a cable's length of her on that side. Then he had the Count put the ladder over the starboard side abreast the control position, where he — Bob — could take a hand in the proceedings — notably, say goodbye to Nadia — without having to stray too far from the wheel. He had the address of McCrae and McCrae scrawled on a sheet of signal-paper in his pocket; nobody else need see him give it to her.

Enzeli might suit the Solovyevs very well. Nick had told him, when they'd been steaming down the delta and before things had become less comfortable, that if there was any way of getting to the Crimea he hoped to take the girls there and — he hoped — leave them under the protection of the Dowager Empress, Maria Feodorovna. And from Enzeli it might well be possible to reach the Crimea by some roundabout route, initially of course through Persia.

So God only knew when he'd see Nadia again . . .

The boat from *Slava* brought him a Russian engineer officer and two stokers, a Russian watchkeeping lieutenant whom he'd met before, two Russian able seamen, a signalman and telegraphist — both Royal Navy — and an Armenian former Russian Navy cook. With about four hundred miles to cover — say twenty-six hours' steaming — this reinforcement would (a) ensure safe navigation, (b) allow one to get a few hours' sleep and maybe a hot meal or two. As there'd been eighteen men living on board there had to be food of some sort down below.

The Russian lieutenant, Ugryamov, had brought him a choice of ensigns, British and Russian. Jimmy Roebuck hedging his bets, Bob thought. But the Schichau was *his* prize — at least until he delivered her at Krasnovodsk: then, if she was to be returned to the Imperial Navy — well, fine ... Dherjakin had appeared on deck meanwhile, leaving Krebst in sole charge of the engineroom, and Bob asked the newly-arrived engineer to take over immediately — realizing that Krebst would have been doing all the hard work — under Dherjakin's direction — for the past eight hours or more.

Nadia and the Solovyevs arrived on deck then, looking nervous of the boat trip awaiting them. Which made one think again about the trip they *might* have had. But he thought they seemed nervous of him, too, as he went out into the ship's waist to meet them. One of the ABs had taken over the wheel by this time, having dumped his gear somewhere below, and Ugryamov came back up as well; the relief in being able to leave the ship in other hands for a minute — or for an hour, or several hours — was tremendous.

But this diffidence — from Nadia ...

From Irina — well, who gave a damn. She'd take her cue from her brother anyway; and he was still sulking — had been in all his waking moments since last night.

Nadia, pale and frighteningly distant, gave him her hand. 'Bob. We owe you so much.'

The artificiality was — painful ... And this was suddenly a bad — really awful — moment. As if nothing had ever happened between them — or as if what had happened had meant nothing to her. Denial of complicity was in her eyes, her voice, her whole manner, and — he thought — nothing to do with being — or having been — seasick. She wasn't even meeting his eyes: it seemed to be that kind of goodbye — an embarrassment, to be got over with quickly. And — *for ever*? He had the tightly folded signal-paper in his hand, but now the moment had come there was no question of trying to give it to her: she'd have rejected it — or asked 'What's *this*?' But when that thought hit him — *for ever?* — the enormity of it, and that there was nothing he could do — that voice in his shocked brain rasped impatiently *Oh, grow up, boy!* One's own conclusion, of course, but stemming from an old habit of asking oneself in certain situations what would *he* think, or do, or say ... Reaching for her hands: he drew her towards him, touched his lips to her cheek. His right hand and her left one meanwhile palm to palm. She'd felt it: her fingers curled, taking the small wad of paper: then they were separating and it was Irina's turn: he kissed her cheek too. Nadia meanwhile had turned away, her manner unchanged, revealing nothing: in his imagination he was hearing his father chuckling to himself while Irina thanked him, wished him — oh, good luck, success — that kind of thing ... He barely heard, he was watching Nadia as she moved towards the rail, two of *Slava*'s boat's crew waiting to help the passengers embark.

'Bob.' Nick Solovyev was pale above his beard, and dull-eyed. Offering his hand somewhat diffidently. 'Robert Aleksand'ich — I have to say this — you were right, last night. I'm sorry. And thank you — for that as well as for so much else. I am — *enormously* indebted.'

'You saved my life to start with — remember?'

'Oh ...'

'And since then we've come through quite a lot together, I agree, but it hasn't been all *my* doing.'

'Well — the plain truth is that without you I'd have been dead, and *they* —' a movement of his head towards the girls — 'God knows ... Robert Aleksand'ich, if ever I am in a position to make recompense, in any way at all ...'

'Thank you, Nick. And I'll remember it. But I'd say we're all square. Truly.'

And if she gives me half a chance, I'm going to steal your girl.

It put a stopper on other things one might have said — such as hopes of meeting again in happier times. For which, if it hadn't been for the Nadia angle, he *would* have hoped ... And — who could tell, in these present circumstances. If she and Nick broke off their engagement first, for instance — and according to her it wasn't a real engagement anyway...

'Nick, I hope we'll meet again. But you'd better get along now. Look after these two — and yourself — and best of luck...'

The four hundred miles took twenty-eight hours' steaming, as it turned out. During which time as well as running the ship he had plenty to think about.

To start with, Nadia. He'd been ridiculously slow in seeing it, but the answer had to be that Irina had either told her brother about Nadia's extrovert behaviour on the Schichau's stern the night before, or she'd threatened to. The threat seemed more likely. If Nick had known about it he wouldn't have been just sulking over the other business, he'd have been — well, murderous ... But Nadia wouldn't have had anywhere to go, unless the Solovyevs took her with them to the comparative safety of the Crimea. It was a repeat of the Petrograd scenario — when Nick hadn't been sure that his sister and mother would take her along — and last night, or maybe this morning just minutes before their appearance on deck, Irina would have told her, *Behave — or else*...

So she'd behaved. Or tried to. And he — Bob — had damn near lost her.

Whereas now — please God...

But the other major question — doubt — while the Schichau plunged on south-south-eastward — through lighter seas now, conditions steadily improving — was what was likely to happen after all this to Robert Cowan, RNR. By and large, he thought the answer might be 'not much'. They could hardly blame him for having been tricked by the Count's lie, when the Commodore and Dunsterville had also fallen for it. And for that same reason — the fact they'd been had — they'd want to keep the whole thing quiet. Including the fact he'd killed a few Bolsheviks and stolen a warship, when the Royal Navy was only here — officially — to fight Turks and Germans. He thought they'd want to forget it, as soon as possible.

No Grand Duchesses, no grateful monarch, no medals or promotions. A small error of judgement, through having been deliberately misled by a foreign national; regrettable loss of a CMB and two lives. No blame attributable: and all of it heavily overshadowed, probably, by the loss of Baku to the Turks.

Krasnovodsk Bay is protected from the open sea to the west by a long south-reaching finger of land, twenty-five miles of it, with the main entrance to the bay between its southern tip and Cheleken island. But there's a small gap in it about halfway down, a lot wider than the Schichau needed.

She was flying the White Ensign now, from the yard of her stubby mainmast. Turning to port, after passing through the gap, into the bay's calm, sheltered water with Krasnovodsk town and port now eight miles to the north. 2 pm on Thursday 18th September: and they'd be docking in half an hour.

Lieutenant Ugryamov had the watch, with one of the Royal Navy men on the wheel. Bob walked back into the Schichau's stern, leant back against the four-pounder gun-mounting, with his hands in the pockets of a pair of white trousers that might have been Bakin's, gazed out over the little ship's frothing wake; thinking about Maroussia — hoping to God she'd have got away with it — and Leonide — whom he'd have to call on — on her or her family, when time allowed — and finally indulging himself in the luxury of thoughts of Nadia.

She'd still be at sea, in HMS *Slava*, would have had a few good meals by now, and a hot bath or two. It would be strange, he thought, even rather daunting in prospect, to meet her when she was dressed and groomed — the Princess Nadia Egorova, looking as she must have done before these horrors started.

They mightn't recognize each other. Like two strangers meeting.

Initially. Not for long. Provided she did — *please* — get in touch. Not have second thoughts, or — out of sight, out of mind . . .

'*Leitnant?*'

Krebst. Wearing the orang-utan's boots. He'd been making himself useful as cook's assistant and general dogsbody, and his service before that in the engineroom had been invaluable. Bob nodded to him, liking him. 'All right, Sergeant?'

'May I ask, sir, do you have any idea what they'll do with me?'

'No — can't say I do ... But if I can help — you've certainly been a big help to *me* ... I imagine what you'd like best is to go home — right?'

'That was Captain Majerle's wish, sir.' Krebst shrugged. 'But — yes, eventually — when it's possible, I suppose ...'

'The war isn't likely to last much longer — according to reports. If you signed on with my people — on the understanding that you'd leave with us when we go — alternatively when the Turks are kicked out of Baku and we get that railway open ...'

'I should be very glad, sir.'

'To serve afloat meanwhile?'

Nodding, smiling, in his luxuriant blond beard. 'If the *leitnant* could arrange it.'

'I'll do my best. Leave it to me, I'll let you know.'

A light had begun to flash from Krasnovodsk's signal station. Leading Signalman Bury was ready for it, acknowledged smartly, and Bob read the message as it flickered out to them: *Berth on* President Kruger *starboard side to. Russian ensign should be flown, or none.*

And what the hell was *that* about ...

'Change the ensign, sir?'

'Yes please, Bury.'

Must be handing her over to the Russian Caspian flotilla, he guessed. It was surprising: with the questionable loyalties of those ships' companies, the talk had been of paying them off and sending their crews home — not augmenting the flotilla. But presumably, he supposed, watching the White Ensign drop like a wounded bird and a moment later the white flag with its blue St Andrew's cross climb up there in its place, there'd be some good reason.

It was good news that the *Kruger* was here, anyway. She'd been the accommodation ship in Baku and all his gear except what he'd taken with him in *Zoroaster* had been in her; with any luck he might soon be able to cease looking like a pirate.

He'd taken over the conning of the ship and sent Ugryamov to prepare on the starboard side for berthing, when the first rocket went up from the harbour. He heard the bang before he saw it: then saw the high, falling trail of orange-tinted smoke. Another rocket soared: then several more.

Ships' sirens, then. Screams, hoots, a fast-mounting cacophony of sound ... Able Seaman Morton muttered, glancing sideways from the wheel, 'Bit of a welcome, like, sir.'

Astounding. His expectation had been to slip in quietly, berth where he'd been told — on the outside of HMS *President Kruger*, thus removed and to some extent hidden from the sight of the general populace. Who in fact seemed to have gone mad. Boats were putting out now, too — they'd be in the Schichau's way if they didn't shift out of it bloody quick — crammed with waving, cheering Russians. Another pair of rockets whizzing up, bursting in sparks and streamers of coloured fire: and the sirens still going full blast.

'Slow ahead.'

'Slow ahead, sir ...'

Clang of the engineroom telegraph ... He glanced up, saw the Tsarist naval ensign whipping in the breeze. Somewhere, he guessed, politicians were at play.

About an hour later — having shaved and showered, and feeling distinctly overdressed in a Number Six white uniform — he knocked on the door of the Commodore's day-cabin, opened it and stepped in over the low sill.

'Ah. Clothed and in his right mind ...' The Commodore, whom Bob had encountered briefly when he'd berthed the Schichau alongside her, had two Army officers with him, a Lieutenant-Colonel Stuart and a Major Barstow. Barstow had something to do with Intelligence. The Lieutenant-Colonel murmured as they shook hands, 'Have to congratulate you, Cowan. Top-hole, absolutely!'

Everyone had been congratulating him. They'd all been on deck to see him berth the little torpedo-boat, had all wanted to stop him and shake his hand, slap him on the back, and so forth, after he'd crossed the plank to go and get cleaned up. His gear including the stuff out of *Zoroaster* had all been here; he'd been considered dead, and it would all have been parcelled up for dispatch to his next of kin, except that the Commodore had known that his only kin was also recently deceased. But even Mr Dewhurst, the normally crabby Gunner, had wrung his hand and muttered a lot of nonsense.

It was all rather bewildering. He felt as if part of him was still somewhere north of Astrakhan.

There was nothing from McCrae and McCrae. But apparently there'd been no mail in the past week. It was thought that because of the uncertainty over Baku they'd have been hanging on to it in Baghdad, waiting for a new pattern of deployment to emerge.

Major Barstow said, 'As much as you've told us so far about that supply base is most interesting, Cowan. We're looking forward to seeing your full report on it. Obviously we've no direct involvement of our own, but—'

'General Denikin has expressed keen interest.' Colonel Stuart had cut in. 'It's been known for some time that they're planning a move on Guriev, but nobody dreamt it was to be on such a scale. And of course it's of strategic interest in relation to Denikin's own plans. You've rendered the anti-Bolshevik forces a considerable service, in that respect.'

'Pure accident, sir. And the second visit was — well, a matter of survival, a way out.'

'Well, never mind *that*—'

'Another fortunate outcome —' the Commodore interrupted — 'is the effect on morale here. The scenes you've been witnessing, your reception by the townspeople — our having to pull out of Baku's been a blow, you see, they start thinking 'We're for it next' — which is rubbish, of course, we can hold this place till kingdom come, if we're allowed to … I know what you're thinking — and you're right, pinching that little Schichau doesn't make two-penn'orth of difference to anyone, but — well, you saw 'em, heard 'em — eh?'

'Rockets supplied by comrade Kuhn, sir?'

Both the soldiers smiled. Kuhn was the political boss, the Social Revolutionary 'Dictator' of Krasnovodsk. The Commodore had shrugged. 'They certainly didn't come from *us*.' He cleared his throat, 'But Cowan — speaking of confidence tricks — Count Solovyev was lying to us, wasn't he?'

'I'm afraid he was, sir.'

'He won't admit to it. We've had a signalled interim report from *Slava* — General Denikin wants to know all about it, naturally — and Solovyev seems to be saying that you misinterpreted what he told us, that he'd only said he thought it was *possible* his mother might have taken the Tsar's two younger daughters under her wing. What d'you say to that?'

'That he's lying again, sir. And anyway, he'd sold that yarn to General Denikin in the first place.'

'Well, no.' A shake of the head. 'That's not so, apparently. He told *us* he had — and it influenced General Dunsterville, of course. But according to Denikin himself, Solovyev only requested leave of absence to go and rescue his mother, sister and fiancée.' The Commodore glanced towards the door: 'Yes, Chief Yeoman?'

CPO Harmsworth had knocked and was hesitating on the threshold. 'Private signal for Lieutenant Cowan, sir, from Lieutenant-Commander Roebuck. I thought while we had him here on board — if you don't mind, sir—'

'Carry on, carry on …'

Bob took the folded page. 'Thank you, Chief Yeoman.' Glancing at the Commodore: 'Would you excuse me, sir?'

A nod … 'Colonel — tell me — if the Turks were to

pull out of Baku — next week or next month, whenever it might be ...'

Bob read, *Name of company in Scottish address is indecipherable. Please inform.*

'We can bung a reply out right away, sir, if you like.'

Staring at the message. Thinking, Oh, you beautiful, fantastic—

'Reply, sir?'

'Yes. Yes, please.' Pulling himself together — or at any rate half together ... He took the board, and the offered pencil, wrote — in capitals this time, having dashed this off on the last occasion in the control position of the plunging and rolling Schichau — *ROEBUCK FROM COWAN — McCRAE AND McCRAE. THANKS.*

He hesitated — thinking of adding *GIVE HER MY LOVE* — and decided against it, not to risk spoiling this when Jimmy Roebuck had been so discreet. He passed the board back to Harmsworth. 'Thank you.' Reacting, then — the reaction triggered no doubt by the thoughts of Nadia — feeling suddenly like a man who'd run a race and had the trophy thrust into his hands before he'd even begun to get his breath back. If Nadia could be thought of as a trophy: it was a fact that *nadyejhda* was the Russian word for 'hope' ... But there again — being out of the trees now, so that one could as it were look back and see the wood — well, that hope was for oneself, and — begging the question, perhaps — for her. But could there be any hope at all in any broader sense — for this country or its people?

The Commodore was still listening to some military dissertation from Colonel Stuart: all three of them noticeably cheerful, the atmosphere in the narrow, sunlit cabin redolent of progress — *achievement*, for God's sake.

And — all right, from *their* point of view ...

'All is well, I trust, Cowan?'

The question, referring as it did to that signal, switched his thoughts back to Nadia, and his smile as he answered the Commodore was real, spontaneous. 'Entirely so, sir — thank you.' He nodded. 'Very well indeed!'

It really was — he thought . . .

When he'd slept for about a day and a half, he'd *know* it was.

POSTSCRIPT

The vastly outnumbered Dunsterforce's defence of Baku ended in evacuation on 14th September, but on 30th October the Turks signed an armistice on board the battleship HMS *Agamemnon*, in Mudros harbour. British forces reoccupied Baku on 17th November, and with the opening of the railway from Batoum twelve forty-foot Coastal Motorboats under the command of Cdr E. G. Robinson VC RN arrived in the Caspian in December 'after an adventurous six-hundred-mile journey during which Cdr Robinson and his officers had to work the train themselves'. The official account adds that 'it was difficult to know which Russians were friends and which enemies, but all were equally determined to appropriate gear and stores belonging to the boats'.

Turning now to a memorandum drawn up by SNO Caspian and headed *Naval Events in the Caspian Sea 1918–19*, under a sub-heading *Possible Naval Activities during the Summer of 1919*, paragraph (c) reads:

> About halfway between Astrakhan and Guriev are reported to be two divisions of Bolshevik Army who were in the late autumn advancing in the direction of Guriev for the purpose of attacking it and obtaining possession of the valuable Emba Oil Fields. The Bolsheviks were using tugs and barges before the ice made that impossible, to convey their stores, and it is possible therefore that operations may be undertaken on this coast.

In the same document the strength of the Bolshevik squadron at Astrakhan is estimated as 10 Armed Merchant Cruisers, 9 destroyers, 8 small torpedo-boats and 4 submarines. Bearing these numbers in mind, it is interesting to turn back to the account of CMB operations in 1919, where it is stated that 'The Caspian *having been cleared of Bolshevik vessels*, the British officers were sent home and the boats handed over to friendly Russians', and that '*CMB officers regretted not being allowed to follow the Bolshevik war vessels when they retired up the Volga*'.

My italics. And my thanks to Naval Historical Branch and the Ministry of Defence librarians for allowing me access to these and other documents.